BISHOP'S LAW

A THRILLER

RAFAEL AMADEUS HINES

*For Kingston and Dakota, who both asked,
"Can you write another one, Daddy?"*

*I also want to offer my deepest gratitude to the Soldiers,
Sailors, Marines, Airmen and Special Operators who
continue to share stories that weave their way into the
Bishop series. I'm so thankful for all your help and
support, and humbled by your service and sacrifice.*

*May God bless you, protect you and
bring you all home safe.*

*Last, but far from least, I want to thank these
great men who recently left us. Each of them
helped guide me through life and kept me
laughing during the most difficult times.*

Sensei Sam Lewis

*Daniel "Danny Boy" Burnette,
USMC and Brooklyn's Best*

*Glenn Williams, St. John's Basketball,
NBA Veteran and LES Legend*

*Coach John "Butch" Purcell, Rucker Park,
NBA, and the Mayor of StuyTown*

CHAPTER 1
TEAM RAZOR

Mosul, Iraq

CHAGO'S MOTHER NAMED him Chao Chen Goh after his great-grandfather, who was a national hero in China for his courage under fire in World War II. She'd been furious when her son's drill sergeant started calling him "Chago" in basic training and her anger soared to DEFCON 1 when the name stuck. The fact that a dozen years later he was a decorated US Special Forces staff sergeant and an elite Tier II operator did little to help her get over it. Chago knew she never would, but that was okay with him. Nickname aside, he was sure there was no better way to honor his great-grandfather's legacy than by being part of America's tip of the spear in the war on terror.

This was Chago's eighth deployment. On several of his tours he'd worked directly with the Kurdish forces in Northern Iraq and spent several years living in and around Mosul. Back then it had been a bustling city with a thriving middle class, thanks in large part to the constant flow of "black gold" being pumped out of the nearby oil fields.

Not anymore, Chago thought as he looked through the

narrow rear window of the M-ATV (Mine Resistant Ambush Protected-All Terrain Vehicle). He saw heatwaves rippling across a flat open area of a once lively residential neighborhood. The streets were now eerily quiet and the apartment buildings had been reduced to rubble by a joint Iraqi and US Coalition attack on ISIS forces in this sector the day before.

Looks deserted... But the tangos are out there... Watching. Just waiting for a clear shot, he thought.

Chago knew there were Special Ops snipers, drones and Joint STARS surveillance planes monitoring their AO (area of operation), but he still scanned the few buildings that remained standing for threats. He was focused on a caved-in apartment complex when he heard Staff Sgt. Bobby Floyd's voice over the roar of the M-ATV's 370 horsepower 7.2 liter engine:

"Just so you know, Chago, inside this here truck we speak our minds," Bobby said from the driver's seat.

Eight tours and this dude's treating me like a Gomer fresh out of boot camp, Chago thought. He wasn't mad though. He was the new guy on the team and was keenly aware that he was the replacement for Bobby's best friend, Staff Sgt. Able Diaz, who had been KIA in an op just a few months earlier.

"That's cool with me," Chago said from his rear seat directly behind Bobby's.

"Well I'm just tickled to death that it's cool with you, because on *this* deployment we ain't gonna be holding your hand and hugging it out when one of us says something that hurts your feelings," Bobby said.

"Good to know," Chago said.

"Why're you breaking his balls?" Staff Sgt. Maceo "Mace" Hendricks asked.

"I'm not," Bobby said. "I'm letting him know how things

work around here. It don't bother me none that he puts soy sauce on his cheeseburgers, but being a Chinaman I expect he's a little more sensitive than the rest of us."

"Asian-American," Chago said.

"Come again?" Bobby asked.

"He said he's Asian-American. Not a 'Chinaman,'" said Chief Warrant Officer Bear Bernstein, who was sitting in the front passenger seat next to Bobby.

"You see! That's exactly what I'm talking about. I call you the Jew and you're not offended because you love your heritage. I call Mace the Black Guy and he may not like it, but he's enlightened. What you call forward thinking, because being the musical prodigy that he is, he knows I may be a Kentucky redneck, but I'm *way* blacker than he'll ever be."

"You've never called me 'the Jew,'" Bear said.

"And you've never called me 'the Black Guy,'" Mace said.

"That's only because you're both so abnormally large I know you'd kick my ass."

"So what's your fuckin' point?" Mace asked.

"I only speak one language. Down home, grade A, good ol' Kentucky boy English. It's my understanding that our new friend, Mr. Chago, here, speaks six."

"And…?" Bear asked.

"He ain't saying it, but he's thinking all kinds of fucked up shit about us in six different languages. That just ain't right," Bobby said with a big grin on his face.

That got them all laughing.

"You're just pissed off and talking trash because you didn't check the AC before we left the base," Mace said. He felt like he was sitting on a wet sponge as he moved from side to side in his seat, then slammed his right forearm and fist against the M-ATV's heavily armored rear passenger door in frustration.

The truck's three-inch-thick bullet-resistant windows, designed to save lives in combat, didn't open out or roll down, and temperatures inside the M-ATV were already up over a hundred and rising. The four elite US Special Forces operators sitting inside the mobile hot box baked in their seats with sweat dripping down from under their helmets and tac vests.

Chago opened a water bottle, tilted his head up and splashed water on his face: "I'm melting in here, man," he said.

"Feels like I'm dipping my balls in a bowl of soup," Bear Bernstein said.

"Matzo ball soup?" Bobby asked.

"Had to go there, didn't you?" Bernstein shot back.

"Yeah, I did and speaking of food," Bobby said as he pulled off his helmet, ran a callused hand across his shaved scalp and felt the heat coming off it: "I can fry a fuckin' egg on my head."

Their SOCOM (Special Operations Command) M-ATV variant was a million-dollar twelve-ton armored truck with a busted AC. Not busted all the way, just enough to piss everyone off when a trickle of chilled air came through the vents every two minutes, then crapped out again.

"You triple checked everything except the Goddamn air, didn't you?" Mace asked Bobby.

Before they left their temporary COP (Combat Outpost) in the desert, they'd done a thorough PCI (Pre-Combat Inspection) followed by a PCC (Pre-Combat Check) to make sure all their comms gear and every single weapon was working. After the radios checked out, they test-fired their 9mm SIG P226 sidearms, M4A1 rifles and the dual roof-mounted 240 Bravo .50 caliber machine guns into the base's firepit to make sure they were all fully operational. The only weapon they hadn't test-fired was the roof-mounted Mk 19 grenade launcher, and as for the AC, well, Bobby could answer that…

Bobby, in the driver's seat, turned and looked over his shoulder at Mace, the truck's gunner, who was sitting diagonally behind him in the right rear passenger seat. Bobby shouted into his lip mic. "I turned the truck on and the fuckin' AC was working. How the hell was I supposed to know it was gonna die on us?" he asked.

Mace used his fingers to hold his nose: "Damn Bobby," he said.

"What?" Bobby asked.

"You got smoke and flames coming out your grill, bro. You brush your teeth since we deployed to Iraq?" Mace asked.

Bobby started to fire something back, but chose the classic non-verbal response instead. He raised his right hand, closed his fist, extended the middle finger.

"Thanks for not speaking. Stick to hand signals from here on," Mace said.

"Asshole," Bobby said.

"Dude, for the sake of the team you gotta work on your oral hygiene. Until then, think of your face as a claymore and keep your Front Towards Enemy." Mace lowered his lip mic, tilted up his water bottle to cover his smile, and then took a few long swallows to keep himself from laughing.

Bear did his best to tune out the bullshit his sergeants were giving each other while he listened to mission updates on his SINCGARS (Single Channel Ground and Airborne Radio System). He was also watching the action in real-time on an 8 x10 inch monitor.

For today's op Bear and his SF staff sergeants were acting as advisors to the Iraqi Army, trailing half a mile behind an

Iraqi Counter Terror Service armored column. The column was working its way towards a sector in Mosul that was still under ISIS control. In addition to Bear, Mace, Bobby, and Chago's M-ATV, there were six larger eighteen-ton MRAPs in a staggered line behind them, acting as rear security for the Iraqi lead elements.

Chago reached over and tapped Bear on the shoulder and asked: "Chief, at your three o'clock, is that what I think it is?"

Bear used his sleeve to wipe beads of sweat off his face, then scratched at his rough beard before turning his head to the right to look through the M-ATV's side window. He didn't detect a threat warning in Chago's voice, so he took his time scanning the neighborhood that had been liberated from ISIS just two days ago. Liberated, in this sector anyway, meant flattened.

When a few hundred ISIS fighters who were dug in and bunkered up in dozens of buildings had refused to surrender, the team's GCC (Ground Combatant Commander) had ordered the coalition bombers to take them out. Bear looked over at the devastating effects of five-hundred-pound bombs dropped from twenty thousand feet up by the B-52s, and from the lower level precision air-to-ground attacks by the F-15E Strike Eagles. The three- and four-story enemy-occupied buildings were gone, pounded into mounds of bricks, concrete, and rebar with pieces of broken furniture and loose wires sticking up at odd angles.

Bear knew there was a whole lot of bad guys buried underneath the piles, but other than some dust swirls and a rangy black mutt with big patches of its fur burned away, he didn't see anything moving. Even from ten yards out, he could see the dog's skin was bright red and probably infected.

"Sergeant, if you think that's a burnt-up dog then yeah, you're right," Bear said.

"Yeah, I know… but, what's in its mouth?" Chago asked.

The dog was shaking its head from side to side, making it hard for Bear to get a clear view. When it stopped moving and turned towards him, he saw why his sergeant was so insistent. The dog had an arm in its teeth and was gripping it by the bicep. The arm was small, with two tiny bangle bracelets around the wrist, just above the little hand that hung limply down towards the ground.

"Shit," Bear said.

Chago: "I'd like to shoot it and bury that arm."

Bear nodded and said, "Know how you feel, but after you open that rear door and get taken out by an ISIS sniper, you'd have animal rights activists pissing on your grave for the next hundred years because you were KIA while trying to shoot a canine."

"No doubt," Chago said just as they all saw three emaciated dogs charge in and attack the burnt-up mutt. It was dead in seconds and the three starving survivors growled at each other as they ripped and tugged at the child's arm.

"Get us the fuck outta here," Bear said to Bobby.

"Copy that," Bobby said, glad to be moving.

"TOC, this is Red One, We're Oscar Mike," Bear said into his radio, alerting the Tactical Operations Center that they were "on the move."

Bear, Bobby, Mace and Chago were part of a twelve-man Special Forces A-Team, call sign Razor, and they'd spent most of the day watching a shootout between dueling ISIS and Iraqi artillery batteries that managed to hit just about everything except each other. Barrage after barrage of 122 and 105mm rounds crumpled buildings and destroyed entire neighborhoods. US F-16 and coalition airstrikes were far more precise in their targeting, but added to the chaos on the ground where fires raged throughout the war-torn city.

The desert sun did its part too, torturing Team Razor along with half a million terrified civilians suffering through another day without power or running water. The Iraqis baked in their homes, their windows shut and sealed to protect them from the late afternoon breeze that guided massive plumes of toxic smoke from burning oil fields across Mosul. The black clouds were nearly as deadly as the artillery shells and had already killed thousands of the young, the old and the infirm. The windows stayed shut until the wind died, while the bombs kept falling.

A fly buzzed around inside the team's truck as they drove slowly through the wrecked neighborhood. Their M-ATV was designed with a V-shaped hull to deflect IED (Improvised Explosive Device) blasts away from the crew, but it was defenseless against winged insects.

Chago swatted at it. "I think I got him," he said, just as the fly landed on his right cheek and took a sharp bite out of him. "Son of a bitch!" he shouted.

"You're screwed, dude," Mace said.

"Whattaya mean?" Chago asked, wiping a trickle of blood from his cheek.

"That's an ISIS fly, bro. They have them bite the mullahs, then send them out to recruit new members," Mace said with a straight face.

Chago looked over with a raised eyebrow and chuckled: "You're so full a shit, Mace."

"Laugh all you want, but we've all seen it."

"Comes on quick too," Bobby said, looking back over his shoulder at Chago as he drove. "In a few hours you're gonna be prepping for your trip to paradise, stuffing C-4 and det cords under your tac vest."

"Better take his ammo," Bear said from the front passenger seat.

"Assholes," Chago said, shaking his head.

It had only been four weeks since he'd been assigned to Razor and he knew the veteran members were still breaking his balls to break the ice. Honored to be a part of this elite team, he had no problem taking a little shit from these legendary warriors.

Chago was briefed on Razor's history and the heavy casualties the Special Forces A-Team had taken over the past six months. Their OIC (Officer in Charge) and four sergeants were killed in an ambush in Afghanistan, another sergeant was killed in a separate op off the coast of Yemen, and John Bishop, their 18B weapons sergeant and one of the most decorated soldiers in American history, left the Army and was now a civilian. Despite these losses, Razor was now fully operational and the replacements, including the new OIC and NCO Chao Chen Goh, were all combat veterans with multiple deployments to both Iraq and Afghanistan.

Bear, Bobby, Mace and Chago were the lead in a line of seven armored vehicles driving a half mile behind an Iraqi column of trucks and tanks. The column was fighting its way through Mosul to rescue a company that was surrounded and about to be overrun by ISIS jihadists. The M-ATV and the big eighteen-ton MRAPs (Mine-Resistant Ambush-Protected vehicles) were tasked with rear security in case any Islamic State fighters tried to sneak in from behind and back-shoot the main column.

"They're looking good," Mace said, nodding his head in approval as the Green Beret advisors watched a live feed delivered to their monitors by a drone flying high above the action.

"Long as they stay on the main road they'll have plenty of room to maneuver," added Bobby.

Right on cue the Iraqi commander ordered the armored column to turn left onto a side street.

"God damn it!" Bear shouted, his voice amplified by the tight confines inside the M-ATV.

"Bad move," said Chago.

The side street was a tight squeeze for the Iraqi armor, and once all the M1A1 Abrams tanks, Humvees and troop carriers were bunched together in the narrow road, thirty ISIS fighters immediately opened up on them with AK-47s on full auto. Hundreds of 7.62×39mm rounds pinged off the steel-plated vehicles.

The Iraqis returned fire, blasting away with turret- and roof-mounted .50 caliber machine guns. Five ISIS attackers were flattened by the heavy rounds, and the survivors ducked into doorways and fled around corners. None of the Iraqis were hit by the small arms fire, but these seasoned soldiers had learned some hard bloody lessons in the battle for Mosul… they all knew what was coming next.

From four blocks away, two technicals (white Toyota pickups with heavy weapons in the truck beds), accelerated towards the lead M1A1. The tank gunner fired his 120mm main gun and the first pickup erupted in a fireball. The second Toyota came to a stop after being riddled with rounds from the tank's .50 cal. There was a brief moment of silence followed by a massive explosion when the dead driver's hand released its grip on the detonator, and fifty pounds of ordnance lit off.

From side streets four more cars raced towards the center

of the column, and again the battle-tested Iraqis blew them to pieces before the drivers got close enough to self-detonate and inflict any damage.

"Not too shabby," Bobby said with pride.

Bear, Bobby, Mace and Chago had spent weeks training the Iraqis in advance of the offensive to displace ISIS from Mosul.

"Didn't like that turn off the main road, but these guys are really good," Bear said. "Way better than what we saw back in '07 through '09," he added.

"Yeah, they got game," Bobby said. "Wonder when these ISIS boys are gonna get tired of gettin' splattered. Only thing they're blowing up is themselves."

"And civilians," Mace added.

Chago made eye contact with Mace and nodded his head in agreement. "Roger that," he said, recalling the intelligence briefing that detailed many of the horrors that ISIS was inflicting on Mosul's civilian population. As ISIS fighters lost more and more ground, they were increasingly targeting the locals, initially through sniper fire and IED attacks, but now they were going house to house, killing the men and abducting the women.

Over the roar of M1A1 cannons and heavy machine guns, all four Green Berets heard the radio warning from a Joint STARS surveillance plane flying thirty thousand feet above the city to the Iraqi commander of the armored column:

"Big Eye to Bravo One. Artillery fire. I say again… Incoming."

CHAPTER 2
MISSION PREP

New York, NY
Manhattan's Lower East Side

FIFTY-EIGHT HUNDRED MILES west of Mosul, John Bishop gazed through the living room window of a twelfth-floor East 10th Street apartment that he was using as a combat outpost for the upcoming battle. During his dozen plus years in Special Forces, he'd always tended to drift away into his own world for a few moments before each mission. Six months out of the Army, he and his family had been in a private war since the day he returned home to NYC, and his military routines hadn't changed much.

John's amber eyes looked out across the Lower East Side neighborhood where he grew up, while flashcards with a lifetime of memories floated before him. Someone had cooked in the apartment the night before. The aroma of pork, garlic, and cilantro still lingering in the air brought up the queen of hearts from his memory deck… His mother's smiling face was on it.

He saw her beautiful dark features, felt her hand on his

head playing with his curls and tickling the back of his neck. The corner of his mouth went up when he replayed her few futile attempts to learn English. So many Panamanians were bilingual, but even after marrying his non-Spanish-speaking Jamaican father, she hadn't really bothered with it.

His slight grin disappeared when the image of Cristina and Michael Bishop's bullet-riddled bodies appeared before him. He was nine at the time. Riding in the back seat of his Uncle Gonzalo's Cadillac with his mom and dad when the machine guns changed his life forever. John reached up and unconsciously touched the deep scar he received during the attack. It started on his forehead, zigzagged through his right eyebrow, and ended in the center of his right cheek. The scar had stretched and lengthened over time, but 25 years later it was still bold and prominent.

Memories after that were colors rather than images. Lots of black, grays, and reds during the sad dark time when he withdrew from the world. Then the colors brightened and he saw his cousin Felix, his Uncle Gonzalo, and his Aunt Grassiella. Together, they had pulled him from the abyss and brought him back to life.

Next was Maria, his childhood sweetheart. An angel. Almost too good to be true. She had waited for him. Hung on for years while he fought his demons, and through all his deployments to Iraq, Afghanistan and Africa. The woman he was lucky enough to marry. His life partner who was almost six months pregnant with their first child.

The images flashed faster through his years as a Green Beret. Contorted faces of team members, friends, brothers, all pleading with him to tell their mothers, fathers, wives, and children how much they loved them, before dying in his arms. Warriors all. The best of the best, their mangled bodies bleeding out into foreign sand and soil.

Lastly came the bad guys. The hundreds of bearded Al Qaeda, Taliban, ISIS, Al Shabaab and Boko Haram fighters he'd killed. Some of the faces were obscure and blurry, far more were clear crisp snapshots of men frozen in time at their moment of death. It was too quick to be sure, but John could swear that every one of them gave him the finger before they silently drifted away. He mentally gave them each a fuck-you right back.

Even though blood and death filled the arc of his memories, Bishop knew he was blessed. The love of his wife, his family and friends had saved his life. They had helped him overcome all the pain and sorrow, and against all odds he'd survived. A born fighter with the scars to prove it.

A heated discussion behind him pulled him out of his reverie. He turned and headed over to his cousin Felix "Cat" Valdez and John's friend Valentino "Bunny" Brown, who were highlighting the many benefits of wearing Kevlar. John listened in for a while, chuckling at first, then quickly started getting annoyed. He never imagined it would be this hard to persuade a sixty-year-old man in a wheelchair to wear body armor, but Speedy Billups wasn't backing down.

"C'mon Speedy. Just put it on," John said.

"Not gonna happen," Speedy said. "I've been in more gunfights than you, war hero. Stood face-to-face and outdrew any man fool enough to test me. Cowards had to back-shoot me to put me in this chair, and even without legs I'm still undefeated."

"This isn't some Wild West showdown, Speedy. These Russians are coming at us with AK-47s. We all need to vest up," John said.

"My brother, ain't no vest in the world gonna save us if we get lit up by AKs, and you know it. Plus, I got a rep to maintain. Can't have people thinking I'm soft and worried about getting hit with a few shells."

Felix gave up: "Speedy does have a point. Dude's been shot three more times since he's been in that chair. Always managed to wheel himself to the ER and have the docs plug the holes. He wants to go to war naked, that's on him."

John wasn't having it. "Enough! Will you just do me the favor and wear the Goddamn body armor," he snapped.

Speedy was about to shout back, but kept his composure and his voice even. "Sure Johnny, I'll wear the girdle. I know this is your fight. I owe a lot to your uncle and I'm just here to help."

John's uncle was Gonzalo Valdez, head of New York's notorious Valdez crime family. Speedy was a lone wolf gangster, but had always respected the Valdez flag and never did any dirt in neighborhoods under Gonzalo's control. As a sign of respect, John's uncle had tracked down the out-of-state hitters who crippled Speedy, and Gonzalo had flown him down to Atlanta so he could exact his revenge. It was a debt Speedy vowed to repay and this battle with the Russian mob was his chance to balance the books.

Felix and Bunny, a former Green Beret and one of John's closest friends, helped Speedy strap on the Kevlar upper body rig.

"What're you packing?" John asked.

"Glock 20s with fifteen-round mags," Speedy said, brandishing a black 10mm semi-automatic in each hand.

"That it?" Felix asked skeptically, raising an eyebrow to emphasize that they all knew Speedy was armed with a lot more than two pistols.

"Hell no. We's the bait, but this here bait is sho' 'nough gonna bite back." Speedy holstered his Glock 20s and lightly tapped the arms of his wheelchair. "I call these babies my night-night guns 'cause anyone standing in front of 'em is gonna be laying down right quick. Each arm is a sawed-off twelve-gauge. Fires four shells in under five seconds."

Bunny and John both whistled and bent down to examine the perfectly camouflaged shotguns more closely. A former Green Beret 18B weapons sergeant, John was an expert in all manner of firearms. He nodded his head in admiration at the creativity and craftsmanship of the master gunsmith who'd customized the chair.

"Johnny, just make sure you ain't standing behind me when the shootin' starts. Firing these babies puts me in reverse, and I don't want you gettin' your legs broke," Speedy said.

"Thanks for the heads up," John said.

"What you got?" Speedy asked.

John smiled and opened his dark blue windbreaker to reveal two SIG Sauer P226s hanging ominously in left and right shoulder holsters. Speedy dipped his chin in respect to the hand cannons. They anticipated that the Russians would attack from Humvees in full body armor and the SIG's .357 rounds packed massive stopping power.

"Heard you got married," Speedy said.

"Yeah, I sure did," John said.

"Baby on the way too," Bunny added.

Speedy looked up at John thoughtfully and said, "Must be more understanding than most."

"What do you mean?" John asked.

"In my experience, single ladies surely do love us bad boy gunmen, but pregnant wives don't take kindly to their baby daddies standing out in the street getting shot at. Those maternal hormones kick in and right away they try turning you into a house cat." Speedy smiled and then added, "Yours must be mighty special."

"Yeah, she sure is," John said, then a voice in his head added, *Maria's more than just special, but if she knew what I was about to do, she'd probably shoot me herself.*

John, Speedy, Felix, Bunny and several Valdez family soldiers were using the twelfth-floor apartment as a staging area. John walked back over to the apartment windows and picked up a pair of binoculars from a small wooden table along the way. Raising the binoculars, he increased their magnification to give him a detailed view of the battlefield. Scanning past the empty Dry Dock Pool on East 10th Street and across Avenue D, he focused on the big oval in the Jacob Riis Houses that would soon become a killing ground.

The Russian mob had been using advanced technology to ambush members of John's family, and it had taken them more than a week to identify the brilliantly disguised mini drones that looked and flew like small birds. Today they were using the Russians' technology against them by giving them an irresistible target and drawing them into an ambush. John was that target and he felt a slight tinge of regret as he thought about the men he was about to kill.

His regret wasn't tied to the Russian hitters themselves, since they had tortured and executed six Valdez soldiers in less than a month. The plan was to try to keep one or two alive for questioning, but now or later they would all die for the atrocities they'd committed. John wasn't losing sleep over that. Killing bad guys didn't bother him much. The fact that he was largely responsible for a whole lot of good people dying over the past several months definitely did.

After voluntarily ending his illustrious career with

Special Forces in June, John had come back to New York to marry Maria, reconnect with his family, and put his violent past behind him. Nearly a decade of constant combat operations had cost him a lot. Too much. He'd been wounded twenty-three times, dozens of his battle buddies had come home in flag-draped coffins, and he'd killed more men than he could count. John had left Team Razor to find peace and vowed never to take another life.

The vow was short-lived. A chance encounter with an Afghan terrorist and his network of cells intent on killing civilians and blowing up several power plants in New York had been the catalyst for all the bloodshed.

"Don't forget to glance up at the building when you walk out so that little bird drone gets a good look at you," Felix said.

Smiling on the inside, John merely nodded as Felix walked him through the battle plan once more. After all, John was the decorated Green Beret, while Felix was a civilian.

Former civilian, John thought. *He's a true soldier now.*

Felix had always been tough. Even before he went to prison for a crime that John committed when they were teenagers, but the constant combat of the past six months had transformed Felix into an urban commando with a natural feel for mission strategies and tactics.

The cousins had the same amber, cat-like eyes, and both were exactly six feet tall. Felix packed more muscle, weighing in around two-twenty. John was leaner at one-ninety-five, but they both moved with the same ease and confidence of super predators. They were the top of the food chain when it came to hand-to-hand combat—Felix from his years in prison and the black belts he'd earned in Kendo and Karate after he got out—John from being one of the most decorated war heroes the US Army ever produced.

John, Felix, and Bunny wore earpieces and mics on their shirt collars, so they heard all the troops checking in from the surrounding LES (Lower East Side) buildings, from a high-rise still under construction across the East River, and from an additional sniper team positioned under the Williamsburg Bridge.

"Alpha One to Bravo One. Give us another five minutes to get set up. We're extracting a few more residents. I'll give you the go signal when they're cleared out and everyone's in position, over," Randall "Christmas" Owens, said over the secure net.

Christmas, a former Navy SEAL, was the head of the Valdez family's elite military wing. He was running the op and had overall command and control.

"That's a good copy, Alpha One. Understood. Five minutes, over," John confirmed.

Even though their radios were encrypted, they were using call signs. The Russian mob they were facing had already shown that they had access to the latest in advanced technology, when they ambushed several Valdez family soldiers by tracking their cell phones. When John and his family switched to more secure communication devices, the Russians had upped their game as well, using the small brown bird-shaped drones that looked and flew like sparrows. After three more Valdez men were tracked, abducted and tortured to death, John and Christmas had devised a plan to go on the offensive and use the drones to set an ambush of their own.

John knew the plan was solid. If the Russians took the bait, they'd find themselves surrounded, outnumbered and outgunned by thirty pissed off men who'd be shooting down from elevated positions. The Russkies were some tough SOBs. No one expected them to surrender, but if any of them tried to make a run for it, two heavily armored SUVs with more Valdez shooters would seal off the escape route. The only possible flaw that John saw in the plan was that the Russians would more than likely die trying to kill the bait. Since he was the bait, it was cause for concern.

Chapter 3
Calling Johnny Bishop

Mosul, Iraq

THE COLUMN BUTTONED up, slamming and locking their hatches shut to keep the troops inside safe from the shrapnel. The first wave of 122mm HE (High Explosive) rounds, fired by two Soviet-made M-30 Howitzers, rained down slightly off target, striking and damaging the surrounding two-story buildings, but missing the column.

Dozens of smoke grenades were tossed from rooftops, windows and doorways by ISIS foot soldiers to help their artillery team hit the mark. The tanks surged forward. Driving through the thick red smoke, they plowed through occupied family homes to escape the kill zone.

From the tower of a nearby mosque, an ISIS spotter radioed his artillery team to adjust fire, and a second wave of 122 HE landed with pinpoint accuracy, slamming the column with one direct hit after another. Several vehicles broke formation and turned onto side streets trying to find a way out, only to face fanatical suicide bombers charging towards them.

Detonating themselves next to the tires and tracks, they disabled two of the Abrams tanks and a Humvee.

TOC, which oversaw both the US and Iraqi elements involved in the op, called in air support and the three Black Hawks that were on station streaked in. With so many civilians in the surrounding houses, the ROE (Rules of Engagement) prohibited the attack helos from using their missiles, but they were weapons-free with their M134 miniguns. The six-barreled M134s delivered over six thousand rounds per minute and once the pilots had targets in their gunsights, tiny pieces of cloth floated in the air like black snow when the ISIS fighters had their uniforms shredded by 7.62x51mm rounds—and then the men themselves evaporated in a red mist.

The ISIS spotter in the tower had a sniper by his side and he directed his shooter to zero in on the Black Hawks. The sniper aimed for the tail rotors with his captured US Army M107 .50 cal semi-automatic rifle. He had known the Back Hawks would come and made his M107 into an anti-aircraft gun by loading it with armor-piercing incendiary rounds. As soon as the first helo was hit, the pilots took evasive measures and disengaged.

Back on the ground, two bearded attackers fired shoulder-mounted RPG-7 anti-tank rounds at the lead Abrams, and the tank instantly erupted into a fireball. Crews from disabled and boxed-in vehicles popped their hatches and doors to escape on foot just as the next wave of 122mm shells landed. Shrapnel ripped through them, tearing off limbs and leaving the survivors screaming for medics.

"They're getting wiped out!" Bobby shouted. "We need to take out that tower. The sniper is hitting the helos and there's a spotter up there calling in the artillery."

"Negative," Bear said. "ROE states we can't destroy any mosques."

Chago focused his binoculars, zooming in on the tower.

"Take a look. Those two assholes are up there laughing at us. We need to blast those fuckers," Chago said.

Bear thought it over. Their mission objective had been clearly laid out for them the night before. Make assessments and send SITREPs (Situation Reports) about the capabilities of both ISIS and the Iraqi army in Mosul. Period. He knew that Team Razor reports were making their way up through the chain and were being used to make tactical, operational, and strategic decisions by CENTCOM (US Central Command), SOCOM (Special Operations Command), the Joint Chiefs, and even the president. Bear also recalled the stern warning given to him by Special Forces Gen. Marcus Palmer:

"Your mission is to advise. Don't jump into any fire-fights… even if you see the Iraqis taking losses. Understood?"

"Yes, sir," Bear had said.

"Remember, the whole world is watching this battle for Mosul on CNN. So stay off camera, protect yourself at all times, and do *not* get killed or captured."

Bear wasn't about to disobey Palmer's direct order, but he wasn't going to sit back and do nothing either. Over the secure net, he listened to the Joint STARS surveillance plane give the three Black Hawks the coordinates of the ISIS artillery team less than five miles away. Bear made a call of his own as he watched the helos dip their noses and race off towards their new targets.

"Red One to Squeezer, over."

"Squeezer to Red One, go."

"Squeezer, we have two targets in the white tower in

sector six. A shooter and an arty spotter that need your immediate attention, over."

Special Forces Sgt. Dan "The Squeezer" Morris and three other SOF snipers were supporting Team Razor from their concealed positions half a mile away. There were several seconds of radio silence as Squeezer put the sights of his Browning M82A1 long-range rifle on the mosque's minaret.

"Targets acquired… break…Your call, Red One… break… We've been instructed to shoot around these types of buildings, not at them, over."

"Understood. Don't scratch the walls or chip any paint, but you're weapons-free on both targets," Bear said into his lip mic.

"Good copy," Squeezer said as he fired.

The sniper in the mosque tower had his crosshairs on a wounded Iraqi major when Squeezer's .50BMG round hit him in the right temple. The ISIS insurgent who had been feeding coordinates to the soon-to-be-dead artillery team bent down to tie his shoe just as his partner's head exploded. Instantly coated with blood, brains and skull fragments, the spotter threw himself to the ground. Squeezer's second shot missed and put a six-inch diameter hole in the mosque wall.

"Thought we agreed. No scratches," Bear said into his mic.

"Quick little fucker. Think he's heading down. See if you can catch him in the street. He'll be hard to miss," Squeezer said.

"Small guy, thick beard, dressed in black?" Bear asked. "Not many of 'em around here."

"The gallon of blood and brain matter sprayed all over him will make him stand out in the crowd."

"Copy that."

F-16s flew in low over the battlefield, doing strafing runs and hosing down ISIS fighters with their 20mm Gatling guns and an Iraqi QRT (Quick Response Team) was on its way to support the column and help with the wounded. Five Sikorski Pave Hawk helicopters were also en-route for CASEVAC (Casualty Evacuation).

With the sniper team and the Black Hawks back on station to back them up, Bear made the decision to go after the artillery spotter. He told Bobby to ease the M-ATV forward with the other trucks following at staggered intervals. They were fifty feet away from the mosque when a lone figure burst through the front door.

"That's our man!" Bear shouted.

The blood-soaked spotter looked back at the line of massive eighteen-ton armored trucks heading right at him, and took off running. He was less than a block from the mosque when the lead armored truck caught up to him.

"Stop! Stop and get down on the ground!" Bear commanded in Arabic, his voice booming through the truck's loudspeaker.

Ignoring Bear's orders, the tango cut across the street and sprinted into the open doorway of a three-story building. Bobby hit the brakes and Mace manned the dual roof-mounted 240 Bravo, rotating and scanning for targets with both .50 cals while Bear and Chago hopped out, pressed their M4A1 rifles to their shoulders, and cautiously approached the building. Six team members from three of the MRAPs also dismounted and ran towards the building to back them up. From the entrance, Bear and Bobby could see a bloody handprint where their man had touched the wall next to the staircase.

"You take the stairs," Chago said to Bear. "I'll go up from here."

Staff Sgt. Chao Chen Goh was born in New York's Chinatown. He grew up climbing buildings and jumping rooftops to evade the cops who regularly chased him as a teenager. Joining the Army at eighteen had changed his life, probably even saved his life. His delinquent days were now only a distant memory, but scaling walls was something he'd never forget.

"Fucking cowboy," Bobby said, not really meaning it. Over the past few weeks, everyone on Razor had come to respect Chago as an operator and seen firsthand just how competent, hardworking and professional he was. Chago was a New Yorker and cocky as hell, but so what? Every operator on the team was cocky. Humble, quiet dudes would never fit in on Razor.

The vacant building that had once housed a thriving street level market and a residence on the floors above was now pockmarked with holes from heavy machine gun and artillery fire. There were plenty of handholds, and Chago made his way up to the third-floor balcony in seconds. From there he wedged his right boot into a crack in the wall for leverage and pulled himself up onto the roof. He unslung and shouldered his M4 just as the blood-covered ISIS jihadist burst through a door to the roof holding a Beretta 9mm pistol.

Chago didn't hesitate. He fired once, hitting him in the right shoulder. The fighter screamed in pain, but managed to stay on his feet.

"Drop it," Chago said in Arabic. "Drop it or die."

After his run up the stairs, Bear came through the roof door and trained his weapon on their target's back.

"Don't shoot! Don't shoot! I have information," the skinny fighter said in heavily accented English. He dropped the pistol and pressed his left hand over the bullet wound. "No Guantanamo!"

"Information? Information is good," Bear said, coming in from behind and thoroughly checking him for any concealed weapons. "We'll talk downstairs."

Bear and Chago went on either side of their prisoner, and each held an arm as more SF operators were on their way up the stairs.

"We got him," Bear said. "Everyone head back down."

They all went down the stairs, out onto the street, and hustled over to Bear's lead M-ATV.

"All right. What do you have for me?" Bear asked as Chago and several other Green Berets searched their prisoner again and used the BAT/HIIDE (Biometric Automated Toolset/Handheld Interagency Identity Detection Equipment) to photograph and fingerprint him, then secured his hands behind his back with zip ties.

"The next attack."

"Here?" Bear asked.

"No, not here. I mean yes… we will keep fighting you here, but the next attack is in your New York City."

"We'll need more than that. Let's start with who you are and where you're from."

"My name is Warid Saif. I am Afghan. I fought for Aziz Khan in Khost."

Bear tried to conceal his shock at what Warid had just said, and the CWO glanced up at Mace, who was still manning the dual .50 cals on the roof of the M-ATV. Aziz Khan was directly responsible for the death of six Team Razor operators. Chago was a new member of the team, but Bear, Mace, and Bobby had been part of the op coordinated by John Bishop that wiped out Aziz and his entire army. Or so they thought.

"Okay, you fought for Aziz. What're you doing here in Mosul fighting Iraqis?"

"After the Americans killed Aziz Khan, many of us followed his second, Tariq Hassan, to join our ISIS brothers here and in Syria. Tariq is working with senior leaders on the New York mission."

"You want to stay out of Gitmo or a Saudi interrogation center, you gotta give us more than that, Warid," Bear said. "We need details. Where and when?"

"I have some, not all, but I know who Tariq's main target is."

"You said *who*, not *what*. Who's he going after, the mayor?"

"No. An enemy far more important than any politician," Warid said.

"Gimme the name," Bear said impatiently.

"You promise to protect me? No torture. No Gitmo."

"I'll need the name before I can promise you anything," Bear said.

"John Bishop. First, we kill him, then we blow up New York."

Bear pulled his iridium secure satellite phone from a front pouch in his tac vest, punched in a few numbers, and got Gen. Palmer on the phone. He gave the general a quick SITREP.

"Yes, sir. We're returning to base with the prisoner now, and I'll send out a preliminary report as soon as he gives us the details…. Yes, sir, I'll remain in the room and call you directly… Very good, sir… General?… Can I call him?… Thank you, sir."

Bear's jaw was tight, flexing with tension as he prepared to make his next call. He nodded at his sergeants. "Mount up and move out," he said as he rapidly hit more numbers on the secure phone.

Chago looked up at Mace: "Who's he calling now?"

"Our brother, Johnny Bishop," Mace said.

Chapter 4
The LES Way

Jacob Riis Houses, LES

BISHOP CHECKED THE streets again to make sure there weren't any civilians wandering around. While the Russian mob was indifferent to collateral damage, John and the Valdez family couldn't have any innocents caught in the crossfire. LES was their neighborhood and everyone in it lived under the protection of the Valdez flag.

John's phone vibrated in his pocket and he smiled when he recognized Bear Bernstein's international number on his caller ID. The smile disappeared when Bear got right to the point and gave him a preliminary report about the imminent attacks coming his way. The slight darkening of the scar on his face, and the change in his eyes that went from their normal deep yellow to a fiery amber were the only signals that he was none too pleased by the news he was getting from his old friend.

"Appreciate the heads-up, Bear. I'm in the middle of something right now, so let's talk again after you get the details. You know the drill. I need the who, how, and when."

"Will do, Johnny. Watch your six, brotha," Bear said before ending the call.

Bishop paused for a moment to process the intel. He'd have to deal with it later since he definitely was "in the middle of something."

"Who was that on the phone?" Felix asked.

John gave him a short summary of the new threat coming their way from Tariq Hassan and ISIS. Felix kicked a chair in anger.

"Man, this whole mess started with Aziz Khan. That fucker ambushed your team in Afghanistan, and when you stopped his nephew Amir from blowing up half of New York, he sent that head-chopping bitch Omar after you. Not sure if Omar's alive after Bunny shot her, but Amir and Aziz are dead for sure. Now more of Aziz's soldiers are coming at us? Partnered up with ISIS? When's this shit gonna end, bro?"

"I don't know, Cat. The good news is Team Razor's on the case, and Spec Ops will stop these assholes long before they get here," John said.

Felix stared at his cousin momentarily before nodding his head sadly and turning away. John knew that Felix was thinking about how much this war had already cost them. Their cousin, Chris Valdez, had been murdered by one of Amir Khan's suicide bombers. Their Uncle Macho, Chris's father, had traveled to Afghanistan to avenge his son, and willingly gave his own life to kill Aziz Khan.

Another uncle, Sesa Valdez, was in a coma after being gravely wounded. Six of his Special Forces brothers were dead. John's wife Maria had been kidnapped and seriously injured in the fight to rescue her, and John and Felix had come close to being killed by Omar, the Tringa assassin.

After all that death, the war was still far from over.

Enemies were coming at John and his family from all sides, but sitting back and waiting for the next attack simply wasn't an option. In order to survive, they had to go on the offensive, and after this battle with the Russians John knew there were many more to come.

"Brava One to Alpha One, we're all set here," Christmas said over the radio.

And so it begins, John thought as he pushed Speedy in his wheelchair down the hallway towards the elevators. They exited the building, went south on Avenue C, made a left on 10th Street, and headed east.

Felix "Cat" Valdez and Bunny Brown moved to the back bedroom of the apartment. Felix watched John and Speedy through a pair of Steiner military binoculars. Bunny had the same view through the scope of his Remington Mk 21 precision sniper rifle.

Bunny was huge. Six-five and a chiseled two-seventy. His father was black, his mother Italian. Bunny looked like an NFL lineman turned TV star with a square jaw and perfect teeth. A former Green Beret, Bunny had four deployments to Iraq until his military career ended when he was shot saving John's life. Their bond, forged in combat, had become far deeper over the years, and they loved each other like true brothers.

"You okay, big man?" Felix asked when he heard Bunny's loud and unstable breathing, then glanced over to check on him and saw that he was drenched with sweat.

"Hell no," Bunny said, his eye never leaving the rifle's scope. "You?"

"Just breathe, bro. Christmas has a lot of shooters out there, but we may need your skills too. Sweaty palms and shaky hands don't hit the mark. Breathe, Bunny. Just breathe."

"Can't believe you're schooling me, Cat. You're right though. Gotta get my head in the game." He rotated his neck and took five deep, steady breaths. "I'm good now. Don't worry. I've got Johnny's back."

Felix and John were first cousins, raised together by their Uncle Gonzalo. Felix had spent almost four years in state prison and was as tough as they come. Despite his calming words to Bunny, his own hands trembled slightly as he watched his cousin, his brother, march into a bloodbath.

Down on the street, John pushed the wheelchair while Speedy did an admirable acting job of transforming himself into an invalid. Wearing a fitted wool Yankees hat, Speedy's head hung down towards his left shoulder, and even though it was unusually warm for early November, blankets were draped over his legs.

"They spotted you, Johnny," Christmas said into everyone's earpieces. "The drone is thirty feet above you doing wide arcs. Shouldn't be long now."

"Roger that," John said.

"You ready, war hero?" Speedy whispered.

"Always, old man," John said with a slight grin.

They moved at a calm and steady pace along East 10th Street, then crossed Avenue D into the Jacob Riis Houses. The nineteen buildings that made up the Riis projects were built in a circle with a large oval-shaped driveway for cars and buses at its center.

They'd planned ahead. All the residents had been told to move their cars the day before so they wouldn't get damaged, and to make today's trip fit into a pattern, every morning for the past five days someone had pushed Speedy in front of building 438 to catch some rays.

With the morning sun at their back, John and Speedy

were alone in the oval. They heard the engines seconds after Christmas announced that three black Hummers were heading their way, coming north up Avenue D.

The Hummers drove in a tight formation and were nearly bumper to bumper when they made the sharp right turn into Jacob Riis. The big utility vehicles roared as their drivers accelerated around the circle towards their target. John and Speedy stood their ground. That should have been a bright red warning flag to the Russian hit teams, but the three trucks confidently stopped fifteen feet in front of the man they came to kill.

John stared at the wide front windows, calmly waiting for his attackers to make their move. He knew it wouldn't be long, and he reached for his SIGs just as the six rear doors flew open and twelve Russians wearing full body armor jumped out onto the pavement. All twelve held AK-47s. Formidable weapons and one of the most reliable assault rifles ever made, but their size gave John a slight advantage.

He picked his targets as he moved to his right, and had his SIGs up and firing before a single AK was leveled at him. He hit the first Russian in the bridge of the nose, and a big chunk of the back of his skull flew off. John shot the second one in the throat and the powerful .357 caliber round went through him, instantly killing him and the man behind him.

"Nice shooting, Johnny," Speedy said while blasting away with his Glock 20s. His 20s didn't have the punch of Bishop's .357s, so he aimed for anything unprotected by armor. The crippled gunfighter didn't miss, and four more Russians were dead before they hit the ground.

The drivers put the Hummers in gear, but in their planning sessions John, Christmas and the Valdez team had all agreed that the Russians would try to run them over as soon as they started taking losses. From third-story Jacob Riis apartments, Christmas and five other marksmen fired down at the trucks with a mix of M4 assault rifles and Barrett .50 caliber semi-auto sniper rifles, penetrating the bullet-resistant windshields and killing the drivers.

John stayed in motion while everything around him seemed to slow down. The years of intense Special Forces training and the hundreds of firefights he'd been in kept his mind at ease and his body almost on autopilot. He wasn't reckless in battle but his fighting philosophy was pretty basic: dominate the enemy with pure aggression and overwhelming firepower. Shooting with both hands, he moved forward.

A six-six Russian, massive and powerfully built, tossed his AK and pulled out a Beretta. He pushed his comrades aside and charged at John, shouting out a war cry and firing as he ran.

John felt the hit to his collarbone. After being shot so many times before, he knew his vest had stopped the 9mm round from penetrating. It was going to hurt like hell after the adrenaline wore off, but he'd take a deep bruise over a hole any day.

Getting shot was something that always pissed John off, so he decided to take his time with this one. He put a .357 round through the giant's left leg, severing it below the knee, and then hit him again in the right shoulder. The Russian's eyes went wide when the bullets covered the short distance at 1,500 feet per second and sent his pistol flying and his three-hundred-pound body airborne. He landed on his back and looked up at John.

"Good fighter for a blackie," he said, in heavily accented English. "Yakov will send more for you. Soon. Very soon, you're a dead blackie."

Bishop glanced down at the Russian but didn't bother responding to the racist threat from a soon-to-be-dead man. If the big boy didn't bleed out, he'd wish he had when Gonzalo's interrogation team went to work on him.

John heard AKs firing a moment before the massive booms from Speedy's "night-night guns" silenced them.

From his elevated position in the Haven Plaza apartment, Bunny saw a Russian creep from behind one of the Hummers and point a handgun at John's back. Bunny fired. Through his scope he saw the puff of red on the shooter's scalp and then watched him topple backwards from the head shot.

Christmas and his men came charging out of the buildings with weapons raised, checking for survivors. They found two more wounded Russians, who were then quickly bound and gagged. Christmas raised his M4, took careful aim, and blew the hovering bird-drone out of the sky. It fell to the ground in pieces a few feet away.

John walked over to Speedy and put his hand on his shoulder.

"Nice shooting, Mr. Billups. Let's get out of here."

"You go on ahead, Johnny."

John looked closer and saw blood pumping slowly from Speedy's neck. He tried to put pressure on the wound to stem the flow, but the crippled gunfighter knocked his hands away.

"Tell your uncle, we be even. My debt is paid."

"Don't you die on me, old man. Let me get you to a medic."

Speedy grinned. "It's the LES way, Johnny. Live hard. Die well."

His head fell forward and John knew he was dead before he checked him for a pulse. John bent down and touched his forehead to Speedy's, whispered a few words, then walked away surrounded by Christmas and a dozen Valdez soldiers.

Six SUVs and two eighteen-wheelers with the Valdez cleanup crew on board raced into the oval to remove the prisoners and sanitize as much of the carnage as they could. All three Hummers were quickly loaded into the Mack trucks, and thirteen dead Russians were unceremoniously tossed in after them. Speedy Billups was handled with the honor and dignity he deserved, his body carefully placed in the back seat of a separate vehicle and driven away. The rest of the cleaning crew used industrial vacuums to suck up the scattered shell casings and big pools of blood, then dumped bags of sand on the blood they couldn't remove before leaving the killing ground. When they left the oval, it was empty and eerily silent. The only sounds came from the blaring of police sirens racing towards the Jacob Riis Houses.

CHAPTER 5
NESTOR

Washington Heights, North Manhattan

GONZALO VALDEZ WAS the head of the Valdez family, but came to his brother Nestor's Washington Heights headquarters to try to resolve their differences… and talk some sense into him. Nestor was the second youngest of the seventeen Valdez siblings, and Gonzalo always had a soft spot for him, despite his recklessness.

Nestor was behind his big mahogany desk in a highbacked leather executive's chair, speaking on the phone with one of his lieutenants while Gonzalo sat facing him in a small metal folding chair. If his brother was trying to intimidate him with such a cliché power move, Gonzalo was unimpressed.

His legs crossed, his back straight, muscled shoulders relaxed, Gonzalo plucked a tiny piece of lint from the sleeve of his black Armani blazer, flicked it away and then casually reset the cuffs of his white Eton dress shirt. Though the shirt, slacks and jacket covered the knife cuts and bullet wounds that marked his body, they did nothing to conceal the deep scars on his face and hands from years of bare knuckle boxing on the streets of Panama when he was a boy.

Gonzalo knew the scars, his dark skin, bald head, and catlike yellow eyes—characteristics that made most people fear him on sight—didn't do anything to intimidate his little brother. Nestor was equally fearsome. More powerfully built, his copper-colored skin was covered by an intricately detailed cobra tattoo from his neck down, and each of the snake's scales was made up of many smaller, baby cobras.

Gonzalo momentarily drifted away while he waited for Nestor to finish his call… Going back in time to when the Valdez clan made its way from the streets of Panama to New York City after their father was murdered, and their mother died from pneumonia soon after. Eleven brothers and six sisters arrived in Alphabet City on Manhattan's Lower East Side with nothing more than their will to survive. Back then, in the 1970s, the neighborhood had one economy: drugs. Gonzalo had made the fateful decision to take control of the market, and with his family behind him, they fought their way to the top. Of all the choices he'd made in his life, it was the one he truly regretted, and the Valdez family had paid dearly for it.

Seeing four of his brothers die in the streets had been hard to bear, but the loss of his baby sister had nearly broken him. Christina was gunned down along with her husband Michael in a failed assassination attempt against Gonzalo. They were John's parents, and he was in the car with them when a rival gang sprayed it with machine guns. John's face and heart were forever scarred from the attack, and from that day on Gonzalo had raised him as his son.

Now Gonzalo glanced at his little brother, marveling at the eerie electric light that surrounded him. Nestor had it since birth and had carried it with him to prison after his murder conviction. Thirty years in a cage had transformed Nestor from a wiry teenager into a muscled power lifter, and the electric light burned brighter than ever.

Nestor was just a kid when the Valdez wars started. He was raised in battle and quickly became a fearless fighter with an insatiable bloodlust. When the bullets were flying and everyone else ducked or found cover, Nestor would charge the enemy with guns blazing. He'd killed half a dozen men before he turned eighteen and never received so much as a scratch. A teenage legend, it wasn't long before he became a lone wolf hunter, tracking down rival gangs on his own without backup.

Gonzalo and the entire family had repeatedly pleaded with Nestor to stop taking unnecessary risks, but he ignored their warnings and became even more reckless. On a dark and rainy night in the 1980s, he'd stalked one of their enemies and opened fire as soon as he had him cornered. Nestor's target was standing in between two police officers when he shot him. Evidently the blue uniforms didn't impress him, because he pumped three more rounds into the body lying at their feet. Witnesses said he was laughing when they took him into custody.

During his thirty years of incarceration Nestor had built his own army. He now controlled all the prisons north of Louisiana and east of Nevada. Gonzalo had ended the Valdez family's role in the drug trade more than a decade earlier, but Nestor was deep in it and his goal was to have complete control of the US market. Gonzalo and his brothers were trying to bring Nestor back into the family, and they'd had several meetings to discuss it since his release. They pleaded with him to walk away from the drugs and to see the big picture… Once again Nestor wasn't listening.

The Valdez family had their own security cameras placed

throughout the Lower East Side, and Gonzalo and Nestor watched the ambush at Jacob Riis in real-time on a 70-inch monitor in Nestor's office.

"The big Russian spoke the truth. Yakov will send more soldiers. Many more," Gonzalo said.

"You have to hit them higher up in their chain of command."

"We're trying to send a message first, Nestor. If it doesn't work, then we'll target decision makers within their organization."

"You called me Nestor. You know that's not my name anymore."

"No offense, Geronimo. I forgot."

"You never forget anything, but none taken, big brother."

Nestor had announced his name change the day he walked out of prison and into the arms of hundreds of his chanting and fiercely loyal followers. His name wasn't the only thing he'd changed. All the Valdez brothers were dark-skinned but Nestor, now Geronimo, was the exception. From birth he'd been a deep rust color, a strange mix of red and brown. In Panama, their mother had once joked that he must be part Indian. That one must have come down from the mountains and ravaged her in her sleep to give him that color. All his older brothers and sisters had laughed long and hard. Nestor didn't. He was five at the time, and looked up at his mother with hard, flat eyes that never seemed to blink, staring at her in silence. She never teased him again about his complexion. None of them did.

Gonzalo thought back to that moment and realized for the first time that they had all been afraid of him, and in his heart of hearts knew that he still was. Maybe more so now since Nestor's transformation, which only added to his strange aura.

As a follow-up to his stark realization, another thought crossed Gonzalo's mind:

I wonder if he's going to kill me.

As if sensing his unease, Geronimo turned away from the flat screen and stared into Gonzalo's yellow eyes. "Don't worry big brother, I'm not going to kill you."

"I wasn't thinking that."

"Yes, you were. Why would I kill you, Zalo? You have nothing I need. You're not even a gangster anymore, but I was surprised to hear you're a government snitch now."

"We don't snitch on anyone. We're businessmen and consultants."

Gonzalo and the family had put their street money to good use, buying real estate and starting several highly profitable businesses. He'd also leveraged his former relationships in the drug trade to assist the United States government. He was now working closely with the CIA to fight the global war on terror and recently helped mediate a ceasefire between warring Mexican cartels, stemming the violence that crossed the border into Texas and Arizona. The fact that his younger brother was now a drug kingpin posed a major threat to Gonzalo and the future of the Valdez family.

"I may use some of your companies to clean my money," Geronimo said. "Oh, and I need you to schedule a meeting for me. We're taking over the Mexican cartels and I want you to do what you do so well. Negotiate their retirement plan."

"Neither one is going to happen, Nes... excuse me, Geronimo."

"Sure, it is. Listen Zalo, I respect you. Despite what you may think, I always have. I saw my path long ago and I followed it. I had to get to prison so I could build my own army. That's why I shot Ray-Ray in front of those cops."

The ravings of a madman, Gonzalo thought, but kept his expression neutral.

"You think I'm crazy, big brother? Think what you want. Just know that I rule this country now. Mexico is next, then we move to Europe. This little skirmish with the Russians is a good exercise and as you said, you want to send a message. You're under my protection now, so I'm going to add a few exclamation points to it so Moscow hears us loud and clear."

Geronimo pressed the remote and the image switched to the crowded yard in Elmira State Penitentiary, the prison where he'd done his time.

"You have access to all the security monitors?"

"Yes, for every facility except for a few in Cali and two in Texas. Watch."

Amazing, Gonzalo thought, finally recognizing just how powerful and dangerous his younger brother really was. The new reality was brought home as they watched a group of seven shirtless men who were easily identified as Russians by the Mafia tattoos that covered their upper bodies.

"That's Sergei and his crew. He's Moscow's top dog here," Geronimo said.

Sergei and his lieutenants were lifting weights and laughing at an inside joke when thirty prisoners charged them with steel pipes and homemade knives. The fight only lasted a few seconds. All seven Russians lay dead, along with two of Geronimo's Apaches.

"We did the same thing in ten other prisons this morning. Forty-eight dead, not counting the ones John and Christmas took care of at Jacob Riis. All the Russian bosses are going to be very pissed off at Yakov for starting this little war with you… Speak with them… as my representative."

Geronimo didn't wait for Gonzalo to respond. He snapped his fingers and one of his men hustled into the office. Geronimo pointed to the bodies of his two fallen soldiers displayed on the monitor.

"Isn't that Hollywood and Smokey?"

His man silently nodded in agreement.

"Go see their families today. A hundred thousand each."

Another silent nod and the man left the office.

"Quiet one," Gonzalo commented.

"No tongue," Geronimo said. "We shared a cell for a few years and he used to talk a lot. It became annoying."

Gonzalo stared at the madman who used to be his little brother, wondering how he was going to handle him.

CHAPTER 6

MARIA

Long Island, NY

"YOU THINK I'M an idiot," Maria said.

"What did you say? I can't hear with the water running," John said from the shower.

"Nothing," Maria said. More of a growl than a word.

She picked his clothes up off the floor and closely examined them.

Most women check their husband's shirts for lipstick or perfume, but here I am checking for signs of a gunfight. And there it is, she thought, finding the bullet hole in his windbreaker.

John got out and dried himself off. Maria stared at his back, her brow knitted, her jaw tight. Some of her anger melted away when she saw the dozens of scars from bullet wounds, shrapnel, knife cuts, and all the other weapons that enemies had used to try to kill the man she'd loved her whole life.

"So, what did you do today, honey?" she asked, setting him up.

She knew he wouldn't turn around and face her when he

started lying. As expected, he kept his back turned, continuing to pat himself down even though he was already dry.

"I told you, babe. Had to go over security details with Christmas, Bunny and Felix."

"You had to go all the way to the city for that?"

"Well, you know, there was a lot we had to review."

"I feel like there's something you're not telling me."

John, getting nervous now, paused a second before answering: "Like what?"

"Like a God damn shootout in Jacob Riis!" she shouted. "And a bullet hole in your freaking jacket!"

"Wait… what? I didn't…"

"Don't bother. I found the Kevlar hidden in the downstairs closet, but you should've burned the jacket 'cause I found the hole. And!… I just got off the phone with my cousin and she told me all about your big fight with the Russians! The whole neighborhood's talking about it, and you come in here lying to me?"

John walked over and gently put his arms around his angry, pregnant, and beautiful wife. Maria got her stunning Asian features and dark flowing hair from her Filipina mother. John firmly believed the only thing her Scottish father contributed to her DNA was a fiery temper.

Maria was five-three, John was six feet, so she tilted her head back to glare up at him. He hugged her a little tighter.

"I'm sorry, baby. I really am. Didn't want to worry you. That's all," he said softly.

"You don't lie to me. Period. No matter what. Understand?"

"I do. Won't happen again, Mrs. Bishop."

She smiled up at him, then leaned in, placing her head on his chest.

"You got shot?"

"Um…technically, well, yeah, but it bounced off the top of my vest."

"No more getting shot either."

"I'll try, honey. I'll really try."

"Let's take a look at it," Maria said. She took him by the hand and sat him down on the edge of the bed.

The bullet had hit the Kevlar above his collarbone, and there was already a dark angry bruise forming in the front of his muscled shoulder. She touched it carefully to make sure nothing was broken. John failed at trying not to flinch as pain shot up his neck and down his arm and spine.

"You need ice," she said, putting her hand gently on his cheek, then leaned in and kissed him.

"It's a long walk for a pregnant mamacita. I'll go."

She wagged her finger at him and smiled, then turned and left the master bedroom to head downstairs to the kitchen.

Right after the war with Amir and Aziz Khan started, Maria had been kidnapped by one of Amir's loyal followers, a mole in the NYPD. John, Felix, Bunny, Christmas and several other Valdez family members had managed to rescue her and save the city, but John knew how lucky he was to get her back alive. He wasn't going to let anything happen to her ever again. Even if it meant keeping her under house arrest here at his Uncle Calixto's Long Island estate.

Calixto and his son Nelson ran all the Valdez family's legitimate businesses that brought in tens of millions annually. They'd purchased the seventeen-bedroom mansion and the surrounding twenty acres of land many years ago and then turned it into a fortress. At least they thought it was. Maria had been standing next to Sesa, another of John's uncles, when the Albanian hitman Connie Belusci tried to shoot Gonzalo from long-range and hit Sesa instead. Sesa was still in a coma and Connie Belusci was still out there hunting for John, Felix and Gonzalo.

John knew Maria was restless, and she was getting more insistent about visiting her parents in the city. He knew it was still too dangerous, and he wasn't about to let his enemies use his wife to get to him again. He rubbed his temples, frustrated that he couldn't do more for her.

Before John quit the Army and returned home, Maria had a high-powered banking career. She took a leave of absence when John's cousin Chris was killed by a suicide bomber six months earlier, and after she shattered her elbow during her kidnapping ordeal, Maria told John she was thinking about making the short-term leave more permanent. He knew she'd worked hard to get where she was: an MBA from Columbia and a determined climb from VP to managing director in just eight years. Then they found out she was pregnant, and after their wedding John broke the news that they were still in danger. At that point the decision to leave her job was out of her hands.

Maria returned with ice packs and Advil and smiled lovingly at the man she'd adored since they first met back in elementary school. She sat beside him on the bed and gently placed a cold pack over the blackish-blue mark that was rapidly spreading across his shoulder. She knew John wasn't some cowboy who liked getting shot at... getting shot. He was protecting her and their baby, and the only way to keep them safe was to go out and kill their enemies. She was going to do everything she could to help and support him in his efforts.

Maria wasn't a military tactician, but she had a highly analytical mind and decided to put it to good use. She got a pen and pad from the dresser and sat back down.

"You know I'm all about lists," she said.

"Don't I know it," John said. He smiled and put a hand on her knee. "What's the list?"

"Everyone who's trying to kill us. No more secrets. No more lies to protect me. How many are there? Who are they? Where are they? How are you going to kill them?"

Her dark almond eyes were clear, her jaw set and determined. John knew it was a waste of time trying to dissuade her.

"I just didn't want you stressing. Not good for the baby," he said and moved his hand from her knee to her belly.

"I know, and I appreciate you trying to protect little old me, but remember… I killed a guy with my bare hands a few months ago." She gave him her best coy and innocent face, batting her eyes to really bring it home. He tried not to laugh, held it in for a few seconds, then lost it to a full deep body shake.

Maria had broken her elbow on the chin of the NYPD lieutenant who'd kidnapped her, and then she'd followed up by shoving him onto a massive transformer at the Con Ed power plant in LES where she was being held hostage. No one was sure if he died from the fall or the hundred thousand volts that burned his body to a crisp, but either way they weren't mourning the death of a terrorist mole.

The pain in John's shoulder ended his laughing fit and Maria put her game face on.

"This is pure analysis, baby. We're in this together, so let's hear it. All of it," she said with pad and pen in hand.

John nodded. "All right here goes. Connie Belusci, the hitman who shot Uncle Sesa is still out there. He knew we were hunting him, so he killed the son of Moscow's most powerful Mafia boss, Yakov Skobelev."

He saw her eyes questioning him about the motive.

"When Connie killed Yakov's son Nicky, he put the bodies of two of our men at his feet to make it look like a Valdez attack."

Maria nodded. "Got it, Connie is one and Yakov two. I assume it was Yakov's men you were fighting today."

John nodded his confirmation.

"Okay, how many Russians are we facing?" she asked.

"Our initial estimate was twenty to thirty, and we reduced that number by more than half today but we're all in agreement that Yakov will send more. A lot more."

Maria nodded as she wrote it all down. "Who else?"

John was really impressed by her clinical approach to hearing all this.

Can't believe how lucky I am to have this woman, he thought.

"Omar. She is, or was, Aziz Khan's top assassin. Bunny shot her in the chest but we still don't know if she's dead or alive. If she is alive, as soon as she's able, she's coming for me. Omar's a Tringa and they've been doing murder for hire for over a thousand years. Rumor is, they've never failed. Who knows if that's true, but it does tell us that even if Omar is dead, they'll send someone else to replace her."

He watched his wife momentarily lose her composure. Her eyes watered, her bottom lip quivered, and her hands trembled. He was amazed by how quickly she regained control. She blinked, took a deep breath, and began writing again with a steady hand.

"How do we destroy them?" Maria asked.

"Good question. Gonzalo has a whole team working on it. The plan is to locate them on their home turf in Pakistan, but we haven't found them yet."

"And if they've already sent Omar's replacement, we don't even know what she looks like," Maria added.

John nodded, agreeing with her assessment.

"Wait…Are all the Tringa killers women?" she asked.

"Doubtful. Word is they train one child at a time, and all indications are that they don't pick them based on gender."

Maria tapped the back end of the pen against her nose to help her concentrate. It was an old habit. John had been watching her do the nose tap since middle school. Sitting two rows behind her. Daydreaming about their first kiss. He wanted to kiss her now, but instead he let her agile mind process all the information. He waited quietly for her next question.

"Omar worked for Aziz and Aziz is dead. If she is alive, doesn't his death void her contract?"

"Hmm… Great question. I'd like to think so…Just not willing to bet my life on it," John said.

Maria held up her left index finger as she added more notes. "Anyone else?"

"Yeah, there is. Mike Meecham's son, Caleb. Mike is the bastard who hired the Albanian, Connie Belusci, to kill me, Felix, and Gonzalo. Now that Meecham's dead, Caleb inherited all his money, which is literally in the billions, as well as his dad's psychotic personality. He's coming at us for sure."

"This is insane. How can this many people want you dead?"

"They don't know how charming I am," he said with a slight smile, not sure whether the joke would land.

"This is a lot. Almost too much to really get my mind around but it's what I do. I'm an analyst. It's how I'm trained and how I'm wired. I'll help you find a way through this."

She put down the pad and pen and hugged him close.

They sat there holding each other for several moments. When she looked into his eyes she could see by his expression that he was holding something back.

"Wait… we're not done, are we?"

John shook his head just as his phone vibrated on the nightstand. Maria was closer, so she picked it up and handed it to him.

"It's Bear," she said.

John nodded. "You wanted to hear it all, so I'm putting it on speaker."

After the quick greetings, Bear got right to it. "Okay Johnny, here it is, and you ain't gonna like it."

Bear gave them a rundown of the new threat coming their way. Maria picked up her pad and added Tariq Hassan and ISIS to her list. Tears rolled down her cheeks. John reached out with a finger and tenderly caught one on her jawline, then brought the tear to his lips as Bear gave them all the terrible details.

CHAPTER 7
CALEB

Trapp, Maryland

THEY CAME RELUCTANTLY. A Texas congressman, two federal judges and three prominent businessmen. Heavy hitters. Power players all. The movers, shakers, and dealmakers in DC politics. Jeff Stamper, the billionaire real estate mogul turned politician who just two weeks ago won the presidential election and would be inaugurated in January, was the last to arrive. Stamper and all the others had initially turned down Caleb Meecham's dinner invitation, but Caleb was relentless. Cashing in chips, reminding them how much his father had done for them, and what a true friend he'd been.

Friend? His father hadn't had any. Caleb's father, Michael Meecham, had been universally hated, and all his relationships were based on bullying or blackmail. And like his recently deceased father, Caleb had a sociopathic lack of empathy for his fellow man combined with a narcissistic determination to get his way no matter what the cost. Once he realized that asking nicely wasn't going to get the president-elect and the others to come to his estate, Caleb had sent each of his dinner guests snippets of video recordings that if released would guarantee them decades in prison.

The pre-dinner cocktail reception was tense and awkward. Most of the men in the room were thirty to forty years older than him, and none of them even tried to hide their disdain for the 25-year-old Meecham. They barely spoke to him while they huddled together in a tight circle, communicating through head nods and knowing looks.

Are they using a secret code? One blink for yes, two for no? Caleb thought.

When they went next-level, turning to the Washington insider's classic lean-in whisper in the ear, Caleb began shaking with rage. He was about to scream, but his dad's voice helped him compose himself:

"Keep calm and get even. Revenge is all there is. Everything else in life is just a distraction."

He made a last attempt to engage his guests, clinking his glass and raising it high.

"To Michael Meecham!" he shouted, louder than intended.

All seven dark blue suits slowly turned to face him. Only two glasses touched lips, but the move was reflexive. The mouths stayed sealed tight to prevent even a sip from passing. The rest of the drinks remained waist high.

There was a soothing click inside Caleb's lizard brain. He thought about what he was going to do to these seven ungrateful bastards. Not yet though. *Soon, gentlemen. Just not yet.*

The president-elect, Jeff Stamper, stared at Caleb and tried to come up with the right word to describe him: *Wet? No… damp. Yes, damp. Slimy?*

Stamper recalled shaking Caleb's clammy hand and unconsciously wiped his right palm on his pants leg while he looked over at the reflection the overhead lights made when they bounced off the sheen on the young billionaire's forehead… and the dark sweat stains in the armpits of his cheap blue shirt.

Doesn't he have the sense to wear white? Stamper thought.

His father may have been a despicable bully, but Mike Meecham was a smart dresser and a fitness fanatic. Caleb, on the other hand, had sunken gray eyes and was so skinny and pale he appeared terminally ill.

Far worse was that he had no sense of how things were done. When Stamper and the other six suits arrived at the Meecham "castle," they were shocked by the absence of party favors. In the past, whenever they had been summoned to the luxurious estate, they were always greeted by dozens of beautiful women wearing nothing but high heels and welcoming smiles. They knew going in that Meecham would demand that they do something shitty, but a few hours of debauchery before he gave them their marching orders had a way of softening the blow.

Now they were here with this emaciated little rich boy who only offered them cheap well liquor, soggy pigs in a blanket, and no women.

"Caleb," Stamper said, "Thank you for the invitation but I really must go."

"We're about to have dinner," Caleb shot back.

"Sorry, young man. Another time, perhaps," Stamper said.

The remaining six began making their excuses and put their drinks down.

"Gentlemen. Before you go, I have something for you."

"What is it?" the Texas congressman asked impatiently.

"Your orders."

There was a moment of silence as they exchanged looks.

Then they started laughing at him. Deep and loud. Caleb stood there watching, mentally recording the moment. Their laughter was cut short when Connie Belusci walked into the room. The six-six three-hundred-pound baldheaded killer handed a manila envelope to each guest. None of them looked inside.

"What's going on here, Caleb?" Stamper asked.

"I'll tell you what's going on. I own you. Every one of you. Including you, Stamper. Just like my father did. You want to actually get inaugurated and stay out of prison…" He nodded at Connie. "Or go in a hole in my back yard, you'll do exactly what I tell you to do."

The kid has balls, Stamper thought. *Balls, but he's a dumbass. Can't believe he thinks he's going to get away with publicly threatening to kill a president.*

Stamper then focused his thoughts on which team of elite killers he would assign to get all of Meecham's files before they made him a distant memory. He knew he could have Caleb killed tonight, but decided he'd wait until after he was sworn in.

Unlike Stamper, the others were nervous now. "What do you want us to do, Caleb?" one of the businessmen asked.

"Mr. Meecham," Caleb said.

"Excuse me?"

"You work for me now, and as your boss we need to formalize our relationship."

Caleb watched the pompous idiot's Adam's apple bob up and down as he swallowed hard and looked around for support.

"What do you want us to do, Mr. Meecham?" he finally asked in resignation.

"The Valdez family fed my father to lions at the Bronx

Zoo, and none of you did a fucking thing about it. I'll decide on the punishment for your inaction, but while I'm pondering I want you to get to work on your first targets."

"Who?" one of the federal judges asked.

"John Bishop and his cousin Felix. I want their lives ripped apart. Special prosecutors. State and federal indictments. Assets frozen. The full Monty. Everything you need to get started is in those packets."

"Okay Cal… Mr. Meecham. We'll get started on this right away," said the judge.

All seven pissed-off men headed towards the door.

"Where the fuck do you think you're going?" Caleb said venomously.

They all froze.

"We're still having dinner. I know you assholes love fine dining, so I had the chef make a special meal for you. Hope you like Kraft Mac & Cheese and chicken nuggets."

It was Caleb's turn to laugh deep and loud as they turned around and followed Connie to the dining room.

CHAPTER 8
NIGHT HUNTERS

Trapp, Maryland

BUNNY AND CHRISTMAS were a thousand yards out from the Meecham mansion, watching through their Steiner binoculars with laser range finders. They were lying on their stomachs on a heavily wooded hill that had a narrow, natural shooting lane through the trees. They each had an M91A2 .300-win mag sniper rifle on a bipod by their side.

During the gunfight at Jacob Riis, a Valdez surveillance team had spotted Connie Belusci at a highway rest stop twenty miles away from Meecham's estate. After they called it in, the team was instructed not to follow, just to determine if Connie was heading south… He was.

Bunny and Christmas had slept in the back of an Escalade for most of the two-and-a-half-hour drive down from New York City. After a little shuteye they were fresh, alert and ready for a night hunt for the Albanian hitman.

From detailed maps of Caleb's estate they knew the general area where they wanted to set up shop, and after a slow approach in the dark using NVGs (Night Vision Goggles) they'd come across their current location. Now it was all about patience. Watch and wait while the skeeters went into a frenzy, trying to find a way past the heavy coating of bug repellent.

Christmas was sipping on a Red Bull and looked over at the big man. "Where you from, Bunny?" he whispered.

"Harlem, bro, Lenox Terrace, near 135th Street."

"For real? Didn't know you were Harlem royalty."

Bunny smiled. "Royalty? Never that. Lost pop to the streets and mom to cancer when I was twelve. Three sisters, one brother. We did it all on our own. The five of us raised each other. Had less than nothing. Turned it into something. We all managed to find our way."

"When'd you enlist?" Christmas asked.

"Nineteen. Everyone said I could walk onto any college campus in the country and get a football scholarship, but I didn't want it. Wasn't sure what. Just knew it wasn't that," Bunny said.

"Found a home?" Christmas asked.

"Man, you know it," Bunny said. "Thought I'd be in and out, get some bennies, maybe learn a trade and move on, but I loved the Army from day one. When I passed SFAS and put on that Green Beret it went next-level. Then, getting assigned to Team Razor and fighting alongside Johnny Bishop was better than hitting the lotto."

"I've only worked with Johnny for the past few months, but hands down he's the best I've ever seen. Must've been something going downrange with him on all those deployments," Christmas said.

"We all thought we were some badass door kickers until Johnny joined Razor. Took one firefight for all of us to realize that he was Michael Jordan and we were his supporting cast. Started calling ourselves the Bulls. The legend is real, brother. There's none better. Man's been surrounded by death his whole life, and he's put down so many bad guys he should have his own graveyard."

"Crazy world. Just glad to be on the team and fighting alongside him… and you," Christmas said.

"How 'bout you? What's your story?" Bunny asked.

"A little different, kinda the same. I came up in Baltimore. Lost my mom and pops to dope. They both OD'ed within a year of each other. Dad went first, then mom lit herself up with a hot shot on my eighth birthday. Ran away that night. Was living on the streets like a wild animal for six months till my Pop-Pop found me. Was just me and him until I enlisted. He saved my life for sure."

"That's heavy. He still around?" Bunny asked.

"Yeah, we don't speak much anymore, though," Christmas said.

"Sorry, man."

"Nah, it's not what you think," Christmas said. "Grandpa Owens was a Baptist minister for thirty years. Devoted his life to saving souls, then one day he gave it all up and moved to a retirement home down in Florida."

"Got tired, huh?" Bunny asked.

"Just the opposite… tried Viagra and literally went buck wild with it. Every time I call him he says he's too busy *gettin'* busy to talk. Says he keeps passing the four-hour erection window, and when they load him in the ambo there's always a "Golden Girl" riding him all the way to the ER."

Bunny held it in for a second, then started shaking with laughter and put both hands over his mouth to muffle the sound. He pulled himself together, then glanced at Christmas and they both started back up again. A few minutes later they were laughed out, wiping the tears from their eyes.

"Man, that's just too good," Bunny said. "Navy SEAL, huh?"

"Yeah. Funny how some things can change your whole life. When Pop-Pop was helping me deal with all that shit, he took me to this pool on the other side of town. Taught me how to swim and the water just seemed to wash everything away for me. It became our thing. We went there two, three times a week. Years later, when I went to enlist I picked the Navy 'cause I thought swimming might help."

"When'd you decide to go for the SEALs?" Bunny asked.

"Two years in. Tried it on a dare and ended up making it all the way through," Christmas said.

"If you don't mind me asking…"

"How'd I go from being a SEAL to the head of Valdez security?"

"Yeah," Bunny said.

"Don Valdez approached me a year after I left the teams. Sat down next to me at a café in South Beach and introduced himself. Laid out his plan and asked me to join his family," Christmas said.

"And that was it?" Bunny asked.

"Nah, man. Even down in B'more his name rang out. I knew who he was and told him to step. After seeing what dope did to my folks, I'd eat my gun before I ever helped a drug dealer… *But…* then he explained how he and his family were out the game and that making the move made them more vulnerable than ever. Did my research and a few months later I joined… on a temporary basis."

"How many years has it been?" Bunny asked.

"Eleven," Christmas said.

"I've been around powerful dudes all my life, but Gonzalo Valdez is a breed apart," Bunny said.

"That he is. First gangster I've ever known or heard of that walked away from the game at the peak of his power. No matter how much money they put away, kingpins hold on to the bitter end. Know they're gonna get life in prison or shot down in the street, but they just can't quit," Christmas said.

"Know what you mean. I've only heard of two that walked away. One found God and joined the NYPD, the other became a writer," Bunny said.

"Cop and a writer, huh? Well, Don Valdez ain't ever gonna be either of those but the man has vision. I get paid, sure, but I'd follow him for free. Wherever he leads."

"Same here," said Bunny. "I started out just wanting to help protect Johnny and get some payback against those fuckers who ordered the suicide attack that killed poor Chris, but it's more than that now. I'm in all the way. Proud to be part of the Valdez family."

They both saw headlights in the distance and went silent. What they initially thought was one vehicle turned out to be four. A luxury car caravan of two big Mercedes sedans, a Rolls Royce, and a Cadillac Escalade went up the long U-shaped driveway and made the wide left turn to the main house. All four vehicles stopped in front of the mansion's huge double doors, and the drivers hopped out to assist their well-dressed overweight white-haired passengers onto the pavement.

Neither Christmas nor Bunny recognized any of the suits going into the house, and they settled back in, waiting and watching. Fifteen minutes later, another group of vehicles, this time seven black SUVs, went up and around the driveway.

"Let's see who else is visiting Caleb and Connie," Bunny said, focusing his binoculars.

The first SUV drove past the main entrance to give the second vehicle space to pull up in front of the massive double doors that Caleb's dad had managed to "acquire" from a French castle. A security team scanned the perimeter and stared blindly into the night before opening the house-facing rear door and escorting the next president of the United States up the front steps.

"That's Jeff Stamper, the fuckin' president-elect," Christmas said.

"This shit just keeps getting deeper and deeper, don't it?" Bunny added.

"Bananas, bro," Christmas said.

"So, the question is, why's the next president meeting with a junior psychopath and an Albanian hitman?" Bunny asked. "Don Valdez needs a SITREP right away," he added.

"Yeah, you call it in. Before you do, I'm letting you know, if I get Connie in my crosshairs I'm squeezing regardless," Christmas said. "I'm still carrying lead in me from when he outdrew me in Barcelona and he shot Sesa Valdez on my watch. Even if Connie's holding hands with Stamper, I'm taking the shot."

"Understood," said Bunny.

Bunny called Antonio, Gonzalo's nephew and gave him an update. Gonzalo never spoke on the phone, and Antonio said he would pass on this important intel right away.

They lay there for another three hours. Then all the guests left, and they watched and waited for three more hours after that. Christmas gave Bunny a tap and they eased back, creeping until they reached the far side of the hill and walked down the rest of the way. Sixteen Valdez soldiers stood waiting for them at the bottom, and Christmas raised his hand over his head and made a circular motion, indicating they were moving out.

Inside the Meecham mansion, Connie stepped away

from the tripod-mounted Accuracy International L115A3 long-range rifle. It was the same long gun he'd used to shoot Sesa Valdez.

"They're gone," he said. "You can turn on the lights now."

"Couldn't you have taken them out?" Caleb asked.

"Christmas for sure. Bunny would've moved, so fifty-fifty on hitting him. Plus, they had a full platoon of Valdez soldiers out there... They tipped their hand and showed us something tonight, though," Connie said.

"What?" asked Caleb.

"They want me so bad they'll follow me wherever I lead them. Now we can lay a trap and really bushwhack these motherfuckers."

Caleb rubbed his hands together in anticipation. "I can't wait," he said, then thought of his father:

It's all falling into place, Dad. I own the next president of the United States and I'm going to kill every Valdez I can find. As for Bishop, I still haven't decided whether I want to visit him in prison or spit on his grave. I'll make you proud, Dad. I promise I'm going to make you so proud.

Chapter 9
Tariq

Raqqa, Syria

"I'M LET BECAUSE I set down and drink a bear," Marwan said.

"No," Gretchen said.

"I'm let because…"

"No!" she shouted.

"How do I say it!?" Marwan asked.

"I'm *late*," she said.

"I'm late because I set…"

"No," she said.

"But you said it was, late!" Marwan shouted, his dark eyes glaring at her.

"Not let. Late. Not set. Sat. Not drink. Drank. Not bear. Beer! I'm *late* because I *sat* down and *drank* a *beer*. Get it?" Gretchen asked.

"Yes," Marwan said, his voice flat but his eyes still blazing.

"Okay, try again," she said calmly.

"I'm let because…"

"Stop! Ugh!" Gretchen shouted as she walked away, frustrated with Marwan's slow progress… and also angry with herself for losing her patience.

She poured herself a glass of water, drank half in one swallow, and took a few deep breaths to bring her temper down. Shouting at the Syrian was counterproductive, and he had to learn this, and learn it fast.

Tariq Hassan watched her from his chair across the room. He respected how hard she worked to overcome the stain of being an American. Despite her lineage he'd grudgingly come to admire her. She was determined to complete her assignment and was committed to giving her life for the Caliphate.

"Can he do it?" Tariq asked.

Gretchen approached him. "A slight accent is no big deal, but he's got to get the basics down or it's going to raise questions when we go through Customs. Do we really need him?"

Tariq nodded yes.

"Then I think you better talk to him. Most of his resistance is tied to me being a woman… and an American. I'm not sure which part of me he hates more, but we both know he feels disrespected because I'm his teacher."

Tariq knew she was right. Marwan was a legendary fighter who'd been on the front lines in Iraq and Afghanistan for a decade. The Syrian was proud, though. Perhaps a bit too proud. This mission was too important to let anyone's ego or short-sighted prejudices get in the way.

He got up and walked over to Marwan. "English is not easy, is it, my brother?" Tariq asked.

"Not my fault. This American pig is bad teacher."

"I heard that," Gretchen said.

"Good," Marwan grunted.

"She is a good teacher and she is part of our team. You are the only one who is…" Tariq searched his memory for the right phrase. "Fucking it up." He looked back at Gretchen for confirmation.

"You got that right," she said.

"Yes, Marwan you are fucking it up, and fucking it up is not allowed. Do you want to be a part of this? Yes or no?"

"Yes Tariq, but…"

"There is no time for buts. You accept Gretchen as one of us, as a true soldier of God, and as your teacher. Otherwise you're out. And if you're out we'll shoot your sons before we do the same to you. Understand?"

Marwan nodded his head in agreement.

"Good. Keep practicing with her. I'll be gone for a few hours. You better be able to say every fucking word when I get back."

He kicked the door open and called Gretchen over before leaving the apartment.

"Make peace with him. Whatever it takes. You understand?"

She said she did. As soon as Tariq left she poured a second glass of water and brought it over to the table. She stood there for a moment while he scowled up at her.

"I'm not your enemy, Marwan and we're going to die together in a few weeks. We're going to kill thousands of Americans, so let's work together and try to get along while we do God's will."

She handed him the water. He huffed as he took the glass from her. She picked up her chair, carried it around to his side of the table and sat next to him, staring at his profile.

A brute, but not an ugly one, she thought. *As Tariq said, whatever it takes.*

She placed her hand on his thigh. Felt his tension as he sat there frozen with his hands clasped on the table staring straight ahead at the wall across the room.

"What do you think of my clothes?" she asked.

"Disgraceful," Marwan said, still not looking at her.

In public, Gretchen and the other four radicalized female members of the strike team wore the mandatory uniform of all ISIS women. Black double veil over their heads, loose-fitting black abayas that covered their entire bodies and long black gloves over their hands. Behind closed doors, they role played in apartments filled with typical American products and furniture and put on the same casual clothes they would wear on the mission.

She was wearing stonewashed Gap jeans, white and blue Nike running shoes, and a tight pink tee shirt from Old Navy with three buttons at the top. She popped the buttons.

"How 'bout now?" she asked.

He turned towards her and stared hungrily at the deep cleavage line.

She took his hand and placed it on her breast.

"Say it."

"I'm late…"

Gretchen reached over and put her hand in his lap.

"Say it."

"I'm late because…" he said.

"Why, Marwan? Why are you late?"

"I'm late because I sat down and drank a beer."

"You knew it all along, didn't you?" she asked.

He smiled then.

Finally, she thought.

"You're a very good student, Marwan. And all good students must be rewarded for their hard work."

She pulled her shirt over her head, unpinned her long blond hair and gave it a shake, letting it cascade down her shoulders, falling just over her pink nipples. Marwan exploded out of his chair, taking her down to the floor.

Gretchen's eyes were hard and her jawline was tight as she unzipped him.

Whatever it takes, she thought.

Tariq Hassan walked through the streets wondering how long the Islamic State would last.

Eventually, US-led forces are coming to Syria, he thought. *The battle will be bloody, thousands will die on both sides. The Caliphate will fall and the stupid American politicians will see it as a victory. In truth, the destruction of the Caliphate will be a blessing from God. Tens of thousands more true believers will rally to avenge the martyred, and then they will spread out and wage a war unlike anything the Americans have ever seen, spreading across the globe and launching attacks in every Western city.*

He wouldn't live to see it. His path was already written and etched in stone.

After Aziz Khan was killed by John Bishop and his family, Tariq had left Afghanistan with five hundred fighters, crossing through Iran and Turkey to get to Syria. The spirit of Aziz had whispered to him along the way. Guiding him. Helping him formulate the plan that would change the world order.

When he had first reached the Caliphate he'd moved through layer upon layer of security. He expected no less and would have been disappointed if it had been easy. By the time he was finally granted an audience with the inner circle he was ready. He'd learned from the best. Aziz had been a master planner and never sent his men into battle without carefully reviewing every detail.

Tariq had given the ISIS senior committee members the most professional mission briefing they'd ever heard, complete with resource requirements, and the estimated American body count. Before he was halfway through, he knew he had them and that his destiny would soon be fulfilled. His plan was solid, but he had no idea how much they were going to improve upon what he'd already laid out.

His jaw had dropped when they escorted Gretchen and the other Americans into the room. Twenty-five young men and women who'd turned their back on their country, their families, and everything they'd ever known. All of them were ready to give their lives to defend the Islamic State.

The twenty-five were special. There were hundreds of other converts from America and Europe fighting and dying here in Syria and in Iraq, but all the others were on CIA, FBI, Homeland Security, Interpol and other counter-terrorism watchlists. This group was invisible. No scent trails of radicalization on social media or anywhere else. None of them showed up on any agency's threat radar.

They'd told him to pick twelve. Eight from the Americans. He could have two Afghans from his own army, and they wanted two of theirs as well. With several days to make a decision Tariq had interviewed them all, rejecting the ones who were too eager, and the others not eager enough. Then he'd drilled them to see whom he could break and which would endure. He'd been the youngest combat commander in Aziz's army, he knew men, and was now learning women.

A week later he had his team and they immediately began the intensive training. Explosives and weapons were a component but the majority of their days and nights were spent in practice sessions. Role playing for Tariq and the other four non-Americans so they wouldn't raise any red flags at the border. Passports, no matter how perfectly forged by the ISIS intelligence unit, just weren't enough. The men needed to be comfortable, relaxed, and able to answer basic questions in case they were stopped.

Then there were the women issues. Marwan needed more work than the others, but even Tariq recognized how uncomfortable he was when they role played a bar scene. The five girls wore outfits that would instantly get them stoned to death in the streets of Raqqa; they spoke their mind, and freely touched the men, pushing the limits to get a reaction. And it did. Every time.

It was Lisa, the short dark-haired girl from California who had a small half-moon scar in between her eyebrows, who suggested they pair up. Tariq and Lisa slept together for the first time that night. Just sleep. No sex. That lasted until three nights later, when she rolled over to him and said: "If you don't do it, no one's going to believe we're a couple. You want the mission to succeed, then you better start banging me."

Banging?

"It's an expression American guys use for, you know... having sex."

They did, and she was right. He instructed his fellow Afghans and the two Syrians to do the same. Marwan had been the last holdout, but that morning Lisa assured Tariq that Gretchen would find a way to help Marwan overcome his objections.

The thing Tariq still hadn't been able to get used to was his face. Because he was on the top one hundred terrorist watch list, over the past four months he'd had two surgeries and worked with makeup artists to cover the last remnants of the scar he'd carried since the American jets destroyed his childhood home. He was clean-shaven, and his once long black hair was cut short and dyed brown. When he looked in the mirror he barely recognized himself.

No one in Raqqa recognized him either, although it was his black ISIS uniform that covered everything except for his eyes and hands that was mostly responsible for that. Every man in a leadership role and many of the fighters kept themselves camouflaged to prevent the US drones and satellite surveillance from marking and targeting them.

When he reached the hospital, he identified himself by pulling his mask down, and a security detail escorted him through the hallways and then down into the basement, where the senior council was meeting today. After a round of greetings, Mohamed El Salim asked the question they all wanted to hear an answer to:

"Tariq, is your team ready?"

"Nearly. God willing, we'll be ready by next week."

"Something has happened that may require us to change your departure date," Mohamed said.

"What?" Tariq asked.

"Your man, Warid. He was captured in Mosul."

Tariq sat for a moment thinking about the repercussions. "Warid does not know any of the details."

"We understand that, but he knows the targets."

Tariq shook his head and said, "No... He only knows about New York, and the Americans know that New York is always number one on our target list."

"Anything else? The women? Your surgeries? The dates?"

"Well..."

Tariq scoured his memory trying to think if he'd shared anything other than vague details with Warid on their journey from Afghanistan. He knew that Warid had been angry when he wasn't selected to be a part of the mission and became sullen when he was assigned to frontline combat in Mosul.

"I'm just not sure how much he knows, Mohamed."

"It's settled then. You and your team leave tonight."

"Tonight?" Tariq asked.

"Yes, tonight. As you said, you're only one week away. If it was a month we would postpone the operation until next year, but a week is easy to make up. Train as you travel."

The reality of the moment was not lost on Tariq. He stood up. "We are ready, and we will not fail," he declared.

"Excellent. Trucks will pick you up in a few hours. Once you reach the border you'll have a Turkish military escort protecting you at all times until you head west."

The goodbyes were heartfelt. Hugs and pats on the back, and the farewell message that they would all see each other again in paradise. A car was waiting for him outside the hospital, and it raced him to the safehouse where his team was role playing.

He hoped Marwan and Gretchen were dressed by now.

Chapter 10
Fox-One

Washington, DC

"WHAT ARE OUR options here?" President Carson asked.

"Airstrike, Mr. President," said Gen. Paul Miller, chairman of the joint chiefs.

"In Raqqa?"

"Yes, sir," said Gen. Marcus Palmer, head of SOCOM.

"Collateral damage?" the president asked.

"It's difficult to give an accurate assessment with the limited intel we have, Mr. President, but based on the satellite imagery and the pics just taken by the Joint STARS surveillance run, the collateral losses may be significant, sir," Palmer said.

"Or none," Miller added. "Personally, I don't believe anyone in Raqqa qualifies as a civilian. If everyone in ISIS-controlled territory is deemed an enemy combatant, then there will be zero collateral damage, sir."

"What about children?" the secretary of state asked.

"That's a gray area. Based on ISIS videos and our own on-the-ground intel, every child over six is being trained to fight," Miller said.

"I can tell you one thing for sure," the president's chief of staff said. "The media won't see it as a gray area if dead kids get pulled from the rubble after we hit the building."

The DNI (Director of National Intelligence) cleared his throat before speaking: "Sir, in addition to the apartment complex where Tariq Hassan and his team are residing there is a second, and perhaps more valuable target."

"Show me," Carson said.

President Carson, the members of his security council, his chief of staff, the White House counsel, and the secretary of state all turned in their seats to look at the seventy-inch wall monitor in the situation room. There were numerous still shots, followed by a thirty-second video.

"Wait... is that a hospital?" the secretary of state asked.

"It is. ISIS senior leaders meet in the basement," DNI said.

"We can't blow up a working hospital filled with... We just can't," State said.

"Again, if there are no civilians, then our standard ROE restrictions can be lifted," Gen. Miller said.

"C'mon, general," the chief of staff said. He was furious and couldn't hold it in. "You want us to stand in front of the whole world and say we approved an airstrike on a fucking hospital? You can't be serious."

Miller was unfazed and unemotional. "If it makes you feel better you can say we—and by we, I mean the men and women in uniform risking their lives to protect our great nation—made a mistake. Tell the media the pilots missed the designated target."

"How dare you!" the chief of staff shouted.

"Enough," President Carson said forcefully. He liked

a healthy dialogue between his top advisors but things were getting out of hand. Ultimately, this was his decision.

"Probability that our intended targets, Tariq Hassan and the ISIS leadership will be at both locations?" he asked.

The CIA director took this one: "Fifty-fifty, sir. Without assets on the ground and time to see our targets entering the building, we just don't know. It's nearly midnight in Raqqa, so the chances that ISIS leaders are still at the hospital seem unlikely. However, since Raqqa isn't known for its nightlife, Tariq and his men should be sleeping in their beds right now."

"What if they're not?" Carson asked his chief of staff.

"If we don't get Tariq, the Republicans will cite this as another example of Democrat incompetence. The Syrian government will scream bloody murder, and of course, so will the Russians. Politically it's a lose-lose either way, but we all know what this is about even if no one else does."

"Keeping America safe," Carson said.

"Exactly," the chief of staff said.

"Okay." The president tilted his chair back and looked up at the ceiling for a moment, then leaned forward and made eye contact with everyone in the room.

"Just to recap, Tariq and a three- or four-man team are about to leave ISIS-controlled territory, somehow enter the United States illegally, and launch a massive attack on New York City. Am I leaving anything out?"

"Yes, sir, they also plan to kill John Bishop, either before or after they complete their mission," Palmer said.

"Is Bishop aware of this?" Carson asked.

"Yes, sir. I authorized our team to update him," Palmer said.

The president leaned over to Palmer and whispered in

his ear, "Arrange a meeting. I want to discuss something with Mr. Bishop."

Palmer gave a slight head nod to indicate he would set it up.

State still had reservations. "We have Tariq's picture. Why not just snatch him at the border?"

CIA responded, "He knows we have his photo and how difficult it is for anyone on the terrorist watch list to cross our borders, and he's coming anyway. He has a plan and we don't know what it is. Are you willing to risk thousands of lives by not taking him out now?"

State couldn't or wouldn't answer that one.

"Last question from me," Carson said. "How will we know whether or not the airstrike gets him?"

"Sir, our asset will be on-site in three hours using the cover of searching for survivors to identify Tariq's body," the CIA director said.

"Okay, I've heard enough. The hospital is out, but we go for Tariq. General, initiate the attack on the apartment complex. Operation Night Light is approved," President Carson said.

Miller punched in a series of numbers on the secure conference call console in the center of the table. He was on speaker when he gave the go order to the Air Force colonel at the US air base in Incirlik, Turkey.

"Colonel, mission approved. Operation Night Light is a go."

"Thank you, sir. Night Light is a go. Birds are fifteen minutes out," the colonel said.

The four F-16 Fighting Falcons had taken off from Incirlik an hour before and topped off their tanks over the Mediterranean when they hooked up with a KC-135 Stratotanker for in-air refueling. For this mission, two of the F-16s carried JDAM (Joint Direct Attack Munition) two-thousand-pound bombs. There was a heavy cloud ceiling over Raqqa, and the JDAMs relied on satellite GPS that made them immune to poor weather conditions. They were the optimum payload for precision targeting in densely populated areas.

The other two Falcons were outfitted with AIM-120 AMRAAMs (Advanced Medium-Range Air-to-Air Missiles) in case any Syrian or Russian jets showed up with bad intentions. Even though the Joint STARS surveillance plane flying overwatch at thirty thousand feet showed the route in from the Syrian coast going east to Raqqa was clear of air traffic, the two additional F-16 escorts flew in a tight formation with the bombers to make sure they got home safely.

The president and his staff listened in and watched the mission in real-time through the Joint STARS and satellite feeds.

"Alpha One to Bravo Six. Target acquired, over," said the flight leader.

"Bravo Six to Alpha One. You are weapons free, over," mission control in Incirlik said.

"Roger, Bravo Six. Weapons free. Going in to attack… Fox-One. Weapons away," said Alpha One.

A second later, the Alpha Two pilot repeated the message when he dropped his payload.

Four 2,000-pound bombs hit within ten feet of each other, instantly disintegrating the eight-story housing complex.

"It's done, Mr. President," Gen. Miller said.

President Carson nodded while he continued to watch the smoke and debris rise from the massive bomb blasts. He wondered how many innocent people he'd just killed in order to take out Tariq and his men. Dozens? Hundreds? He bowed his head and said a prayer for them. Then he prayed that Tariq Hassan was among the dead.

CHAPTER 11
A BIG ASK

HIS SON, CHRISTOPHER. Three, maybe three and a half, running through an acre of bright yellow flowers. The bulbs reached just above his shoulders, tickling his chin as he ran. Maria danced behind him, singing. Twirling with her eyes closed, smiling up at the sun. Pregnant with their second child. Eight months now. Everyone eager to see the little lady. They knew it was a girl.

He sat on the porch. *Their* porch. Looking out over their grassy fields. He wanted to mow. Maria told him not to. At least not this year. Let it grow, she said. Like the life growing inside her.

A series of low green mountains rose out of the open valley where they'd built their home. He took Chris deep in the woods a few times a week, showing him the land and the animals around them. Mostly day hikes, with overnights under the stars sprinkled in whenever he could swing it.

"Here I come!" John shouted.

"Uh oh. Daddy's coming to get you," Maria warned.

Chris squealed with joy. Running faster now. Looking

back over his shoulder. Tripping once, then hopping right up, taking off again.

John laughed as he ran. "I'm gonna getcha. I'm gonna getcha!"

"Johnny."

"Hmmm…."

"Johnny…. Wake up hun, you're talking in your sleep."

He looked up at Maria, blinking himself awake… "I was dreaming."

"About what?" she asked, caressing his face.

He interlocked his fingers with hers with one hand and gently rubbed her belly with the other, then told her the details. Painting it so she could see and feel their future.

"A beautiful dream. I can't wait to live it, Mr. Bishop."

"Coming soon, Mrs. Bishop." He pulled her close. Their kisses were soft and gentle for about three seconds, then quickly heated up. Maria put her hand on his chest and pushed away. His eyes asked, what's wrong?

"Gonzalo's here. He said you need a suit and tie." She rubbed his chin. "And a shave."

"He's here? Now? What time is it?" he asked.

"2AM," she said.

Has to be something major, John thought.

"Did he say where we're going?" he asked.

She shook her head. "But he's wearing the blue Zegna, so it must be important. Get your ass in gear, Sergeant."

John hopped up and hustled into the shower. With Maria's help, sixteen minutes later he was crisp, clean, and heading downstairs to meet his uncle.

Gonzalo was out on the patio. John saw him standing with his head tilted down. Thought he was praying, then quickly realized his uncle was staring at the spot where his brother Sesa was shot in the head.

Gonzalo heard John walk over but didn't look up. "It's time to let him go," he said.

John put his hand on his uncle's shoulder. Although all the Valdez brothers were close, John knew that Sesa and Gonzalo had shared an even stronger bond. Gonzalo was head of the family, and his older brother had been his guiding hand and counselor for forty years.

"He's not coming back, is he Tio?" John asked.

Gonzalo shook his head. "The doctors confirmed what I already knew. He died six months ago. The machines are just keeping his body alive."

John's hand gripped his uncle a little tighter. "Silvi and Antonio. Do they know?"

Silvia "Silvi" Valdez and Antonio Valdez were Sesa's children. Antonio was Gonzalo's protégé, being groomed to become the next head of the family.

"I saw them before I came here," Gonzalo said.

John asked what they wanted to do.

"They both said the same thing. 'Keep his body breathing until all our enemies are dead. Then he can rest in peace.'"

It was the Valdez way. Had been for centuries. Harm one and other family members would exact revenge. No matter what the cost. Even if it meant their own deaths.

Gonzalo straightened up. "You ready?" he asked.

"Of course, Tio. Where to?"

John's eyebrows rose and his eyes went wide when Gonzalo told him where they were heading. They both turned towards the wump-wump-wump of rotors in the distance. The sound grew louder as the Sikorski S-92 flew in fast and low, then did a quick stop and drop for a perfect landing thirty feet away. John and Gonzalo trotted across the great lawn, instinctively ducking their heads when they got close to the helicopter.

The high-speed luxury helo headed south and made the two hundred fifty-mile flight in forty minutes. Security was tight at the airfield in the Maryland woods. On their approach John counted a dozen soldiers carrying M4s and the landing lights went out a moment after the wheels touched down on the helipad.

Once their feet hit the ground, John and Gonzalo were escorted to a non-descript three-story building that was a flight control center and a security screening facility, where they were frisked by hand before going through a full-body scanner. Ten minutes later they were sitting in a large living room sipping good coffee. John and Gonzalo nodded to each other, both impressed by the rustic décor and the history that surrounded them.

Their host's security team came in first, and he followed a moment later wearing loafers, jeans, and a dark blue V-neck sweater over a white dress shirt.

"Gentlemen, it's good to see you again. Welcome to Camp David."

His tone was welcoming, yet formal.

They both stood up. "Thank you, Mr. President," they chorused.

Carson came over and gave each of them a solemn, knowing look as they shook hands. A silent connection, acknowledging the pain they still carried from the heroic death of John's cousin, Chris Valdez, just a few months earlier. The president had pinned a medal on Chris and was in the hospital room when he died from his wounds.

Carson lightened the mood: "Looks like someone forgot to tell you about the dress code around here."

Can't imagine throwing on jeans and a tee shirt for a top secret presidential meeting, John thought. "Don't worry about us. We're fine, sir," he said.

"Okay. We have a few more people joining us, and I need some caffeine," the president said, then walked over to the wooden service table that had a simple setup of coffees, a few tea choices, and an impressive display of fresh baked cookies and muffins.

During their flight, John and Gonzalo had brainstormed about why they were being summoned for a face-to-face. If news of the meeting got out, best case was that the president would be embarrassed, but in all likelihood it would result in a major scandal followed by congressional hearings.

Still unsure of the reason, they stood there watching the most powerful man in the world pour himself a cuppa. Touch of cream. No sugar. He paused over the desserts, shook his head no, then came back gesturing for everyone to take a seat.

"The chef here is pure evil. Knows I'm trying to drop weight and he's waving cookies in my face at three in the morning." He paused for a moment, looking them over. "You mind if I ask you a personal question?"

"Of course, Mr. President. Anything," Gonzalo said, answering for both of them.

"Your eyes. I've never seen anything like them. When we met at the hospital, um…" He shook his head sadly, mentally replaying the moments before Chris Valdez died, before continuing with his question: "I think I remember your cousin Felix had the same yellow eyes. Is it a family trait?"

"Evelio Valdez is the first that we know of. He died around 1790," Gonzalo said. "Since then, in each generation, one family member has been born with yellow eyes, but usually not until the prior carrier has passed away. This is the first time we know of that three of us have them."

"Fascinating. Only males?" Carson asked.

"Pilar was the one exception. She was head of the family from 1840 to 1852," Gonzalo said.

"Incredible. Wish there was time to hear all the details about your family's history, but we need to get started."

"Of course, sir," John said.

Clayton Unser, the CIA's deputy director, walked past the Secret Service detail, followed by Gen. Marcus Palmer. John and Gonzalo had years of history with both men. Back when Palmer was a colonel he'd been John's GCC (Ground Combatant Commander) on dozens of ops, and after he got bumped up to general he'd pinned medals on John's chest on multiple occasions.

Gonzalo began the transition from LES crime lord to government consultant fifteen years earlier when Clayton Unser had approached him, asking for help with the war on terror. Initially there was mistrust and uncertainty on both sides, but over the years the two became more than just allies, and mutual respect had grown into a true friendship.

After quick hellos and handshakes, the president sat back down and everyone else followed his lead. The president, Palmer and Clayton on one well-worn brown leather couch, John and Gonzalo sat facing them on a matching one with a narrow coffee table in between.

"Well, I'm guessing you're both wondering why we asked you here," President Carson said.

John nodded.

"In a nutshell, we need your help."

Clayton chimed in, "Before we get into it, you both

have to sign these." He handed over iron-clad non-disclosure agreements.

"What does it say?" John asked, signing without reading the three-page doc.

"That if you tell anyone other than the people in this room anything about this meeting, or repeat anything that we're about to discuss here, you're one hundred percent guaranteed to die in a federal prison."

"Understood," John said.

Gonzalo remained silent, but nodded his head, then signed and handed his NDA back to Clayton.

"Okay, now that that's out of the way… John, as I was saying, we need your help."

"How, Mr. President?" John asked.

"We're a nation at war and we've got terrorists, both foreign and domestic, trying to incite fear and destroy our democracy by killing as many American citizens as they can. Bottom line, your country needs you, John."

"You want me to re-enlist, sir?" John asked.

"Yes and no. We want you to head a special unit. Deep cover. As Black Ops as it gets. Run by the next director of CIA, reporting directly to the commander-in-chief and the director of National Intelligence."

Gonzalo was about to speak, then pulled back, waiting for the president to explain the obvious challenges. John had a long list of questions, but he too waited for more details.

"I know what you're thinking. How do we set this up when I've only got a few months left in office?" Carson said.

The prior week's election had been a tight one, but Jeff Stamper, the Republican candidate had won the day, and he would replace the two-term Democratic president in January.

"Here's the deal," Carson said. "The debates and the

election were ugly and the country is deeply divided. Despite that, we've been having bi-partisan behind-the-scenes meetings. We presented our plan to President-elect Stamper after he signed a top-secret NDA identical to yours, and he's on board."

"Won't Stamper pick his own people for National Intelligence and CIA?" John asked.

"That is correct, and he agrees that Clayton has CIA, and General Palmer is the DNI."

"Forgive me for saying so, Mr. President, but that's hard to believe," John said.

The Congress and the nation were deeply divided ideologically and along party lines. The thought of a new Republican president agreeing with the outgoing Democratic commander-in-chief to pick the same two men for these senior positions seemed absurd.

"Look, despite all the insanity there are true patriots on both sides, and the country needs a smooth transition so we can focus on the road ahead. I took office with two wars and a global economic collapse, but I believe the next president will face far greater challenges than I did, and he's going to need a lot of help… That's where you come in, John."

The president took a sip of coffee and then continued.

"Aziz Khan was a perfect example. He was the number two bad guy on our top one hundred most wanted list, and a lot of good men died on my watch trying to kill him, yet you and your family took him out in a matter of days… So, here's the deal, we want you to plan and execute similar operations against enemies of the United States. Wherever those enemies are… here or abroad. Pick your own men and build a dedicated team of operators. CIA will provide funding for training, weapons and equipment. Whatever you want or need to get the job done, name it and it's yours."

"With all due respect, sir, the op we set up to kill Aziz Khan was unique and not something that can be replicated. Our family has its own way of doing things, and as you know, my Uncle Macho volunteered to sacrifice his own life to kill Aziz. Sergeant Able Diaz was killed too. I'm not doing anything else that will put my friends or family members in harm's way," John said.

"From what I understand they're already in danger. Hasn't the Russian mob killed seven of your family members in the past few months?" Carson asked.

John nodded his head slowly, his scarred face a grim mask of anger and sadness.

"We're offering you unlimited resources to help you from here on. You'll have access to any intel the CIA, NSA, DHS and FBI has on anyone you're going after," Clayton Unser said.

John looked at Clayton, then turned back to the president and stared at him for a few seconds. John noticed for the first time that the commander-in-chief had a few razor bumps on his neck and needed a shave. Bishop tilted his head back, looked up at the thick wooden beams along the ceiling, then took a deep breath and followed with a long exhale.

This was a big ask. Too big really, John thought.

Pregnant wife at home. His family at war. John was a patriot, but he'd already given and sacrificed so much. Love of country had its limits, especially when he finally had a shot at a life. A real one, with marriage, home, kids. Granted, there was an impressive list of assassins trying to crush his dreams, but even with all these enemies coming at him, he could still see a way forward. Everything he'd ever wanted was within his grasp, and all he had to do was kill them before they killed him to reach the finish line.

Taking on this role... *As what? Captain of the USA's all-star hit squad?* Whatever you called it; it moved the line. Maybe even erased it. There was an endless supply of bad guys ready to die trying to destroy America and willing to kill as many innocents as they could along the way. How could he do this to Maria?

I can't. Not if I want to keep her. Eventually she'll leave to protect the baby. Not right away, but one day I'll come home from a mission and she'll be gone.

John came back. Realized the president had been staring at him the whole time he was running through the pros and cons, and so far, it was a lopsided ledger.

"Mr. President, you've clearly been briefed on the, uh, *challenges* our family is currently facing."

"I have, John, and it's an important part of why you should accept our offer. Every one of your enemies poses a clear and present danger to our country, and we may have actually eliminated one of the threats earlier today," Carson said.

"Tariq Hassan?" John asked.

"Exactly. General, can you fill him in?" Carson asked, turning to Palmer.

Gen. Palmer gave John a complete AAR (After Action Report) on the Raqqa air strike.

"General, are there assets in place to positively identify Tariq?" John asked.

"On-site, but with the amount of damage and the high body count it may take some time to get confirmation," Palmer said.

"I'd appreciate it if you let me know as soon as you get it, sir. There's a long list of bad guys coming at us, and checking off even one name would be helpful," John said.

President Carson leaned forward to emphasize his point: "John, your list is our list. We'll help you with every name, and once your team takes them out, we'll add new ones."

Quite an offer, John thought.

He looked over at Gonzalo, who'd been sitting quietly, taking it all in, processing the information and working through all the implications for John and the Valdez family.

"Sir, why is my uncle here?" John asked.

The president nodded at Clayton Unser.

"Great question, John, with a fairly simple answer," Clayton said. "We know you're a package deal. We admire your loyalty and appreciate the unique skills that the Valdez family can provide."

Clayton shifted slightly to address Gonzalo directly: "We've been working together for a long time now. Besides risking your own life to save mine on two separate ops, you've helped CIA gain a tremendous amount of intel that's aided us in the war on terror. Up to now, and due to the nature of your business, your role has been off the books and unofficial. We want our relationship to change, but there's a prerequisite…"

"The Valdez family has to be completely legitimate," Gonzalo said.

"Yes, exactly. That's part one and it's non-negotiable."

"Part two?" Gonzalo asked.

"You set up a security contracting company," Clayton said.

"Like Blackwater?" Gonzalo asked.

"They're Academi now. But yes, similar. Only you'll be more specialized. Your company will be the logistical arm of John's team."

Clayton handed over a folder and Gonzalo quickly scanned the proposal. The key points had been highlighted with a light green sharpie, and the initial contract proffered by a CIA dummy corporation was for a hundred million dollars.

"You're going to need a lot of equipment," Clayton added, nodding at the check in Gonzalo's hand. "Encrypted comms to liaison with me and a small trusted group within CIA and NSA, as well as land, air and sea transportation and of course weapons and a training facility."

Gonzalo's brilliant mind ran through all the calculations. He was already working towards legitimizing the family business, and taking this deal would accelerate his plans, but there were two major obstacles. First and most important was John. Gonzalo loved him like a son and knew how much he'd suffered throughout his life. Now, for the first time in a long time, John was whole again. Despite the losses and all the challenges they still faced, Gonzalo knew that his adopted son was finally truly happy. He didn't want anything interfering with that.

Second was that politicians were emotional. More often than not, they acted irrationally under pressure. This president seemed fairly levelheaded, but he was on the way out. Who knew how this next one would behave? Any pre-inauguration commitments to protect John could easily be tossed aside. He wasn't going to gamble with his adopted son's future or the future of his family without more information.

"What guarantees do we have?" Gonzalo asked.

"Honestly my friend, for you, we can't provide any," Clayton said. "If you're prosecuted for any of your past crimes, whether it's state or federal, you're on your own. We can't help. Wouldn't even if we could. That's the cold hard truth of it."

"John is a different story," President Carson said. He

handed John a folder, identical to the one Gonzalo received. "That's a *get out of jail free* card. A presidential pardon for anything you may have ever done or will do while you're working for us."

"How do I know Stamper will honor this?" John asked, holding up the folder for emphasis.

"You can ask him yourself," the president said.

"Ask him? When?" John asked.

"Now," Carson said. "Gonzalo, if you don't mind, we're going to ask you to leave the room with Clayton before the president-elect comes in."

Gonzalo nodded his agreement and stood up. Clayton rose to do the same, but the president tugged on his arm, pulling him close for a private word. "Make sure Mr. Valdez agrees to that other thing we talked about. It has to be done, or there's no deal."

Clayton's expression changed slightly, from stoic to sad as he looked into the president's eyes. He paused for a moment, then regained his composure, stood up and escorted Gonzalo past the Secret Service and through a side door.

CHAPTER 12
DECISIONS

Camp David
Frederick County, MD

A FEW MINUTES after Gonzalo and Clayton left the room, President-elect Jeff Stamper walked in. Like President Carson, Stamper was wearing jeans, loafers and a dress shirt, but instead of a V-neck sweater Stamper wore a dark blue blazer. Even though Stamper was overweight and out of shape, he exuded so much confidence that he seemed much taller than his actual height of five-eleven. He had intense dark brown eyes and a shock of brown curly hair that bounced a bit as he moved, and on the left side of his chin he had a half-inch scar he got playing lacrosse in high school.

Stamper strode over to the group and shook hands with Carson first, then Palmer, and then Unser before he turned to John and gave him a well-practiced pump, hold and release. He plopped down heavily on the couch and politely declined the president's offer of coffee or tea.

John had been too busy killing bad guys to follow the election or even vote, but he knew that the real estate mogul and former two-term Virginia governor sitting next to him had left a bloody trail in his bid for the White House. John also knew that most of Stamper's rhetoric had been aimed directly at the current leader of the free world. Despite being keenly aware that these guys were professional politicians, he was still a little surprised that neither man displayed any animus, and that they both seemed relaxed and comfortable sitting three feet across from each other.

President Carson got the meeting started by summarizing where they were in the discussion, adding that John needed to hear guarantees before he left to consider their proposal. Stamper, still in campaign mode, began by spewing out slogans and then started outlining his aggressive agenda for reshaping the country.

Carson shot him a look and said: "Jeff, it's late and you already won the election."

Stamper smiled, nodded in agreement and got down to it. He promised to support John and his team, and said he looked forward to working with him in January when he was sworn in. John listened politely, maintaining eye contact and nodding his head when Stamper vigorously drove home a point. When Stamper was done John felt less confident than he did before the discussion started.

"Sir, I'll be frank," he said, turning slightly to his right to look Stamper directly in the eyes. "I don't see how anything you've said here guarantees protection for me and the men I'd bring in. As General Palmer knows, I served my country to the best of my ability, but I did it knowing that the Army and the country had my back. You're asking me to risk my life and a lot of other lives. And if things go bad, as they often do in combat... if there's collateral damage, or an international incident, I can't just take you at your word that you'll take the heat and not leave us dangling. Or worse yet, throw us under the bus."

"I'd feel the same way if I were you, John," said the president. "That's why there's a MAD contingency here."

Carson held up another folder and John raised his eyebrows questioningly.

"Mutually Assured Destruction. None of us are perfect. We all make mistakes. Some more egregious than others and our friend here has made some big ones. These files contain details regarding his businesses that the FBI and the press haven't uncovered. If Mr. Stamper breaches the terms and guarantees of our agreement, this report will be leaked. At best his career and reputation will go up in flames, and in all likelihood he'll end up in prison."

"Presidents don't go to prison," John said.

"Not yet," Carson said.

Stamper shrugged.

The president handed over the file. John opened the folder and started reading. Glanced over at Stamper and noted that he was surprisingly cool and relaxed.

Stamper was indeed calm and composed on the outside, but inside he was laughing at this fortunate turn of events. It had only been seven hours since Caleb Meecham threatened the Virginia governor with a similar folder, and he was now sitting next to the man Caleb tasked him with destroying. Stamper gave John his best "I'm on your side, we're in this together" smile while he plotted how he'd have the scar-faced trouble-maker quickly terminated once he took office.

A few minutes later, Stamper said his goodbyes. The president walked him to the door with his hand on Stamper's shoulder. A temporary ceasefire. Hostilities would undoubtedly resume in the morning.

John was left with the president and his former combat commander, Gen. Palmer. They both encouraged him to take some time to think things over. Some, but not too much. They also reminded him that he was still a civilian, and they'd really appreciate it if he and his family would stop firing automatic weapons on city streets… at least until after he officially joined the team. John said it wouldn't happen again, but knew it was a promise he just couldn't keep.

Clayton and Gonzalo had walked outside and away from the lights of the main house. It was a dark night. An hour before dawn. No moon. Cool, but not cold. Quiet except for the wind blowing through the trees and rattling the last of the late autumn leaves. The two men strolled over to a large rock near the edge of a stand of white birch. The rock had a bronze plate with an inscription, but it was too dark for either of them to make out what it read.

"Zalo, just so you know. Even if John doesn't accept our offer, we still want you to set up the company and work with other teams that I'll put together myself," Clayton said.

Gonzalo thought about that for a few moments, as his yellow eyes bored into Clayton's.

"Quite a generous offer," Gonzalo said, breaking the silence. "Now, tell me my friend. Tell me what the president of the United States wants me to do."

Clayton told him, expecting a reaction. Gonzalo nodded, recognizing that despite all his experience, he'd let the president's calm demeanor and easy-going smile disarm him. No longer. He now knew just how ruthless and calculating the most powerful man in the world truly was.

There wasn't enough light for Clayton to clearly see his face, but Gonzalo turned away anyway. A single tear rolled down his cheek while he stared out into the night.

CHAPTER 13
SHARING

Calixto's Estate
Long Island, NY

JOHN GOT BACK from Camp David at 7AM and hurried into the house to find Maria. He thought she'd be sleeping, but she was in the kitchen, sitting at the breakfast table sipping a cup of chamomile tea. He kissed her and asked her if they could talk upstairs so he could change out of his suit. She nodded, and they walked together up the wide staircase and then down the carpeted hallway to the master bedroom.

He only managed to take off his jacket and tie before she made him tell the story. When he was done he reached into his inside jacket pocket, took out a copy of the NDA he'd signed, and handed it to her.

"What's this? she asked.

"Basically, it says that I've got to turn myself in today and start serving a life sentence in Leavenworth or Gitmo for what I just told you," he said.

She didn't bother reading it. Tossed it on the nightstand,

then sat down on the bed. Stared at him for a full minute while she digested it.

"So, just to be clear, the president of the United States asked you to lead a super-secret anti-terrorist kill squad, in front of the next president, who represents a party that's basically at war with the current administration, who then promised you immunity from future prosecution," Maria said.

"Umm, yeah… doesn't have much of a flow to it when you say it like that, but that's the gist of it," he said.

Maria punched him in the arm. "Ouch," John said, rubbing it and feigning injury.

"You're not considering this, are you?"

"I wanted to run it by you first. 'Cause, you remember how the other day you said no more secrets? … Remember when you said that?" He couldn't resist smiling at that one.

She raised her fist, ready to punch him again.

"Okay, okay. Just kidding. Bottom line, I don't trust any of these guys. I appreciate what the president did for Chris, but he's on his way out. If he wasn't… then yeah, maybe. With this other dude, I can't see it. He's not a soldier. He's a politician, which means deep down he's really just a gangster," John said.

"If you did do it what would it mean for us? For our baby?" Maria asked.

He moved closer, taking both of her hands in his.

"That's just it, honey. It would be bad for us. Really bad. Things are messed up enough now with all these crazies coming at us, but at least we can see an end game. I take this on, I'll be taking off to hunt people all over the world at a moment's notice. It'll be like I was deployed again, only this time there wouldn't be a return home date."

"No! No way. You can't. Not after you just got back. Not

after all the years apart. You gave them too much already. I love you, but I can't do it again, Johnny. I just can't do it."

"I know, baby. You're my wife and my life. Now and forever. I'm not giving you up for anyone, not even the president," John said.

She exhaled deeply, relieved to hear him say it.

"Good. You know, you're about to say no to some very powerful men. That's a word they don't take well," Maria said.

"Yeah, I get it. I've got a solid relationship with General Palmer. I'll talk to him first. Get a feel for whether there's gonna be some blowback."

"Sounds good, baby. I'm glad we're sharing. A good foundation for a happy family," Maria said.

"Speaking of sharing…" he said.

She smiled up at him, the beautiful disarming smile that had made his knees shake the first time she laid it on him and still made his heart melt more than twenty years later. She tried to unbutton his dress shirt while he tugged at her blouse, trying to pull it over her head. Hungry and eager, their efforts were only slowing things down, and they pulled apart to get undressed on their own. Clothes hit the floor and they attacked each other on the bed. Having fun with it. Newlyweds who'd been in love for a long, long time.

Afterwards, Maria slept, curling up next to him with her hands cupping her protruding belly. John did a quick run-through of his long to-do list and soon followed, finally going down at nine in the morning to get himself recharged.

Early that afternoon they showered together. Lathering each other up led to more loving. A quickie this time. John had to get to the city. She got out and dried off before him. He shaved and followed her out a few minutes later.

She'd laid out his clothes. Black rubber-soled ankle-high

boots, dark blue jeans, black tee, a thin black sweater to go over it, along with a black bomber jacket. Both his .357s were there too, with extra magazines and the double shoulder rig. So was the Kevlar he'd stashed in the downstairs closet.

"You don't go anywhere without body armor. Not till this is done," she said.

"Whatever you say, Mrs. Bishop."

Hustling now. Gonzalo had called a meeting for the entire Valdez family back in LES, and he couldn't be late for it. Dressed. Velcro straps pulled snug. Safeties on. He kissed her again, then turned and rushed out the door.

Maria's smile faded as soon as he left the bedroom. She lay down on the bed, hugged a pillow to her chest and started sobbing. She was still crying long after he was gone.

CHAPTER 14
THE TRINGAS

New York, NY

DAVID WAS THE last of his kind. A pure Tringa. Genetically selected. Bred from the best fighters. Bred to become the greatest assassin to ever live. His forefathers were brilliant in their psychosis. No labs. No blueprint. Just time and commitment. Over a thousand years to tinker with DNA, a millennium before the term even existed.

The ancient Tringas mated their best pupils, manufacturing children who were faster, and stronger, more intelligent and cunning. Failures far outweighed their successes, but their will to engineer assassins never wavered. Those who were weak or lacked the will and discipline to become true Tringas never survived. They all died in training. Cut down by their stronger, more determined siblings during the daily sessions that began on their fifth birthdays and lasted for the next sixteen years.

Through centuries of genetic testing and tinkering, they kept meticulous records. The elder scribes wrote everything down. Every minute detail of life from birth to violent death.

Now there were no more scribes, and David's father had been the last Tringa librarian. On his deathbed he pleaded with David to preserve their family legacy, to find and train new students. To rebuild the Tringa army of assassins.

His father recognized that everything he'd worked for was gone, and was bitter and angry when he died. His son was the best the family had ever produced, but he was also the last. When David told him that John Bishop was his final mission, his father summoned his strength and struck him hard in the face. David didn't move or block the blow and was impressed by the power of the punch. His father tried to say something after that, but died before delivering the message.

An apology? I'd be disappointed if it was, David thought.

He understood his father's anger. In twelve hundred years the Tringas had never failed to complete a contract. It was an impressive track record that became harder to maintain in the modern age of technology. Many assassinations became suicide missions that required two, three or four Tringas to die in order to get to the target. The family began losing more students than they could train, and in an effort to replenish the ranks, had stopped the breeding program.

Elders scoured the countryside searching for strong and defiant four- and five-year-olds they could train at a faster rate. They found two hundred children, but made the fateful mistake of training them all together in one location instead of separately as they'd done in the past. The Tringa school was high in the mountains, and a winter avalanche in 2012 killed them all.

David, his father, his grandfather and his grandfather's student Omar lived and trained separately. It was the only reason they survived. His father just died, he buried his

90-year-old grandfather a month before, and Omar was killed trying to complete her mission.

David was going to start a new life. Change his name. Travel the world in search of a path that led him away from being a genetically engineered killer. First though, he would close the books and complete his family's final contract. Tringa honor demanded it.

He walked down St. Marks Place in Manhattan's East Village, taking pictures, casually moving towards the Valdez family's Lower East Side stronghold. Moving towards the man he traveled seven thousand miles to see.

Five-eleven, light brown hair, brown eyes, strong jaw, good looking, but not handsome, David was bred to blend in. To be the perfect chameleon. His black Chuck Taylors, worn jeans, black tee shirt, dark blue fall jacket, light backpack, and the Canon camera hanging from a neck strap, all created the perfect camouflage.

The small pillow strapped inside his shirt, a lazy stride, slight slouch, and a spot-on Australian accent to match his visa, all brought the performance home. If you had told any of the people he'd spoken to throughout the day that he was a highly trained Pakistani killer, they'd all have said you were out of your mind.

David crossed Avenue A and into Tompkins Square Park. He was getting eager. Too eager. He paused to take a few pictures of red-tailed hawks dipping and diving for park rats, to stay in character and slow himself down.

I'm looking forward to meeting you, John Bishop. You're the last. The last to ever die by a Tringa hand. For such a momentous occasion, your death must be truly spectacular.

Just then a hawk caught a fat gray rat in its talons and flew over to a low-hanging tree branch with its meal. David was only ten feet away and the red-tail looked at him impassively, as fearless of him as it was indifferent to the rat's squealing. The hawk took one last look around, then casually lowered its head and began ripping the rat's fur and flesh apart with its sharp beak.

David saw it as a sign: *Yes, I'll peel Bishop's skin before I kill him.*

He took a few closeups of the hawk, and then continued strolling and taking pics while thinking about how much John was going to suffer before he died.

Café Mogador
Manhattan's East Village

Omar the Blade rented an apartment on East 11th Street and had been going to Café Mogador a few blocks away on St. Marks Place for the past few weeks. She sat for hours by the window, sipping Moroccan tea, pretending to read a thriller by her favorite author, John Sandford, while she watched and waited.

Watched for David Tringa and waited for her body to heal after the big black man she now knew was Bunny Brown shot her in the upper right chest. It had taken her five months to recover from the surgery. The .45 round had done a massive amount of damage and stopped her from killing both John and Felix. Felix wasn't on her hit list, but he had cracked her skull with a steel handle while defending his cousin. She still hadn't decided whether Felix would live or die. For John there was no question, her blade would end his life.

Like David Tringa, Omar was perfectly disguised. Her long black hair was hidden inside a gray-haired wig; cotton pads in her mouth changed the shape of her face; makeup, contacts and small pillows transformed her from a lean strikingly beautiful 30-year-old killer into an overweight woman in her late fifties. She told the friendly Mogador waitresses that she was a recent widow seeking a quiet corner where she could read and think about her late husband. They gave the sad, heartbroken lady plenty of space, keeping the tables around her empty whenever possible to let her mourn in private. A fresh pot of tea arrived every hour or so, but otherwise they left her alone.

David was easy to spot, and if not for the sun reflecting off the restaurant window and the book held up to her face, he probably would've recognized her too. They grew up sparring against each other and had nearly killed one another numerous times during their countless combat drills. He'd regularly bested her fighting hand-to-hand, but she had dominated him whenever they used blades… He had the scars to prove it.

Omar and David knew each other intimately. Sex and seduction were important parts of their training, and they began practicing together in their teens while Tringa teachers made corrections and Tringa scribes took notes. They never made an emotional connection. That was not what sex was about for them. Rather, it was just another weapon to be mastered and used to get closer to a target.

She knew they were the last of their kind, but her instincts told her to remain invisible. She knew David. Despite her legendary status in the world of assassins, he was pure blood Tringa while she was born to peasant farmers, and he never let her forget it.

David had come to complete her mission and kill John Bishop. If he knew she was alive, Omar suspected he would try to kill her to protect his right to complete the Tringa contract.

She paid her check, put her book in an oversized purse, and slowly walked down St. Marks Place. A sad and broken woman trailing a block behind the Australian tourist.

CHAPTER 15
YAKOV

Moscow, Russia

AFTER THE MASSACRE at Jacob Riis and the multiple attacks on Mafia leaders in US prisons, the consortium of Russian bosses in Moscow conducted their own investigation into the murder of Nicky Skobelev and his wife in Brooklyn. The evidence was clear. The Valdez family had nothing to do with it. The Albanian hitman Connie Belusci, working for the young billionaire Caleb Meecham, had killed Nicky to start a Russian-Valdez war to help Meecham avenge the death of his father.

Yakov remained uncharacteristically calm and quiet as he listened to the private security team share the details of his son's murder in a PowerPoint presentation. The deck included photos taken from a restaurant's security camera. Connie had disabled all the other cameras in the area, but was unable to get to the live feed from the twenty-four-hour deli in Brighton Beach. The still shots showed the big bald-headed hitman standing over Nicky's body. Then the bright light from the

Uzi's muzzle flash when Connie fired a dozen rounds into Nicky's face.

Yakov felt his rage building. He ran his hands over his thick curly hair and gave the back of his neck a light squeeze to help keep his temper in check. He reached into the pocket of his black silk vest, pulled out a platinum cigarette case, and lit one with his diamond-covered gold lighter.

The other bosses watched him smoke. Waiting for him to speak. They had all fought their way to the top. Climbed over mountains of bodies to get where they were. They were all equals. Sort of. Yakov was a little more equal than the rest, since the army of Mafia soldiers under his command slightly outnumbered that of all the other bosses combined. He also had a direct line to the Kremlin. Shared the same blood with Russia's president. Second cousins, but blood was blood and the president hadn't held back his tears when he kissed Yakov on the cheeks at Nicky's funeral.

Despite his position, Yakov was no fool. After ten years of fighting there was finally peace in Moscow. The Kremlin had intervened, dictating which bosses would remain, adding a few of their own, and killing anyone unwilling to accept the new balance of power. His cousin had ordered the shakeup prior to winning the election and had personally ordered Yakov not to do anything to rock the boat once he took office.

Yakov knew his war with the Valdez family had just cost the other men in the room a lot. Prisons were a huge source of income. The "managers" kept the cash flowing from US facilities and shipped it directly back to Moscow. Losing close to forty Mafia managers in a single day was going to have a big impact, probably in the millions.

Yakov exhaled deeply, sending a heavy plume of smoke above the meeting table.

"Gentlemen, it seems I have made a mistake. I was tricked by this Meecham and the Albanian. My error has cost you men and money. The men I cannot replace. I can only convey my regrets and mourn with you. As to the money, there I can be of assistance."

He snapped his fingers on his left hand. The snap was a loud crack, and the overhead lights caught the twenty-carat diamond on his pinky, sending dazzling bright dots around the room. Seven men entered, carrying briefcases. Each boss had a case placed in front of him.

"Ten million each… To ease your pain and suffering," Yakov said, looking each man in the eye and holding the stare until he received the necessary nod of acceptance.

He wasn't worried about the money. He would get it back a hundred times over. It was more of a short-term loan. When his president/cousin told him not to rock the boat, he'd added that it would only be for a year or two. After that he would personally help Yakov eliminate all seven of these men and make him the boss of bosses.

A few more months and they would all be gone, but for now he wanted them relaxed and happy.

"Thank you for finding my son's true killers. It is a debt that I owe to each of you. I will not forget it, and one day soon I will find a very special way to repay you all. In the meantime, I'll put an end to this misunderstanding with Valdez. Restore peace… and our reputations."

The bosses clapped loudly. Now that the business was concluded, the drinking began. They took shot after shot of the smooth Tovaritch Vodka, talking about the glorious future they would all share. The evening ended with somber toasts to Nicky before the bosses went home, leaving Yakov alone with his brother Sasha and a few of his top lieutenants.

"I will handle the truce, Yakov. I'll call Gonzalo myself," Sasha said.

"Not yet, Sasha," Yakov said. He pointed to one of his men standing by the door. "Call in Vorovka."

"Why do you want The Thief?" Sasha asked.

Yakov ignored the question and didn't meet his brother's disapproving eyes.

"The Thief" did not steal money or jewelry. Only lives. Some said his "heists" numbered in the thousands. Now in his sixties, the master sniper had been shooting people from long range since he was a teenager. He was semi-retired, yet always willing to return to work for the right price.

No one spoke when the seemingly harmless old man was escorted in. He wore a cheap charcoal suit with a sweater vest and tie, and although he still had perfect vision, added non-prescription glasses with small round frames to complete his librarian impersonation. He walked towards Yakov and stood casually a few feet away from the Mafia boss.

"Cigarette?" Yakov asked, holding up the platinum case.

"I quit."

Yakov nodded. "Bad for the health."

"Who?" Vorovka asked, getting right to the point.

Yakov couldn't say the name right away. He knew now that he'd been fighting the wrong people. Right or wrong though, once a war starts it's hard to end it. Too much blood had been spilled. He was going to spend months torturing Caleb and Connie before he killed them. That was separate. The problem was that he couldn't just forgive and forget all the men he lost to the Valdez mob. He thought back to the video from the drone in Jacob Riis and the man standing over his comrades.

"John Bishop," he said finally.

"Yakov, don't do this," his brother pleaded.

"He will be the last. His life for all the men we lost today. After Vorovka completes his mission, you can call Gonzalo Valdez and tell him the war is over."

Sasha Skobelev shook his head sadly.

Wars don't end with the death of cherished sons, he thought.

CHAPTER 16
LIFE IS CHANGE

Campos Plaza, Lower East Side

JOHN AND HIS uncle had been the only passengers on their short pre-dawn flight back from Camp David. Sitting side by side, Gonzalo shared his vision for the family's future. Twelve hours later, John was seated next to Gonzalo again, only this time in a room full of Valdez family soldiers silently waiting for their leader to speak.

This is gonna be interesting, John thought.

Two adjoining apartments in Campos Plaza had been gutted, their connecting walls knocked down to create a three-thousand-foot open space for larger Valdez family meetings. Usually, there was more than enough room. Gonzalo, his brothers and a few trusted advisors would gather around the mahogany conference table. This meeting was different.

Gonzalo sat at the head of the table with his nephew Antonio to his right. In honor of Antonio's father, Sesa Valdez, the next seat over remained empty. A somber reminder that the man who had given so much to the family was gone, but never forgotten. John was on Gonzalo's left, then Felix, and then Bunny. Four of Gonzalo's surviving brothers—Carlos, Victor, Fiero, and Calixto—sat close as well. Nestor, now Geronimo, was doing his own thing with his Apaches and was not invited.

Christmas, the former Navy SEAL and head of the family's military wing, also had a seat at the "high table," and several of his soldiers stood a few feet behind him. The last seat went to Benji Medina. Benji was a top Valdez enforcer who reported directly to Antonio.

For the rest, there were chairs along the walls in case anyone wanted them, but all 80 men remained standing. Everyone knew this was an important meeting. It was rare that Gonzalo gathered everyone together in one location, and they all wanted to be there to see him and hear what he had to say.

Gonzalo looked around the room, making eye contact with each of them, remembering all the battles they fought together over the years. He was proud of these men. They'd forged a bond in blood in the streets and built an empire based on loyalty above all else.

Gonzalo stood up to bring the meeting to order. Regal in a black three-piece Brioni with a gray tie and a gray shirt, he lightly tapped his gold ring on the table to get everyone's attention. He knew it wasn't necessary since the room was already silent, but it was an old habit, so he did it anyway.

"Gentlemen. Thank you all for coming. I have news to share with you and I wanted you all to hear it from me in person." He paused and took a small sip of water.

"We started this family forty years ago, right here in LES. Just me and my brothers at first, but every one of you chose to join us and swore an oath of loyalty. An oath, not just to me, but to each other. Together, we fought back to back and side by side. Throughout all our years at war, against all enemies, against all odds, not one of you has ever hesitated or failed to do your duty.

You are all true warriors and more importantly, true brothers. Our enemies are money-hungry mobs, while we stand alone as a true family. La Familia Valdez!"

The room went wild. Cheers, whistles, and applause. Once the room calmed, he continued.

"Before I say anything else, we must honor the fallen," Gonzalo said.

He said every name aloud. The list included his four murdered brothers, his baby sister Christina, and thirty-two other members of La Familia Valdez. He didn't read from a paper. He remembered every face and the name of every man who died in his service. He paused at the end. Was about to say Sesa's name, but just couldn't bring himself to do it. Antonio, Sesa's son, saw his struggle, put a hand on his shoulder and whispered in his ear.

"It's okay, Tio. We'll say his name soon. When our enemies are all dead, we'll say his name."

Gonzalo hugged him close. The men in the room all understood what Antonio had just done. He'd proven himself time and time again, and this was another sign of a true leader. He put his own pain aside and helped his uncle get through his. They knew he was ready.

Regaining his composure, Gonzalo raised a glass. "To our fallen. May they rest in peace."

The solemn toast was echoed around the room and everyone took a drink.

"So, you are all asking yourselves, what is this big news? Here it is. No more street. We got out of the drug trade years ago, and we're making millions more now than we ever did back then. Now we put it all behind us. The gambling, everything. It all ends today."

There were lots of questioning looks around the room. Even Antonio and Gonzalo's brother Fiero had shocked expressions on their faces.

"You have questions?" Gonzalo asked.

"Many," Fiero said. "First, what is our new business?

"Security consultants."

John watched his cousin Antonio closely. He was a serious gangster. The real deal. Old school. He'd spent nearly half of his life training to be the head of a crime family. If that was not who the Valdez family was anymore, John figured that Antonio wasn't really sure where that left him. From the look on his face, John knew the heir to the throne wasn't happy with his uncle's decision.

"What kind of security?" Fiero asked.

"Paramilitary. We're taking our existing global network, infrastructure, and years of experience with guerilla warfare to assist the US armed forces and intelligence agencies. We will also leverage John, Christmas, and Bunny's relationships to build our own army of Special Ops veterans."

John scanned the room. There was confusion, but above all else these soldiers were wondering how'd they fit into Gonzalo's new business venture. Gonzalo saw it too.

"My brothers, this is for all of us. The street is the street, but the street has changed. LES now has more million-dollar condos than low-income housing. The Wild West days are over, with or without this deal. And if you want it, there's a place for every one of you… As the head of this family I can command you to join me, but I won't."

Gonzalo turned to Benji Medina. Five-seven with a deeply pockmarked face, Benji was a man of few words. A quiet and unimposing killer. One of the most feared enforcers New York had ever known.

"I've already spoken to Benji in private, and given him my blessing to start his own family. I do the same for all of you."

Benji, thoughtful and deliberate as always, took an eight count before responding.

"Thank you for the offer, Don Valdez, but this is my family. I follow you. Wherever you lead us, I follow. My oath stands."

John was impressed, though not surprised. Benji was loyal, and he and Antonio had been inseparable since the first grade.

John's Uncle Fiero seemed to be having the most trouble wrapping his mind around the move away from all criminal activity.

"I have many questions about working with government agencies. They know our history. How will they now partner with us in this new business? And what about the competition? Blackwater or whatever they're called now. They'll come after us. Not with guns, but politically and in the news. We'll be an easy target and they will fight to keep those big government contracts in their own pocket," Fiero said.

"All good questions, mi hermano. Shall I answer now?" Gonzalo asked.

"Not yet. First, what about our money on the street? As of this morning it's just over two point five million."

"We leave it," Gonzalo said.

"Just like that?" Fiero asked.

"Yes, exactly like that. We walk away and don't look back."

"I… I don't understand, Zalo. How can we?"

Gonzalo knew it was a bold move and yes there were risks involved, but the opportunity far outweighed the downside. He pulled some folded papers from the inside pocket of his Brioni, held them up for effect.

"This is how we can. Our first contract. One hundred million. Fifty in advance for setup costs."

Fiero smiled for the first time. "Well done, Don Valdez. Well done. You never cease to amaze me, brother."

Antonio was equally impressed, but didn't lose sight of the realities they still faced.

"Tio, business aside, we're still at war, and our enemies don't care how we make our money," Antonio said. "Or maybe they do. This move may make them even bolder. Either way they're coming for us. How do we kill them if we become law-abiding citizens?" he asked.

"Our enemies are enemies of the United States. Our job is to help create the list. Then assist in the capture or killing of anyone who's on that list, in a support role or when appropriate through a more... hands-on engagement."

"Hands-on? I don't know much about the support part. I know we're real good at being hands-on, though," Antonio said. He rarely smiled, but came close to it when the corners of his downturned mouth lifted slightly. There was a short round of laughter from around the room.

"Understand something, all of our enemies are getting wiped out, and the fact that we've always been so careful over the years really helps us now," Gonzalo said. "Only Felix and three others here have felony convictions. As security professionals, all the rest of you will have concealed carry permits, good in every state, including New York."

John could see his uncle won them over, as he knew he would. They were a tight group and keeping the family together, even within a new corporation, while getting rich at the same time wasn't really a hard sell.

Gonzalo wasn't done. "Life is change, my friends. If we stick to our old ways we risk death and prison, but if we adapt, if we evolve, and seize this opportunity your families will be set for generations to come. Who's with me?"

Every man shouted his allegiance. The applause didn't end until Gonzalo gestured for them to stop.

"This is day one of our new journey. We are still a family, but you will all receive employment contracts within the week. In the meantime, here are your first paychecks." He nodded to his brother Calixto, who removed a bundle from his briefcase under the desk.

He held it up: "Two hundred and fifty thousand each."

The room exploded, and this time Gonzalo let them run with it. High fives, hugs and cheers. When they finally calmed down, they lined up to receive their checks. To a man, after Calixto handed each of them a personalized envelope, they turned to Gonzalo, bent down and kissed his hand. "Don Valdez," was repeated by all.

Antonio was the only one who still wasn't happy. His dream of running a crime family was gone, and he just couldn't wrap his mind around becoming a civilian. He didn't get up from his seat or pick up the check when Calixto slid it across the table to him.

Gonzalo knew his nephew would be upset, and he planned to meet with him in private to explain the senior leadership role Antonio would have in their new venture.

"What's next?" Fiero asked.

"Classes," Gonzalo said.

"What?"

"To be successful we must learn our new business the

same way we learned the streets. We all have to educate our-selves and we have to do it quickly. Classes begin in a few days."

John was amazed by his uncle's vision and how he could come up with all this in less than a day. He'd put his phone on mute before the meeting started, and he casually glanced down to check it. He froze when he saw ten missed calls from Maria and a dozen texts that repeated the same message over and over:

911 911 911 911 911 911 911

John's hand shook when he pressed her number. She picked up on the first ring:

"Johnny!"

He kept his voice calm: "Maria, what's wrong?"

"It's my dad. He was supposed to come here today, but never showed. His cell goes to voicemail and there's no answer on the home phone."

John knew her instincts were right. Her father was a stickler for being on time for everything, and he was always reliable. He'd never miss a visit with his only daughter unless something was very wrong.

"Maybe he just…"

"Don't bother. Something's happened to him. I can feel it."

"Maria, where are you?

"I'm in the car. Almost to the city."

"Maria, no! Turn around right now!"

The line went dead. He frantically redialed, got her voicemail, glanced at his uncle, then took off running out of the room. Felix, Bunny, and Benji Medina chased after him.

Antonio stood up. At six-four he towered over Gonzalo.

"Looks like school's gonna have to wait, Tio."

Gonzalo nodded: "What are you all waiting for? Go! Find out what happened."

Except for a few of his brothers and his personal bodyguards, everyone raced out. Gonzalo stood for a moment, then collapsed into his chair and put his head in his hands.

.

CHAPTER 17

VOROVKA

Manhattan's Upper East Side

VOROVKA HAD SO many fake identities and characters that he played to perfection, that he sometimes forgot his real name. Boris. Boris Vasiliev.

When was the last time anyone called me Boris? Too far back to remember.

For this short visit to America, his cover was a low-level translator of Russian literature working on a project for the United Nations. He did his analysis on the flight from Moscow to New York and found what he was looking for. The weak link. The pressure point that would deliver his target right into his crosshairs.

It was a skill he'd mastered over the decades. If a person had no idea someone paid to have them killed, then they were easy to stalk. Those were the civilians. Sheep that he could take at any time.

When it came to professionals, people who knew there were enemies hunting them, he took a much different approach. Instead of stalking them or trying to predict where they'd be at a certain time, he made them come to him.

Most of his peers, the elite shooters who killed for money, wanted to keep all their targets, regardless of training, relaxed and comfortable in their routines.

Not Vorovka. He saw life as purely unpredictable, with random events keeping the world in a constant state of chaos. He simply added to the chaos by making his targets emotional and unstable by finding their weak point. One glance at the Valdez family org chart and John's was easy to see… Maria.

Yakov's small army of soldiers in New York hadn't done much besides get themselves killed, but they were good at providing summary backgrounds on John and his entire family. The report stated that Maria never left the fortified compound in Long Island, so Vorovka quickly figured out a way to draw her out.

The Russian Mafia had started a massive buying spree of New York real estate four years earlier, and that hadn't slowed down despite the soaring prices of Manhattan condos. Most of the purchases were part of a global money laundering operation, and the majority of the fully furnished apartments sat empty. Vorovka told Yakov what he needed, and two hours later he was directed to the forty-story building on East 83rd street. The doorman handed him the keys, and when he entered the three-bedroom condo, his "tool box" was waiting for him, lying flat on the dining room table.

He opened the gun case and smiled down at the bolt action Winchester 300 Magnum. He was comfortable shooting any long gun and preferred using a Russian-made Dragunov semi-automatic sniper rifle whenever he could, but he was more than satisfied with the Winchester. He didn't have an exact count of how many lives he'd taken with variations of the 300 Win Mag over the years, but knew it was north of a hundred.

Vorovka spent an hour setting up his shooting stand, assembling and sighting his weapon and calculating the range to target. After he was done, he headed down to create some chaos.

He sipped a grande coffee, black no sugar, while he observed the twenty-two-story building from a Starbucks across the street. Watching the flow of traffic going in and out, after thirty minutes he'd seen enough.

Wearing black slacks, a dark brown suit jacket over a green sweater vest, and his standard round-rimmed glasses, Vorovka timed his entrance perfectly, walking in alongside two elderly tenants. The doorman tipped his hat to the trio, thinking they were all together, and even if Vorovka had come in alone he would have registered as a zero on the doorman's threat meter.

He got off the elevator on fifteen, walked down the hallway and lightly knocked on the door. He heard movement inside and stood back a few feet in front of the peephole to give the resident a clear view of him.

For years Alastair Williams had dreamt of having grandchildren. He knew his daughter was madly in love, but it had broken his heart to see her suffering for more than a decade while John was deployed. Now that she was married and pregnant, Maria's mother joked that it was a coin toss as to who was happier, father or daughter.

He'd spent the day shopping. Bags of clothes and toys lined the hallway near the front door. Boy or girl, it didn't matter, he bought outfits for both. Maria had told him she was having a huge baby shower at the estate and begged him to stop the madness. This would be his third delivery in less than a month. He realized this haul was a bit larger than he'd planned, but he felt it was his right, *nae* his duty, to spoil this baby rotten.

And Gaelic. He'd start the lessons right away. This one would be fluent, and when they traveled back to Scotland everyone would light up when the wee lad or lass spoke like a true highlander.

A Scottish-Filipino-Panamanian-Jamaican who speaks Gaelic, English and Spanish? Now that's as badass as it gets, he thought.

Alastair was hustling. He saw Maria only once a week at the Long Island estate and didn't want to lose a minute for being late. He scolded himself for almost forgetting the bags in the fridge filled with his daughter's favorites: smoked Scottish salmon with bagels, cream cheese, tomatoes, red onions and capers... *she had to have the capers.*

He was heading to the kitchen when he heard the soft knock on the front door. His brow wrinkled. He wasn't expecting anyone, and John had briefed him on the dangers surrounding them and walked him through the security protocols. Alastair had served in the British para forces 30 years earlier and he was smart enough to check the peephole to see who was knocking.

Although the gentleman looked harmless enough and even waved his hand in greeting, Alastair remained cautious. He unlocked the door and opened it slightly. No more than a foot. Just enough to see the elderly college professor he assumed was lost and got off on the wrong floor.

"May I help you?" Alastair asked.

"Yes, Mr. Williams. You can," Vorovka said.

The move was quick. Too quick for Alastair to get out of the way or close the door.

The Scotsman looked down and said, "Oh."

The dagger went in between his top two ribs, just below his breastplate. Vorovka kept it there, twisting and angling it upwards to make sure he punctured the heart. Saw the resignation in Alastair's face, then shoved forward to keep the body and the blood in the apartment.

Alastair Williams felt himself falling, but didn't feel any pain when his back slammed into the floor. He stared up at Vorovka, the thief who'd stolen a thousand lives. Didn't see the Russian's face. All Alastair saw was the image of his daughter. He tried to force himself up to somehow warn her, then he let out a soft moan when he realized there was nothing he could do.

Vorovka watched him struggle, gave his dagger another wiggle, tickling and tearing more of Alastair's heart with the point of the thin blade, and then watched Maria's father take his last breath. He died with his eyes open.

The Russian took out his dagger and wiped it on Alastair's shirt before carefully putting it back into the sheath attached to his left forearm inside his suit jacket. Then he grabbed his victim by the ankles, dragged him across the living room and over to the windows.

It took some effort to get the body up onto a chair and keep it balanced in a sitting position. Vorovka opened the curtains and the big windows all the way, and then walked to the front door to admire his work. Alastair was sitting with his back to the door and appeared to be staring out the window.

Vorovka used the paper towels from the kitchen counter and some Windex he found under the sink to clean up all the blood on the floor. He did a final inspection and gave a satisfactory nod before leaving the apartment.

It took just five minutes to get back to the Mafia-owned

condo, and once inside he washed his hands and poured himself a cold glass of water. Then he pulled up a chair. Through the Winchester 300's scope, he looked into Alastair Williams's open eyes 800 yards away and wondered how long it would take his daughter to get there. Once Maria arrived, Vorovka knew John wouldn't be far behind.

"I better piss now," he said out loud. "My bladder isn't what it used to be."

Vorovka smiled on his way to the bathroom, thinking about the shot he would make, then wondered if his flight back to Moscow would be on time.

CHAPTER 18
LITTLE PRINCESS

MARIA KNEW SOMETHING was wrong and she'd felt more and more uneasy as the minutes ticked past her father's scheduled arrival time. She kept getting his voicemail, but told herself not to panic. Phones die, and the Long Island Expressway was notorious for its random traffic jams. She called her mother, who was visiting a friend just north of the city in Scarsdale. Her mom said there was no reason to worry, but Maria could tell she was lying.

Mom knows too.

Maria ran to the closet and got the SIG 9mm that John made her practice with… *in case, just in case*. She shoved it into her purse, almost tripped running down the stairs, then charged through the house and into the attached garage. She fired up her BMW and nicked the slow opening automatic double doors on the way out.

The four Valdez guards at the gate were taken by surprise when she blew past them. It took them a minute to get in their SUV and give chase. By the time they made it to the highway she was already miles ahead of them, and they had to use binoculars to spot her.

Maria was doing 95 on the Expressway, deftly maneuvering the powerful BMW 750li around cars that were driving closer to the speed limit. She weaved in and out, pressing the gas pedal down to the floor whenever there was a clear path, leaning into it as the Bimmer lurched forward.

Desperate to get to her father, she used the car's Bluetooth to call him, then tried John, going back and forth between the two of them each time she heard their recorded messages.

She was on the Queensboro bridge, crossing the East River into Manhattan when John finally called her back. Heard him shouting, telling her to turn around.

No way, Johnny. Not while my Daddy's in danger.

She slowed for traffic on the exit ramp, crossed Second Avenue, saw there was congestion going west on East 60th Street so she drove onto the sidewalk. She used her horn to clear the pedestrians, who cursed and pounded on the car as she raced past them.

John kept calling. She ignored him. Took a sharp right onto Third Avenue, saw it was clear in the center lane and floored it again. She heard the sirens. Glanced in her rearview and saw flashers several blocks behind. No stopping now.

Have to get to Daddy. Have to.

Tears flowing, trying to calm herself with deep breaths, and chanting the mantra in her head over and over again, *He's going to be okay. Everything's going to be okay.*

Made it to 83rd Street. No place to park so she screeched to a stop in front of the building and left it in the street, motor still running. Racing now. Didn't realize she had the gun in her hand until people started screaming and backing away. Eddie the doorman shouting after her as she ran to the elevators.

The ride up to fifteen took too long. Maria was shaking now. Holding the SIG's grip tightly with her right, while her left was balled into a fist, thumping against her thigh. The doors opened and she raced down the hallway. The same hallway where her daddy first taught her to ride a bike. Precious moments of their life together flashing before her eyes as she reached the door. Key in, a quick turn, she raised the SIG and got into a shooter's stance when she stepped into the apartment.

"Daddy? Daddy, where are you?"

Then she saw him in the chair.

"Oh, thank God," she said, lowering the gun. "You really had us worried."

John ran out of the meeting at Campos Plaza with Felix, Bunny, and Benji right behind him. Christmas and twenty more Valdez soldiers were running down the stairs chasing after them. Felix called the security team as they ran, and there was a black 500 SEL waiting for them on the corner of 12th Street and Avenue C by the time they hit the pavement. The Benz was running and all four doors were wide open.

Benji got behind the wheel and took off the second their asses hit the seats. They flew past the Con Ed plant where only a few months ago the four of them had been in a life and death battle to rescue Maria.

John was in the front passenger seat frantically hitting redial, trying to reach her while they ran through red lights on their way to the FDR Drive. A beat-up red Honda was moving slowly in front of them, blocking their way. Benji accelerated, rammed it with their front bumper, and used the power of the big German eight-cylinder engine to push the obstacle out of their way.

Six more cars filled with Valdez soldiers followed them up the FDR Drive while Christmas and three more vehicles tried an alternate route and roared up 1st Avenue.

"This can't be happening," John said.

All the security. All the contingency plans. His constant warnings. He told her not to leave the house.

Why didn't she listen... and why the fuck isn't she picking up?

Bunny was sitting behind John in the rear passenger seat. He reached forward, put his massive hand on John's left shoulder and gave it a squeeze.

"Almost there, Johnny," he said. "Game face, brother. We go in tactical. You lead, I'm on your six just like always. Benji and Felix take nine and three, watching the corners. Good?"

John nodded, but didn't say anything.

Benji rammed another car, crumpling the front bumper this time. Both side mirrors got knocked off when they muscled through a tight gap and kept going, cutting over to the left lane to make it onto the 63rd Street exit and off the FDR. He sat on the horn as he ran through light after light going north on York Avenue until they hit 83rd Street and banged a sharp left.

"Thirty seconds. Check your loads. If there's any cops on the scene, my men will deal with them," Benji said.

They were 50 feet from the corner of Third Avenue when they hit a log jam. A Farmers Market delivery truck was double-parked, blocking half the street, and a city garbage truck was stuck behind it with no room to get by.

They all hopped out and ran to the avenue, guns drawn, pointed down. When they reached the corner they saw a dozen people milling about in front of Maria's parents' building. Two police cars with lights flashing and sirens blaring were racing towards the scene, still half a block away.

John had both his .357s up now, scanning for threats as they ran to the entrance.

"Down, down, down," Bunny said to the terrified civilians. Not shouting, but loud enough for everyone to hear. "Everybody down. As soon as we get inside, all of you get the fuck outta here."

John saw the doorman, blanked on his name, then remembered it a second later.

"Eddie, did Maria go inside?"

"Yes sir, Mr. Bishop. She had a gun… I tried to stop her, but…I just didn't know what to do."

"Anyone else go in or out?" John asked.

"No sir. No one."

Bunny leaned into the wide front door, pushing it open with his shoulder so John could run in past him.

Twelve of Benji's men made it to the building just as the police cars pulled up.

"Benji, have eight of your guys take the stairs. Four in each of the two stairwells. The other four guard this door. No one gets in or out," John said.

Benji gave the order and they all took off. Four cops with guns drawn cautiously approached the now-closed and locked front door and started shouting from the other side of the glass:

"Police! Drop your weapons! Drop your weapons!"

John, Bunny, Felix and Benji ignored them, glanced back at the screaming cops for a second, and then stepped into the elevator. On fifteen, John led the way, running flat out with Bunny right on his shoulder while Benji and Felix walked backwards, protecting the flank with their guns pointing down the opposite end of the hallway.

John saw the sunlight coming from the open door and barely slowed down when he made the quick turn into the apartment.

"Maria? Maria, where are you?"

He saw her then. Sitting on Alastair's lap. Swaying slightly. Making a sound he'd never heard before. Not a hum or a hiss. More like a high-pitched E that kept going.

He moved towards her while Felix watched his back and Bunny and Benji cleared the other rooms.

"Honey... Baby, look at me."

Maria lifted her head off of her father's shoulder. Looked towards John. Didn't seem to recognize him. He saw her face clearly now. Her cheeks smeared with blood. He knew she was in shock.

"Johnny? Is that you?"

"I'm here. I'm right here," he said. Moving closer. Speaking softly to keep her calm and keep her where she was until he could get his arms around her.

"My Daddy... My Daddy's dead, Johnny."

"I know, sweetheart."

"He's dead and it's my fault. All my fault."

"No, baby. Not yours. Mine. I'm the only one to blame here."

"He's such a good man. You know what he called me?"

"His little princess," he said.

John knew Maria was close to the edge. Should've realized that hearing her father's pet name would break her. She screamed then. Her pain echoing off the walls. The sound was heartbreaking, but it also brought John back into focus.

Something was wrong. Couldn't put his finger on it. Almost there.

Benji saw it before John did. He'd been in the apartment twice before to discuss security measures with Alastair.

The curtains… and the windows.

Alastair had said they pulled back the heavy drapes every morning to let in light, but never the thin lacey ones. And the big bay windows. Benji had personally helped remove the glass panes and install the bullet-resistant Plexi panels.

Bullet-resistant glass only works if the windows are closed, Benji thought as he moved up behind John. *Alastair promised he'd keep them closed and locked, but they were wide open.*

"Maria, I need you to listen to me very, very carefully. Can you hear me?" John said softly.

She nodded her head, but stared down at her hands and saw they were covered with her father's blood.

"Baby? Sweetheart… stay right where you are. Don't move, okay? Don't move."

She looked at him now. Saw him for the first time. "Johnnnnny!" she screamed, then jumped up and reached for him.

"No!" he shouted, diving towards her.

From a block away, Vorovka watched and waited for his target to appear as he knew he would. Through the scope attached to the Winchester he saw Maria enter the apartment with her pistol and then run to her father. Vorovka was almost touched by the scene when she carefully sat down on her father's lap. Almost.

She ran her fingers through Alastair's hair and from the movement of her head, Vorovka could tell she was speaking to him. Not long now. Not long.

I can feel you coming, Mr. John Bishop.

From his angle he couldn't see far into the apartment. That was okay. As long as Maria stayed near her father's body, John would come to the windows to comfort his grieving wife.

Vorovka saw her look up and knew his prey had arrived.

"Closer. Just a bit closer," Vorovka said aloud.

His finger caressed the trigger, anticipating the command. A slight glare from the sun reflecting off a glass vase on the window's ledge momentarily obscured his view, but he could still see clearly enough to know that someone was there, talking to Maria. Talking to her and moving closer.

"And there you are," Vorovka whispered when he saw John. Saw his curly hair and the top of his head as he dove towards Maria, and that was all the master sniper needed as he squeezed the trigger. Vorovka knew he had him. Felt the big Win Mag buck slightly when the 150 grain .308 round left the barrel. The bullet reached the window in three tenths of a second and hit its mark. The blood spray from Bishop's head confirmed the kill.

Vorovka whistled while he disassembled the rifle and wiped everything down.

A well-deserved nap on the plane and I'll wake up in Moscow, he thought as he left the building and looked for a cab to take him to the airport.

CHAPTER 19
REGRET... RELIEF

THE MEETING WAS wrapping up at CIA headquarters in Langley, Virginia and the news wasn't good. Tariq Hassan's body was not among the seventy-three that were pulled out of the rubble, so they had to assume he was still alive. That meant the airstrike was a failure and everyone involved, from the president on down, was getting smeared with shit over this one.

Clayton Unser was far less concerned about the blow-back from the talking heads on major news outlets than he was about Tariq. The terrorist had to be stopped before he reached the United States, and every available DHS, CIA, FBI and NSA resource had just been re-tasked to find and terminate the Afghan.

Clayton was listening to his messages when his phone vibrated against his ear. He looked at the number, saw it was Antonio Valdez, was about to send him to voicemail, but then decided to pick up.

"What's going on, Antonio?"

"It's me."

"Gonzalo?" Clayton asked.

"Yes. Where are you right now?"

Clayton stood up. Immediately on high alert. He knew Gonzalo never used phones and hadn't spoken on one in over forty years.

"I'm at Langley. What's happened?" Clayton asked.

Gonzalo gave him the details. Clayton felt the rush of emotion, but kept his breathing under control and his mind focused.

"Zalo, I'm so sorry. What do you need, my friend?"

"The police have the building surrounded and SWAT teams are on the way."

"How many men do you have at the scene?" Clayton asked.

"Forty so far. Many more are coming. The last thing we want is a shootout, but this is beyond my control. They won't let the police inside and they'll die before they let anyone come near him."

"Understood. I'm on it."

Gonzalo was gone. While scrolling through his contacts Clayton quickly prioritized the calls he needed to make.

Tensions were rising. They'd taken Eddie the doorman's keys and locked the building's wide double doors from the inside. Five Valdez soldiers were lined up shoulder to shoulder, arms at their sides, calmly staring through the reinforced glass at the police who were screaming at them to open up and get down on the floor. Twenty more Valdez men were stationed around the lobby, their weapons concealed, but jackets open and hands ready to reach for them if the police tried to force their way in.

Upstairs in Alastair Williams's apartment, Bunny inched

his way along the wall to the windows, not sure if the sniper was still searching for targets. Thought the shooter was already in the wind, but there was only one way to know for sure.

He took a deep breath, then said, "Fuck it," as he reached out quickly and pulled the windows down.

Felix was on his knees screaming, "No! God, please no!" as his fingers frantically checked for a pulse.

Bunny wiped his eyes, then knelt down next to Felix and put a hand on his shoulder.

"He's gone," Bunny whispered, looking down at the massive head wound.

Outside the building, police blocked off 3rd Avenue and the surrounding sidewalks. More squad cars were arriving from the 19th Precinct on East 67th Street and from the 23rd Precinct on East 96th. A uniformed NYPD lieutenant took control of the scene and was getting an update from his command sergeant when four men in suits approached him.

"Lieutenant? Can we have a minute?" one of the suits said, flashing his FBI credentials.

"You are?" the lieutenant asked as he walked over to the group.

"Terry Hall, Special Agent in Charge. We met a few years ago down at One PP."

'Yeah, you look familiar. How can I help you?"

"We need you and your men to stand down. We're taking control of the scene," Terry said.

"Who's *we?*" the lieutenant asked.

Terry nodded to the balding man to his right. "This is NSA Deputy Director Bill Simpson."

"I don't suppose these other gentlemen want to introduce themselves," the lieutenant said. He was a former Army Ranger and had seen enough shit in Iraq to recognize spooks when he saw them. Their suits and ties didn't do much to hide the fact that these were elite CIA killers.

The two Delta Force members remained silent.

"This is a matter of national security. We need you to clear out," Bill Simpson said.

"But there's been a shooting and the building's been taken over by armed men. With all due respect, sir, we can't just leave."

NYPD Capt. Jimmy Ryan arrived on the scene and trotted over.

"Hey Terry," Jimmy said.

There were quick introductions, then SAC Terry Hall pulled his old friend Capt. Ryan off to the side and gave him a quick and private update.

"Shit," Jimmy said, and looked up at the building. "I can't fucking believe this. What floor is he on?"

"Fifteen. Help me defuse the situation. The Valdez men aren't gonna let a bunch of your guys go in there. If you don't clear out this is only gonna escalate, and none of us want that to happen," Terry said.

"Agreed." Jimmy went back over to the lieutenant. "I'm giving you a direct order. Move everyone out."

"But Captain…"

"Do it now!" Jimmy snapped.

The lieutenant started shouting orders. The cops were angry and confused, but they holstered their weapons and backed away from the building.

Capt. Ryan positioned two of his trusted officers from his own precinct on either side of the front doors to calm any residents, and several more at each end of the block, then went back over to speak with Terry Hall.

"Nice job, Jimmy," Terry said. "Johnny's entire family is

at DEFCON 1. If you hadn't moved the troops out, a whole lotta people might've been hurt."

"I agree, but there's bodies up there. People are dead. National security or not, your guys, my guys, someone has to get up there to examine the scene."

Terry just shook his head. They stood together on the sidewalk, waiting. Each trying to figure out their next move when the front doors opened. Bunny came out with several armed men in tow and waved Terry and Jimmy over. They started walking, then momentarily froze when a dark blue Range Rover screeched to a stop half a block away. A small Asian woman jumped out of the driver's seat. Her long dark hair was matted to her forehead, makeup streaked down her face.

"Shit," Jimmy Ryan said.

"Who's that?" Terry Hall asked.

Ryan didn't bother to respond. *You'll see*, he thought.

They both watched Isabelle Williams charge the building. She lost her left Cole Haan black pump halfway across the pavement, kicked off the other one without breaking stride, and kept going through the open door. The wall of Valdez soldiers parted to give her a wide lane to the elevators.

Bunny picked up Mrs. Williams's shoes, then turned and gestured for Jimmy and Terry to follow him. They all ran after her. She was already on her way up by the time they reached the second elevator. Terry pressed fifteen and they rode up in silence, the three of them preparing themselves for what was coming.

Isabelle tore down the hall. She slipped and fell when she tried to stop at her apartment door. Ignored the outstretched hands of the two Valdez men who tried to help her up. She saw the door was cracked open, crawled a few feet towards it, then slowly got up onto her feet. She hesitated for a second, took a deep breath in and then pushed it open all the way and went inside.

Felix and one of Benji's men stood completely still with their heads bowed, like stone pillars on either side of the apartment's hallway. Isabelle didn't see them. She went slowly across the living room … towards the big windows.

Bunny, Ryan and Hall got to the apartment door just as Isabelle reached her family. All three unconsciously made the sign of the cross as they watched her trembling hand touch her husband's cheek. Alastair was still slumped in the chair with his head tipped down to his chest. She tenderly placed her arms around him and kissed him several times.

The blood was thick on the floor and already congealing. All the men at the door saw the bright red line on her skin-colored stockings slowly rising from her feet, and then a darker color coming down when her bladder released the moment she let go of her husband. Her whole body shook as she looked at her daughter.

Isabelle knelt in the blood. "Give her to me," she said softly.

John didn't want to let go. His muscles ached from hugging Maria so tightly, and he knew instinctively that the moment he let go she'd be gone forever. He had to force his eyes open.

He carefully sat up, holding Maria more gently now. She was limp in his arms. Her face as calm and as beautiful as he'd ever seen her. The calm would soon be over. He kissed her tenderly, fearing in his heart of hearts that it may be for the last time.

Isabelle watched him. Reached for her daughter, then pulled back. Terry and Jimmy jumped when she screamed at the top of her lungs, then swung her arm back and slapped John in the face with all her might.

"You did this! You killed my husband!"

John never looked up. He couldn't face her. Knew she was right. Maria was waking up as he passed her over to her mother. He sat there in the pool of blood while Isabelle cursed him.

"You scar-faced monster. You fucking bastard. You see what you've done?" Isabelle screamed.

Felix and Bunny crept forward. Each took a side, hooked John under his armpits, picked him up and pulled him away. He didn't resist, a dead weight in their arms.

They knew what was coming though. Both were tense and ready for it when John surged forward, fighting them to get back to the love of his life. They held him tightly, speaking softly to him. He couldn't hear them, but they kept talking as they dragged him towards the door with his arms stretched out, reaching for Maria.

Jimmy and Terry helped guide him into the hallway. Gonzalo and John's Aunt Grassiella were waiting there, and he collapsed into their arms.

"He's gone, Auntie," he said. "I killed Alastair. I killed him… and Benji. Benji's dead. He saved my life. Took a bullet for me."

It happened so fast. He remembered diving towards Maria, then Benji knocking him flat from behind. Felt Benji's body convulse on top of him from the head shot.

"I killed them both," John said.

"No, my son. Not you. Never you," Grassiella said.

Gonzalo kissed John on the top of his head, gave his adopted son another squeeze, then released him. Gonzalo wiped his eyes as he turned towards everyone else in the hallway. He pulled Felix and Bunny close, his hands tightly gripping their forearms.

"Take him home. We'll get Maria to a doctor and take care of everything here," Gonzalo said.

"Not happening," John said.

He gently pushed away from Grassiella, but she kept her hands on his cheeks, looking up into his eyes.

"We'll stay here together, but you're bleeding. You need a doctor," she said.

"It's Benji's blood, not mine," John said, waving his hand dismissively. "Even if it was, no way I'm leaving my wife and baby."

Gonzalo nodded his head in understanding, gave instructions to one of his men about the doctor, then went to speak with Jimmy and Terry.

"What do you need, Mr. Valdez?" Jimmy asked.

"Quiet," Gonzalo said. "No press and no cameras."

"Okay. We've been fortunate that there's only been a few residents trying to get in or out. Let's clear the building. We'll say it's a gas leak and the Crime Scene Unit will put on FDNY jackets before they come in."

Terry saw Gonzalo was about to say something, but he raised his hand as a sign of understanding. "Jimmy and I will be right here, Mr. Valdez. Let us take care of Mr. Williams and Mr.?..."

"Medina. His name is Benji Medina."

They spoke for another minute working out the logistics, and then Terry and Jimmy started making calls to put everything in motion.

It took another three hours before Alastair and Benji were slowly wheeled out of the apartment on stretchers by FBI crime scene investigators wearing FDNY and ESU jackets.

Maria and Isabelle held each other up as they walked slowly behind Alastair's body bag. Neither of them looked at John as he stood against the wall, his body trembling, eyes wild, mouth moving, no words coming out. Gonzalo and Felix were on either side of him.

They took the bodies down to the basement so they could wheel them out through the freight entrance on East 83rd and away from the crowds on 3rd Avenue. John hung back, giving Maria and her mother their space, staying close enough to keep his wife in sight, and watching to see if she would turn back to make eye contact with him before getting into a black Escalade with Gonzalo's security team.

She never looked back, and John felt something die inside him. Not love. His love for her would never die. Hopes and dreams did. Hope for a life of peace and his dream of chasing his son through a field of flowers while his wife danced in the sun…Those were gone and he knew they weren't coming back.

He wiped his eyes, took a deep breath and turned around. He nodded at Gonzalo, Bunny and Felix, then looked past them at the stretcher carrying the body of Benji Medina. John's cousin, Antonio Valdez, had unzipped the body bag and was gently touching the cheek of his lifelong friend.

"Let's go see his mother," Antonio said.

"We have cars outside waiting to take us to her," Gonzalo said.

"Does his brother know?" John asked.

"He's off the grid," Antonio answered. "No phone, no internet. We'll drive upstate and see him tomorrow.

"Okay," John said. "I'm so sorry, Antonio. He gave his life for me. Pushed me down and took the bullet."

"That's who he was. Who we all are. That's why they'll never beat us," Antonio said.

Antonio said a final goodbye, kissed his friend on the cheek, then zipped up the body bag and headed out to the street. John and the rest of the Valdez crew followed him out.

It was just past 7PM and already dark. As dark as New York's Upper East Side gets at night anyway, with big bright streetlights glowing along every block. A few people were gathered across the street from the freight entrance discussing the afternoon's events. The elderly woman who'd joined the group of neighbors pretended to be listening while she kept her eyes on John.

He looks so sad, she thought. *Almost broken.*

Omar felt something shift in her as she watched the man she was going to kill. A feeling she'd never known before. She wasn't sure where it came from, but she knew what it was… Regret.

From half a block away on 3rd Avenue, David Tringa watched John through the telephoto lens on his camera. He snapped a few pictures of his prey and then turned slightly to get a pic of Omar. David felt something shift in him when he saw her. He wasn't sure where it came from, but knew exactly what he was feeling… Relief.

I'm glad she's alive, David thought. *I'm the last pure Tringa, and every breath that peasant bitch takes is a crime against my family. A shit stain on my legacy. I can't wait to kill her.*

CHAPTER 20
TRAVELERS

IT STARTED RAINING just as the Syrian delivery truck reached the Turkish border. Big drops slapped the truck's windshield and bounced off the metal hood as it was waved through the border gate and drove past the line of Black Tiger tanks with their gun turrets and cannons all facing out towards the Syrian desert. A platoon of heavily armed soldiers surrounded the vehicle, and a Turkish captain stepped up onto the running board. He pointed to a large warehouse a hundred yards away and instructed the driver to move his vehicle there for a private inspection. The captain held onto the door frame and came along for the ride while his men trotted along on foot.

Once inside, the driver realized it was a much larger building than it appeared to be from the outside. More of an armory than a warehouse, eight Turkish APCs (Armored Personal Carriers) and three more tanks were parked neatly on the main floor, and more than a dozen wheeled artillery pieces were lined up along the far wall.

Before he stepped down off the running board the captain used the universal hand swipe across his throat to tell him to turn off the truck. Once the driver got out of the cab, he was momentarily confused when the captain repeated the hand swipe signal. The confusion was replaced by a brief moment of clarity when the Turkish sergeant behind him plunged the six-inch blade of his combat knife into the driver's throat and gave it a full twist.

Tariq and his twelve disciples piled out of the back of the truck. Tariq with a briefcase in each hand, everyone else held an AK, their weapons ready, but the barrels pointed down and away from the line of twenty-five Turkish soldiers who stood watching them with their own weapons shouldered and holstered.

Tariq led the way, sidestepping around the driver's body and the expanding pool of blood as they walked over to the captain.

"All is ready?" Tariq asked.

The captain nodded. "Yes. I see you received the clothes and the passports," he said.

"We did and my compliments. Our documents team in Raqqa examined the passports and they're perfect." He held out the briefcases. "These are for you."

"One point five?" the captain asked.

"We made a last-minute adjustment," Tariq said.

"What?" the captain said, moving his hand to his holster. His men all followed his lead and instantly leveled their weapons at the jihadists.

"We doubled it to three million… For any difficulties the new timelines may have caused you," Tariq said, which brought a wide grin from the captain as his hand left his sidearm and he greedily reached for the briefcases. He turned and lifted them onto a table behind him and popped them both. Paused for a moment to stare at all the hundred-dollar bills neatly stacked and bundled into packs of ten thousand dollars each. His men stared open-mouthed into the cases as well.

"Very fortunate you survived the airstrike, my friend. Very fortunate indeed," the captain said, casually fanning a stack of hundreds as he spoke.

"Airstrike?" Tariq asked.

"Last night American F-16s bombed the housing complex where you were staying."

Tariq kept the shock off his face. "Must be a coincidence," he said.

"The American president personally ordered the strike," the captain said.

"How do you know this?" Tariq asked.

"The F-16s flew from Incirlik directly to your house, but as you said, it's probably just a coincidence," the captain said, smiling at Tariq as he repeated the lie.

"Our route is secure?" Tariq asked.

The captain nodded his head. "It is. My men will escort you to the airport and get you on board," he said, then turned back to the table and rubbed his hands together as he stared at the money.

Tariq and his team climbed into a dusty and dented Mercedes Benz twenty-seat van and settled in for the eight-hour drive to Antalya. Making it out of Syria and across the border into Turkey was only the first phase of their operation, but there was a palpable release of tension for having made it this far. Several team members closed their eyes and quickly nodded off, their heads bobbing up and down with each bump in the road. Although Tariq hadn't slept in nearly twenty-four hours, his mind was racing. The news of the airstrike could only mean one thing: Warid had betrayed him.

They didn't even have to torture you, did they, Warid?

Cowardly dog. You told them everything without even a slap. Before I die, I will send word to our brothers in Afghanistan to rape your wife and daughters before they kill them.

Tariq pulled himself back from his moment of rage and got refocused. The Americans knew he was coming and feared him enough to launch an attack that must have killed hundreds of civilians.

Do they know that they missed and I'm still alive? he asked himself. *Probably. If not already, they'll know soon.*

He smiled at the thought, realizing that he was now the most wanted man in the world. It was better this way. He was glad they knew he was coming because with all their military might and the trillions of dollars at their disposal, the Americans couldn't stop him. He was coming, and he wasn't coming alone. He glanced around at his team, all sleeping now except for the ever-vigilant Marwan, who sat near the front of the van watching the road ahead for any threats.

Thank God I didn't tell Warid about them, Tariq thought as he stared at Gretchen and the other radicalized Americans.

He managed to stay on high alert for another thirty minutes before he too felt the need to recharge. He walked to the front of the van, leaned close to Marwan, and quietly told the Syrian to wake him in two hours.

When Tariq opened his eyes five hours later, he realized Marwan had let him sleep much longer than instructed. Tariq didn't berate him for it. He woke up feeling sharp and refreshed, and twenty minutes later they reached the airport just outside the ancient city of Antalya on Turkey's Mediterranean coast.

Their military escort bypassed customs and drove them right onto the tarmac, where their chartered flight to Costa Rica was revved and waiting. An attendant and two Costa

Rican nationals greeted the team at the top of the stairs, welcoming them aboard the Gulfstream G650. The pleasantries were brief. They stowed their gear, took their seats and buckled up as the pilots throttled forward and the jet picked up speed down the runway.

The direct flight from Antalya to San Jose was a long one—fourteen hours long—and even though the ISIS pipeline to Central and South America had been up and running for the past few months, and small cells of Mujahideen fighters were already training in Costa Rica and several other countries, Tariq instructed his team to maintain their cover. They all played the part of wealthy Turks taking a much-needed vacation and chatted about their plans to get massages, mud baths, face peels and cold plunges at a luxury spa.

They were treated like VIPs at the San Jose airport, and the Costa Rican customs agents barely glanced at their tourist visas and Turkish passports before stamping them and waving them through. From there it was a two-hour drive to a private beach house near the town of Jaco on the Pacific coast.

Alone for the first time since they left Syria, once they settled in, Tariq allowed the team to have a brief celebration with high fives and hugs all around. Costa Rican customs had been the chokepoint where they were most at risk. It was the only border crossing. The only one where they were actually on the grid anyway, and it couldn't have gone smoother.

"How long before the ship gets here?" Gretchen asked.

"It's already here," Tariq said, extending his arm and pointing his index finger past the open patio doors towards the beach and deep blue open ocean. "Six miles out. Our brothers will pick us up on the beach after sunset. You have a few hours," he added.

"Anybody up for a swim?" she asked.

"I think we all need one," Tariq said.

None of them hesitated. They ripped off their clothes and ran naked to the beach, laughing as they raced each other to the water. They pushed and splashed, playing like children in the waves... *children* who were dedicated to committing mass murder.

It was almost 9PM when members of the local Mujahideen cell arrived in two small fishing boats. The team was all business now. No one spoke as they waded waist high into the water holding their gear over their heads and climbed aboard.

It was a windless, warm and clear November night. Once they got past the breakers, the ocean was calm and flat all the way out to the massive eighteen-thousand-ton Panamax cargo ship that sat in the water with nearly five thousand containers strapped to its deck.

The ship's captain greeted them at the rail, then took them below deck to their quarters. The few crewmembers they passed in the hallways either looked away or stared down at their own shoes, instinctively knowing it was better for their health to pretend these thirteen travelers never existed.

Tariq smiled when the captain showed them their quarters. A big rectangular room with cots laid end to end along the rusty walls, with an open toilet and a shower with no curtain in the far corner. After their playtime at the beach he wanted his team to get refocused, and these spartan conditions were perfect.

"Settle in," the captain said with a deep Southern drawl. "It's two weeks to Vancouver. We'll set y'all up with a schedule so you can go topside at night in shifts. No more'n three at a time. Satellites are tracking every cargo ship at sea. Chances of anyone zoomin' in for a closeup are slim to none, but slim does come knockin' on the old barn door every now and ag'in."

As suggested, they settled into a regular routine. Tariq drilled them mercilessly, waking them at five each morning, role playing and constantly testing each of them on every aspect of the mission.

CHAPTER 21
GOODBYES

Manhattan's Lower East Side

A FEW DAYS after the coroner's office completed autopsies, the bodies of Alastair Williams and Benji Medina were released to their families. The services were scheduled a day apart. Some of Alastair's family and friends were traveling from overseas, so Benji went first.

The pockmarked Valdez enforcer was an LES legend. Feared and respected by thousands, and truly loved by all who knew him. People started lining up along 1st Avenue and Houston Street hours before the wake at Pedroza's Funeral Home, and by early afternoon the police had to divert traffic from the area to accommodate the massive throng of mourners who came to pay their respects.

Benji's brother, Lulu Medina, approached John and Gonzalo at the wake: "John, Antonio, thank you for all you said about my brother."

Antonio had given a moving tribute to his lifelong friend, and John told everyone about what happened at the apartment, and how Benji had sacrificed himself to save his life.

"I shouldn't be alive, Lulu. Wouldn't be if Benji hadn't done what he did. Don't know how you thank and honor a man for doing that, but I'm damn sure gonna try every day for the rest of my life," John said.

Lulu nodded his appreciation then turned to face Gonzalo.

"Don Valdez, my brother was as much a part of your family as he was mine. Think he was more Valdez than Medina actually."

"My deepest condolences, Lulu. It was our honor to have him with us all these years. I loved him as my own blood and always will," Gonzalo said.

Gonzalo knew that Benji's younger brother had something important to ask, and he let him take his time. Lulu was a Marine. Not *was*, since once a Marine always a Marine. He'd been through hell fighting for six years in Iraq and Afghanistan, and when he came back after his last deployment he simply withdrew. From friends, family, everything. He now lived alone and isolated deep in the Adirondack Mountains, in a small house on a few acres of land. No electricity. No phone or internet.

"Thank you, sir," Lulu said.

"You don't *sir* me, young man. Benji was family and so are you. Remember that. Anything you need. I… all of us… We are here for you."

"I really appreciate that. Can I ask a favor?"

"Name it," Gonzalo said, placing a hand on Lulu's shoulder.

"I was going to take him back to Panama and bury him there, but this is our home now. Can he lay with your family at the estate? I know it's a lot to ask. I just don't want him to be all alone."

There was a graveyard at the Long Island Valdez estate where all the family members who'd died violently over the years, including John's parents, were buried.

"We were going to ask you the same thing," Gonzalo said, "but we didn't want to impose or put any pressure on you in case you had other plans."

Lulu looked skeptical, glancing down and flexing his jaw. John placed his hand on Lulu's left shoulder.

"It's true, hermano. Let us care for Benji and bring him home," John said.

Lulu looked up and held John's gaze for a moment before nodding his agreement. His eyes told John there was something else.

"What is it, Lulu?" he asked.

"I want in. Let me help you."

"We're at war, brother. You sure you're ready to go back to that?" John asked.

"I'm good, bro. Needed some time away from the world to get my mind right, but I'm solid now."

"We're a family and there's no halfway. If you're in you're in all the way," John added.

"Understood," Lulu said then focused on Gonzalo. "Don Valdez, I'll take the oath if you'll have me."

Gonzalo paused for a moment before responding. "Let's talk after we bury your brother. You need to know what we're facing before you join us."

"Fair enough," Lulu said.

They buried Benji the next day, placing him high on the hill amongst the Valdez dead. This was more of a private ceremony for hundreds rather than the thousands at the wake in LES.

Geronimo and several of his Apaches came to pay their

respects. After the services he approached Lulu and the inner circle of Valdez men who stood by his side.

"I'm sorry for your loss," Geronimo said, taking Lulu's hand in his. "If you want to avenge Benji's death, I know where to start."

"Tell me."

John, Antonio, Gonzalo, and several of Gonzalo's brothers leaned in to hear what Geronimo had to say. They all nodded their heads in approval, and even Gonzalo smiled when he heard his younger brother's plan of attack.

Maria and her mother sent flowers but did not attend Benji's funeral. They were suffering and no one blamed them or felt any resentment towards them for not coming. A day later they buried Alastair.

It was a chilly November day. Cloudy, gray and wet. When John, Gonzalo and the Valdez family arrived at the funeral, they were instructed to stay off to the side and keep their distance. After the service, Maria pulled away from her mother and walked over to John.

All of John's calls had gone straight to voicemail and he hadn't been able to speak to her at all since her father's murder. Maria's expression was flat and her eyes were cold as she approached him, but just being this close to his wife made John hopeful.

"Hi sweetheart," he said, trying to read her.

"Hi Johnny," Maria said.

"When're you coming home?" he asked.

"Home? We don't have a home. Just a room. A jail cell really, in your uncle's house."

"You're my home. Wherever you are," he said.

"Not anymore," she said.

"Please don't say that," John pleaded.

"We killed my father, Johnny. He's dead because your enemies used me and my Daddy to try and kill you. Who's next? My mother? Our baby?"

"I'll protect you, Maria. I'll…"

She shook her head. "Empty words, Johnny. You know you can't."

"So, what now? Where does that leave us?" he asked.

"I'm sorry, baby, but it's over. I'm leaving the country tonight."

He was trying to hold it together, but couldn't stop the tears from flowing down his cheeks.

"Where will you go?" he asked.

"Some place safe where our child can grow up without blood and death all around him."

"Him? It's a boy?" he asked.

"I think so," she said.

"My dream. I saw him running in the field of flowers."

"He will, Johnny. He'll be there in that field… only you won't be there to chase him."

"Please, Maria. Please… don't leave. Please don't take my son from me."

She hugged him close. Felt a moment of hesitation, then quickly pushed it aside. She took his hand and placed it on her belly.

"Feel him, Johnny."

"My son… *our* son," he said.

"Now say goodbye to him."

John fell to his knees and pressed his head to Maria's belly.

"I'll find you. Wherever you go. I'll find you," John said.

"Don't. Otherwise your son and I will both be dead. Sooner or later it'll happen. Let him live, Johnny. Please.

Don't look for us. Hold your love for us in your heart, but promise me you'll never come near us."

"You're the love of my life. How can I promise that?"

"You know it's the only way," she said.

They stayed there for a few moments. Two LES kids who'd loved each other their whole lives. Maria pulled them back to reality.

"One last thing. Don't go seeking revenge in my father's name."

"We're at war," John said.

"Wars end. Use my Dad's death to end this one."

He nodded his head and said okay. She took his face in her hands and looked down at him.

"Goodbye my love," she said.

"I… I just can't…"

She put a finger to his lips.

"Remember what we had," Maria said.

"Had?" he asked.

She nodded, wiped the tears from her eyes, then turned and walked away. She was ten feet from him when she stopped and turned around. John hopped up and hurried towards her.

"I changed my mind," Maria said.

"Thank God," he said.

"Kill them all. Anyone who was a part of it. You kill them all for me," Maria said.

He failed at trying to hide his disappointment as he realized his misunderstanding, and his eyes welled up again.

"I'll find them. Every one of them," he whispered.

Maria wiped the tears from his cheeks, nodded, then turned and walked away. This time she didn't stop or look back and John knew she was gone forever.

CHAPTER 22

GRETCHEN

IT WAS NEAR midnight, their fourth day on the cargo ship, when the five women put on baseball hats and windbreakers to disguise themselves from any possible satellite surveillance, then went up on deck together to get some fresh air.

"I wish Tariq would give it a rest," Melanie said. She was tall and thin, a deceptively strong brunette from Flint, Michigan. "We all know what to do. Why is he riding us like this?" she asked.

Lisa knew Mel was a bit of a complainer, and ignored her. Gretchen knew it as well, but she had too much respect for Tariq to let it go:

"Don't you realize how big this operation is, Mel? We're the tip of the spear and Tariq is keeping us sharp so when we cut it's so deep it's gonna shake up the whole fuckin' world. Don't you see that?" Gretchen asked.

"C'mon. You know I do. It's just…" Mel said.

"It's *what*, Mel?" Gretchen asked her.

"I dunno. You ever wonder how we got here?" Mel asked.

Gretchen didn't say anything.

Damn right I know how I got here, she thought, flashing

back to when her mother's third husband raped her for the first time on her eleventh birthday. Gretchen's alcoholic mother either didn't believe her or didn't care, and the assaults continued until she finally told her teacher two years later.

Gretchen thought the system, the police, someone… anyone, was going to protect her. She was wrong.

When the news got out, Gretchen's classmates taunted her, nothing happened to her stepfather and *she* was removed from the house and sent to foster care for "her safety and protection." A week later she was sexually assaulted by her counselor at the group home and she ran away the next day.

She'd always liked the name Cincinnati, and took a bus there from Iowa to find her way in the world and make a better life. Somehow, some way, she knew Cincinnati would save her.

A month after she happily skipped off the Greyhound at the Gilbert Avenue bus station, she was on the streets turning tricks. From there her life became a drugged-out living hell where she was regularly sold or traded from one pimp to another, and then used and abused in every way imaginable by her customers.

Six years later, Gretchen was twenty, standing on *her* corner searching for her first trick and jonesing for her second dope hit of the day when a light-skinned, clean-cut man walked over and changed her life forever. His name was Adeeb Elahi. She'd never seen him before and didn't know his name when he said in a soft voice, "Let's go."

He started walking and she robotically followed him, her clear five-inch heels clacking loudly along the sidewalk. After a few blocks he hailed a cab and took her to his house on the other side of town, a two-family unit that he rented from his cousin. She immediately started reciting her menu options and what she charged for each service. Adeeb wagged a finger in her face, then gently took her by the hand and led her down to the basement.

"This is yours," he said. "There's a shower and a full kitchen down here. Groceries in the fridge if you're hungry."

"What?" she asked. "What kinda game you runnin' here, man?"

"No game," he said. "Every now and then we all need a friend. Many have helped me and I'm here to help you… if you want it."

She reached for his crotch, but he shook his head and pulled away.

"That's not what this is. Like I said, if you want all that shit to end, if you want to kick the dope and get off the streets, you have a home. There's some clothes for you in the dresser and in the closet. Here's your key," he said, placing it in her palm. "I live upstairs. The door is always open. You need anything or just want to talk, come on up."

And that was it. A complete stranger had saved her life. Gretchen got clean and Adeeb helped her find a job. They ate together every night and it was a year later when she finally kissed him. Turned out there were knights in shining armor in Cincy after all.

Adeeb was Pakistani, in the States on a student visa, studying to become a doctor. Besides being the kindest, gentlest man she'd ever known, he was also a practicing Muslim. Curious, she asked him to teach her about his religion. Gretchen knew he wasn't trying to push anything on her, but the more she read, the more fascinated she became.

When he left on a trip to Pakistan to tell his mother about her, he gave her his worn copy of the Koran. A book that had been in his family for three generations. A week later, Adeeb's cousin Fawad came to the house and told her that a US drone strike had hit the family house. Adeeb, his parents and several other family members were all killed. No one knew why. They couldn't get any answers.

"Adeeb told me how much he loved you. A while back he took me to see you," Fawad said.

She wiped the tears from her eyes. "When? I don't remember."

"It was a few years ago. When you lived that other life. We sat together in my car watching you. He told me that he was going to marry you," Fawad said.

"Bullshit," Gretchen said.

"That's exactly what I said to him back then," Fawad said. "I thought he was joking. I think we both found out that he wasn't. Anyway, I just want you to know that even though he didn't live long enough to make you his wife, you are and always will be part of the family. You can stay here as long as you wish. No charge."

"Thank you, Fawad."

He got up and reached out to shake her hand and said, "We won't see each other again. Goodbye, Gretchen."

"*What*? Where are you going?" she asked.

"Pakistan first… for the funerals. Then I'm going to Syria to fight and avenge my family," Fawad said.

Gretchen stared at him for a few moments. Then she wiped the tears from her eyes and the expression on her face changed from one of deep sadness to fierce determination.

"I want to come with you," she said.

"For the funerals?" he asked.

"No. I mean, yes. That too, but what I really want is to go with you to Syria to join the fight. Now that Adeeb's gone, there's nothing left for me here," she said.

"You better be sure. There's no turning back once you commit, *and* I can promise one thing," Fawad said. "You'll die bloody, and you'll probably be dead within a year."

"So, you know you're gonna die, but you're still going?" Gretchen asked.

"My family was murdered. All I have is vengeance now," Fawad said.

"Adeeb is... *was*... the only person who ever loved me. Like I said, there's nothing left for me here. I'm coming with you," she said.

"Be sure, Gretchen. This will be a rough and dangerous road and I won't be able to protect you."

She held his gaze for three seconds, then nodded: "I'm sure," she said.

"Okay. It's much better if you travel off the radar. I'm going to have someone from our mosque come over tonight to talk to you. If he agrees, you'll go to Canada and then we'll get you to Morocco and from there into Syria... but he has to approve you."

"Okay, whatever you say, Fawad."

"Be truthful with him, Gretchen, and make sure he knows you're committed... that you're willing to give your life to avenge Adeeb. If he's not convinced...if he thinks you're bullshitting him, he'll fucking kill you right here in this house and then he'll call me to come back and clean up the mess."

Later that night she met her handler, Abu El Salim, and based on Fawad's warning he was definitely a surprise. Not that she thought Abu was going to be some terrorist from central casting, a dark turbaned giant holding a scimitar, ready to chop off her head at any moment. Abu was well-dressed, nothing flashy, casual in light blue 7 For All Mankind jeans, a dark blue slim fit dress shirt and dark blue driving mocks with no socks. Clothes aside, the fact that he was white was what really caught her off guard. He looked white anyway, clean-shaven with straight brown hair and light brown eyes.

Despite his appearance, Gretchen had been around enough cold-blooded killers during her years on the street to know that Abu was the most dangerous kind there was. Not some hot head that had to work himself up to do something. He was one of those calm and relaxed killers. The ones whose expression never changed when they pulled the trigger or stuck a blade in your heart. She could tell that most people never recognized the dude for what he was until the life drained out of them and their eyes clouded over.

Abu's voice was soft and quiet. He asked her for a pen and paper to take some notes, and after she went and got them and handed them over, he asked her a lot of questions about her past and what had brought her to this moment… to this crossroads in her life. She was freaked out at first, hands sweating, talking too fast, wondering whether he was going to strangle or stab her to death. His shirt was too fitted to hide a gun. She knew he had a weapon on him, though. Probably a knife, she thought.

She never realized she'd handed him the weapon. Didn't notice that Abu wasn't writing anything down. Just held the pen in his hand, rolling it between his thumb and forefinger as he listened…. deciding whether to grab the back of her head with his left hand to hold her steady and shove the pen tip into her carotid artery with his right.

Hours later, Abu put the pen down on the table. Convinced that she wasn't a mole, a Homeland Security, FBI or CIA deep cover agent trying to penetrate his network, he told her to pack a few clothes, no electronics, and get a few hours' sleep.

The next morning she was heading west with him on I-94, on their way across country, driving to Seattle with nothing but a bag of clothes, a bar of soap, toothbrush, hairbrush, a picture of Adeeb and the copy of the Koran that Adeeb had given her. They made the 2,300-mile trip in three days while Abu read to her and asked her more probing questions, continuously testing her commitment as they drove. Hearing her history of abuse, at home and on the streets, he promised her that she would never be violated again. She was now a member of the family, a family of true believers, and she would be protected as a beloved sister or daughter.

Gretchen knew Abu was taking his time with her, bringing her in slowly. She let him do his thing. She didn't want to sound too eager, but she was ready... Ready to do whatever was asked of her, to kill or be killed, to avenge Adeeb. A tiny voice deep down inside her, a voice that rarely spoke, said it wasn't just about the love of her life getting blown up. It was about her too. Her mom, her school, the system, her country, had all failed her, and she was going to get some serious payback before she died.

The closer they got to Seattle, the more comfortable Abu was with her. He told her that American intelligence agencies were foolishly using racial and religious profiling to track their enemies, searching for the brown faces who publicly made radical statements and threats on social media.

"We are the new front-line soldiers, Gretchen. White faces, no public profile, no travel history to Muslim countries. We are Clean Skins, as they say in the intelligence business. Invisible assets that can come and go as we please, penetrate US government agencies, gather intel and strike at any moment."

She was driving, took her eyes off the road to glance over at him and asked, "What will I do?"

"Watch… Listen…and learn."

She did all three.

From Seattle they simply hiked through the woods and crossed the border into Vancouver. A few days later, Abu gave her a forged Canadian passport and delivered her to a new handler, a dark-haired Egyptian woman who would escort her on the next legs of the journey. Abu said goodbye to her at the airport and they flew to Morocco. From there to Istanbul and once in Turkey, they drove for days until they crossed the border into Syria, where they were picked up and driven to Raqqa.

When she got there, she expected that some of the men would demand sex from her. She'd prepared herself psychologically for it, telling herself she'd do whatever it took to avenge Adeeb. She was relieved and a bit surprised when no one touched her. Abu had been right. She'd been treated with respect and the only requirement was that she work her ass off… which she did.

She spent fourteen months training, all the time watching, listening, and learning. Learning to speak Arabic, learning how to shoot and build explosives, and studying the Koran. Then she met Tariq and once she was selected to join his team, the training became far more intense. He tried to break her, constantly testing her commitment to the Caliphate. She never wavered. Passed every test. She was ready to die for the cause. She knew it and more importantly, Tariq knew it too.

Sleeping with Marwan on their last day in Raqqa hadn't bothered her either. She knew she'd be dead in a matter of weeks and until then she was Tariq's to command. There wasn't anything she wouldn't do for him.

Gretchen came back to reality, heard Mel say that she wished she could see her mom one last time before they got to New York.

"Michigan is on the way. You think Tariq will let us make a quick stop? Mom is a great cook and we can all have a last meal," Mel said.

"That sounds wonderful, Mel. You should ask him in the morning," Gretchen said.

Mel nodded eagerly and started telling Lisa about how wonderful her hometown of Flint, Michigan was.

Gretchen turned her back, stared out into the night, the horizon barely visible, a black line against the wide expanse of black ocean. She took a deep drag on her cigarette, flicked it out into the night and told the group she was heading back down for some sleep.

She moved quickly through the ship, hustling down the four flights of stairs to their main room. The lights were out, but she saw that Tariq was still awake, lying on his cot, reading a map with a narrow penlight.

He heard her coming and was already turning when she tapped him on the shoulder and sat down on the edge of the cot.

"What is it?" he asked.

"It's Mel. She's going to betray us."

"You're sure?" he asked.

Gretchen nodded: "She may just try to run, but I think she's gonna turn us in… Tell her mother anyway and then the mother will call the authorities."

"You have done well, Gretchen. I will handle this…" Tariq held her eyes, placed his hand on hers. "Are you okay with Marwan?"

She held his gaze. "I am yours to command, Tariq. Whatever you need me to do, it will be done," she said.

He looked over at Marwan, who was snoring loudly, then Tariq got up, turned on the lights and clapped his hands once to wake him and the others. All nine of his soldiers, including Gretchen, were instantly alert and on their feet with weapons up. They held their 9mm Berettas with two hands, their arms outstretched, searching for targets, ready to aim and fire at any threat.

Even though Tariq was impressed with their response time, his surgically repaired face didn't show it. Only Gretchen, the once-upon-a-time drugged-out street hustler whose day-to-day survival had depended on her ability to see and sense imminent threats, picked up on the momentary spark in Tariq's usually hard and flat eyes when Lisa, Karen, and Mel rushed into the room.

"Is everything okay?" Lisa asked.

"Yes… Weapons down," Tariq said. "Time for a special training exercise. Everyone form a circle. I'll be right back."

Tariq left the room and went down the hallway to the freshwater generator that converted saltwater into drinking water. He grabbed a big bucket, turned on the hose attached to the 500-gallon holding tank and filled the bucket with ocean water that hadn't been desalinated.

He remembered the warnings the senior council had given him about the Americans on his team before he left Syria.

"Watch them closely," they'd said, "and if any waver, kill them as an example to the others."

Mel was actually doing him a favor. He'd been planning to kill Lisa. He was tired of sleeping with her and she was starting to become affectionate and informal with him.

Nothing overt, but she had a toe over the line. He didn't like it and more importantly, he couldn't allow it.

Tariq carried the bucket into the room. The team opened the circle to let him in and then closed the gap when he placed it on the steel floor in their center. Standing in the middle next to the bucket, he looked around at his team, taking his time with it. Finally, he pointed at Mel and used his hand to call her over.

"Come, Mel," he said.

"Yes, Tariq," she said, standing before him. Her voice was even, but her eyes... Her eyes betrayed her fear.

"On your knees, Mel," Tariq said.

Trained to follow orders, she went down quickly.

"Hands on each side of the bucket," he said.

She did... her hands were shaking now.

"Why are you afraid, Mel?"

"I'm not scared, Tariq. I just don't know what I've done wrong," she said.

"Done wrong? Why would you say that? You've sworn to give your life for this mission. To die for the Caliphate and in the service of God. Have you forgotten your oath, Mel?"

"No. Never. I am ready to do whatever you ask of me, Tariq."

"Good. Put your head in the bucket and keep it there until I tap you on the shoulder," he said.

Mel looked up at him, her eyes defiant, her lips quivering. She started to say something, must have thought better of it because no words came out. She paused for a moment, took a deep breath in, then plunged her head into the cold salty water.

The entire team stood there watching Mel and flicked glances up at Tariq as the seconds flew by. Mel started shaking at the one-minute mark. They all watched her struggle when she ran out of air, yet still fought to keep her head under.

Tariq didn't move until Mel finally pulled her head out of the bucket and collapsed on the floor, coughing and gasping for air. He leaned over her and said: "You disobeyed my order, Mel. You didn't wait for the tap."

"I … I tried, Tariq," she croaked, coughing and choking on the saltwater she'd inhaled… "I tried my best."

"Your best? I don't believe you, Mel. Let's try it again… and this time, you must give us your very best," he said.

"Please no," she said, but mechanically got back up on her knees and once again faced the bucket.

She coughed, spat, then took five deep breaths in and out, held it on the sixth, and then plunged her head back under the water. Her eyes open, there was just enough light coming in around her head and hair to see the dents at the bottom of the metal bucket and the rust lines along its sides. The rust brought back the memory of an old barn where she used to play with her sisters. Inside, there'd been a broken-down tractor that had been rained and snowed on for years after the barn's roof collapsed. The tractor was rusty… rusted clean through in some places.

Can't believe I remember that, she thought.

"Lisa, Gretchen, Danny, Thomas, Karen," Tariq said to five of the Americans. "Can you please help Mel? Make sure she *does* give us her best this time…and don't let her up until I tap her shoulder."

Mel panicked as soon as she felt the many hands holding her down. She fought with everything she had to raise her nose above the water line, then tried to knock the bucket over, but they were above her, had the leverage and the five of them easily held her head under. Out of air, she finally sucked the saltwater into her lungs. Her body convulsing, she saw the rusty tractor one last time. Her mother and sisters sitting on it. Waving goodbye.

The Americans waited for Tariq. They kept holding her down for a full minute after she was gone. Tariq finally bent down and tapped Mel's shoulder. They all stood up, unsure of what to do and what would happen next. All of them hoping and praying that none of them were following Mel into the bucket.

"No one is above the mission. This one," he said, looking down at Mel's body, "was going to betray us."

He went to each of them, holding their eyes with his, watching to see if any of his soldiers would blink or look away. None of them did.

"I demand only one thing from each and every one of you... Absolute loyalty. Do I have that?"

"Yes, sir!" they shouted in one voice.

"Good. Toss her overboard. Empty her pockets, but leave her clothes on," Tariq said. "Let her drift out with the garbage as food for the sharks."

At first, he was going to strangle her to make it personal, but he'd put his own anger aside and thought ahead. If the sharks that trailed behind the cargo ship didn't eat her and another ship happened upon her body, she'd have saltwater in her lungs. Tariq knew it was a million to one that she'd be found, let alone identified by her fingerprints, but even if that longshot came in, Mel would just be another unfortunate drowning victim... One of the thousands that the oceans claimed each year.

"We'll take care of it, Tariq," Marwan said.

"One last thing. I'm making a change. Lisa, you're with Marwan now. Gretchen, you're with me. Questions?"

Marwan nodded his approval. So did Lisa.

"We are yours to command, Tariq," Gretchen said as she searched Mel's pockets. Inside Mel's bra she found a tiny piece of paper, carefully rolled into a narrow tube. No name. Just an address and a phone number.

No one had any doubts now. They all knew she would've betrayed them. Gretchen handed the paper to Tariq. He stared at it for a moment, memorizing the number before putting it in his pocket.

"Get rid of her. Then all of you get some sleep. We have an early start tomorrow," he said, then went to his cot and lay down on his back, looking up at the ceiling.

Seven miles off the coast of Northern California, the body of Melanie Donaldson floated on the dark surface of the Pacific, bobbing in the wake of the massive cargo ship. Tariq was still thinking about her when the first of several great whites took a test bite out of her right thigh.

The mystery number bothered him. If it was for a family member, Mel should've known it by heart. Was she a deep cover operative and if so, had she been in contact with any of the ship's crew?

He was running through all the different possibilities when Gretchen came to him. Already naked, she stood over him, waiting for orders. Tariq lifted his blanket to invite her in.

CHAPTER 23

THE NUT SHOT

AFTER ALASTAIR WILLIAMS'S funeral, Felix and Gonzalo rode with John back to the Long Island estate. It was a quiet ride. Felix broke the silence:

"I'm sorry, man. Maria's hurting. She just needs some time and space, but she'll be back, bro."

John knew his cousin was trying to help… trying to soften the blow of his marriage ending. John looked away. Didn't bother to respond.

When they arrived, he went upstairs to his room and looked around. Maria had sent a friend over to gather up some of her clothes, pictures and a few mementos. Everything else was still there hanging in the closet. He looked down and saw her neatly stacked rows of shoes in different styles and colors.

No way she'd leave her shoes. No way. Means she's coming back… doesn't it?

His eyes drifted over to the nightstand and saw the envelope with his name on it. His hands shook as he carefully opened the flap and began to read:

Johnny,

I'm sorry we had to end this way, but there's no coming back from this. Take care of yourself and don't let the end of us be the end of you. Remember, Johnny, you're a fighter. Don't ever forget who you are or stop being that because of us.

Also, please don't get reckless. You're at war and your family needs you now more than ever. Especially Felix, Bunny and Zalo. They love you more than life itself and without you they'd be completely lost.

I made some notes about your list of enemies that we worked on last week…Last week? Feels like a lifetime ago… Not sure if anything I jotted down will help, but who knows.

Don't worry about Chris. I'm going to hug and spoil our little man every day of his life and keep him far, far away from the blood and death that destroyed us and so many around us.

On the business side of things, you can give my clothes and shoes to charity and please sign the no contest paperwork you'll get from my attorney in the next few days.

Bye baby,

Maria

John read the letter again and then glanced at Maria's three pages of handwritten notes about his long list of enemies and how to kill them. He didn't bother reading the notes, but told himself he'd get to them tomorrow.

Is she really gone? he asked himself.

He tossed the envelope back onto the nightstand in frustration and heard a clunk from something a lot harder than paper. Reached down and opened it back up. Felt around the bottom and found what had made the noise.

John stared at Maria's wedding ring. "Asked and answered," he said aloud, then flopped onto the bed and closed his eyes.

They checked on him after eight hours, and every two after that, and finally eighteen hours after they'd arrived, Felix gently shook him awake.

"Hey cuz," Felix said.

"Hey yourself," John said. "What time is it?"

"Four o'clock."

"In the morning?"

Felix shook his head. "Afternoon. Time to get up, bro. You've been down for nearly a day."

"No way," John said, still foggy as he came out of his coma.

"Yes way. Everyone's downstairs for a mission prep. We all understand if you wanna sit this one out, but thought I'd better wake you so you can decide for yourself."

"You know I'm in. Do I have time to shower up?" John asked.

Felix said he did and there was food and coffee ready for him after he got cleaned up. Felix looked over at the nightstand. Saw the letter… and the ring.

"You wanna talk about it?" he asked.

John picked his head up for the first time and held his cousin's gaze, their two sets of identical yellow eyes staring back at each other for a moment.

"Not now," John said. "Someday, just not now."

"I'm here, primo. We all are. Whatever you need," Felix said, then he turned and left the room.

Thirty minutes later John came downstairs, grabbed a

cup of coffee and joined everyone in the main dining room. Christmas was laying out the details of their next mission, but he paused and nodded his head in greeting. Gonzalo, Antonio, Bunny, Felix, Lulu, the Valdez brothers and several other Valdez soldiers tipped their chins towards John as well.

"John, we're just getting started so you haven't missed anything, and there's a packet for you on the table with high res pics of the target," Christmas said.

John said thanks, took another gulp of coffee, then put his cup down and picked up the packet.

After Benji's funeral service, Geronimo had gathered Lulu, John, Christmas, Gonzalo, Antonio and the rest of the Valdez men together and laid out the rough plan of attack. Everyone had agreed the plan was solid. It would give Lulu and the family some serious payback for Benji and Alastair's murders with a high Russian body count, and hit the bosses in Moscow right where it hurt the most. Below the belt. Back of the pants, not the front. In their wallets, which would definitely be the nut shot for the Russian mob.

Geronimo had offered twenty of his own men to join the attack, but Gonzalo had politely declined the offer. This was a Valdez fight and the Apaches were a different tribe. Geronimo said he understood and had only one request, which he shared privately with Gonzalo.

Christmas continued, "As you can see in the photos, they've got four lookouts on the surrounding rooftops. Dudes ain't trying to hide either. They're standing up there in plain sight, smoking butts while they watch the streets. There's also security cameras on every corner within a six-block grid. Eight cameras face out from the warehouse itself, and there's four more on the fence that surrounds it on three sides and runs all the way down to the river."

"So, we'll need four shooters to take out the roof guards," John said.

Christmas nodded. "And our techs will hack into the camera feeds and freeze 'em so they won't see us coming."

"How many men inside the warehouse and on the docks?" Antonio Valdez asked.

"We've spotted fourteen so far from across the river. There may be a few of 'em in there sleeping or watchin' TV that we haven't seen yet, but not a whole lot more. Our estimate is sixteen to twenty bad guys," Christmas said.

"Lulu, you want a long gun for the lookouts, or be part of the assault team going through the main gate?" Antonio asked Benji's brother.

Lulu looked at Antonio and then at John. "I'm kickin' in the front door."

"I'll be right behind you," John said.

Felix, Bunny and Christmas made quick eye contact with each other, collectively and silently expressing their concern. They all knew about his military record, but none of them had seen Lulu in combat. He'd been a badass snake eater for sure. A life-taker and widow-maker in Iraq and in the Stan, but he'd been living alone in the Adirondack Mountains for a year and a half. To this core group of men who'd been fighting together for the past six months, Lulu was definitely a wild card.

He picked up on the vibe. "Look, I get it. We've never fought or trained together. Most of you don't even know me and never seen how I get down. So, let me go in first. If I fuck up, I'll be dead, and you guys can clean up the mess. Good?"

"Fair enough," Bunny said. "No disrespect, Lulu."

"None taken. Roles reversed; I'd feel the same way."

"Ask you a question?" Bunny said.

"Sure, man."

"Where'd you get the name?"

"Lulu? I got it from Benji. He's three years older. Was, I mean. Anyway, he stuttered when he was a kid. My name's Luis and he could never say it. Always came out Loo Loo. After a while everyone, including mom, started calling me that."

"Never knew that," John said.

"Cool," Felix said.

"Okay, it's 5PM now. We hit them in seven hours, and there's a lot of work to do so let's get to it," Christmas said.

Chapter 24
Welcome Back

Red Hook, Brooklyn
11:55PM

THE WAREHOUSE IN Red Hook was right on the East River, with a long loading dock in front for heavy trucks coming in through the main gate and another one in the back for mid-size cargo ships loading and unloading from the river side.

"How we looking, Danny boy?" Christmas said into his mic.

"Five by five. All set here," said Danny Jones, the Valdez hacker who could get into any computer or breach any security system. "Say the word and I'll disable the cameras and put in a false loop."

"Do it," Christmas said.

Christmas was set up in his shooter's blind on the sixth floor of the Red Hook Self Storage Center eight blocks away from the warehouse. The Russian sentry in the crosshairs of his night vision scope was 750 yards out, smoking an unfiltered cigarette while he stared down at the street. The man was completely unaware that his life was about to end when Christmas fired his sound-suppressed .300 Win Mag rifle and sent the 165-grain expanding bullet towards him at 3,000 fps (feet per second).

Down in the street and several blocks away from the warehouse, John and Felix were sitting in the back of an armored-up black H2 Hummer, Bunny in the driver's seat and Lulu next to him up front. Two more identical H2s were idling right behind them. All three heavy SUVs had their front windshields replaced and all the bullet holes plugged after John and his team confiscated them from the Russian hit squad following the massacre at Jacob Riis.

"Nice touch rolling in these Russkie Hummers," Felix said, glancing over at John, waiting for a reaction.

John kept quiet, his eyes forward, holding his MP7 with the barrel pointing down. After Felix turned away and stared through his darkly tinted side window into the night, John said, "Yeah, it's a nice touch, but these fancy-ass trucks didn't keep any of those Russians alive when they came at us last week."

"I'm gonna need you to eighty-six that negative energy, my brother," Bunny said. "Those Russians ain't us. They fucked up and paid the ultimate price for it. Long as we stay on point and go into this op with a positive attitude and bad intentions, we're all gonna be okay. Got it?"

"Got it," John said. No smile. His face tight with a deep scowl between his eyebrows.

Felix watched. Worried that his cousin wasn't at all on point and didn't have his head in the game.

"You good, bro?" Felix asked.

John nodded. Still tight.

Felix tilted his body to the left, raised his right butt cheek and let one rip.

"How 'bout now?" he said, looking at his cousin with a big toothy grin.

John shook his head in disgust, but his face relaxed a bit. Glanced at Felix, then quickly looked away. Realized he was focused on Maria instead of the mission. Shook his head again to clear out all the clutter just as the smell hit him in the face.

"Oh my God. The fuck did you eat?" John asked.

"Some leftover Thai," Felix said, laughing.

"Damn that's nasty," Bunny said. "You can leave your guns in the truck, Cat. That ass gas is all you're gonna need," he added.

John leaned over to Felix: "I'm good now. Thanks, cuz." Then he tapped Bunny on the shoulder with his fist. "Got my bad intentions and positive vibes flowing again," John said, smiling for the first time in days.

"Glad to hear it," Felix said.

"My man. Welcome back, Johnny," Bunny said.

"Let's go kill these fuckers," Lulu said.

"That's what I'm talkin' 'bout. Man up front knows why we're here. I'm liking you more and more, Lulu," Bunny said.

Over the secure net they all heard Danny Jones announce that the security cameras were neutralized.

"Copy that," Christmas said. "Echo team, on my mark. Three, two, one, execute."

Christmas and the other three Valdez snipers fired simultaneously. Veteran shooters, they anticipated the recoil and kept their scopes on their targets. Each confirmed his man was down after seeing the blood spray from the head shot.

Christmas's voice came through their earpieces, telling everyone that he and the three other snipers were in position.

Now that the Russian sentries were off the board, all four Valdez shooters were sighted in on the warehouse.

"We're going in," John said into his mic.

It was midnight when Bunny threw the truck in gear and pulled out into the empty street. This part of Red Hook was always quiet at this time of night. Not many apartment buildings in the immediate area, mostly auto repair plants, small factories, storage facilities and waterfront dockyards. They didn't see a single car driving or anyone walking in the street during the ten-block drive to the warehouse.

Bunny slowed when he sighted the four Russians at the main gate. All four reached for their weapons when they saw the three H2s coming their way.

"Take 'em down," John said.

From their elevated positions Christmas and his men again fired as one and the sentries silently crumpled to the ground.

Bunny went wide, driving all the way over to the right side of the street, then made a sharp left turn and put the gas pedal down to the floor. The 8,900-pound H2 surged forward and didn't slow when it rolled over the dead guards, smashed through the gate, and took down a 20-foot section of the hurricane fence topped with razor wire.

Speeding towards the warehouse, Bunny pulled up in front of the steps to the loading dock while the two other H2s went left and right around the main building to launch their assault from the back. Bunny, Lulu, John and Felix all hit the ground with their MP7s pointed up and ready. Three Russian gunmen surged through the big double doors. Before they could fire a shot they were all flattened by the Valdez sniper team.

"Clear," Christmas said over the radio.

"Going in," Lulu said as he sprinted up the concrete steps.

He ran across the wide platform, past the three bodies, and through the big double doors without slowing, scanning for targets as he ran. John followed him in with Bunny and Felix bringing up the rear while the rest of the Valdez troops attacked through the back door on the river side of the warehouse.

"Watch your corners," John said. "There's a lot of shit to hide behind in here."

There were big wooden pallets stacked high with boxes and four big rig cargo containers placed haphazardly all around the main floor.

"Copy that," Lulu said.

John saw the barrel of an AR-15 coming around the edge of a six-foot-high crate. He waited for the man to peer out, then fired his sound-suppressed MP7 and put a 4.6x30mm round into the Russian's left eye. There was a shout from behind the crate and a second Russian charged out to avenge his comrade. John fired three times, hitting his target twice in the chest and once in the forehead before the man thumped down, flat on his back with his arms spread wide.

John heard the footsteps before he spotted four sets of legs running behind one of the big cargo containers that was sitting on a flatbed trailer.

"Four targets at my three o'clock. I'm going low," John said.

"I'm going left," said Bunny.

"I'm going right," Felix said.

John squatted down, took a knee, and zeroed in on the lower legs of the two men edging past the trailer's front tires and moving toward the left corner of the container. He fired his MP7 in short bursts on full auto, hitting each man four or five times in the shins and thighs before shifting his sights to the right and flattening the other two Russians with another dozen rounds to their feet and ankles.

Bunny and Felix both ran forward as soon as John started shooting. They came around either side of the container at the same time, firing down into the men on the floor before they could raise their weapons.

"Clear," Felix said. "They're all down."

John knew he was running low on ammo, and kept his gun up and pressed into his shoulder with his right hand while reaching into the ammo pouch of his tac vest for a fresh thirty-round mag with his left. Swapped out his near-empty for a full load without looking down or thinking about it, the same way he'd done countless times before in training and in combat.

"Moving up," John said, just as they heard the loud blasts from multiple AK-47s firing from farther back in the warehouse.

"Lulu? You okay?" John asked.

There was radio silence for two beats before Lulu responded.

"Got a little scratch," Lulu said while firing his MP7 on full auto. "We've got five or six bad guys dug in back here," he added.

"On our way," John said, moving forward as the tip of the spear with Felix and Bunny five steps behind and evenly spaced on his left and right, all three scanning for targets as they quick-stepped towards Lulu.

"Damn," they heard him say.

"What?" Bunny asked.

"Another scratch," Lulu said.

They saw him now. Twenty feet ahead. Three dead

Russians at his feet. 7.62x39mm AK-47 rounds hitting the steel support beam he was using for cover. John saw blood flowing down from the hole in Lulu's left shoulder and another in his right leg—the two "scratches" he'd mentioned.

"We see you, bro. Stay put. We're circling around to flank 'em," John said into his mic.

"Copy that," Lulu said.

They moved fast, using the crates as cover. A final quick dash through a natural pathway between the boxes and they saw the storage room where the Russians were making their final stand. The eight-foot-high four-foot-wide door was open, but the room was dark with the only light coming from the AK muzzle flashes.

"They're dug in and we're not risking lives trying to dig them out," John said, then pulled an M67 grenade from another pouch in the front of his tac vest. Bunny moved up beside him ready with his own M67.

There was more firing from the back of the warehouse as the rest of the Valdez troops fought their way in. John gave them a warning.

"Cover, cover, cover. Fire in the hole," he said into his mic as he and Bunny pulled their pins, released the grenade handles and held for a second before throwing them overhand twenty feet in a straight line through the storage room door.

The blasts went off simultaneously, immediately followed by high-pitched screams when the fragmentation grenades' steel casings ripped through the Russians.

Resistance in the back of the warehouse was neutralized and several Valdez men charged forward, shooting as they ran through the storage room door. There was no return fire and John, Bunny, Felix and Lulu could hear the pop, pop, pop of suppressed MP7 shots from the Valdez soldiers finishing off the wounded.

"We're all clear here," John said into his mic, "but check every corner just to make sure. Lulu's hit. Anyone else hurt?"

It was Chepe, the leader of the Valdez assault on the back of the warehouse, who responded. "We lost Manolo and Eggy. They're both gone," he said over the radio.

"Fuck!" Felix shouted.

John shook his head sadly, then looked down at his boots for a moment before he followed Bunny and Felix over to check on Lulu while the rest of the men spread out to do a thorough search.

They found Lulu sitting with his back to the steel beam, his legs splayed out in front of him.

"How're them scratches?" Bunny asked, as he knelt down to examine the bullet wounds.

"Starting to tingle a bit," Lulu said, trying to smile, but the pain made it more of a grimace.

"I bet," Bunny said. He took off his belt and cinched it around Lulu's leg to slow the bleeding.

Lulu groaned when Bunny pulled it tighter.

"That hurt, La-La? Thought you Marines were tough," Bunny said.

"La-La has a nice ring to it," Felix said, laughing.

"Fuckin' assholes," Lulu snarled, but started laughing too.

John bent down to examine Lulu's shoulder, put pressure on the hole in front, turned him to look at his upper back and saw the exit wound.

"Shoulder is through and through, but we gotta get you to a medic ASAP," John said to Lulu. Then speaking into his mic again he said, "Christmas, send in the trucks and the backup teams so we can evac Lulu and our KIAs and clean this place out."

"They're inbound now, Johnny," Christmas said.

Four SUVs pulled into the open lot in front of the warehouse, followed by an eighteen-wheeler that backed its way in and stopped when its rear trailer tapped the loading dock. Sixteen more soldiers led by Antonio Valdez made their way up the stairs and hustled over to John.

Antonio had been listening to the action through his earpiece and gave quick orders. Pointing to the two men closest to him and then down at Lulu he said, "Get him to the doc now. Four of you go to the back and bring out Manolo and Eggy."

They lifted Lulu, who gave a thumb's up as they carried him out, while the others ran to the back to retrieve the bodies of their fallen brothers.

"The rest of you start opening these crates and see what's in 'em," Antonio said.

They worked quickly, cutting through the strapping that held boxes on the pallets, prying open lids and calling out what they found inside.

"Guns here. AR-15s, AKs and 9s," one of the Valdez men said.

"Got a lotta drugs in this one. Looks like coke and X," said another.

A Valdez soldier with a thin goatee opened up the big container. He stood there for a moment with his mouth open before saying, "Holy shit."

John, Bunny and Felix walked over with Antonio to take a look.

"Holy shit is right," Felix said.

They all took in the sight, staring at the clear plastic

bundles stacked almost to the roof. Antonio's man pulled one down. The packages, four feet long and two feet wide, were filled with hundred-dollar bills.

"How much do you think?" Bunny asked.

John hopped up into the back, walked over to the side wall of the container, and pulled off the clipboard that was hanging on a nail.

"According to this," he said, reading the manifest that fortunately was written in English, then he paused for a second as he looked down at everyone... "There's sixty-seven mil sitting here, ready to get shipped back to Moscow in the morning."

"Damn," Bunny said.

"Damn is right," John said.

"Can we take the whole trailer?" Felix asked.

"We gotta check for booby traps before we do anything. Doubt they'd risk blowing up their own cash, but you never know. There's definitely trackers in there though," Antonio said. "Let's get to work," he added.

John jumped down to give Antonio's men more room to operate. They brought in scanners and quickly found several electronic tracking devices. Two were in the container's roof and five more had been buried deep in the money stacks. They carefully removed the trackers and laid them out on the floor of the trailer.

"Okay, as soon as we move this box, a whole bunch of Russians are gonna be heading our way," John said. "But, maybe that's not a bad thing. Let's bring them in and take 'em out before we torch this place."

Antonio nodded in agreement. "Load up all the dead Russians so no one finds all the bodies, but move all the drugs and guns to the parking lot as a gift for the cops, and then get this place rigged to blow. Take phone vids when it goes up. We want Moscow to see what happens when they fuck with us," he said.

CHAPTER 25

CROSSING LINES

Red Hook, Brooklyn

ALL NINETEEN OF the dead Russians were loaded into the back of the Mack truck while John and Bunny set the explosives and Valdez soldiers poured gasoline on all the crates still inside the warehouse. Then they got the keys to the cab of another big rig and backed it up to the loading dock. Using forklifts, they took turns pulling each of the five pallets out of the money container and quickly transported them into the Mack's trailer. Antonio had four of his men climb into the back to guard the cash from the inside before he watched the doors swing closed and the truck pulled out.

They all watched the fortune turn into the street with a caravan of Valdez cars leading the way and several more following.

"All right, grab the trackers. Drive them around the front lot and up and down the street, and let's see who shows up," John said.

"How long do you think?" Felix asked.

"Ten minutes? Fifteen max," Bunny said.

It only took seven. Christmas and his shooters, still on overwatch, let everyone know their guests were arriving. Three black Mercedes SUVs and another big H2 came roaring down the street. They slowed when they saw the wide section of the fence and the front gate were down, and the boxes of drugs and guns dumped around the lot, but then sped in and screeched to a stop in front of the main building.

John and the troops, parked half a block away with a clear view of the warehouse, waited for the Russians to get out of their vehicles. As soon as the car doors opened and the armed men hopped out, John hit the detonator. The initial explosions weren't that loud. Just a series of thumps, but once the gas and fuel lit off a second later, the whole building went up.

"Let's go take a look," John said.

They drove slowly across the street and stopped at the gate looking for movement. Only moments before, twelve men had been standing out in the open with their guns drawn facing the warehouse. None were standing now. The fireball had sent dagger-like pieces of wood, chunks of concrete and shards of metal in all shapes and sizes flying directly at them. They were all blown backwards and lay scattered across the lot, most of them in a twisted pile of broken arms and legs.

"Any survivors?" Antonio asked.

"Four, boss," one of his men answered. "It'll be three in a minute. This one's bleeding out," he added, pointing down at a Russian with a massive wound who was pressing his intestines back into his belly with both hands.

"Search the others, then bring them over here," Antonio ordered.

Several of his soldiers did a rough and thorough search,

then dragged the three survivors over to face Antonio, John, Bunny and Felix.

"Who's in charge?" John asked.

The three remained silent, staring back defiantly. The Russian in the middle spat, not directly at John, but the bloody gob landed close to his feet. Before John could say anything, Antonio raised his .45 Colt Commander and shot the spitter in the mouth.

"Who's in charge?" Antonio repeated.

"Me," said the thickly bearded and heavyset Russian standing to Antonio's right.

"You have Yakov's number?" Antonio asked.

The Russian nodded.

"Call him," John said, "and put it on speaker."

The Russian found the number on his speed dial list and hit send. After three rings a voice on the other end said, "Da?"

John took the phone: "Yakov Skobelev?"

"Who is speaking?"

"John Bishop. The man you tried to kill."

"What is it you want?" Yakov asked.

"I'm at your warehouse in Red Hook."

"So?" Yakov said.

"Your assassin murdered my father-in-law Alastair Williams and Benji Medina, another member of our family, and nearly killed my wife. Today, we killed all your men, burned your drugs and weapons and took your sixty-seven million. I want you to know we're just getting started."

"How do we fix it? End our hostilities?" Yakov asked.

"Start with giving me the name and location of the old man you sent," John said.

Gonzalo and his security team had reviewed the surveillance footage at Maria's parents' building and zeroed in on the seemingly innocent elderly man who snuck in through the lobby and killed Alastair.

After a long pause, "We call him Vorovka, the Thief, but his real name is Boris Vasiliev. He has a farm outside of Minsk," Yakov said. Another pause, then: "Mr. Bishop, I apologize for your loss and any misunderstanding."

Antonio didn't care about apologies. Benji Medina, his friend, his brother, was dead and words couldn't bring him back. Antonio shot the bearded Russian high in the stomach and watched him double over, screaming in pain. The last man standing put his hands up and said, "No," just as Antonio shot him in the neck.

"Misunderstanding!" Antonio shouted. "You wanted a war, Ivan. Now you've got it."

"This is not Bishop. Who is speaking?"

"I'm Antonio Valdez and I'm coming for you and anyone you know or love. You crossed the line when you went after our family, motherfucka. Now we're gonna find you and wipe you out."

"Wait!… we can…"

John cut him off, "We know you lost a son, Yakov. We also know you're smart enough to figure out that we had nothing to do with it. Connie Belusci killed your boy."

"I know," Yakov said.

"You knew and you still came after our family… killed civilians? Why the fuck would you do that?" John asked.

"I mean, I know *now*," Yakov said. "I was informed after we sent Vorovka. I am truly sorry for any misunderstanding, Mr. Bishop."

"Sorries don't bring our people back," Antonio said. He took the phone from John, hit the end button, then took a step towards the bearded Russian he shot in the stomach. The man was still alive, barely, lying on his back, groaning in pain. Antonio stood above him, paused for a moment, shot him two more times, then turned and walked away.

John watched him go. He knew Antonio was hurting over Benji. Still, there was a line and Antonio just crossed it. John was a warrior, but he'd never killed a man like that… wounded and unarmed.

Line or no, there was no turning back now. Yakov and his whole organization were going down and John was glad the call gave him a crucial piece of information. The name of the man he was going to travel a long way to see… Boris Vasiliev, AKA Vorovka.

"Let's go," Felix said, guiding John by the arm.

They all got in the H2s and drove off into the night. When they were three blocks away, a line of fire trucks raced past them heading towards the burning warehouse.

CHAPTER 26
PARTNERS

Campos Plaza, LES

"TELL THE PRESIDENT, I'm in," John said to Clayton Unser.

"You mean *we're* in," Gonzalo added.

John nodded in agreement: "Yes, *we're* in… temporarily."

Clayton Unser wrinkled his brow and looked at John and Gonzalo for answers.

"Why temporarily?" he asked.

"Jeff Stamper's gonna be our next president, and he met with Caleb Meecham the same night we met with you at Camp David. He's in Meecham's pocket and Meecham's sworn to kill us all," Gonzalo said.

"When Stamper's in the White House he may forget all about the promises he made to you," Clayton said, looking at John as he walked through the logic.

"Exactly," John said. "We'll sign on until the inauguration in January *if* and only if all the men I bring in get the same presidential pardon that you gave me… *and* as long as we don't actually have to sign any CIA employment contracts."

"What happens when Stamper gets sworn in?" Clayton asked.

John shrugged his shoulders, the move sending a blast of pain down the back of his neck and his right arm from the bullet that hit him at Jacob Riis, but his expression remained neutral, his eyes flat: "Hard to say," he said.

"Can you expand on that a bit?" Clayton asked.

"We now know Stamper is our enemy," Gonzalo said. "In the next three months either we'll both be dead," Gonzalo tapped his hand on John's knee, "Or our enemies will be."

"You're not suggesting…" Clayton said.

"Stamper? No… No, of course not," John said, shaking his head. "Meecham and his hired gun, Connie Belusci, are going down for sure, though. Once they're off the board we can assess the situation with Stamper, but it's hard to imagine working for a president who's actively plotting to have us killed or incarcerated."

"Fair enough," Clayton said. "How many guys are you bringing in?"

"I have three in mind, but I haven't asked them yet," John said.

"Bear, Mace and Bobby?" Clayton asked.

John nodded in agreement.

"You may want to add a fourth name. Staff Sergeant Chao Chen Goh. He's a top-tier operator." Clayton reached into his briefcase, pulled out Chago's OMPF (Official Military Personnel File) and handed it to John. "I added notes and assessments from the dozen plus black ops missions he's volunteered for. Also, he's in Iraq with your team now. Goh was assigned to Team Razor three months ago."

John glanced down at Chago's file, nodded at Clayton and handed it to Gonzalo, who put it in the briefcase at his feet. John made a mental note to read the file later, but he didn't know the man and there wasn't going to be enough time to build a relationship. If his three Team Razor brothers were in, along with Bunny, Christmas and Felix, he'd have a rock-solid team that would be operational and hunting targets within a week. He'd definitely ask Bear about Chago. For now, though, the man was a maybe at best.

"I need to see them face-to-face," John said.

"In Mosul?" Clayton asked.

"Djibouti, if you can get them there," John said.

"How soon?"

"How about the day after tomorrow?" John asked.

Clayton said they'd be there.

"Also, for the active duty guys I bring in, their DD-4s gotta remain in place," John said. "I don't want their Army contracts and bennies getting jacked up over this."

"Not a problem, John. That it?"

Gonzalo leaned in. "There's one thing we need him to do," he said.

"And by *him*, you mean the president of the United States?" Clayton asked.

"Yeah, *that* him," John said.

Clayton looked from John to Gonzalo, questioning them with a raised eyebrow.

"Okay, what?"

John told him.

"That's a big ask. Not sure I can make that happen," Clayton said.

"It has to happen," John said. "He wants us, you tell him we need this."

Clayton stared into John's yellow eyes for a moment, then nodded his agreement.

"Assuming he says yes, anything else you need to get started?" Clayton asked.

"Space. A big private place to train. Somewhere close to the city," John said.

"Ready and waiting for you. Five thousand acres in the Catskills, just two hours north of here," Clayton said.

"We're gonna be doing a lot of shooting. Any neighbors close by?" John asked.

Clayton pulled out maps and aerial pics of the property… "You're really going to love this place. Nearest neighbors are fifteen miles away. It was originally built by a bunch of meth dealing, Mad Max type, end of the world Neo-Nazis and sat empty for a few years once the DEA and ATF busted in and locked their asses up. After 9/11 it was upgraded and rede-signed as a training facility. The anti-terrorism task force used it for rapid response scenarios and training ops to counter attacks against big cities and small towns. It's a state-of-the-art covert ops facility. Hasn't been used in five years, so it may be a little dusty but the lights still work."

John looked over the maps and photos, Gonzalo leaned in to see as well, and they both nodded their heads in agree-ment… Clayton was right, the site was perfect. It was basically a small town, several levels up from a Hollywood movie set because all the buildings looked solid. There was a depart-ment store, a hospital, a school, a police station and several other structures made to look like residential and state or fed-eral government buildings, all designed to simulate terrorist bombings, rocket, mortar and vehicle-based attacks, suicide bombings and hostage rescue scenarios.

"You're gonna need some bad guys to train against," Clayton said.

Gonzalo bared his teeth, which made him look scarier

than usual… Clayton knew from years of working with the man that it was his attempt at a smile.

"Bad guys? You're offering us bad guys? We've got plenty of those, my friend," Gonzalo said.

Clayton nodded, smiling back: "Yes, you certainly do, Don Valdez."

John looked at his checklist. The weapons, a cache of long guns… HK MP7s with sound suppressors, M4A1s, HK416s, M1014 semi-auto twelve gauge shotguns, two Mk 46 machine guns, four Mk 12 special ops sniper rifles, and the handguns… a mix of SIGs—P226s, P228s, P239s—with a few HK45CTs and Glocks thrown in.

Spec Ops soldiers were trained and proficient in all manner of firearms, but most had their individual preferences as to what weapons they wanted to carry into combat. John had spent enough time downrange with Bunny, Bear, Mace and Bobby that he'd built the list around their favorites, and added a few of his own.

They spent another two hours sorting out the details, going over logistics and travel arrangements before Clayton said his goodbyes and showed himself out of the Valdez stronghold in LES.

A few minutes later, John and Gonzalo were drinking strong black coffee when Felix opened the conference room door and escorted their next guest in.

John got up to greet him: "How are you Uncle… Geronimo?"

Geronimo held John's hand in a tight grip and looked into his eyes for a good five seconds. Long enough for it to feel awkward, John thought.

"I'm good, John. Very, very good," Geronimo said. He was dressed casually, wearing black jeans, black Nike running shoes and a black Hugo Boss tee that looked one size too small. His shoulder muscles stretched it out and his triceps bulged out of the short sleeves.

John stepped away to pour a coffee for his tattooed uncle and another one for Felix. He came back with the steaming mugs, watched his uncle take a sip, and then all four of them sat down at the big conference table.

"The mission went as planned?" Geronimo asked.

"You know it did," Gonzalo said.

"Where are the drugs?" In exchange for the information on the Russian warehouse, Geronimo had told Gonzalo that he could keep any money they found, but that he, Geronimo, wanted all the drugs stored there.

"They were destroyed in the fire," John said.

Another long stare. John didn't look away. Waited ten seconds this time for his uncle to speak.

"That wasn't what we agreed to," Geronimo said.

"It was a firefight, Tio. I wasn't going to risk my men's lives to save your drugs," John said.

"Really? Why not?" Geronimo asked.

"Seriously? I… I don't even know how to answer that," John said, trying not to lose his temper.

Gonzalo stepped in: "Look, hermano, the drugs are gone and there's no bringing them back, so let's move on."

Another long pause, Geronimo turning his head to look at each of them, not blinking, just going back and forth.

Is he insane? John thought.

"So, the drugs were lost, but you saved the money," Geronimo said.

"Yes," Gonzalo said.

"Okay," Geronimo said.

Another silence.

"Okay what?" John asked.

"Okay, I'll take the money."

It was Gonzalo's turn to stare.

"The drugs were valued at a hundred mil," Geronimo said. "But they were worth more than just money to me. I'm going to control the global markets, and this is a setback... A minor one, but a setback, nonetheless. We're partners so it's only fair that you make up the loss," Geronimo said.

"Partners? How are we partners?" Zalo asked.

"You're right. We're not partners. I was just being nice. The truth is you work for me now, and from here on I'm taking a more hands-on approach. I wanted to see how you'd handle some semblance of autonomy, and you completely fucked it up."

"Hermanito, you can't be serious," Gonzalo said, his yellow eyes burning bright and both his hands pressed hard onto the table. "The Valdez family has been out of the drug business for over a decade, and we're not getting back in. We're completely legitimate now."

"Zalo, *you're* done. The family is mine to do with as I choose. You can keep a seat at the table if you can handle being a puppet, otherwise you're out. I don't want you or anyone else getting hurt. Especially when we share blood. There's no need for it. Do as I say and you'll be fine, but what I'm about to do is too big. I'm going to make Pablo Escobar look like a small-time corner kid."

"Escobar, and every other drug kingpin dies bloody or in a cage. Why're you chasing that dream, Tio?" Felix asked him.

"Because I can, nephew. Did Caesar, Genghis Khan or Alexander the Great take a pass on conquering the world? Even if they knew they'd die bloody after they'd won every battle, you think it would've stopped them?... Not a fucking chance."

"Geronimo, you know how many people are coming at us?" John asked. "We're not just fighting the Russians. We've also got ISIS, Pakistani killers and an Albanian hitman all trying to kill us. We don't have time for a family feud right now."

"Family feud?" Geronimo raised his left eyebrow and smiled incredulously. "There is no feud. Deliver the money and we'll all get along just fine."

"As John said, we don't have time for this," Gonzalo said. "We'll deliver the sixty-seven million this week."

"One hundred million," Geronimo said.

"We only got sixty-seven from the Russians," John said.

"And as I said, the drugs were worth a hundred, and I need you to make me whole," Geronimo said.

He got up from the table and stood there looking at the three of them for another five count and then said, "Okay, we're done here. It was good seeing you all. Make sure you drop off my money by the end of the week."

He turned and walked out without looking back.

"What the fuck is wrong with him?" John asked after he left.

"I told you, Johnny, he's a fuckin' lunatic. Saw it first-hand when I was doing my time with him up in Elmira," Felix said.

Felix had served four years in prison with Nestor, now Geronimo, and even before the name change he'd seen just how deadly and dangerous his uncle was.

"I had no idea. This is bad. How're we gonna handle him, Tio?" John asked Gonzalo.

Gonzalo didn't say anything. Looked at his nephew for a

moment, then he looked away and stared out the window for a long time. Neither John nor Felix broke the silence. They waited half an hour for him to speak.

"Where's Antonio?" Gonzalo asked.

"We haven't seen him since he shot the three Russians at the warehouse," Felix said.

"I knew he was gonna take Benji's death and everything else that's happening pretty hard. Probably needs some time alone to get his mind right," John said.

"And you, my son? How are you handling Maria and all this?" Gonzalo asked him.

"I put it in a box, Tio. Put it in a box and hid the key. At least till all this is done… after that? I just don't know," John said, staring down at the table.

Gonzalo reached out and placed both hands on top of John's.

"We're here for you. Whenever you want to talk about it, we're here."

"Thank you, Tio," John said.

"We need to find Antonio," Gonzalo said.

John nodded. Didn't say anything. He was deeply conflicted about his cousin. Antonio had executed the three Russians in cold blood. John had his own code about killing. He knew that Yakov and his assassin, Vorovka, had crossed the line when they targeted Maria and her father, and he'd taken out a few Russians himself when they stormed the warehouse, but he'd never shot a man who had his hands up in surrender… Hoped he never would.

John knew the law didn't see much difference between a civilian putting bad guys down in a gunfight and killing them in cold blood, but he sure did, and it made him realize something about his cousin… Whether Gonzalo saw it yet or not, Antonio wasn't fit to lead the family.

Then there was Antonio's openly hostile reaction to Gonzalo's move to make the family completely legitimate. The more he thought about it, the more uneasy he felt, but there was too much to do so he made a mental note to take a closer look at the Antonio situation when he got back from Djibouti.

"I'm on it," Felix said to Gonzalo. "I'll find Antonio and tell him you need to see him," Felix said.

"Good," Gonzalo said. "Okay, here's what we're going to do…"

Washington Heights

It took Geronimo thirty minutes to drive uptown from Campos Plaza to his headquarters in Washington Heights. Unlike Gonzalo's HQ at Campos, Geronimo didn't have any civilians living in the four six-story buildings where he'd planted his flag. They were fortified with exterior and interior surveillance systems, reinforced steel doors, hidden rooms, tunnels below ground, rope ladders on the rooftops, and fifty of his soldiers lived in apartments spread out across the four buildings.

When Geronimo walked into his office, Antonio Valdez was already there waiting for him. Geronimo clapped Antonio on the shoulder then went around his desk and sat down in his high-backed black leather chair.

Antonio was a big man, the largest of the Valdez family at six-four. Balding, he'd started losing hair in his early twenties, and now at age 42 he was down to a few curly scraps above his ears and at the back of his head. The hair he'd lost on his dome had somehow transferred to the rest of him, because his body was covered in a thick kinky mass that poked out from every opening of his dark blue collared shirt.

"How did it go with my uncle?" Antonio asked.

"As expected, Antonio. As expected... I was hoping he would walk away, but knew in my heart it wasn't gonna happen."

"He still loves you, Tio. Despite it all he won't try to kill you," Antonio said.

"That's why he's not fit to lead anymore. He's weak now," Geronimo said.

"You thought he'd try?" Antonio asked.

"Was more curious than anything else. In a way I hoped he would. Better to see my big brother die like a man than have to be put down like a lame horse."

"He was a man in his day," Antonio said.

"Yes, he *was* a man. Not anymore, though," Geronimo said.

Geronimo stared at his nephew for a while, looking past the eyes, and into the heart of the man who sat before him.

"And you, my nephew. What are you?"

"I'm a man. You know I am and I'm ready, Tio." Antonio said.

"Have you thought it through?"

"How I'll kill him?" Antonio asked.

Geronimo nodded.

"Has to be face-to-face. By my own hand. I owe Gonzalo that much at least after all he's done for me."

"And your cousins?" Geronimo asked.

Antonio looked confused: "What about them?"

"What about them? You know what about them. If you want this you'll have to kill John and Felix, too."

Antonio tried to hold his uncle's stare, but this time looked away, his mind racing.

"Heavy is the head that wears the crown, Antonio. Most men are too weak to make the hard choices it takes to be a king, and fewer still can handle the weight once they take the throne. To become a king… a true king, every man swims through a sea of blood and climbs over mountains of the dead… Think of the bodies as a ladder. The more bodies you make, the higher you'll climb."

"Never thought of that," Antonio said.

"Few do. And remember, any soldier can kill his enemies, but sooner or later, every true king must slaughter those he loves the most. That's the price that every great ruler has to pay."

"You paid?" Antonio asked.

"I have, many times over," Geronimo said. He drifted for a moment, thinking back to his early years in prison when he was still finding his way and unsure of his true path. Two brothers, Tuckey and Nino Martinez, and their cousin Didi were lifers in El Mira who ruled the prison together. The three of them were a tight unit and they'd been running things at "The Hill" for twenty years. Geronimo saved Didi's life in a hit that he himself had orchestrated. Five years later, on the night when Didi, Tuckey and Nino officially made the then Nestor Valdez their blood brother, he killed all three of them.

He'd killed many more friends and trusted lieutenants over the years, but those kills were never as difficult as his decision to wipe out team Martinez and take everything they had. He loved those dudes. Especially Didi. Geronimo came from a big family, but somehow he'd never really felt a part of it. But Didi? Man, he loved Didi like a true brother, and that night Geronimo slept in his bed with his arms wrapped tightly around Didi's head. The rest of Didi remained where it had landed on the floor after Geronimo separated his head from his body with a hatchet.

"Tio," Antonio said, bringing Geronimo back. "I have to ask. What's in this for you?"

"A partner," he said, simply.

Geronimo saw that his nephew was skeptical, so he went on: "Deep down I'm a sentimental man and I want the Valdez family to survive. I also know I can't be the one who eliminates Zalo and takes his place... None will follow me. That said, my big brother is working against me now, and for that he has to die."

Antonio noted there was no emotion or even a hint of remorse in Geronimo's voice when he talked about killing his own brother.

"John and Felix, too," Geronimo said. "Those three yellow-eyed demons are a package deal. If you don't kill them, I'll have to do it. After that, I'll have to wipe out everyone else, and then the Valdez family will be no more."

He leaned forward over his desk towards his nephew. "And when I say *everyone,* Antonio... that includes you too."

Geronimo held out his right hand. "Partner?"

Antonio reached out with his right and squeezed his uncle's tightly. "Partners," he said, his eyes watering up as he fought to hold back his tears.

CHAPTER 27

THE BORDER

Vancouver, Canada

THE CARGO SHIP dropped its anchor three miles off the coast of Vancouver at just past 2AM. Minutes later, a twenty-foot fishing boat with a cuddy cabin and twin outboard engines approached the ship. Tariq and his troops hurried down the cargo ship's ladders with their gear and climbed aboard the fisherman as it idled alongside. Tariq questioned the boat's captain and the first mate, both Saudis, who assured him that there wasn't a surprise attack waiting for them on the beach, and that they had their own people surveilling the area to make sure.

During the short ten-minute trip to a deserted stretch of Pachena Beach on the west coast of Vancouver Island, Tariq and the team took off their shoes and socks and rolled up their pants legs. Tariq knew he didn't have to say it, but told his team to stay alert and have their guns ready in case of an ambush.

It was low tide and the boat had to anchor a good fifty feet from the beach. The team walked barefoot through the freezing waters of the north Pacific, the light surf up to their knees, wearing their backpacks with their boot strings tied together, the boots hanging down from their necks to keep them dry… and to keep their hands free in case of a shootout.

Two women met them on the beach and led them into the woods. No flashlights, they put on their socks and boots in the dark and moved out. None of them said it out loud… They all felt relieved to be back on dry land and to have made it this far without any incidents. Except for the Mel incident, which they weren't looking back on. As a group they were completely focused on the now and on the road ahead.

Tariq wore the deluxe version of the LL Bean hiking ensemble. Jeans, flannel shirt, North Face down parka, waterproof hiking boots, backpack with tent and sleeping bag strapped across the top. The rest of his team of seven men and four women were dressed in the same "ready to face the outdoors" fashion.

They started their trek on Vancouver Island, heading southeast into Washington's Wenatchee National Forest. On day three the tour group of twelve terrorists and two guides reached the Canadian-US border. There wasn't a gate or a wall or even a sign. The US trees were identical to their Canadian brothers. They found the line on Google maps. All of them smiled as they dramatically hopped across it. Even Tariq felt a surge of adrenaline when he placed his feet on American soil. The whole world was hunting him, yet here he was.

Gretchen leaned over and whispered to him, "Do you know how epic this is, Tariq?"

"Epic?" he said.

"Epic is like, *incredible*. We're the most wanted people on the planet and we just walked into America. That's epic," Gretchen said, smiling.

"Epic? Yes, epic. Very epic," Tariq said.

"About as fucking epic as epic gets," she said.

The celebration was a quick one. They had to keep moving and the guides led the way along narrow trails, always heading south through the forest, and the farther south they went, the more people they came across. Hundreds of hours of role playing with the native-born Americans before they left the Islamic State had paid off. They all smiled, waved and said hello to fellow hikers walking along the intersecting paths, appearing to be a close-knit group of nature-loving friends instead of trained killers on a suicide mission.

That night they sat in a circle around their evening fire, silently staring into the flames. After walking for fourteen hours, they were more interested in rubbing and warming their feet than talking. None of them lingered long, and after a few minutes they all made their way to their tents.

Before heading to his tent, Tariq instructed one of their guides and Marwan to take the first watch. When he climbed in, Gretchen was already there, lying naked on top of her sleeping bag, her body covered in goosebumps and her nipples hard and erect from the cold. Tariq congratulated himself on making the change. He'd grown tired of Lisa, and Gretchen was far more skilled at the art of lovemaking.

He knew women were weak, and Americans in general were bred with a sense of arrogance and self-importance that made them question everything. He respected Gretchen's loyalty, but now that they were on American soil he would use every tool at his disposal to keep her committed to their cause. He instructed his three ISIS brothers who were also paired up with American girls to vigorously service them each night to help keep them fully focused and indoctrinated.

After he rolled off her, they lay quietly together for a few minutes. Gretchen usually liked to stay close to him afterwards so he could whisper in her ear, reviewing the plan, her excitement growing with each detail. Then she would reach down and start stroking him, using her mouth, whatever it took to get him to mount her again. Tonight, she quickly drifted off to sleep and Tariq thanked Allah for the reprieve.

He dressed and left the tent, walked away from the camp, following the beam from his flashlight along the trail until he found the rock formation they passed near the end of the day. A round mound protruding from the earth, rising only fifteen feet above the ground, flattening out at the top.

Even in the dark it was a safe, easy climb. The top was surprisingly smooth, polished by thousands of years of wind and rain. He lay down, staring up at the stars, thinking about his life, and how it was about to end. Imagining the glorious eternity bestowed upon martyrs in paradise.

His thoughts then turned to the man he revered above all others. The man who'd mentored him as if Tariq were his own son. He pictured Aziz Khan at his peak. Poised to rule Afghanistan and defeat the Americans just as he'd beaten the Soviets years before.

Then he pictured Aziz as he last saw him. Body broken, large wooden splinters in his eyes, a bullet hole in his forehead, the bastard John Bishop standing over him. Bishop. The man he hated above all others.

Tariq had sworn an oath to avenge Aziz and that promise would soon be fulfilled. Thousands of New Yorkers were going to die, but John Bishop would lead them down into Jahannam, the eternal pit of blazing fire.

Tariq used deep controlled breathing to calm himself. The many mistakes made by Aziz Khan's nephew, Amir Khan, in New York six months ago were lessons to be learned and they would not be repeated. Amir had all the men and resources to launch multiple attacks on Manhattan, but he'd been blinded by his rage at John Bishop. For Tariq, Amir's lack of sight helped him see.

Bishop would die, but not at the expense of the mission. He was a bonus, and Tariq knew that when he stood over Bishop's body he would smile up at the sky, knowing that Aziz could finally rest peacefully.

All the pieces were in place and he mentally reviewed everything once more, trying to poke holes in the plan. His greatest fear had been the border, and now that they crossed it, he couldn't see any way the Americans could stop them.

Satisfied that he'd prepared himself and his team for every possible contingency, he clicked on his flashlight to check the time on his watch, and was surprised to see that it was past midnight. Surprised that he'd been on the rock for two hours, Tariq stretched and made his way back to the camp.

Over the next several days the tour traveled through rich, fertile valleys with majestic green mountains towering above them. Tariq and his jihadists saw them as barren rocks compared to the beauty they would all soon find in paradise.

At the end of the hike a bus took them to Seattle, where they said their goodbyes to their guides. Several cars were there to pick them up and take them to five separate safe-houses. Twelve strangers arriving at one location would draw unwanted attention so they split up for the night to get show-ered, have a good meal, dump all the camping equipment and gear up for the next leg of the trip. After the long journey from Syria and the many nights of sleeping on the ground, they welcomed the soft beds and comforters. The team members were up at dawn, refreshed and ready to meet the children.

Traveling separately in twos and threes, they arrived as scheduled at Lincoln Park at 9AM. The RVs, each loaded with plastic explosives hidden under the floorboards, got there an hour later. The mothers stepped out of the vehicles with their babies and there were introductions all around. The children were all between nine months and three years old. The kids were carefully selected for their easy-going temperaments, but the team also brought mild sedatives in case the little ones got cranky during their ten-day drive across the United States.

The strike team was quiet, mentally walking through the plan as they held the babies. The perfect plan created by Tariq. All eleven of them looked upon him with love and adoration for what he was about to do for them. Lying in the grass, chest pressing one of the two-year-olds up and down while the toddler laughed and laughed, Tariq was smiling too. But not at the child. It was the image of the thousands who would die while the entire world watched in real time that made his lips curl up. Tariq's smile broadened a bit more as he pictured how he was also going to kill John Bishop.

Even though it was cool and cloudy, more and more day hikers and tourists were arriving at the scenic park. Many people smiled, waved and said good morning to the large gathering of calm and committed terrorists relaxing in the grass before they headed off to New York to commit mass murder.

CHAPTER 28
THE TEAM

Djibouti, Africa

Camp Lemonnier, Combined Joint Task Force-Horn of Africa (CJTF-HOA)

"CAN'T BELIEVE IT'S ninety-five degrees in November," Felix said as they waited for their ride outside the single terminal building at Djibouti's Ambouli International Airport.

"Be happy that it's November, Cat. This is cool and comfortable compared to July," John said.

Bunny nodded his agreement and said, "Summers here are no joke."

"We did SEAL sniper training here one summer," Christmas added. "One of our guys almost died from lying prone out in the heat all day."

Their ride, a dusty and dented white Toyota minivan, pulled up in front of them. They stowed their gear in the back and the four of them climbed in through the sliding doors that opened on both sides. It was only a four-minute drive to

Camp Lemonnier and it took longer than that to get past the Marine Security Force at the camp's main gate.

Lemonnier is the US military's only permanent base in Africa, and John, Bunny and Christmas had all spent time there in the past, either training or launching ops from the five-hundred-acre camp into Somalia, across the Red Sea into Yemen, and even farther points north, into Iraq, Kuwait and Syria. Felix had never been on an active military base before and he couldn't keep the excitement out of his voice as they drove through it.

"What's all the shooting?" he asked, hearing the crack, crack, crack of multiple weapons being fired in the distance.

"Gun range," Bunny said.

"So cool that you guys got to do all that Army shit… I mean, not the getting shot at and the killing people stuff, but just the training part. Getting to shoot all those weapons must be fun," Felix said.

"The Army has a way of sucking a lot of the fun out of it," Bunny said.

"How?" Felix asked.

"Don't get me wrong, the gun range, the tactical training and all that can be a blast, but unless you're actually *in* combat, you've got to account for every round fired," Bunny said.

"Bunny's right," John said. "When you're done shooting, the team leader shouts, 'Police Call the Range' and everyone has to help pick up thousands of spent casings off the ground. Then we weigh the brass to make sure every single round has been fired and is accounted for."

"Policing the area?" Felix asked.

"Exactly," John said. "And don't worry, we've all seen you shoot, but you're gonna get a crash course in weaponry and we'll be shooting and blowing up a whole bunch of shit together."

"And picking up brass?" Felix asked, smiling.

"That job's all yours, Cat," Bunny said. "You're a newbie on this squad and newbies pick shit up and carry the bags."

"Happy to," Felix said, meaning it. He was eager to prove himself and let everyone on the team know he was there to learn from them. They were the pros and he definitely was the newbie, but newbie or not, he was on the squad and that was all he cared about.

"Just make sure you don't wrinkle my tightey whiteys when you put 'em in my drawers today," Bunny said.

"You want them folded along the shit stain?" Felix asked.

Even Christmas was cracking up from that one.

"We're here," John said as they pulled up to the double stacked CLUs (Containerized Living Units). The CLUs were basically shipping containers made into living quarters, hundreds of them laid out in neat rows. The single stacked "wet CLUs" were for sergeant majors and officers, E-9s and above, with a single bed, toilet and shower. The double stacked CLUs where John and the crew were staying were primarily for NCOs and some senior NCOs, sergeants and higher ranking sergeants, E-5s to E-8s, with two beds in each unit and community toilets and showers.

"Couldn't get us rooms at the ODA Hilton?" Bunny asked.

In addition to the CLUs, Lemonnier had communal barracks for junior enlisted, E-4s and below, and a separate fenced-in compound designated for the Special Forces ODAs (Operational Detachment Alpha), or A-Teams. With so many A-Teams planning and launching ops from Lemonnier into West Africa and Yemen, space was limited, and before leaving the States John checked in with the base commander to see where they could rack out for the night. John had added that he'd be happy to take any bunks that were available.

"Sorry, Bun. No Spec Ops room service for you on this trip," John said.

"Gonna miss the mints under my pillow and the heated towels," Bunny said, laughing.

"Felix, you bunk with me," John said. "And don't touch my underwear… Let's all just dump our gear and head over to the Galley."

Christmas and Bunny had the CLU right next to John and Felix, and after tossing their bags they all headed over to the Galley, Lemonnier's largest restaurant. John spotted the operators from his former ODA, Team Razor as soon as he walked in. CWO Bear Bernstein and Staff Sgts. Bobby Floyd and Mace Hendricks were sitting together at a round table apart from the dozens of other soldiers and civilian contractors who were eating a late lunch.

There were high fives and hugs all around before they all sat down to talk.

"All right Johnny. You pulled us out of combat in Iraq and you guys flew all the way here to meet face-to-face, so we already know it's important," Bear said. "Lay it on us."

"Not in here," John said. What he was about to say was top secret and there were too many people within earshot.

They all walked to the empty soccer field and formed a tight circle.

"Okay, here it is…"

John laid out the proposal. The request that came directly from the president of the United States, the CIA backing, the logistical arm managed by his Uncle Gonzalo's new company and the buy-in from Jeff Stamper. He also filled them in on

Stamper's ties to Caleb Meecham and the threat that the relationship posed for all of them.

"Wow," Mace said. "Just… wow."

"Johnny, you're our brother and you know if you need us we're always gonna be there for you," Bobby said, "but what about…"

"Your military contracts and time towards your pensions remain intact," John said. "I told them that had to be part of the deal. This is classified as a temporary assignment, but still active duty. You'll still be pulling your Army pay, and even though I know money's not a factor here, you're also getting sign-on bonuses and contractor's pay as long as you're on the team… Also, you each have a signed presidential pardon in case we catch any public heat for what we're about to do."

Bear looked at John and then around the circle: "Just the seven of us or are you bringing in more guys?" he asked.

"One or two more would be ideal, but I haven't asked them yet," John said.

"There's a guy on our team you should talk to," Mace said.

"Goh?" John asked.

"Yeah, Chago is definitely one of us and he'd be down for sure," Mace said.

"Okay, I've already read his file a few times and if you vouch for him we can break it down to him and see if he's interested," John said.

"What about Neville?" Bear asked. "He's CA, but he knows his shit and he's a monster in a firefight."

"What's CA?" Felix asked.

"Army Civil Affairs," John said. "CA guys train just like us and they're often the first ones in and some of the last ones out of hostile environments. They figure out who the players are, who the people rely on to solve their problems and who they rely on for essential services."

"Guys like Master Sgt. Neville Martin know the local culture and the economy, and tell us who we should or shouldn't target and what we should or shouldn't blow up," Bear added.

"Sounds pretty badass," Felix said.

"That he is," Bobby said.

"Is he here?" John asked Bear.

Bear nodded. "Saw him this morning, doing PT on this very field."

"Okay, I'll talk to Nev and to Chago, but first I gotta ask…"

"Yeah Johnny, we're in. No matter what, we roll with you, brother," Mace said, speaking for all three of them.

"What's next?" Bear asked.

"Thought it was gonna take at least two bottles of Johnny Walker Blue to talk you into it, so we were planning on leaving tomorrow. Since you're already in we'll all fly back this afternoon. Let's see what your boy Chago has to say and then we'll sit down with Neville, but whether it's seven of us or nine of us, we gotta figure out how to kill Tariq Hassan before he launches his attack."

"And while we're working on that, we also have to take out the Albanian hitman, Connie Belusci, and kill an invisible Pakistani assassin," Christmas said.

"Invisible?" Bobby asked.

"We have no idea what he… *or she* looks like," John said.

"Don't forget the Russians," Felix said.

"Yeah, if you even hear a Russian accent, you'd best shoot first and ask questions later," Bunny said.

"That it?" Bobby asked with a raised eyebrow.

John didn't want to go into the details around Caleb

Meecham and the mob boss in Moscow, Yakov Skobelev, until they were heading home. "There's more, and we'll give you a full briefing on the plane."

"Let's move. Chago's taking a Spanish pause over at his CLU. Let's go wake his ass up," Bear said.

The team split up. Christmas, Bunny and Felix went back to the Galley to get sandwiches, cold sodas and hot coffee while John and the rest went to find Chago. Sgt. Goh was sharing his two-man CLU with Mace and when they got there, John, Bear, Bobby and Mace crowded into the tight space. He was already awake, sitting on his bunk, using a sharpening stone to put a razor's edge on his MK3 combat knife.

After the introductions, John got to the point and broke it down for him. They all stood there waiting while Chago continued sharpening his knife and thinking it over.

"Why me?" Chago asked.

"They vouched for you," John said, waving his hand towards Bear, Bobby and Mace. "And so did the CIA's Deputy Ops… soon to be the new Director."

"For real?" Chago asked.

Johnny nodded and said yeah.

"Okay, fair enough, but it sounds like there's two sides to this deal," Chago said.

"How so?" John asked.

"The first target, Tariq Hassan. That's a no-brainer. He's heading to my hometown to kill civilians. I'm in all the way and I pray I'm the one who puts two in his dome… But… all those other targets you mentioned… Aren't those personal vendettas against you and your family? No offense, but we just met. I mean, I know who you are and coming from NYC, I know your uncle's rep, and again no offense, but you're asking me to risk my life for a family feud."

"None taken, sergeant," John said. "If I were you, I'd pass too. We're facing multiple threats, some national, some are absolutely… more personal, and we're outnumbered and outgunned. Honestly, you'll be a lot safer on the front lines back in Mosul."

"Pass? Who said anything about passing? I just wanted a clear picture of what I'm signing up for. Hundred percent, I'm in," Chago said.

"There it is," Mace said and gave Chago a fist bump.

"Why'd you make the man sweat like that?" Bobby asked.

"Hey! No, I didn't mean to…"

John held up his hand like a stop sign. "All good, bro," he said. "Glad to have you aboard. Pack up. We're heading to the airport in two hours."

"Packed and ready, sir," Chago said.

"Don't call me sir! I work for a living!"

"You got it," Chago said.

Bunny asked around, tracked down Neville Martin and brought him back to Mace and Chago's CLU. There wasn't enough room for all nine of them to talk inside, so they headed to the community room and asked the two sergeants who were shooting a game of pool if they could have the room for a few minutes to talk privately. As soon as the sergeants left, John made his third pitch of the day.

Never Say Nev was wearing camo cargo pants, Army desert boots and a beige tee shirt. Born and raised in New Orleans, he was tall and wiry with a narrow Clark Gable mustache and had an ever-present smile that showed off a chipped front tooth. He looked white, but came from a motley mix of French, American Indian and West African roots. He talked like a gang banger from the 9th Ward, which was where he was from and maybe in part to disguise how "wicked smart" he was. Nev spoke five languages and was one of the most competent soldiers John had ever served with.

"My brotha, what you need ole' Nev for? You got enough killas right cher' to take out an army."

"We're gonna be working in some hot zones that you know better than any of us, Nev," John said.

"I hear you, J dog, but first we gonna double tap some fools coming at you and your peoples, is that right?" Neville asked.

"That's it. Know it's short notice, but we leave in an hour," John said.

"Damn son, not givin' me much time to ponder..."

Nev looked around at the team and said, "Okay, I guess they call me Never Say Nev for good reason. I'm down. Let's do this."

There were handshakes, high fives and daps all around. When Nev got to Chago he stuck out his hand and said: "I finally get to meet the unicorn."

"The what?" Chago asked.

"The *unicorn*. Been hearing about the badass dude from NYC who climbs buildings like Spider-Man, don't miss when he shoots, and speaks twenty languages. You's a living legend, son," Nev said.

"Someone's been telling you some tall tales, master sergeant. I'm just another door-kicker. Only thing special about me is I like soy sauce on my cheeseburgers," Chago said, smiling before he turned his head slightly towards Bobby and winked at him.

"If you were just an average door-kicking Joe you wouldn't be here, my man. Look forward to rolling with you," Nev said.

"Likewise," Chago said.

"Let's move out," John said. "Nev, you're the only one who needs to pack. Twenty minutes?"

"Make it ten," Nev said.

On the Gulfstream flying back to New York, John went over the threats in more detail and asked the team for their thoughts on how to face them. The Q&A lasted three hours before John yawned, then tapped out to get some sack time. He tilted his leather seat back and was snoring lightly a few seconds later.

Felix was exhausted and tried to sleep too. Tried, but couldn't get himself to go down. He got up and walked to the service bar, where Nev was filling a mug with steaming black coffee. Felix waited his turn, and then poured one for himself.

"Never heard of Civil Affairs before John told me about you," Felix said. "How long you been in?"

"It'll be twenty years next March," Nev said.

"Wow. That's amazing. So, CA. It's kinda like Intelligence?"

"All the SOCFOR branches specialize in unconventional warfare," Nev said and Felix noted that the ghetto slang was now gone while Nev continued… "That's why we live in the vills and hang out in the hood with the locals. Instead of trying to win hearts and minds we try to change perception whenever we can. That's always our first option…When that don't work we give 'em option two."

"What's that?" Felix asked.

"Let them know that we can fuck 'em up and wipe 'em out anytime we want to, but we'd really rather not."

"Damn," Felix said.

"We do a lot of PSYOPS…Psychological Operations, too. You know what the most successful PSYOPS missions ever executed was?"

Felix shook his head and said he didn't.

"In your family's home country. Panama. 1989. The invasion was basically over and Noriega was bunkered up in his palace with a bunch of his most loyal personal guards. Bush One wanted him alive and we weren't allowed to blow up the palace, so we figured how to get him to come out."

"How?" Felix asked.

"We knew ol' Pineapple Face hated rock 'n roll so we surrounded him with the biggest speakers we could find. Blasted his ass with heavy metal tunes instead of metal shrapnel."

"You're shittin' me," Felix said.

"True story," Nev said. "Google it. He surrendered twenty-four hours later and none of our guys got hurt."

"That's insane!" Felix said.

"Guns N' Roses should've won a Nobel Peace Prize for their part in it. We played 'Welcome to the Jungle' at least fifty times… Noriega chose life in prison over ever hearing that tune again."

After a good laugh Felix said, "Doubt there's gonna be much PSYOPS here."

"Doubtful, but you never know… Either way, I'm a fair hand when it comes to gun work," Neville said.

Felix knew it wasn't an idle boast and that Neville Martin, like every other soldier on John's hand-picked team, was a trained and seasoned killer. He went back to his seat, closed his eyes and thought about how much work he had to do.

A CA master sergeant, a Navy SEAL and half a dozen Green Berets? How am I gonna keep up with these guys? Felix thought. *You're gonna watch, listen and learn… and make damn sure you don't do anything stupid that gets any of these war heroes killed.*

CHAPTER 29
CHECKPOINTS

THE HIDDEN COMPARTMENT in the floor of the RV was a tight narrow space, and Tariq and Marwan barely fit together inside it. They lay on their backs, shoulder to shoulder, hip to hip with their noses brushing the carpeted roof of their coffinlike hidey hole. They felt the vibration from the feet of troopers stepping up into the RV and walking across the floor inches above their heads.

This was the third checkpoint they'd come to and although the local police, state troopers, FBI and highway patrol officers were on high alert, they weren't prepared to rip up the floorboards of every one of the thousands of mobile campers that were heading east across the country. Even if the officers initially came in prepared to do thorough inspections, the scenes they encountered inside this set of vehicles definitely put them at ease.

Inside each of the four RVs that were traveling together were three American moms. All of them wore small wooden crosses tied with string around their necks, and they each held an infant on their lap while they sang gospel songs. There were also boxes of bibles placed on the floor above Tariq and

Marwan that the Jihadists handed out to any officers who came inside or stood by the door.

This inspection went just like the first two: a quick glance around followed by a few "sorry to bother you, folks" and "drive safe."

"We'll pray for you," Gretchen said from the steps of the RV, holding a two-year-old in her arms as the troopers walked away. "God bless you," she called after them.

When Tariq's caravan of RVs left Seattle they headed southeast, crossing through Oregon, then Idaho and Wyoming before heading farther south into Colorado. They stopped for several days outside Denver at the Colorado chapter of the Jesus Loves You Christian Mission, where they mingled with the other jihadists posing as missionaries. Tariq had anticipated that vehicles with Seattle plates or worse yet, stolen plates, heading to the East Coast might draw unwanted attention to them, so they switched to another set of RVs and six cars that were all legally registered in Pennsylvania, Maryland, New York and New Jersey.

The cars were the scout vehicles. Each car had one of his men and a woman in the front seats and a baby in a car seat in the back. Tariq had two of the six cars traveling a few miles ahead of him along the main route, making sure the road was clear. Two more were heavily armed follow vehicles driving in the slow lane a few miles back and ready to charge up and engage officers if his RVs ran into any trouble. The last two were his roaming patrol cars, traveling along the secondary routes in case the main caravan needed to get off the highway.

They all communicated using smartphones that were all legally purchased by the American jihadists who remained invisible to the CIA, NSA, FBI and Homeland Security terrorist hunters. Even though the phones were clean, on the off chance their calls were somehow randomly monitored, they talked freely and openly, using a simple code about the health of an aunt, cousin or grandparent to notify each other of police activity or checkpoints ahead. So far the warnings had given Tariq and Marwan plenty of time to climb down into their hidey hole before any officers got close to the lead RV.

Once they were waved through the checkpoint, Tariq and Marwan waited patiently for a few miles until the boxes were moved out of the way, the rug was pulled up, the floorboards were removed and helping hands reached down to pull them out.

"Well done," Tariq said to them all when he got to his feet.

Tariq stretched deeply, careful not to lose his balance from the gentle rocking of the RV as he touched his toes and then lifted himself and extended his arms straight over his head.

"All vehicles are safely through the checkpoint, Tariq," Gretchen said with a smile.

"Excellent," he said, and then asked, "I wonder how many more we'll have to pass through before we reach our targets?"

"At least three more, but probably more like five," said Michael, the 24-year-old radicalized American with red hair and freckles who was driving.

"Five more would be a lot," said Gretchen. "Then again, if they're checking vehicles going west to east, the closer we get to the targets, the more frequent the checkpoints," she added.

"I don't think so," Tariq said.

"Really? Why?" she asked.

"It is easier to have these... *choke points?*" Tariq asked.

Gretchen confirmed it was the correct term with an approving smile and an eager nod of her head.

"Making the choke points here in the country, on the big highways, this is more easy, but not so easy to choke in the big cities. Once we are closer to our targets, we will have more safety," Tariq said.

Gretchen ignored his poor phrasing and again nodded her agreement.

"Once again you're right, Tariq. Creating checkpoints in and around the cities would mean delaying truck deliveries of necessary food and equipment, and more importantly making commuters late for work. Business owners would flip out and there would be a media frenzy," Gretchen said.

Tariq nodded, but didn't add that he had backup plans in place in case they encountered roadblocks at any of the numerous routes into the cities. Instead, he stretched again and said:

"I'm going to sleep for a few hours."

He headed to the RV's back bedroom and paused in the doorway. Without looking back he said, "Come, Gretchen."

She smiled greedily, handed the two-year-old baby boy to Marwan, then hopped up and walked quickly past Tariq. She pulled off her jacket and tee shirt and tossed them both on the floor before Tariq could slide the accordion door closed.

Tariq wasn't sure how long he slept, but he felt refreshed when the door slid open and Marwan came in.

Instantly awake and on his feet, Tariq asked, "Another checkpoint?"

"No, Tariq. We are here," Marwan said.

"Here? Where?" Tariq asked, a little confused.

"Outside Philadelphia," Marwan said.

"What? How? How long did I sleep?"

"About nine hours," Marwan said. "The roads were clear and you needed to rest," he added.

Tariq nodded, slightly annoyed that they disobeyed his order to wake him.

Did I give them an order? he asked himself. *No, I only said I was going to sleep for a few hours. That is not an order.*

He went into the bathroom, relieved himself, then washed his face and hands before brushing his teeth. When he stepped back out into the RV's combined dining and living room area, he felt a sense of pride when he looked upon the members of his team whom he had trained so relentlessly. They stood facing him, waiting for his orders.

"You have all done your duty and done it well. We have come far, but we have not yet reached our targets or accomplished our mission. Keep focused and let nothing get in our way during this last phase of the operation," he said.

CHAPTER 30
FELIX

Phoenicia, NY

"CLEAR," FELIX SAID.

"Nice work," John said.

Felix looked back at him and nodded.

The team had been training for three days in their compound in Phoenicia, NY. Most of the training was focused on CQC (Close-Quarters Combat) drills. Kicking doors, clearing rooms, dropping and inserting magazines, with a lot of controlled fire, rapid fire and stress fire shooting scenarios. Then they would shift to the worst case CQC: street fighting with bad guys who were hiding amongst large groups of civilians.

They all *hoped* they'd be able to locate and kill Tariq in an isolated safehouse, but everyone on the team knew that hope wasn't a strategy. With that in mind their training was laser focused on how to prevent or at least minimize civilian casualties in a shootout on the crowded streets of New York.

Before they'd headed to Djibouti, John had placed an order with his Uncle Gonzalo for one hundred fully dressed standing rubber mannequins, seventy men, with the other thirty a mix of women and children. The mannequins were set up in and around the buildings along either side of the main street of the compound, in a toy store, a bar, a hospital, a school and a police station.

The drills were live fire. Felix looked down at the two rubber terrorists he'd just killed, and the three others that John had taken out. This had been the last exercise of the day, and although Felix was going to be in a support role on their planned ops, the team had agreed he needed some trigger time as the first man through the door.

Felix didn't know that Christmas and Bunny would toss firecrackers into the room the moment he stepped into it, but he managed to keep his cool, scan the faces and identify the bad guys despite the noise and the haze of gunpowder rising up from the floor.

In two days he'd killed twenty terrorists and only four civilians. Four was four too many, but the only team members with perfect scores were John and Neville. All the other seasoned soldiers had at least one bad kill on a course that John and Bear had designed to push them all to the limits.

The rest of the team came into the smoke-filled training room and did an after-action review. Christmas, Bunny and Bear each gave Felix a few additional pointers about footwork and lining up angles. Mace and Bobby simply gave Felix the thumbs up sign, and Chago put his hand on Felix's shoulder and said, "Nice work."

"If you remember anything, remember this," John said… "Slow is smooth, smooth is fast."

Neville nodded his head and added, "Felix, you've already been in a few gunfights, you never panicked and I can see how well you move. Didn't even flinch when we hit you with that wildcard with the firecrackers. That's some good shit right there, brotha. Past that, the only piece of advice I can give you is what you kinda already know… Calm wins, bro… most of the time anyway. If you can keep your cool when someone's shooting at you, keep breathing and keep your heart from beating out of your chest while you bring your weapon up and put the enemy in your crosshairs, nine times out a ten you're gonna kill that motherfucka."

"Slow is smooth, smooth is fast and calm wins," Felix said.

"That's it," Neville said.

"Guys, gather 'round," John said.

They all walked over and formed a circle around him.

"Look… With the exception of Chago I've fought and bled with all of you, and I know you all wouldn't have vouched for Chago if he wasn't a top-tier operator."

"What's your point, Johnny?" Bunny asked.

"You've all trained together and fought side by side for years. Felix doesn't have the training or the skillsets. You all know it and I know it, but despite that I added him to the team," John said.

"We trust you," Bear said.

"Not good enough," John said, shaking his head. "Even though he's my cousin, my brother, I wouldn't have him here if I didn't think he could cut it. I've seen him under fire and I trust him with my life, but I don't want any of you to think he's here just because he's family."

John turned to Felix. "Look Cat, we all know you can fight and you're a decent shot, but I want to make a few things crystal clear for you *and* for the whole team."

Felix stood straight and tall waiting for it.

"First. We all know we've got one mission here. Our job is to kill bad guys. Period. But while we're taking these fuckers off the board, we're gonna have to rely on each other so we live and they die. That said, since Felix doesn't have the tactical training and the experience the rest of you do, I want to make it clear that he takes orders from each and every one of you. If one of you needs him to do something you just tell him. Understood?" he asked.

They all said they did.

"Good… Felix? This work for you?"

"Definitely. I know I've got a lot to learn, but I'm no fuckup and I'm not gonna do anything stupid to get you guys hurt. Just tell me what you need me to do and it's done," Felix said.

"That's good enough for me," Neville said.

"Same here," Chago said, looking Felix in the eyes and extending his fist for a dap.

The rest of them nodded their agreement.

"Okay, now that we've got that out of the way let's grab some chow," John said, and led the way to the mess hall.

On the walk over, Felix leaned in and whispered into John's ear. "How was that?" he asked.

"Perfect," John replied. "These dudes are warriors and I didn't want them having any doubts about you."

"Thanks, Johnny," Felix said.

The mess hall, communications center and HQ were all in one location. It was a long rectangular one-story brick building a hundred yards away from the main street, with the taller buildings used for the training exercises. The team walked through the front door and dumped their gear on and around the tables and chairs, and a few couches in the center of the wide open area that was a combo dining and meeting room. They all made their way over to the kitchen that was next to a few small offices and bathrooms at the far end of the structure, and most of them went to the fridge to grab water and sandwiches.

John saw Chago and Mace look at their water bottles and shake their heads. He knew all the guys would love a few cold beers at the end of a hard training day. He'd actually love a few himself, but he wanted them all razor sharp and ready to roll out at any moment. He was pouring coffee when the secure phone on the dining room table started ringing.

Christmas was closest and picked it up and answered it.

"It's for you," he said, holding the phone out to John.

John walked over, spoke for a few moments, then put the phone on speaker, placed it back on the table and told the team to gather 'round. They all sat down as Bishop pressed a button on the phone's main console and a four by six-foot monitor came down from the ceiling. It took another minute to get the video conference up and for Clayton Unser's face to appear on the flat screen.

"Go ahead, Clayton," John said. "We're all here."

"Okay gentlemen, here it is. We caught a break and now we know how Tariq Hassan is getting into the country… *Think* we know, anyway," Clayton said.

"How and where?" John asked.

"The how is pretty fucked up," Clayton said. "Two days ago a body washed up on Baker Beach in northern California. A twenty-eight-year-old Caucasian female who authorities at first thought was the victim of a shark attack…"

"How is she tied to Tariq?" John asked.

"The victim was identified as Melanie Donaldson, from Flint, Michigan. That is in fact her real name. CIA decided to build her creds as a radicalized American around her actual background so the jihadists could easily verify her and her family history," Clayton said.

"How long was she a deep cover operative?" Christmas asked.

"She went under four years ago," Clayton said.

"Her mission?" Neville asked.

"At first she was tasked with penetrating Al Qaeda, and then with the rise of ISIS her mission expanded to include that organization as well," Clayton said. "Her last contact was two years ago. From Syria. She managed to get a message out... said she was trying to join an elite jihadist hit squad that was going to launch attacks outside of the Caliphate."

"Sounds like Melanie had some big brass balls," Bunny said.

"That she did... She's... She was one of the most committed agents I've ever met," Clayton said.

"You *knew* her?" John asked.

Clayton nodded his head solemnly. "I did."

"Very sorry, Clayton," John said... "Is there anything else we should know?"

"Yes, quite a bit actually. We know she drowned. There was saltwater in her lungs, but there were also trace amounts of rust and steel."

"Rust?" John asked.

"Yes, and that leads us to believe she was drowned on a ship, not in the ocean. In a steel drum or some kind of holding tank. Bottom line, she was murdered and then tossed overboard as shark bait. The fact that we found her body and that there was enough of her hands and teeth left to identify her was a million to one."

"So now the question is, how'd she get from Syria to northern Cali?" Bear asked.

"We believe ISIS has established a pipeline. Not confirmed yet, but indicators are that they're funneling hit teams through Turkey to Central America. From there they travel by boat… Gulf of Mexico, up the Pacific coast and into Vancouver."

"How do they cross into the US?" John asked.

"Just walk right in. There's a lot of big forests up there. National parks that overlap each side of the border," Clayton said.

"Shit," John said.

"Yeah, that sums it up," said Clayton. "We think Tariq and an unknown number of bad guys walked into the country near Seattle, Washington. We also have to assume there are *actual* radicalized Americans, both men and women traveling with him on their way to New York."

"How do your analysts think he's getting here?" Neville asked.

"Our assessment is that Tariq and his team are driving cross country. We know what he looks like and there's no way he'd risk public transportation. We're dropping a net on the East Coast. We've already got multiple checkpoints at every highway from Chicago to Jersey," Clayton said. "We may get lucky and grab him up at one of the choke points, but we're talking about millions of cars and trucks. Unless he's sitting in the front seat with his burnt-up face looking out the window, confidence is pretty low that we'll spot him."

"Any chatter about chems or biologicals?" Christmas asked.

"Negative. There's zero chatter and that's got us all really nervous. It's never been this quiet… Ever," said Clayton.

"What the fuck is he going after? I mean, besides Johnny," Bear said.

"John's the only confirmed target. We're going through hard and soft target analysis and running simulations 'round

the clock, and we just can't agree on a location. We've hard-
ened security at all the New York power plants and reservoirs,
as well as all the symbolic sites… Statue of Liberty, Empire
State Building, 9/11 Memorial and the Freedom Tower, but
beyond that we just don't know."

"Since I'm the only confirmed target, we'd better make
me easy to find," John said.

Everyone nodded their heads in agreement, and John
suggested that they all move to his Uncle Calixto's Long Island
estate to be closer to the city.

Clayton liked the idea and added: "We can have one of
our news affiliates run a story on you. Say you've been a recluse
at the estate since your father-in-law's death, but that you
visit his grave every weekend… Something like that, anyway.
It won't be headline news or anything too obvious. We'd just
want it popping up as the most recent hit in a John Bishop
Google search."

"Makes sense," Christmas said. "And even if Tariq doesn't
bite, we may be able to take some Pakistani and Albanian contract killers off the board as a consolation prize."

They all knew Christmas was talking about Omar, the
Tringa assassin who came from Pakistan, and Connie Belusci,
the Albanian contract killer who was hired by Mike Meecham
and now worked for Meecham's son, Caleb.

"Probably see some Russians tryin' to crash the party
too," Bunny added.

"John, we all know there are a bunch of really bad people
gunning for you. Do what you've got to do to eliminate them
and protect your team. That said, Tariq Hassan poses a grave
and imminent threat to our country and thousands of innocent people…"

John was about to speak. Clayton held up his hand to

stop him and said, "I know you already know that, but with everything that's happened and everyone that's coming at you, the president asked me to repeat this message to you word for word… 'Your only mission right now is to eliminate Tariq and his entire network. Kill them all and make them disappear. If the world finds out that ISIS has successfully sent a team from Raqqa into the United States and even one civilian dies, then you and your team will have failed.'"

Everyone around the table made eye contact with one another. They all knew what was at stake. Failure was not an option. They were the tip of the spear, ready and eager to hunt and kill the enemy.

"Message received, Clayton," John said. "We've already started specking out our plans for when we get eyes on Tariq, and we'll go over them again factoring in what you've just told us. We'll pack up tonight and head back to the city in the morning… Anything else?" he asked.

"One last thing. You remember that request you made?" John said he did.

"It's approved. Does he know?" Clayton asked.

John shook his head and said no.

"Then I'm happy to be the first to tell him… Felix?"

"Yes sir?" Felix asked, a look of confusion on his face.

"By order of the president of the United States, you've been granted a full pardon," Clayton said, holding up a letter in his hand.

"What?… But, how?" Felix asked.

"Ask your cousin. He'll fill you in. Your felony conviction has been vacated and all your records are officially cleared. You can vote and legally own firearms. Check your email. A copy of this letter and your full carry permit are both in your inbox. We'll get you the originals, but you're covered for now."

Despite his best efforts to hold it together, Felix couldn't stop himself from tearing up. He and John got up at the same time, walked around the table towards each other, both with their arms outstretched. Hugging each other tightly, in that moment they both briefly flashed back to the night of John's eighteenth birthday. A night that radically changed the course of both their lives when four college kids attacked them.

The biggest and strongest of the group had picked up a bottle and smashed it over Felix's head. John charged in to protect his cousin, and after exchanging a few quick jabs he connected with a powerful uppercut to the jaw. It was a knockout punch. Unconscious as he fell backwards, the college kid cracked his skull on the crown of a fire hydrant and died in the street. The cousins took off running, but Felix was apprehended by the police and then quickly confessed to the crime to protect John and the Valdez family.

The day Felix went away to prison, John walked into an Army recruiting station and signed up.

"Thanks, Johnny," Felix said. "Thank you so much."

John kept his hand on Felix's shoulder when he pulled back, so he could look his cousin in the eye when he spoke.

"You gave up nearly five years of your life for me, Cat. I'll never be able to repay you for it, and getting your record cleared doesn't come close to making up for the time you lost."

Felix, always ready with a snappy comeback or a quick joke, had no words. He was also very aware of the other guys at the table. He knew there was no shame in showing his emotions, but he didn't want to be breaking down in front of them either. He blinked a few times then looked up at John, their matching yellow eyes locked, both understanding the moment.

Felix nodded, thanked Clayton and asked him to convey

his gratitude to the president, then walked towards the bathroom at the far end of the building. When he got there he closed the door, turned on the tap and splashed cold water on his face. Seeing himself in the mirror, he smiled and pumped his fist.

When he was arrested 14 years ago, he didn't hesitate. He knew he was going to take the fall and protect John the moment the cuffs went on. Time in a cage completely sucked, but the reality of life after prison was hard too. His felony conviction had affected so many areas of his life, and now that his record was washed clean, he felt he could finally start living again for the first time since he was a teenager.

When he got back to the table, Felix kept quiet, listening and taking everything in while the experts around him discussed several different scenarios for killing or capturing Tariq and his team of terrorists. They ate cold sandwiches while they worked and three hours later they called it a night.

John and Felix were sharing a room in the bunkhouse that was right next to the main building. The cinderblock walls, concrete floors and steel doors made it feel more like a bunker than a bunkhouse, but the mattresses were thick and comfortable and the water in the showers down the hall was piping hot.

Felix could see how exhausted John was. He knew his cousin was trying to manage everything and keep everyone alive while doing his best not to think about Maria. For the past few nights they lay across the room from each other while John pretended to sleep. Felix didn't say anything. Knew his cousin wasn't ready to talk about it, so he maintained the silence and forced himself to stay awake until John's breathing got deeper and he finally went down.

Tonight was different. Felix watched John stow his gear,

take off his boots and drop heavily onto the bed. Still fully dressed, seconds later he was snoring lightly. Felix moved quietly. He grabbed a towel and walked down the hall to the showers, where he got undressed and let the overhead water jets pound down on him, washing the day's dirt into the drain at his feet.

Fifteen minutes later, he stepped out of the showers. Barefoot, wearing blue boxers, and carrying his clothes and boots in his hands, he froze for a split second when he saw Omar standing outside John's room. The moment of shock was gone and he charged forward, dropping his clothes as he ran down the hall.

Omar watched him come. She stood there motionless until Felix was right on top of her. He never saw her move. Wasn't sure how he went from running to lying on the floor looking up at her. Knew he'd been hit. Didn't know where or how. Felix knew he was about to die, but wasn't thinking about himself as she hovered above him.

"Please don't kill him, Omar. Johnny's a good man," Felix said. "Take me, but please don't kill him."

Chapter 31

Omar

SHE GOT LUCKY. With no sign of John or Felix since the funerals for Benji Medina and for John's father-in-law, Alastair Williams, Omar had been casually observing the movements of Valdez soldiers around the Lower East Side. There was nothing unusual until two days ago, when she saw a group of Valdez men packing up several SUVs with boxes of food and water.

Walking between them, she fell dramatically off the curb, dropping her bag of groceries. Oranges rolled into the street, and none of the men who helped her up noticed it when Omar placed a GPS tracking device under the rear bumper of one of their cars.

An hour later when they drove off they made a solid attempt at detecting any surveillance by splitting up, repeatedly changing direction, and suddenly stopping to observe the cars around them. Watching the convoy use counter-measures from a distance with the GPS tracker on her dashboard, Omar knew they would lead her right to John. Following them from two miles back, they took her north all the way up to the compound in Phoenicia, and she spent the first day and night in the woods making wide arcs around the fenced-in property deciding how and when she would get inside.

Omar liked the woods. It was a calming place that took her back to her childhood and the very beginning of her training. Just five years old, she spent months walking barefoot with her new Tringa master on the long journey from southern India to his home in Pakistan's northern mountains. Each day had been a lesson. The months on the road with her teacher were happy times for her. That was the early and gentler stage of her new life. Before the deadly aspects of her training began when she learned to survive each day, day after day, for the fifteen years it took her to become a true Tringa assassin.

Her years of training—and all the lives she'd taken since she left her mountain home as Omar at age twenty—felt like a lifetime ago. She knew that her teacher and all the others were dead. She and David Tringa were the last of their kind, and the family legacy that had thrived for over a thousand years was now over.

Where does that leave me? she thought.

Just six months ago, the Afghan warlord Aziz Khan sent her from his headquarters in the mountains of Khost to New York to kill his nephew Amir Khan and John Bishop. She'd cut off Amir's head at the Con Edison power plant on East 14th Street, where Amir had been holding John's wife hostage. Omar was about to take Bishop's head as well when Felix cracked her skull with a metal pole, and then John's friend Bunny shot her in the chest.

During her months of recovery, she'd been singularly focused on completing her mission and killing John, though she still wasn't sure about Felix and Bunny. Killing them would be something more personal than fulfilling her contract and restoring Tringa honor. The two of them had interfered with her mission and delayed the inevitable, but she decided that as long as they didn't get in her way again, she would give them both a pass.

Omar knew something was different... that she had somehow changed over the past few weeks. A year ago, even a month ago she wouldn't hesitate to take a life. Now there was a part of her, some unknown voice inside her, that was actively thinking of how to avoid it.

She initially felt it during the weeks she spent reading and sipping tea in the East Village restaurant, Café Mogador. There was a kindness there that was almost contagious. Everyone who worked in the café was thoughtful and caring, and for the first time in her life Omar went from feeling proud of being the most lethal assassin on the planet to suddenly seeing herself as a soulless monster. That feeling grew stronger when she saw John outside his father-in-law's building after the murders, and again when she saw him at the funerals. He looked so broken that she actually thought about walking away and letting him live.

Walk away to what? she thought. *I am Omar. Omar is all I'll ever be...*

No, an unfamiliar voice said, *in this world you can become anything or anyone. The old man taught you more than just how to kill. He showed you the world...*

The voice was right. The majority of her daily training involved combat skills, mastering multiple martial arts disciplines and weaponry of all kinds, but at night the "old man," her Tringa teacher, sat her down at an ancient wooden table in his tiny cabin high in the mountains. There he taught her about the world. They studied history, literature, the arts, languages and even cooking.

Get a job. Start with something simple, the voice said.

Welcome to Café Mogador. I'm Omar, the legendary Tringa assassin. How would you like your eggs?

Omar smiled for the first time in a very long time at her joke. Then she shook her head, as if the physical movement would clear her mind and silence the voice that was making her so uncomfortable.

"Focus," she whispered as she moved forward into the compound.

The middle-aged widow disguise she wore on the drive up was in a hidden compartment in the trunk of her car, and she was now dressed in her fighting gear…

All-black running suit, black socks and sneakers, her long dark hair pinned up inside a black ballcap, her hands covered with thin black gloves that had a soft layer of padding over the knuckles and a deadly layer of molded titanium sewn in over that. Fifteen feet of black nylon rope was wrapped around her waist, a silenced .40 S&W Beretta Px4 subcompact with an extra mag was nestled under her left arm in a custom-made shoulder holster, and a curved short sword similar to the one she used to decapitate Amir Khan was in a thin scabbard and sling that held it down her back, tight against her body. Four razor-sharp throwing knives were concealed on each of her forearms, and in the narrow leg pouches of her track suit she had several wads of C-4 and separate detonators in case she had to blow a hole in something.

Omar easily defeated the compound's security measures, bypassing the exterior motion sensors and cameras. The property was encircled by double hurricane fences topped with concertina wire, so she moved quickly to the fifteen-foot-high main gate. The gate was made of two wide double steel doors that opened outwards to allow vehicles large and small to go in and out, with a guard tower on each side.

The only part of the outer defense without razor wire, Omar quickly climbed over the gate and then scaled the guard tower on her right. The sentry was up and alert, scanning the area below him with NVGs (Night Vision Goggles). He never saw her, never heard her... didn't even sense the blow coming from her right hand that hit him in the back of the head and turned his lights out.

Omar hit him with a short jab and pulled the punch just enough to put him to sleep, but not hard enough to do any permanent damage.

You didn't kill him? Why? she asked herself.

Omar didn't wait for an answer. Ignoring the ladder, she jumped down from the gun tower platform, landing silently on the cement twenty feet below. Hustling now, she ran to the second tower on the other side of the main gate. Launching herself upwards, she grabbed the top rung of the permanently imbedded steel ladder and brought her legs up and around like a pole vaulter to land feet first on the platform.

The Valdez family sentry either heard or sensed something behind him and turned towards her as she took two quick steps to close the gap between them. The guard was a bit out of shape—that was why she'd taken out the other one first—but this one's reflexes were faster than she expected. He managed to get his sidearm, a black .45 SIG P227, out of the holster on his right hip and raise it towards her in one swift and practiced motion.

Slicing down with her curved short sword, Omar rotated the blade at the last second and smacked him in the right hand with the flat of the sword like a Catholic school nun reprimanding a kid by rapping him on the knuckles with a ruler. The "reprimand" shattered the bones and knuckles in his thumb and index finger, but she'd purposefully hit him with the flat side of the sword to avoid severing his hand altogether.

The guard's eyes bulged from the shock and pain. He looked down at the SIG that hung limply from his broken fingers, and reached for it with his left hand. Omar stepped closer, reversed the sword and hit him in the forehead with the hard leather-wrapped steel hilt. She held him as he sank to his knees, and then she gently laid him down so he wouldn't split his head open on the edges of the metal wall. She then checked his hand, felt the broken bones, did her best to reset them with a quick pull and some pressure, then ripped his shirt to make a tourniquet to hold the bones in place.

A lifesaver and a medic? the voice said.

"Shut up," she said softly, then went down the ladder like a fireman, sliding along the side-rails.

Moving silently through the compound, she hid in the shadows when three more heavily armed Valdez soldiers walked right past her towards the main building. She heard them laughing and arguing over who was going to get the last of the roast beef sandwiches, and who was getting stuck with ham and cheese. Once they went through the door, she made her way along the main path to the bunkhouses.

There were four of them. Cinderblock and concrete one-story buildings in a neat line, forming a T at the end of the path that ran the length of the compound. Omar had no way of knowing which one John was in, so she followed her gut and went into the second door from the left.

Inside, there was a long hallway with two rooms on either side of it, and the bathroom and showers at the far end. She heard the shower running and saw that three of the doors were closed, so she went to the room whose door was cracked. The lights were out, but there was enough of a glow bleeding in from the hallway that she could see in.

There he is.

She padded in and stood over him. John Bishop. The man she swore an oath to kill. The only target who had ever survived her attack.

John opened his eyes, blinked once, thought he was dreaming before he realized that Omar was in fact standing over his bed. He'd looked up at her like this once before... when she'd tried to cut his head off. Felix had saved his life when he busted her head open and then John had stabbed her multiple times in the legs from his prone position.

"How're your legs?" he asked.

"Better," Omar said. "Took a few months."

"Felt my blade scrape bone. Thought you were gonna bleed out," John said.

"Between the cuts and the .45 Bunny put in me, I almost did," she said.

John looked at the sword Omar held in her right hand, the tip pointing down towards the floor.

"Got yourself a new one," he said, nodding towards the blade. Felix still had the sword she dropped when Bunny shot her six months ago.

Omar didn't say anything more. Her mind was racing. Part of her, the voice of the Tringa assassin, the only voice she'd known for twenty-five years, demanding that she raise the blade and kill him. Another voice, this new voice, telling her to let him live and walk away.

John wasn't sure what she was waiting for. Her dark eyes drilled into his, but he had no idea what she was thinking or what she was going to do. Determined to die on his feet, he held her stare as he lifted his head off the pillow and slowly eased himself up.

Her move was so quick he barely saw it. No time to react. Using a Dim Mak pressure point strike, she hit him with two extended fingers on her left hand. The blow hit John just below his ribcage on his right side, instantly paralyzing him. He couldn't move, couldn't breathe and felt himself falling back down onto his pillow and losing consciousness. Omar reached out and touched his neck, applying just enough pressure to put him to sleep all the way, but not enough to permanently damage John's carotid artery.

"I can't do it," she said to him as she placed the sword back in its sheath and swung it back over her shoulder.

Omar placed her hand on John's chest. Felt him breathing.

Who are you? a voice inside her head asked.

I don't know… but I can't be Omar anymore.

She stepped into the hallway and saw Felix coming out of the shower room in his underwear, carrying his clothes and boots in his hands. She saw the fear in his eyes… Not for himself, but for his cousin.

That's love, she thought as she watched Felix toss his clothes aside and charge down the hall towards her.

She waited for him to get close, then reached out and touched him with the same index and middle finger Dim Mak attack she'd used on John. She wanted Felix to stay awake, so she hit him with a much lighter pressure point strike. He was flat on his back, his eyes pleading as she knelt over him.

"Please don't kill him, Omar. Johnny's a good man," Felix whispered, barely able to talk. "Take me, but please don't kill him."

"I won't," she said. "I'm breaking my oath and letting

him live. You have nothing to fear from me now… but David Tringa is hunting him, and David will never stop until John is dead and Tringa honor is restored."

"What does he look like?" Felix asked.

Omar reached into one of her leg pockets, took out a photo and handed it to him.

"He's a master of disguise and he'll pick a spot that you least expect," she said.

"You swear Johnny's alive?" Felix asked, still not sure he could believe her.

She held out her hand. Felix was still shaky from the two-fingered strike, and extremely wary of grasping the hand of the woman he'd seen cut a man's head off in front of him just a few months ago before she'd nearly killed him and John.

"Fuck it," he said in resignation, not sure if she was toying with him yet keenly aware that if she wanted him dead, he'd already be gone. Felix reached out and grasped Omar's hand. He felt her strength and power as she effortlessly pulled him up off the floor, and then they walked together into the room. Felix stiffened when he saw John unmoving on the bed, and he tensed further when Omar placed her hand on his shoulder.

"I hit him just a little harder than I did you," Omar said softly. She was so close Felix could feel her breath on his ear and neck.

"Don't worry, he'll wake shortly," she said.

He turned to face her, staring into her dark almond eyes, taking in her high cheekbones and cupid lips. She was just as beautiful as the first time he'd seen her… and he knew just as deadly. He looked up at her hairline below the black baseball cap and saw a long thin scar at the top of her forehead from when he cracked her with a steel jack handle the last time he saw her. She'd already been bleeding badly from where John had stabbed her multiple times in the calves and thighs before Felix had cracked her head open, but if Bunny hadn't shot her in the chest a moment later, Felix knew she would've killed him for sure.

Omar reached out and gently ran her fingers over the scar that ran horizontally across Felix's right cheek.

"I'm sorry about your face," she said. He got the scar when she threw a knife at his head.

"It was the leg that gave me the most trouble," he said. She'd thrown a second blade that lodged deep in his quad, barely missing his femoral artery.

She looked down at his hairy leg and the scar on his thigh, but didn't say anything. Both of them aware for the first time that they were having a casual conversation while Felix was standing there half naked.

"Will I see you again?" he asked.

She was about to say something when they heard footsteps hurrying towards the bunkhouse and men shouting. She grabbed his wrist and pulled him close.

"You're very brave, Felix, but don't fight David. He'll kill you for sure. Also, there's a big man in the woods. He's watching you from over a mile out."

"Connie?" Felix asked.

"I don't know him, but he's big and bald," she said.

Connie Belusci, Felix thought.

"He's a hitman," he said. "Shoots people from long range. Killed my uncle six months ago," he said quietly, thinking of his Uncle Sesa, who was still on life support, but died the moment Connie shot him in the head at the family's Long Island estate.

"Sorry," Omar said. "If this is the same guy he seems

pretty incompetent. He's moving around a lot…making lots of noise. I heard him from half a mile away."

Strange, he thought, then quickly dismissed it.

"Thank you," Felix said, then leaned in and quickly kissed her. "You better go," he said.

Omar nodded, then came in and kissed him back. They held it this time, their bodies pressed together wanting it to last. Then they pulled apart, stared into each other's eyes for a moment and smiled.

"To be continued," Felix said.

"Yes," Omar said, unsure of why her heart was beating so fast.

Felix led her out just as all three doors opened and armed team members burst into the hallway.

"What the fuck!" Bunny shouted, bringing his HK .45 up and angling for a shot at her.

"No!" Felix said. "Back the fuck off! She's helping us."

Felix pushed Omar behind him while Bunny, Neville and Bear moved towards them with their pistols up. Chago, Mace and Bobby hung back, each looking for a clear shot with their MP7s. Felix saw what they were doing and moved his body back and forth to shield her.

"Helping? We've got two men down at the gate!" Bunny said.

"I didn't kill the guards and I don't want to hurt your friends," she whispered in Felix's ear as they kept backpedaling together towards the showers.

"Where the fuck is Johnny?" Bunny shouted. "Johnny!!!"

John stumbled out of his room, still off balance and disoriented.

"Thank God," Bear said.

Bunny grabbed him, put his arm around John's shoulders

and pushed him back, shielding John with his own body. Then Mace and Chago ran up and did the same.

John's head was clearing… just not enough to understand what was happening.

"Let him go, Omar. You're not here for him," John said, as he held out his hand and Chago passed him his Colt 1911 .45 sidearm.

"You don't get it, Johnny," Bunny said. "He ain't a fucking hostage. He's protecting her."

"What? Felix, what're you doing?" John asked.

"Johnny, you know she could've killed us both," Felix said. He held the photo up to show everyone. "She gave us a picture of David Tringa and she just told me that Connie Belusci is outside waiting to bushwhack us."

"Where?" John asked.

"North-northwest on a high hill in the tree line over a mile out," Omar said.

"You can't fucking trust her," Bunny said.

John wasn't sure what to do. He knew Felix was right. She let him live, but what if it was some kind of trick? Or what if not killing him was just a whim and she suddenly changed her mind again?

Felix wasn't backing down. "Look, guys, I know this is one of those crazy moments in life when the world turns upside down and nothing makes sense, but nobody's shooting her today. You understand?"

"Okay, Cat, we get it," John said.

"Guns down," Felix said. "I'm walking her out."

They all lowered their weapons and stood against the walls on either side of the hallway as Felix led her by the hand. She nodded at John and Bunny when she passed them. Everyone on the team noticed when Felix and Omar made a subtle switch from him simply holding her hand to the two of them intertwining their fingers as they walked out the front door.

"Couldn't make this shit up if you tried," Bunny said.

Felix came back five minutes later, his arms crossed, rubbing them with his hands to warm himself from the night chill. The team was still standing where he'd left them. No one knew what to say.

"Are you guys dating?" Neville asked, breaking the awkward silence.

Felix shrugged. "I have no idea."

"No doubt she's the most pulchritudinous chick I've ever seen," Neville said.

"Pulcri what?" Chago asked.

"*Pulchritudinous*," Nev said.

"The fuck is that?" Christmas asked.

"Means she's a fine-ass woman," Nev said. "You don't know, you better ask somebody."

"Yeah, ask who? Fuckin' Google?" Chago asked.

Bunny wasn't having any of it. "You realize she fuckin' decapitates people," he said, looking at Felix as if he was a crazy man. "In the long list of relationship dealbreakers, isn't that number one? My girl is really cute, but she wilds out every now and then and cuts someone's fuckin' head off with her sword."

"There's that," Chago said. He shivered dramatically, then rubbed his throat with his right hand.

"People change," Felix said.

"Yeah, everyone does have a past," John said… "and we've all done some shit in life we seriously regret, but head chopping assassin? C'mon, Cat."

"Gotta say, her name's a close second to head chopping on *my* dealbreaker list," Christmas said. "My girlfriend Omar?

Not sure I could say that out loud." He kept his eyes down when he said it. Knew if he looked up at Felix he'd start laughing, and it was going to be really hard to stop.

Felix shrugged again, then walked over to John, stopping in front of him.

"Dude, we really need to talk," John said.

"Yeah, we do, but we're gonna go kill Connie first," Felix said.

John nodded. "All right. Gear up and let's get eyes on that Albanian motherfucker."

John and Felix went back to their room so Felix could get dressed and they could both throw on some body armor and cold weather gear, and gather their weapons. John reached down for his MP7, grabbed it by the barrel and almost lost his balance.

"You okay?" Felix asked.

"Your girl kicked my ass with two fingers," John said, holding up his index and middle fingers. "Did it casual, too. Like, she just kinda flicked me in the side and I was fuckin' paralyzed. Then she did it again to my neck and I was out cold. She scares the shit outa me, Cat."

"You and me both, brotha," Felix said. "Didn't even see her move and she put me on my ass, paralyzed just like you," he added. "Honestly though, the fact that she didn't kill us both is the best news we've had in a while. Means she kinda likes you... and of course she's got the full-on hots for me."

John knew his cousin was smiling, but kept his back to him while he put on his tac vest and loaded the ammo pouches with extra magazines for his MP7 and his SIG. When he finally turned around, Felix was waiting there with the same goofy grin he'd had since they were kids.

"Bet she's walking through the woods singing right now," Felix said, smiling.

"*Singing*? Singing what?" John asked.

Felix held his arms out wide and his body started swaying:

"Felix, Iiii… love you… you know I do… love you mooore than you'll… eeever know… baby, that's fo' sho'…."

"You're such an asshole," John said, cutting him off.

John tried to fight it, then smiled back at Felix for a second before they both started laughing.

It was the first laugh they'd shared since Alastair and Benji were murdered and Maria left. Once they started up, they couldn't stop. They were both doubled over and howling when the rest of the team came to the door.

"Glad you two are enjoying yourselves," Bunny said, his brow wrinkled, trying his best to be angry without anything behind it.

John exhaled deeply, wiped his eyes and got himself together. Looked back at Felix and busted out all over again. Bunny and the rest of the team were in the room now, all of them standing there belly laughing over John's close call with death at the hands of Felix's head chopping new girlfriend.

CHAPTER 32
CONNIE

Phoenicia, NY

THE COMPOUND WAS originally built by a Neo-Nazi survivalist/paramilitary group that was cooking and selling meth to finance its end of the world arsenal of weapons and ammo. It wasn't until after the FBI, DEA and ATF jointly raided and busted the whole operation that the network of underground tunnels was discovered. Most of the tunnels went out a few hundred yards into the surrounding woods to allow shooters to pop up behind anyone attacking the compound, but two of the tunnels were escape routes that ended a few miles away at the base of the nearest mountains.

John and the team used the tunnel network to go under the bunkhouse and come up through a stairway that led them into the main building. They stood around the same round table where they had the conference call with Clayton Unser just a few hours before, now studying maps and high res photos of the area where they figured Connie Belusci was hiding out.

"Omar said he's north, northwest, which would put him right here," John said, pointing to a photo that showed a high hill just over a mile from where they were standing. "That's the only spot within maximum gun range."

Bear frowned at the photo. "Can he even see us from there?" he asked.

Connie's hill was heavily wooded on the side facing them, and inside the fenced-in compound the Neo-Nazi meth dealers planted a ring of high trees to prevent any prying eyes from seeing what was going on inside their HQ.

"Good question. Bobby, this look right to you?" John asked.

Bobby Floyd was one of SF's best trackers. He grew up hunting in the mountains of Kentucky and had a knack for finding bad guys and sniffing out danger. Bobby, along with his friend and partner Able Diaz, used to be the Team Razor comedy duo. The two of them never shut up and through the toughest times they kept everyone laughing, but after Able was killed in action six months ago, Bobby changed. Still the same guy, only a lot quieter. He'd laugh at someone else's jokes, just didn't make many of his own anymore. The team knew he was still grieving and they were doing everything they could to help him work through it.

"No, it ain't right. Ain't right at all," Bobby said, picking up one of the maps and scratching his chin as he scanned it. "Why would he camp out there?" The question more to himself than anyone else.

"You know, Omar said he was moving around on the hill and making lots of noise," Felix said. "Why would Connie do that?"

"Setup?" Neville asked.

Bobby looked at Neville and nodded his head. "For sure," he said. "We know Connie's a long-range shooter so he wouldn't waste his time in a spot without clear sightlines."

Another chin scratch, followed by a finger snap. "Here!" he said, putting the map back down on the table and pointing to a mountain that loomed up behind Connie's hill.

John came around behind Bobby to get a better view and leaned in to see. There was a flat treeless side on the knoll of the hill where they thought Connie was hiding. You couldn't see it from the compound, but anyone on the slopes of the mountain behind the hill would have a clear unobstructed view of it.

"Whoever's up there on that hilltop is a patsy. Bait to draw us in so the *real* Connie, and probably a few more shooters, can pick us off from behind as soon as we get to the ambush site," Bobby said, his finger tapping the hill on the map and then moving to the elevated slopes of the mountain looming half a mile behind it.

"This motherfucker shot our uncle and got a lot of good men killed when he set us up with the Russians," Felix said. "I get that he's on the high ground waiting for us. So, how do we kill him?" he asked, looking at each of the combat veterans around the table.

"He's expecting to see us on the hill," John said. "Not on the mountain."

"He picked a good spot though," Bobby said. "Guarantee you he's on this plateau about a thousand feet up. It's a pretty steep incline, so climbing up in the dark ain't gonna be easy and the mountain itself is surrounded by open fields… A lot of flat ground. Gonna be hard to sneak up on him."

John smiled. "He doesn't know about our tunnels, though." He leafed through the papers on the table until he found the map of the tunnel system and laid it down next to the topographical map of the area.

"Wait…does this tunnel exit right below the plateau?" Bobby asked.

Everyone crowded in to see.

"Damn right it does," Christmas said.

"Looks like we're gonna pop out about five hundred feet below him, so we've gotta be stealthy on our approach," John said. "Assume Connie's got several guys up there with him, and if they hear us coming they'll be shooting down at us from the high ground,"

"I've still got bullet fragments in me from when Connie backshot me in Barcelona a few years ago," Christmas said. "Can't wait to put this motherfucker down."

Bunny gave Christmas a dap and nodded. "Let's do it," he said.

"Okay. Here's how we're gonna do this," John said…

He broke the team down into twos. When they exited the tunnel, Mace and Chago would go right to flank Connie and his men, while Bear and Bobby would go left to get above the plateau. John and Bunny were going to take a straight line up the slope while Christmas and Neville trailed 50 feet behind them.

"Where do I go?" Felix asked.

"We need you to carry this pack, and when we get there I need you to stay at the tunnel's entrance," John said, handing his cousin a small camo backpack.

Felix felt his anger rising, but put himself in check. "What's in here?" he asked, hefting the backpack that was surprisingly light, only weighed a few pounds.

"Pressure packs, bandages and morphine. We need you ready to help evac the wounded in case any of us gets hit," John said.

"You don't think?…"

"This is combat, Cat. Every man here is praying that we all come back safe, but war is a motherfucker. That's why we train our asses off to be the best and at the same time be prepared for the worst."

Felix nodded, glancing around the table at the seasoned soldiers. None of them spoke. Their eyes said it all.

"Anything you say, Johnny. Just tell me what to do and it's done," Felix said.

SF Staff Sgt. Mace Hendricks had been quietly taking it all in. He was in complete agreement with the mission and John's tactics. There was one thing bothering him though:

"How does everyone know where we are?" he asked.

"I was thinking the same thing," Chago said.

"I mean, Omar showed up and walked right into our camp, and Connie's out there waiting to ambush us," Mace said. "How'd they find us?"

"They must have tracked the guys coming up here from LES," John said… "And that's on me. I've been so eager to go on the hunt, I dropped the ball and forgot there's a whole lot of professional killers hunting us too. I'm sorry for putting you all at risk."

"Don't beat yourself up, Johnny," Christmas said. "I didn't think of it either."

"None of us did," Bear added.

"Maybe we should just hang out here and wait for Tariq, ISIS and the Russians to join the party," Bunny said, which got everyone laughing again.

"Okay, grab water, armor up, do a weapons and radio check, and make sure your NVGs are working," John said. "We'll move out in ten minutes. Add another fifteen to walk through the tunnel and we should be on target at 0100."

They were jacked up and eager to get moving as they did their standard PCC (Pre-Combat Check) of everything they'd need in a firefight.

John walked back over to Felix and handed him a Red Bull.

"Thanks, but I really don't drink that stuff," Felix said.

"I don't care for it either," John said, still holding the thin blue and silver can out towards his cousin. "You've been going hard all day. None of us have slept, you're still on an Omar adrenaline rush, and we're about to take a two-mile hike. Believe me, you don't wanna be coming down when we go at Connie."

Felix reached for the can and mentally scolded himself for not taking it right away.

John and all these guys know what they're doing. Don't get cocky, he thought.

"My bad. Thanks, J," Felix said.

John put his hand on his cousin's shoulder, gave him a squeeze, then turned away to make the final preparations and to make sure everyone else was locked in.

Like Green Beret Staff Sgt. Bobby Floyd, Connie Belusci had been raised as a hunter. His father and grandfather regularly took him deep into the Albanian forests for days at a time as soon as he was old enough to walk. Over the years his time stalking animals in the woods helped him develop his PPQ philosophy when it came to hunting and killing men. Preparation… always be prepared for the worst-case scenario. Patience…be patient and eventually the target will make a fatal mistake. Quiet… train yourself to sit in silence for days at a time. Preparation, Patience and Quiet…PPQ.

Connie's daily mantra helped him become a top-tier operator in the German Special Forces, Kommando

Spezialkräfte, and later when he was recruited by the German Federal Intelligence Service, the Bundesnachrichtendienst, as a covert assassin. Once he realized there was a lot more money in private contracting than in government-sanctioned wet work, he went out on his own and his PPQ helped propel him to the top in the competitive world of murder for hire.

For this operation he had the first P covered. He prepared meticulously, studied the terrain and arranged his team of snipers on the mountain so they had the hilltop completely covered. Connie's lookalike was a dim-witted baldheaded bouncer from a bar in Brooklyn. He paid the big dummy fifteen hundred bucks to sleep on the hill with a long-range rifle for two days and nights.

It was the second P in his PPQ, patience, that he was running out of.

How long is it gonna take John and his merry band of fuckups to see a six-eight knuckle dragger walking around a mile away from them? Connie thought.

He couldn't make it too obvious, but he'd grown so frustrated that he had the guy shaking bushes and doing everything short of building a bonfire to get their attention. If there was no movement tonight, Connie was going to have his stooge fire a few rounds at the compound at first light. Even though the bouncer was a puncher, not a shooter, gunfire in the morning should drive Johnny and his team to the killing ground.

Connie leaned against a boulder thirty feet back from the edge of the plateau. His Accuracy International L115A3 long-range rifle was covered by a waterproof gun slicker and cradled in his arms like a baby. He looked up at the night sky and the thunderheads that blocked out the stars. Figured the temp was below 40. Too warm for snow. Cold enough to make it suck for night hunters like him and his crew when the sky took a piss on them. Thought about checking his iPhone to see when the rain would start, then pictured his grandfather silently shaking his head in disgust.

Imagine that tough old hawk looking at a phone to check the weather, Connie thought.

He felt the night chill on his face, but the rest of his body was well-protected. He wore a heavy sweater under his body armor and a lightweight all-weather parka over that, and thermal leggings under his pants that were tucked inside his shin-high mountain boots. Connie heard the first drops bouncing off the leaves in the trees behind him the same moment he felt the rain hitting his camo colored baseball hat.

He looked around at the four shooters he had positioned on the plateau. The four of them were closer to the edge. They had their gear at their feet and their long-range rifles resting on several chest-high boulders that were perfect shooting stands. They were all professionals, all ex-soldiers from eastern Europe, and Connie knew a bit of weather wasn't going to bother them. Still he made a mental note to give them each a bonus when the job was done and they got back to the city.

He stood up and stretched, pulled his hands behind him and rolled his shoulder blades down to open up the muscles in his neck and upper back, then hopped down into a pushup position. Held himself there for five seconds then slowly lowered himself until his nose touched the short grass, and held there for another five count. Repeated it 49 times, working the massive muscles in his arms and shoulders and keeping his mind sharp.

Fifty pushups can cure just about anything, he said to himself. *Tired? Get down and do fifty. Angry? Fifty. Hungry? Fifty. Your girl left you? Fifty…*

He was just getting started on his *fifty list* and wiping his hands on his pants legs when he glanced over at the silhouette of the Ukrainian member of his shooting team who was positioned on the far right of the plateau. Connie saw the man's head move unnaturally to the side a second before he slumped forward onto his shooting stand.

Connie dove to his left just as a high-velocity round pinged off the rock he'd been leaning against. He felt a sting in the back of his neck as he reached for his rifle with his right hand, missing it as he dove behind the boulder. He pulled his Beretta M9 out of a leg holster strapped to his right thigh, and a second later he was up and running hunched over through the thick brush between the trees.

He didn't bother shouting a warning to the others, and didn't look back to see if any of them were still alive as he ran. Connie had already processed what happened… He knew John and his team had somehow made their way up the hillside and ambushed him.

Connie ran flat out. Felt the guns tracking him and heard the rounds hitting all around him while he scrambled higher, charging through the thick brush towards the secondary position he'd set up just in case everything went to shit…

Preparation.

He saw it. Ten feet away. Took two long strides and was reaching out with his free hand to pull himself over the natural rock wall when he felt a hard slap in his side above his left hip.

"Motherfucker," Connie said as he dove over the wall and landed in a heap at the bottom of the pit he dug out two days ago. He knew he'd been hit, but there wasn't time to assess the damage. He moved quickly, unzipped the matching gun carry bags leaning against the interior wall, pulled out the MP7s, slapped in the magazines, and then reached down into a separate canvas bag and grabbed four M67 fragmentation grenades.

"Supper's ready," he said, baring his teeth to push away the pain in his side that had gone from a dull ache to a white-hot burn.

Connie glanced down at his wound. Couldn't tell in the dark how bad it was, but the searing heat that was spreading across his stomach and the wetness in his groin told him that blood was flowing steadily. Just a few more minutes. If he could quickly kill a few of Johnny's crew and hold off the rest, he'd have time to tend to his wounds.

Connie felt them coming. Even though he held the high ground in a fortified position, he knew he was outnumbered, and in a killing game like this, numbers mattered. He figured they'd take their time and surround him and then lob grenades over the wall. That was all it would take to end it.

He closed his eyes to help him concentrate and visualize the land around him.

Bishop and Christmas won't be crashing through branches and bushes like I did, Connie thought, feeling the scratches on his hands and face for the first time. *They'll be coming in stealthy, sneaking around the boulders and hiding in the tree line.*

Connie smiled. He mentally mapped the distance to his targets, then squatted down so he was well below the lip of the rock wall. He pulled the pin on the first grenade and made a high arcing throw to his left and then grabbed a second one, yanked the pin and chucked that one to his right. There was a two-second delay between the explosions, followed by a scream.

"Gotcha!" Connie said as he reached for another pair of M67s and sent them sailing out into the night.

CHAPTER 33
LOSSES

Phoenicia, NY

BOBBY ASKED JOHN if he could take point. John just shook his head and said no. They'd all fought together in the past, and Bobby definitely was the best tracker in Special Forces, but John knew this op was different. Chago's comment when they were back in Djibouti was spot on. Tariq Hassan was a madman. A terrorist coming to America to slaughter as many innocent men, women and children as he could and going after him was a no-brainer. This fight with Connie Belusci on the other hand… This was far more personal and no less dangerous. John wasn't about to do anything reckless, he was there to kill Connie, not the other way around, but he'd be leading from the front and was going to do everything he could to protect his team.

The tunnel was well lit, the floor flat and dry, so they moved fast for the first mile, jogging single file with John in front, Bunny on his six as always, followed by the rest with Felix as the caboose. The tunnel steadily angled upwards the closer they got to the mountain, and John slowed the pace down to a fast walk. When they made it to the end, they used hand signals to communicate down the line, and each of them pulled down and activated their NVGs a second after John pulled the handle on the breaker switch to turn off the overhead lights.

John climbed halfway up a six-foot ladder positioned below a three-foot by three-foot trapdoor in the ceiling, then slid the four locking cross bars made of rough cut rebar out of their holes and passed them one by one down to Bunny. He tested the door's hinges to make sure they didn't squeak and then slowly let the door swing down, careful not to let it slam against the tunnel's wall when it was fully open.

Dead leaves and twigs cascaded down through the hole as John took another cautious step upwards. Leading with his MP7, he did a thorough scan of the area before climbing out of the tunnel, then moved a few feet away and aimed up the hill to cover his men as they followed him into the cold wet night.

The lower slopes of the mountain were densely forested with white pine, birch, maple, red and white oaks, ash and even a few pockets of hemlock trees, so there was plenty of cover for the four two-man teams. Years of training and countless missions taught them all to use the land to their advantage. Despite the steady rain there was still a thick noisy layer of dry dead leaves on the ground, especially around the oak and maple trees, and as they split up they instinctively walked on the soft and silent pine needles below the evergreens wherever possible.

John raised his hand to hold everyone in place and then pointed to Mace and Chago, using hand signals to have them move out to his right. Mace and Chago, call signs Bravo Five and Bravo Six, had the longest route to the top, traveling below the plateau to come up through the woods to the right of Connie's forward-facing positions. John directed Bear and Bobby, Bravo Seven and Bravo Eight, to move left and make their way to the high ground in the trees above the plateau.

He held himself, along with Bunny, Christmas and Neville for several minutes until they all heard the whispers in their earpieces:

"Five and Six in position," Mace said.

"Seven and Eight in position," Bear said.

"Good copy," John said. "Bravo One and Two moving up," he added, aiming up the slope as he headed up towards the plateau with Bunny three steps behind him.

Christmas and Neville watched John and Bunny advance, covering them from below for a ten-second count, then followed them up the hill, fifty feet back.

"Three and Four moving up," Christmas said.

John and Bunny were just below the crest of the hill when Bear gave them a SITREP:

"One this is Seven. We have eyes on three shooters spaced twenty feet apart to your right. No sign of Connie yet, over."

"Bravo Five to Bravo One. Confirmed. We have sights on three standing snipers and the fake Connie on the hill below us, over," Mace said.

"This is One. Take them now," John said.

"All four targets are down," Bear said. "Seven and Eight moving higher," he added as he ran behind Bobby up the mountain through the tree line.

As soon as he gave the order, John raised his head and his sound-suppressed MP7 over the top of the hill, got a glimpse of a big guy with his back against a rock formation about fifty to sixty feet back, and fired a three-shot burst just as Connie rolled to his left.

"I see Connie. He's heading up through the woods right above you, Bravo Five," John said as he ran.

"This is Five. We're moving up through the trees at your 3 o'clock, Bravo One," Mace said.

John and Bunny ran forward with Christmas and Neville behind them. When they got to the rock where John spotted Connie, they saw a sniper rifle lying in the grass. Neville picked it up, quickly fieldstripped it, taking out the bolt action and the ammo, and then tossed it aside.

They heard him now. Crashing through the brush and trees higher up the slope. Then there was silence. Nothing but rain drops and their own breathing.

"Listen up," John said into his mic. "He's found a hole and dug in. Careful now. He's close. We've got his long gun, but assume he's still got weapons on him."

"Copy that," Bear said over the radio and Mace repeated the confirmation a second later.

John pointed to Christmas and Neville and using hand signals, instructed them to move to the left and then head up. They spread out and the four of them moved up the hill with John in the lead, cautiously quick-stepping with their guns up searching for a target.

They'd gone about thirty feet when the hair on the back of John's neck stood up a second before he caught a glimpse of something sailing through the air.

"Grenades! Cover!" he shouted as he dove behind a fallen tree.

The explosions hit with a wump, wump, in quick succession, followed by a scream.

"Who's hit? Who's hit?" John said, not realizing he was shouting into his mic.

Two more grenades blew, rocking the ground and shaking the trees. Leaves and branches came down all around them.

"Shit," Bear said. "Bobby's down."

"Fuck! How bad?" John asked.

There was a five-second pause when everyone knew Bear was checking Bobby's wounds.

"Not good," Bear said.

"I'm okay," Bobby said. "I can still fight."

"Bullshit," Bear said. "I'm bringing him down. Bravo Nine, have that med kit ready."

"This is Nine. I'm coming your way," Felix said.

"This is One, everyone pull back out of Connie's throwing range," John said.

"One this is Five," Mace said over the radio. "Connie is holed up twenty meters above you. Looks like a reinforced foxhole. Stay put, we're gonna frag his ass."

"Do it," John replied just as the dark clouds dumped their loads. The rain went from a light drizzle to a torrentially loud downpour. The driving rain muted the sounds of the grenade blasts but John, Bunny, Christmas and Neville all felt the vibrations.

John aimed up the slope, scanned above and said, "Five, we're heading up. Don't fuckin' shoot us."

John knew he had to calm himself. His heart was beating out of his chest and his mind was racing, wondering how badly Bobby was injured. When an SF operator says a wound is "not good," it usually means it's fucking awful. John slowed his breathing to get himself to calm down and compartmentalize what he had to do. Bear was taking care of Bobby and

Felix was on his way to help. John's and the rest of the team's job was to take out Connie.

The rain suddenly slowed back to a light drizzle when they approached Connie's foxhole from three sides. They scanned for the slightest movement through their NVGs, and each of them tracked the red dots from the CCOs (Close Combat Optics) on their MP7s, hoping to use the targeting system to put one in Connie's head.

John used hand signals to warn everyone not to peek over the walls of the three-sided defensive position, in case Connie survived the grenade blasts and was lying in there playing possum. Christmas, John and Neville reached their MP7s over the chest-high rock walls and fired into the hole, just as Mace swung around from the one open side of the foxhole and tore up the interior with several bursts of 4.6x30mm.

"Clear," Mace said. "He ain't in there," then quickly turned to face the woods thirty feet behind him.

"Shit," Christmas said.

John ran forward. He sprinted towards the trees, the team following close behind, instinctively spreading as they moved. They all stopped just inside the tree line, searching for any movement and listening for any manmade sounds.

They were at the top of the small mountain now, looking down the gentle slope with only a short-range view…the trees were much bigger and denser on the backside.

John finally found what he was looking for. A blood trail, glowing green and bright through his NVGs.

"There, at my 1 o'clock. Blood trail. Connie's hit. Guns up. I'm on point," he said and started moving forward before anyone could question his decision.

He'd gone ten feet when a woman's voice cut through the silence:

"Stop. Don't take another step."

"Omar?" John asked.

"Yes. You're about to hit a tripwire. The big guy is hit and bleeding badly, but he covered his trail with a line of claymores."

"Jesus," John said, shaking his head at his own stupidity as he backed up.

How did I not think of that? he asked himself.

He knew they all heard Omar's warning and there was no need to tell them all to back up, but he did it anyway.

"Thanks, Omar," John said… "For everything," he added as they backed away with their guns up, still searching for their baldheaded target as they retreated.

He didn't expect a response and wasn't surprised by the silence that followed as they stared out into the trees trying to get a glimpse of her or Connie.

"You thanked her for not killing you?" Bunny asked when they paused and took cover behind Connie's bunker.

John looked at Bunny, shrugged his shoulders and said, "Felt like the right thing to do."

Then he looked over at Christmas and saw his jaw clenched and his whole body rippling with tension.

"I want Connie just as much as you do, Christmas, but we've got to let him go and take care of Bobby," John said.

Christmas nodded. "I know. Just never wanted anyone dead this bad in my whole life," he said.

John put his hand on his shoulder and said, "We'll get him, brother. We'll get him… Now let's go!"

He turned and ran down the hill to get to Bobby, with Christmas and the rest of the team racing behind him.

CHAPTER 34

IT AIN'T ON YOU

THE LIGHT SHINING up through the tunnel's trapdoor was their homing beacon, and the six of them ran and slid down the hill towards it. John was the first man down the ladder and he hustled over to Bear. Bear was leaning over Bobby, who was sitting in a folding plastic chair. Felix was next to Bear, gripping Bobby's hand to hold him steady with his right and aiming his flashlight down with his left so Bear had more than just the tunnel lights to see what he was doing. There was a pile of bloody bandages and pressure packs on the tunnel floor.

As the rest of the team made their way down into the tunnel, John made room for them and edged closer to Bear, but careful not to interfere with the chief warrant officer, who was also a trained medic.

"Pass me the light," Bear said, taking it from Felix.

He shined the bright beam into each of Bobby's eyes.

"Good news is you ain't fuckin' blind, Bobby boy. The shrapnel hit your MP7 and blew up the optics, but as far as I can see you've got nothing in either eye," Bear said, his voice steady and clinical as he gave his assessment. "That's the good news, brother. Bad news is you got a bunch of glass and metal shards in your cheeks and chin, and you lost your left pinky and most of your left ring finger. More good news is that nothing hit you in the throat. The biggest grenade frags hit you in your helmet and your chest armor and none of them penetrated."

John leaned in and saw the blood dripping from Bobby's cheeks and chin and asked, "Are we gonna wrap his face to stop the bleeding before we get him to the hospital?"

"Negative," Bear said without looking at John. "Looks like most if not all of this shit is glass and metal slivers from his gun scope, and the wraps would probably just push everything in deeper and make it harder to get out... Tilt your head back, Bobby."

Bobby did as instructed and looked up at the ceiling. Bear reached into the med pack that Felix had been carrying. It was unzipped and fully opened in a second plastic folding chair next to Bobby's. Bear ignored the iodine swabs that he normally would use to clean a wound and pulled out a bottle of iodine instead. He opened it and told Bobby to close his eyes, then he poured half the bottle down Bobby's cheeks and chin. The rest he poured on Bobby's missing fingers before he wrapped those tightly with bandages.

"Okay," he said. "That'll get us back to base camp." Bear looked over at John for the first time and added, "Then we can either drive him or medevac him in a helo to the hospital for x-rays to make sure I didn't miss anything more serious."

Bobby grinned up at John. A ghoulish red-brown mix of his blood and the iodine dripped from his face as he smiled.

"Who's the fucked-up face guy now?" he asked pointing to John's scar. "You're done, son. The scar face title's gonna be all mine, city slicker, and the chicks are gonna be lined up ten deep to get a piece of this ol' country boy," Bobby said in his deep Southern drawl.

John laughed and said, "Yeah, you earned it, dude. The title's all yours… You gonna be okay walking back to HQ?"

"No sir. We got wheels," Bobby said, pointing with his good hand back down the tunnel.

John forgot about the three bicycles they'd passed on the way out that were leaning against the wall about two hundred yards back down the tunnel.

"Let's do it," John said as Felix helped Bobby up from the chair and onto his feet.

All eight of them watched Bobby closely to make sure he was steady as he moved.

"I'm good, boys," Bobby said.

They all nodded and moved out, Bear leading the way this time with Bobby behind him and John in the third spot. They all noticed how Felix instinctively moved off to the side, then packed up the med pack, slung that on his back, and then grabbed Bobby's MP7 and all his gear before following. Every one of them mentally checked a box acknowledging that although Felix had never served, he was a valued member of the team and he was more than holding his own.

Bear, Bobby and John rode the three bikes in single file down the tunnel, and Bobby did a solid job of keeping his balance while he kept his left hand elevated towards his shoulder and steered the whole way with just his right. The rest of the team jogged along behind the bikes. None of them spoke as they ran.

Every one of them was thinking the same thing: *we got really lucky.*

It sucked that Bobby lost a few fingers and that he was going to be pockmarked for the rest of his life, but it easily could have been way worse. Even though they all knew they were in a life and death war with many more battles to come, this initial skirmish with Connie was a stern warning to all of them about what was at stake here.

When they got back to the compound, Bobby wanted to make the three-hour drive back to NYC so he could get worked on by "real doctors." Bear vetoed the request. He wanted Bobby x-rayed right away and it was only a twenty-five-mile drive from the compound in Phoenicia to the ER at the hospital in Margaretville.

Bear's instincts were right. The x-rays showed forty plus tiny metal shards and glass slivers in Bobby's cheeks and chin, but also revealed three far more dangerous and deeply imbedded half-toothpick-sized steel spikes that had penetrated deep into his left jawbone, and another one that was right below his left eye socket.

The on-call ER doctor at Margaretville had served two tours in Iraq. His last deployment was over a decade ago, and even though Bear, John, Felix and the rest of the team left their heavy weapons and helmets in their vehicles, the doctor instantly recognized the elite soldiers for who they were.

"You boys active duty?" the doctor asked John and Bear as he observed how the other three dangerous-looking men inside the ER were spread out and on high alert, while two more of them were standing outside for perimeter security. The doc knew there was another armed soldier in the room with his patient who had ignored all the requests for him to leave while they examined Bobby.

John stared back at the doctor and didn't answer.

"Okay. I don't know what you're doing way out here and I don't wanna know, but you gotta tell me if my staff and our other patients are at risk. Are my people in danger?" the doc asked.

"There is a bad guy in the area," John said. "He's wounded. Highly doubtful that he'll show up in an ER, but we've alerted state and local law enforcement to cover your facility and all the hospitals within a hundred miles as a precaution."

The doctor nodded and saw the flashing lights from five or six squad cars racing towards the main entrance.

"What's my man's condition? How bad is it?" John asked.

"Serious, but not critical," the doctor said. "This isn't a trauma center, but I can get everything out of his face including the four fragments that are lodged in pretty deep, if you want to keep him here."

The doc held up the x-ray of Bobby's face and tapped the spots that were most worrisome.

"If he's okay to fly we'll get him on a helo," Bear said.

The doc nodded, unable to hide his relief. "As long as he doesn't move his head around too much and you don't wait more than a few hours to operate, that shouldn't be a problem."

"Thanks, doc," John said, extending his hand just as half a dozen state troopers hustled into the ER. They shook hands and then John and Bear walked over to fill the staties in on the situation.

John had called Clayton Unser on the way to the hospital to fill him in, and Clayton then alerted the state and local authorities that there was a group of men working on a mission in their area that had national security implications. He added that the men would remain anonymous, and they were not to be detained or questioned for any reason. Clayton also emailed pictures of Connie Belusci to the state troopers and local police departments. He added a stern warning not to let any of their officers directly engage Connie, or it would result in a lot of casualties.

The Air Force helicopter, a Sikorski HH-60G Pave Hawk, that had lifted off from Stewart Air National Guard base near Newburgh, NY arrived ten minutes later, touching down smoothly on the elevated helo pad outside the Margaretville ER. John instructed Bear, Mace and Chago to fly back to New York with Bobby while he would go with Felix, Bunny, Christmas and Neville to pack up their gear and then drive it all back to the city in the morning.

Bobby refused a wheelchair and the eight of them formed a loose circle around him as they walked him up the ramp to the Pave Hawk.

"See you in a few hours," John shouted over the noise and downdraft from the helo's rotors and twin turbo engines.

"Hang in there, pretty boy," Bunny said to Bobby.

Bobby smiled through the light bandages and the clear plastic bag the doctor had placed over his face like a bandana to help prevent his open wounds from getting infected. He gave Bunny the finger before being helped up into the Pave Hawk by an airman reaching down from the doorway.

John and the rest of the team bent down and hustled back out of rotor range as the helo took off. They all stood watching it for a moment before John broke the silence:

"He's alive. That's all that matters," he said, looking down at his boots.

"Head up, Johnny boy," Bunny said. "Bobby getting hit ain't on you. Don't even think about trying to carry that shit," he added.

Neville nodded and said: "You know he's right, JB. We're

going up against some hard hitters and we need you on point and your game tight."

John nodded and said, "Okay, it's 4AM and we've been going flat out for twenty hours."

"Can't believe we went from shooting drills, to getting our asses kicked by Omar, to a gunfight with Connie, to this," Felix said.

"Don't forget about your presidential pardon and your make-out session with the girl who put you on your ass," Christmas said to Felix.

"Quite a day," Felix said.

"Okay, let's get back to the compound. Mandatory three-hour team nap, then we pack, and then we head back up to the plateau before we drive back to the city," John said.

"To bury Connie's shooters?" Felix asked.

John shook his head no and said, "The security team at the compound already went to the plateau and got rid of the bodies. Our job is disabling Connie's claymores so a family of hikers or some deer hunters don't get wasted when they hit the tripwires."

"Jesus," Felix said. "I forgot all about that."

Neville lightly punched Felix on the shoulder, letting him know without saying anything that he was still new to this and he wasn't expected to see every detail.

When they got back to the compound in Phoenicia, they immediately saw that Gonzalo had significantly increased the security measures. There were at least twenty more armed Valdez soldiers and several dog teams silently patrolling both inside and outside the fence line.

"Doubt Connie is gonna charge the main gate, but we can definitely sack out for a few hours without worrying about anyone getting near us," John said.

"I bet Omar walked right past the dogs and all these guards, and she's snuggled up in Felix's bed waiting for him," Christmas said.

They all chuckled, too tired to give it a real laugh, but when John and Felix got to their room, they both gave Felix's rack a onceover to confirm it was empty. They took off their coats, kicked off their boots and fell onto their beds.

John heard Felix mumble something, looked over at his cousin, and saw that Felix had already passed out from exhaustion.

"Great job today, cuz," John whispered.

He spent the next fifteen minutes doing a mental AAR, reviewing all his decisions during his team's first combat mission. He knew the guys were right. Bobby getting fragged wasn't his fault, and it was dumb luck that he wasn't critically wounded or even KIA. John did recognize that he'd made a major tactical mistake, though. He should have split his team and sent four of them up the backside of Connie's mountain, so they would have owned the high ground and had the big Albanian surrounded.

Would they have hit the tripwires in the dark and been blown away by the claymores? he asked himself. There was just no way to know.

What he did know was that he'd been too eager and way too emotional. Being emotional and anything less than being laser focused would get his team hurt or killed. He wasn't going to let it happen again, and from here on he was going to slow things down and think things through. That was his last thought before he blinked once and then the alarm on his iPhone woke him up three hours later.

They quickly showered, shaved, brushed their teeth, got dressed and had a quick breakfast with strong coffee before they packed their gear, and then headed back through the tunnel and up to the plateau. When they got there they saw that the cleanup crew had done a thorough job of picking up spent shells and disposing of the four bodies.

"Those guys must have used metal detectors to police all the brass," Neville said, as they walked through all the places where shots had been fired.

"Yep," Bunny said. "No other way they could've sanitized this place in the dark."

Even the bunker Connie threw the grenades from was completely clear and empty.

John led the way, with Bunny a few feet back, Felix in the third spot and Neville watching their backs trailing them all. The four of them continued in a staggered line past the bunker and walked towards the tree line on the far side of the bald bluff until John raised his fist. They all froze where they were.

Once they paused, they could hear the large group of men moving slowly through the woods. John had followed up on his assessment of where he'd failed last night and had Christmas lead twenty men up the backside of the mountain. Their job was to make sure Connie wasn't hiding out in the trees trying to get off a last shot before he bled out.

"Two, this is One. In position, over," John said into his mic.

"Good copy, One. We're one hundred yards below the peak. No sign of target," Christmas said.

"Hold your position, Two. I'm heading in to locate the claymores," John said, then turned to look back at Bunny, Felix and Neville and said, "Hold here. I'll be right back."

John moved slowly into the tree line, checking every branch and bush for tripwires. He was fifteen steps into the woods when he found what he was looking for… sort of.

"All clear, guys," he shouted. "Come on in."

He stood in front of a tall birch tree and waited for the teams behind and below him to converge on his position.

"Wow," Bunny said when he got there and stood next to John.

"Nice," said Neville.

"What happened?" Felix asked.

"Looks like your girlfriend left us a present," Bunny said.

Four claymores were stacked at the base of the tree and the disconnected wires hung down from a head-high branch. When they moved forward John noticed a folded piece of paper that was stuck between the claymores. He bent down and pulled it out. After reading it, he handed it to Felix and said:

"It's for you."

The message read:

I tracked Connie to his car. It looks like he's shot in his lower left back above his hip and he's driving a Black Chevy Tahoe- license #ABF 8347

Call me xoxo

John took out his phone, called Clayton, gave him the plate numbers, and asked him to see if the Tahoe showed up on GPS.

Felix handed the note to Bunny, who read it with Neville looking over his shoulder.

"Jesus," Bunny said.

"She's a keeper," Neville said, nodding his head in appreciation.

John's phone vibrated. He saw it was Clayton and picked up on the second buzz.

"That was quick," John said.

Christmas and his team of hunters came through the trees waving hello as John listened to Clayton.

"No way. He's ours. We can't sit back and watch HRT take him down," John said, then listened for another fifteen seconds while Clayton was speaking. "All right Clayton, we're packed and ready. We can be on the road in thirty minutes, but my team is split. Bear, Mace and Chago are in the city with Bobby."

There was another pause while John listened, and then he said, "Understood. Let me know how it goes with Connie."

John hung up and faced all the men, who instinctively made a semi-circle around him while he was on the phone. He first spoke to Chepe, the head of the Valdez soldiers who'd marched up the backside of the mountain with Christmas.

"Chepe, lead your men back to the compound. Leave a few guys and a dog team to guard it in case we need to come back in the next few days, but you and the rest of your men should head back to the city right away."

Chepe nodded in agreement and ordered the sixteen men under his command to move out.

Once they were on their way down the front side of the mountain, heading towards the plateau and out of earshot, John spoke to the four members of his team who stood in front of him:

"Okay, here it is. They found Connie's truck about twenty miles from here. It's a few blocks from a local doctor's house, and the thinking is he's in there getting treated. They're sending in an FBI Hostage Rescue team to take him down."

"Why HRT and not us?" Christmas asked.

"Because there's a lead on Tariq, and Tariq is priority one," John said.

"Copy that," Christmas said. "Hope those HRT boys put a hundred holes in that Albanian motherfucker."

"Where's Tariq?" Bunny asked.

"Philadelphia," John said.

"How're we getting there?" Neville asked. "Philly's gotta be at least a six-hour drive from here."

"Our uncle's been busy," John said, looking at Felix. "We've got our own air force now and our helo is on the way. Bear, Mace and Chago are already airborne, so they'll be on the ground about ninety minutes ahead of us. We'll get more details about his exact location before we get to Philly."

He paused and made eye contact with each of them.

"We know Tariq is here to kill thousands of innocent people. Let's go get him," he said, holding out his fist.

They all touched fists and moved out, hustling back down the mountain as the distant rumble of a helicopter's rotors echoed through the woods.

CHAPTER 35

BULLETPROOF

Washington, DC

PRESIDENT-ELECT JEFF STAMPER sat in an overstuffed leather recliner in the study of his Georgetown townhouse, a lit Perez Carrillo cigar in his right hand and a glass of Macallan Lalique single malt in his left. Stamper's eighty-pound black rottweiler lay at his feet and his personal attorney, Paul Simms, was in a padded wooden chair at his side. Facing them was Damir Goncharov, Russia's US ambassador, who sat on a dark brown and rustic leather sofa.

Damir had always preferred vodka over scotch, but thought he may have to revise his thinking when he raised his glass and tasted the Macallan's smooth delicious flavors.

"My compliments. This is the best scotch I've ever had," Damir said.

"It better be," said Paul Simms, smiling. "That's a twenty-thousand-dollar shot you're sipping on."

"Worth every penny," the Russian said.

"So, Damir, what's this big problem that has you and

your boss all worked up?" Stamper asked, getting down to business. "This about Crimea?"

"No, nothing to do with Crimea, Mr. President," Damir said.

"Not officially president for a few months yet and we go way back, Damir. Call me Jeff... especially when it's just the three of us having a friendly drink by the fire," Stamper said.

"Very well. *Jeff.* Jeff, President Sukov is very concerned about threats coming from one of your citizens against his, umm, family," Damir said.

"Threats against his family? By who?" Stamper asked.

"John Bishop," Damir said.

"What!? Bishop?" Simms shrieked, his voice nearly cracking and his eyes bulging from a combination of shock and anger.

Damir glanced at Simms and nodded his confirmation.

"Who specifically is he threatening?" Stamper asked.

Damir paused for effect. The Russian was a big man at six-four and a hulking two hundred sixty pounds. His intimidating size was just a part of why President Sukov had given him the ambassadorship. Size did matter when you met with smaller men over drinks in smoky back rooms, which was where most of the world's major policy decisions were made. But Damir had also led men in combat, had advanced degrees in psychology and engineering, was a world class poker player, and was the son of a Soviet-era KGB senior officer. He was a skilled negotiator and dealmaker.

"I misspoke," Damir said. "We're way past threatening."

Damir paused again and leaned forward, getting closer to Stamper to emphasize the importance of his next few words.

"You remember your business associate in Moscow?" he said.

"I do," Stamper said.

Stamper actually had a twinge of pride at how he managed to keep his voice flat and steady despite his increased heartrate, and the fact that the temperature in the room was suddenly rising and his skin felt way too warm.

You're the fucking president! Don't you ever let this asshole see you sweat, he thought.

Stamper knew the "business associate" Damir was talking about was Yakov Skobelev. Skobelev had been Stamper's silent partner for more than twenty years in many of his domestic and global real estate deals.

"Bishop has already killed many of Yakov's men in New York, and Bishop's murderous Uncle Nestor has assassinated dozens more inside your prisons," Damir said.

"I had no idea," Stamper said.

Damir ignored the lie.

"Jeff, I have no doubt that you already know this, but I will say it anyway. Yakov is President Sukov's most favored cousin. In truth, they are more brothers than cousins. Your business relationship with Yakov goes back decades, and in truth the relationship has… *expanded…* beyond just business."

Stamper took a sip of his Macallan and then took a long pull on his cigar. He pursed his lips, exhaled a thin gray cloud and then asked:

"Expanded? Expanded how?" he asked as he carefully examined the cigar's ash.

"Let's just say that based on your long-term business relationship with Yakov, you now have friends at the very highest levels within the Kremlin."

Simms was known for his fiery temper, and Stamper raised his hand like a stop sign as his personal attorney and nearly lifelong confidant exploded up from his seat. Simms's face was beet-red and his index finger pointed at Damir like a short-barreled gun.

"Damir, are you suggesting that as president of the United States, I am in any way indebted to President Sukov or anyone else?" Stamper asked.

"Jeff, that is not at all what I'm saying. I am merely emphasizing that we have a longstanding relationship that we believe is both business and *personal* in nature. If we are mistaken in our belief in our friendship, please let us know."

"You are not mistaken, and one of the goals of my administration will be to shift from our two countries being adversaries to strategic and global partners," Stamper said.

"Excellent! Excellent! President Sukov will be very happy to hear this, and he wants the exact same thing," Damir said, smiling. "And as partners, President Sukov is hoping you can be of assistance with this very personal matter… A US citizen is killing Russians on American soil and threatening to kill our president's family members in Mother Russia. What can you do to stop this madness?"

The question hung in the air for a few moments until Stamper stood up and extended his hand. The Russian ambassador stood as well and reached out to shake Stamper's hand.

"Don't worry about a thing. Please tell President Sukov that the Bishop problem will be *eliminated*, and I look forward to meeting him in person next year."

"Thank you Je…" Damir paused for effect. "I mean, thank you, Mr. President, and please let us know when the Bishop situation is permanently resolved."

"Will do, Mr. Ambassador. Paul here will keep you updated," Stamper said.

They shook hands again and then Paul Simms walked Damir out of the room and through the townhouse. Simms returned a few minutes later and plopped down on the couch where Damir had been sitting.

"We're fucked," he said.

"No, we're not, Paul," Stamper said, shaking his head.

"How do you figure? The Russians have a ton of dirt on you. So does Clayton Unser and so does that asshole who's sleeping in your bed at the White House right now."

"I'm surprised you of all people are missing the big picture here, Paul."

"What's that?" Simms asked.

"I was just elected president of the United States. If they'd released their files on me during the primaries or the general election, I would've been done. Glad my predecessor has some twisted sense of morality and held them back, but now it's too late. I'm fucking bulletproof now, and I had to stop myself from laughing in his face when he threatened me with that mutually assured destruction bullshit in front of Bishop at Camp David."

Simms nodded his head. "You're right. You're absolutely fucking right. How did I not see that?"

"You're slipping, Paul," Stamper said jokingly. "Look, we're going to change the game and start making our own rules the moment I'm sworn in. I need you razor-sharp because you're going to be my wartime consigliere."

"I'm on it," Simms said.

"Can't believe they really think I'd even consider giving the CIA to Clayton Unser and NSA to General Palmer. How fucking stupid can they be? We're bringing in our own people, and they better be ready to bend the knee and kiss the ring. If anyone's not on board, I want you to rip their lives apart and utterly destroy them. Understood?"

"Yes, sir," Simms said. "What about Bishop?"

"As far as I can see, John Bishop is our only real problem. Hopefully, he'll do us all a favor and get himself killed trying to stop Tariq Hassan. If he doesn't, we'll have to step in and do it ourselves. One way or another, Bishop is a dead man. Reach out to some of your contacts to give us options and have a team on standby," Stamper said.

Simms nodded, got up and left the room to execute the orders just given to him by America's next president.

CHAPTER 36
BEST LAID PLANS

King of Prussia, PA

AT JUST PAST 4:30PM it was nearly dark when the team's helo landed in a remote field outside Bala Cynwyd, a small town about twenty miles northwest of Philadelphia. Bear, Mace and Chago had arrived a half hour earlier and were already waiting for them, standing next to four dark non-descript vehicles: a Toyota Camry, a Ford Fiesta, a Honda Accord and a Volkswagen Tiguan.

John, Bunny, Christmas, Neville and Felix walked over, each carrying his weapons, ammo and helmet in a black duffle bag. They wore their tac vests and comms gear on the flight south from Phoenicia, and kept them on over their winter parkas.

"Any movement?" John asked Bear as he got within a few feet of the chief warrant officer.

Bear knew that John had been listening in to live updates from the surveillance team just as he had, but didn't hesitate to replay it.

"Heat signatures from the drone on overwatch shows

six tangos inside the house," Bear said. "Two of them haven't moved in over an hour, so they're either napping or they were killed within the last ten minutes, because their bodies are still warm. We've seen movement from the other four and right now they're pretty much stationary in the kitchen area, so they're probably having a late afternoon snack or an early dinner."

"Copy that," John said. "The CIA analysts say all six are males, but can't confirm whether Tariq is one of them."

"How do you want to do this?" Bear asked.

"It'll be full dark in another fifteen minutes, so we'll use cover of night to walk right in," John said.

"Be nice if it was still raining, but even without it we'll get close enough to smell 'em," Christmas said.

For Special Forces and SEAL team operators like Christmas, the rain was an ally. Most bad guys stayed indoors or found shelter from the rain. Even for those targets that stayed on high alert in bad weather, the rain acted as a sound suppressor for these Tier 1 and Tier 2 operators who were some of the most highly trained soldiers in the world. Regardless of the conditions, Christmas and everyone on the team knew they could get as close as they wanted to Tariq and his men. The real challenge was that these terrorists came to America to become martyrs. No one wanted to be standing too close to them in case they were wearing suicide vests and self-detonated.

"We'll observe from a distance before we move in. If there's a real opportunity to creep inside and take one or two of these dudes alive, we'll go for it, but we can't make that call until we're on target," John said.

"Photos show the curtains on two of the downstairs

windows are closed, but three are partially open… probably for them to peek out," Bear said.

"Room enough for targeting. If they can peek out we can peek in," Christmas said.

"Peek in with steel jacketed AP," Mace said, referring to the Heckler & Koch MP7 AP (Armor Piercing) DM11 ammo they would be firing through the windows. The steel encased DM11 rounds traveled at 2,362 feet per second and could penetrate twenty layers of Kevlar from two hundred yards out.

"Roger that," Christmas said.

"Okay, gather round," John said.

He held out an iPad to do a final review of the surveillance photos and mark where he wanted each of them positioned.

"Christmas, Mace, you're our designated shooters. The woods around the house will give you good cover going in, and you should be able to get within fifteen or twenty yards from the target," John said.

Christmas and Mace both nodded and examined the landscape from the overhead photos. They each pointed to a different spot where they would establish their shooting positions: Christmas behind the large barn-like structure in the middle of the big back yard, and Mace in a stand of trees close to the side of the house.

The big barn that Christmas would use for cover may have once held horses, but the horses were long gone and now there were three big RVs parked inside.

Christmas pointed to what looked like a shed or a workshop right behind the house.

"This structure will be my only blind spot from the woods behind the house," he said. "Mace, if any tangos bolt out the back door, that's where they'll go and you can take 'em out from your spot in the tree line."

"I'm on it," Mace said.

"You want me here?" Bear said to John, pointing to the woods across from the main road and facing the front of the house.

"Exactly," John said. "Looks like you'll be about a hundred yards out. You're our overwatch in case our best laid plans go to shit. Assuming everything goes smoothly and once the six tangos are down, the two entry teams will go in. Me, Bunny and Felix through the front door, Chago and Nev go in through the back."

He looked at each of the team members.

"Last thing. Everyone, and I mean *everyone*, wants in on this. Clayton had to meet in person with the FBI and DHS directors to persuade them to let us handle the takedown. His argument was that we'll be sure to keep Tariq, or at least some of his men alive, so we can take them someplace private for interrogation. Last thing we want is for him to lawyer up before we can question him."

"When are the troops gonna sound the bugle and come charging in?" Nev asked.

"As soon as we're on-site there's going to be a couple hundred cops and agents, as well as an FBI SWAT team locking down the area to make sure no one gets out," John said.

"So, they're hanging back to see if we all get wasted before they make their move?" Chago asked.

John smiled. "That's one way to look at it, but we all know that ain't gonna happen. Clayton bought us ten minutes to take Tariq and his team down, gather intel and leave with a few live tangos… Any other questions or suggestions?" he asked.

Everyone was silent.

"Okay. Check your thermal scopes and remember to watch your background so we don't have live rounds flying all over the neighborhood."

They each did a final PCC (Pre-Combat Check) of their weapons and targeting systems before giving a thumbs up.

"We'll separate by teams and take all four cars. Bear, you'll drive solo and follow me, Felix and Bunny. The rest of you will break off and head here to Sweetbriar Park," John said, switching to Google maps and pointing to a dirt road a quarter mile behind the target house. "Then you'll walk in through the woods and take up your positions."

"There's a lot of houses along our walkthrough," Christmas said.

"That's why we're wearing these," John said, pointing to the Homeland Security HSI SWAT patches on the front and back of their tac vests. "If you see anyone along the way, order them to get back inside their homes."

"Copy that," Christmas said.

"Let's mount up and move out," John said.

Bear took the Ford Fiesta, John, Bunny and Felix got in the Acura, Mace and Christmas took the Honda, and Chago and Nev had the Tiguan. They disabled the interior lights and trunk lights in all four vehicles before pulling out behind John's car and heading towards I-76 West. All of them were quiet and focused on the twelve-mile drive from Bala Cynwyd to Tariq's hideout in King of Prussia.

Even though they fought in their first combat mission together against Connie the night before, they all knew this was a different type of fight. As always, last night was a kill or be killed op, but the fight with Connie was compartmentalized and personal. Tariq was different. He was a clear and imminent threat to national security, and his goal was to murder thousands of innocent civilians on American soil. Every man on the team knew what was at stake, and each of them was mentally locked in and eager to kill or capture the ISIS terrorist.

When they took the exit off I-76 onto North Henderson Road, no one in the four-car caravan noticed the gray minivan trailing them. As planned, the two cars with Christmas and Mace and Nev and Chago stayed on North Henderson to come in behind the house through Sweetbriar Park. John, Bunny and Felix took a left onto Hawthorn Road along with Bear in his follow car so they could press their attack from the front of the house.

John and Bear both checked their rear and side mirrors, and noticed when the gray minivan a hundred yards back took the same left onto Hawthorn.

"We may have a tail," John said into his radio.

"I saw it too," Bear said into his.

"Could just be a neighbor," Bunny said.

"Could be, but I don't think so," John said. "Instead of a right on Hansen Road, let's go left and see what he does," John said.

"Roger that," Bear said.

Both cars turned left away from their target. They watched the minivan stop and take a long pause at the intersection before it made a very slow right turn in the opposite direction.

Bunny was monitoring the feed from the surveillance drone hovering high above.

"Yeah, you're right, Johnny. We're blown. There's a lot of movement from all six tangos. They're running all over the house," he said.

"Our best laid plans definitely just went to shit," John said.

"No way they knew we were coming. Gotta be a coincidence, but whoever's in the minivan must have called the house," Bear said.

"All right, team, they're on high alert so we're going in heavy. Christmas, Mace, Nev and Chago… you guys spread out and come in through the park… Make sure you get good triangulation," John said. "And all of you watch out for anything heavy in case they've got RPGs or a .50 cal in there."

"Will do," Nev said over the radio.

John called Clayton, who was standing by at CIA HQ in Langley, VA waiting for a SITREP.

"How's it going?" Clayton asked.

John didn't bother with pleasantries. "They had a spotter car and they know we're coming."

"You standing down?" Clayton asked.

"Negative. We're going in hot and it's gonna be loud so expect a whole lotta 911 calls from the neighbors," John said.

"Not too loud, I hope," Clayton said.

"Our weapons are silenced, but Tariq's won't be. Our goal here is to take them down hard and fast before they can light off any explosives," John said.

"Local police are already moving in behind you and sealing off the area. FBI SWAT is a mile out and ready to back you up if you need more firepower," Clayton said.

"Good. Just make sure the responding officers don't fucking shoot at us. We're wearing HSI patches, but the last thing we want is to see anyone in law enforcement getting hurt because we gotta defend ourselves," John said.

Since it was technically against the law for the CIA to operate inside the United States, Clayton said the local PD and state police had been notified that a Homeland Security SWAT team was engaged in a major takedown. He added that he was also sending in an NSA team to invoke national security protocols and throw a blanket over everything once the smoke cleared.

"John... one last thing," Clayton said.

"We know... You still need a live body for interrogation," John said.

"Yes."

"We'll do our best," John said, then ended the transmission.

He slowed down, made a quick U turn and headed back in the opposite direction towards the house, with Bear following close behind him.

"The minivan pulled into a garage in the house next door," Bunny said, looking down at the live feed from the surveillance drone.

"Shit," Bear said.

"Two houses?" Felix asked from the back seat.

"Looks like it," Bunny said.

"How many heat signatures are you getting from the second house?" John asked.

"We've got three people inside and it looks like they're all standing near the front windows peering out towards the street... Lights just went out in both houses," Bunny said.

They were driving along a dark and isolated stretch of Hansen Road when John pulled over to the right and drove onto a narrow strip of hard packed dirt that had a dense row of leafless bushes alongside it. He killed the lights just as Bear pulled in and parked behind them.

The four of them put on their helmets and checked their NVGs.

John keyed his mic and said, "This is Bravo One. You copy?"

Bravo Five, Six, Seven, and Eight (Nev, Christmas, Mace and Chago) all responded individually, saying, "Good copy, Bravo One."

"Okay, listen up. I'm with Bravo Two, Three, and Four. We're a quarter mile from the two target houses. We are proceeding on foot through the narrow strip of trees along Hansen Road. We'll position across the street from the front of the targets. Once in position we will determine how many tangos we can see with our thermal scopes. I want all of you to do the same from behind and along the sides of the targets. If we get crosshairs on most of these guys, we'll all execute on my command. Understood?"

The team members next to him all nodded their agreement and all the others said either "roger that," or "copy that," over the radio.

"Last thing. Bear's taking the IAR and I'm bringing a few 67s just in case," John said.

The IAR was the Heckler & Koch M27 Infantry Automatic Rifle that fired 5.56x45mm NATO rounds. The IAR was that just-in-case bully gun that once unleashed would make any "ready to die for the cause" bad guy hit the floor, grab his knees, go fetal and start screaming for his mama as soon as the rounds ripped through the walls.

The 67s John mentioned were M67 grenades that he retrieved from the trunk of the car. Bear slung his MP7 behind his back, reached into the trunk and picked up the IAR. He rammed home a 30-round magazine and grabbed another five mags of M27 ammo. Bunny grabbed six more mags for the M27 to back Bear up in the unlikely event the op went longer than expected and they ended up needing more suppressive fire from their big gun.

Except for Felix, all the seasoned soldiers understood that the "just in case" scenario John was referring to was if Tariq and his men had some kind of reinforced bunker in the basement or in a room inside one of the houses.

"We're Oscar Mike," John said, indicating that they were On the Move. "Let me know when you're in position and make sure you watch your asses on your approach to both target houses," he added.

John made eye contact with Felix. Gave him a quick nod and then lightly tapped him, Bunny and Bear on their helmets before turning away. He pointed the index finger of his right hand up to the night sky, made the "wind up" signal and then walked ahead into the tree line. The rest of them knew what to do without being told. Bunny waited three seconds and took up his follow position ten paces behind his team leader, then Felix followed Bunny, and finally Bear moved out last to guard everyone's back.

As John walked through the trees towards Tariq, all his senses were on high alert, his mind focused, but while he scanned ahead for threats he had a brief moment of introspection. He knew he had a gift that few other men possessed. Whether he was born to kill or it was the early traumas of his life that had molded him into who he was, there was no way to know. Either way, his unique ability to navigate a battlefield and terminate the enemy with extreme prejudice was something that made even the hardest of the special operators he'd fought with gape in awe.

He understood it, but he wasn't walking through the woods thinking about what a badass he was. Far from it. He looked inside himself and understood clearly for the first time that he just hadn't been the same since Maria left. The pain of losing her and their unborn child had been a distraction that had dulled his senses and compromised his warrior skillset.

No more, though. He had men's lives in his hands. Men who he was bound to for life. Their bond had been forged in death, blood and fire through their countless operations in Iraq, Afghanistan, Yemen, Syria and in the many central African nations that harbored terrorists. These men were his brothers. They believed in him and they would follow him wherever he led… no matter what the risk.

John knew he couldn't alter the past week. He wasn't getting a redo of last night's fight with Connie or the battle with the Russians at the warehouse in Red Hook. Bobby was maimed for life; Lulu was seriously wounded, and John knew he'd nearly killed his entire team by walking them into the deathtrap of Connie's claymores. There was no going back, but the cloud was lifted and he'd returned to his true self.

John felt a surge of power flowing through him that was more than just a spike of precombat adrenaline. The reconnection with his inner self cleansed him of doubt and sorrow, opened his mind and electrified every part of his body. He returned to who he was. An unstoppable force of nature ready to visit violence upon those who threatened the innocent or threatened his family.

Once again he was the man killer… The yellow-eyed God of war.

CHAPTER 37
BISHOP'S LAW

King of Prussia, PA

JOHN FELT THE change in temperature and guessed it must have dropped five or six degrees since they landed at Bala Cynwyd less than 45 minutes ago. The wind ripped through the trees, shaking branches, rattling bushes and swirling the dead leaves off the ground. All that blended into a loud crackling chorus that sang of the death of fall and the deep barren chill of the coming winter.

Bishop was glad it was windy, dark and cold. If it were a warm summer afternoon, there probably would have been a horde of neighborhood kids bike riding or scootering along Hansen Road, and he would've had to tell the team to stand down. As it was, the streets were completely empty.

The two target houses were a bit isolated from the other homes along the street, and John figured that was probably why Tariq picked them as safehouses. The nearest neighbor was about a quarter mile away, and that house had a long driveway and a big front yard that made the distance to the actual residents even farther.

Despite being isolated, Tariq and his crew had managed to draw enough attention to themselves that somebody saw something and said something. When Clayton briefed John and his team on the way down from New York, he said that an anonymous call came into a tip line about strange comings and goings and the arrival of an unusually large number of cars and a caravan of RVs. That tip hadn't galvanized the county Sheriff's Department to investigate, but it did set off a minor alarm bell at the NSA, whose supercomputers were monitoring every phone, website and database in the US and hundreds of millions more around the world.

The minor alarm got a lot louder after an NSA analyst got curious. The analyst followed up by calling her brother-in-law, who was a light colonel at Dover Air Force Base in charge of the Air Force's Remote Early Warning Reconnaissance and Surveillance Systems. Remote meant drones, and Dover kept hundreds of them in the air at all times. The surveillance drones combined with the high-flying AWACs (Airborne Warning and Control systems) aircraft provided a 24-hour-a-day layer of protection along the East Coast of the United States against threats from both land and sea.

Dover was only eighty-eight miles from King of Prussia, PA and the colonel readily agreed to task a drone to do a flyover. An hour later, the diligent NSA analyst received an email from her brother-in-law that contained thirty-two still photos. When she saw all the military aged males in and around the house and the RVs partially hidden in the backyard barn, she flagged the house for a high-priority review. All the intel was then sent up the chain of command, and finally an NSA senior officer who had been briefed on Tariq Hasan sent it over to the CIA.

Two days later, it eventually made its way into the inbox on Clayton Unser's desk for further analysis. Once he opened the red flash folder and examined the NSA writeup along with the photos, Clayton's gut told him this was the break they'd been waiting for. He immediately tasked John and his team to go onsite and either capture or terminate Tariq before anyone knew a terrorist on America's Top 100 kill list was in a safehouse thirty miles outside Philly.

John stopped walking and raised his fist just above his shoulder to alert Bunny, Felix and Bear that he was in visual range of the targets. With no streetlights along this desolate stretch towards the end of Hansen Road, the world glowed pea soup green through John's NVGs. He stood completely still, searching the final two hundred yards of the woods ahead for movement and mentally marking all the locations where he would deploy booby traps if he were a murderous terrorist fortifying a temporary command center.

One of the many valuable lessons that his Uncle Gonzalo taught him over the years was to think like the enemy. Throughout his childhood and teenage years, Gonzalo spent countless nights with him and Felix sharing his knowledge of the streets, and how to lead men in war, but his uncle always reminded them of what he believed was the most important aspect of any conflict: think like your enemy.

Bishop's fourteen years of Special Forces training and operations only reinforced Gonzalo's message. As a member of his twelve-man ODA (Operational Detachment Alpha) or A-Team, Team Razor, he was constantly being deployed to execute one or more of the Green Berets' doctrinal missions: unconventional warfare, foreign internal defense, direct action, counter-insurgency, special reconnaissance, counter-terrorism, information operations, counter-proliferation of weapons of mass destruction, and security assistance.

To successfully execute any of those missions, Special

Forces operators had to understand what motivated their adversaries strategically, operationally and tactically. Because Green Berets were the tip of the spear and the most actively deployed members of the US Spec Ops community, John had been on thousands of black ops reconnaissance, counter-terrorism and HVT (High-Value Target) kill missions against Al Qaeda, the Taliban and ISIS in Iraq and Afghanistan, and against Al Shabab and Boko Haram in Africa. All those missions left John with an invaluable level of insight into how members of these groups fought.

Bishop knew that the majority of the ready-to-die-can't-wait-to-be-martyred terrorists were poor and uneducated kids. Kids who were either recruited or liberated (kidnaped) from their homes and from the refugee camps throughout the Middle East and Africa. Those kids were then thoroughly brainwashed in mosques and madrasahs by imams who distorted the teachings of Islam to breed a new generation of martyrs and mass murderers.

Although John didn't actually know Tariq Hasan, he did know a few things about him and what motivated him. Revenge for the death of Aziz Khan was one, and the desire to kill thousands of Americans was two. That led John to the next logical step. Tariq knew he was on the 100 Most Wanted terrorist watchlist, yet he was still able to travel halfway across the world to try to execute both missions. That meant that Tariq brought his own A-Team with him. Everyone hiding inside the two houses was a highly trained and experienced fighter.

You may think you're good, John thought, *but you're about to find out the hard way that we're way better.*

John changed direction, carefully moving to his right for 50 yards and then slowly angling back in towards a spot that set off his alarm bells when he first scanned the area. There were two fallen dead trees in front of a shallow depression that made it a perfect sniper's hide or an ideal observation point for anyone surveilling the houses from the woods.

He crouched down below the level of the fallen trees and crept towards where his gut told him the explosives were buried. Then he saw the taut tripwire running two feet above the ground across the length of the depression for about five feet. He smiled when he saw the alarm system.

Not my first rodeo, John said to himself.

He recognized the design from Taliban and ISIS ambush teams who specialized in maiming and killing American soldiers from long range. Once the tripwire was hit, it pulled out a pin and created a connection between two electrified fields that would then send a radio signal to the bombers. Those assholes then remotely detonated the IEDs that ripped through flesh and bone and tore off limbs. The Army, Navy, Air Force, Coast Guard and Marine combat troops who managed to survive the loss of hands, feet, arms, and legs and often horrific head trauma were considered the lucky ones. For thousands more heroic men and women, it was left to their battle buddies to stuff what was left of them into body bags before they were flown home in flag-draped coffins.

"Team, this is Bravo One," John whispered into his radio mic. "They've got at least one remote IED in the woods facing the house. Odds are there's more in the back yard and along the sides. Watch for the tripwires. The tripwires are just an alarm because they wouldn't want some kids or a deer to set off the explosives," John said as he looked past the taut line of thin string and found the black gallon-sized cooking pot covered by dead leaves and branches. He didn't have to lift the pot's lid to know it was packed with explosives, and probably filled with screws and nails.

John closely examined the device to make sure there weren't any secondary wires before he pulled his KA-BAR fixed blade fighting knife from the sheath on the front of his tac vest. He used the serrated edge at the bottom of the seven-inch black blade to cut the wires that went to the IED from the small three-inch by four-inch plastic box that was the remote trigger.

"Disabled," John said into his mic.

"Ours too," Christmas said over the radio. "I found one behind the barn and there was another along the side of the house just like you said there'd be. Both devices are disabled," he added.

"They're gonna be surprised when nothing goes boom after they hit the play buttons," John said.

"Roger that," Christmas said. "Bravo Five, Six, Seven and Eight in position and ready to engage."

"Bravo One, Two, Three and Four moving up. Once we acquire targets we'll execute on my command," John said.

At two hundred yards out, John could see parts of each of the two houses from where he was. He refocused his NVGs to give him a better view, but there were still some trees in the way, and he wanted to get as close as possible before ordering his team into action. He got low and crawled for fifteen feet with his MP7 in his hands, pulling with his elbows and pushing himself along with the treaded soles of his black Salomon Quest 4D tactical boots.

When he got to a thick stand of pine trees, he stood up and moved through them, silently gliding from one to the next. Bunny, Felix and Bear followed him through the evergreens at ten-foot intervals. The thick branches covered in pine needles provided excellent cover as they crept forward. Even with John's signals to stop and hold their positions, several times they were able to cover a hundred and fifty yards in just a few minutes.

The trees and bushes were thicker here, but they had a much clearer view of the targets from just half a football field away.

John scanned the front side of the house to his left and got heat signatures from two of the four front windows. The overhead drone showed this two-story house contained a total of three bad guys, so John assumed tango number three was either in the basement or looking out the back windows.

He then moved his head slowly to the right and scanned the front of the wooden three-story colonial that was a hideout for six more terrorists. He got partial heat signatures in one of the downstairs front windows and two more behind curtains of the second-floor windows.

He turned to see his cousin Felix and the two Green Berets behind him. He used hand signals, pointing to Bear and Felix, directing them to move to their left and be ready to take out the two visible targets in the smaller house. He motioned for Bunny to move to his right and zero in on the single downstairs tango in the larger house, and that he would take out the two tangos on the second floor.

"This is One. In position. Target acquired. Two tangos in target two. Three tangos in target one," John whispered into his mic.

"Good copy, One. We see three tangos. One in target two and two in target one," Christmas said.

"That leaves a tango in target one unaccounted for," John said as he scanned the other windows hoping to find the missing terrorist.

"On my mark," he said, switching from his NVGs to the thermal scope on his MP7. "Three, two, one, execute."

CHAPTER 38

SAFEHOUSE

ALL EIGHT OF them fired at the same time. John's first shot hit his target just off center in the right side of his forehead. He moved his thermally infrared sighting laser onto the torso of the second man, who seemed frozen by the sound of glass breaking and probably from the guy with a hole in his head crumpling to the floor a few feet away from him. John fired again, saw the blood spray from what looked like a shot to the right lung, and watched his man fly backwards and out of sight.

John heard Felix and Bear confirm that they'd hit their marks and they had two tangos down. Bunny silently confirmed his kill with a thumbs up sign.

"Five tangos down in front," John said.

"Three down in back," Neville said. "No movement from either house, but we've still got a missing tango in target one."

Just then a series of loud explosions blew out the front and back windows of both houses. The blasts blew through some of the walls and smoke was billowing through several barrel-sized holes in each of the roofs.

"Fuckers were wearing S-Vests," Bunny said, meaning suicide vests.

John nodded. "With dead man switches," he said, referring to the thumb depressed triggers that many suicide bombers used.

If a suicide bomber was shot and killed before they could self-detonate, the dead man's switch would ensure that they still went boom. Once the bomber's palm opened and the thumb's pressure released from the trigger, the explosives in their vest rigs would light off.

"This is One. Hold your positions. We're going in the front door of the big house to take a look inside," John said.

'Copy that, One. We are holding here," Christmas said.

John stood up from his kneeling firing position, still searching for targets as he moved forward with Bunny ten feet back on his right and Felix ten feet back on his left. They moved out of the woods and crossed the street with their weapons up, and pointed at the front door and the front windows.

Bear stayed in his firing position just inside the tree line as the three of them walked across the street. He was their overwatch, searching for movement through the thermal scope of his MP7 with the M27 IAR leaning in the crook of a knee-high branch to keep it within reach.

John crossed the street and started walking up the short pathway in front of the house. He paused and raised his left hand while holding the MP7 in his right. He was five feet away from the three wooden steps that led up to the porch that went across the front of the house.

Something's not right, he said to himself.

He stood there for another second, and then his instincts kicked in and a voice inside him said: *Back the fuck up.*

He backed away with Felix and Bunny following his lead. All three had their weapons up, searching for something to shoot at as they stepped backwards. They made it off the path and into Hansen Road when an explosion under the front steps and the porch mowed them down, and two of the three RVs in the backyard barn erupted in a huge fireball.

Bear caught a slight glimpse of movement from the tiny basement window near the far right corner of the house, a second before the porch and stairs blew up. His nearly twenty years of tactical training and frontline combat operations kicked in and he didn't flinch from the roar of the explosions or from the pieces of wood, glass and other blast debris that flew directly towards him. He dropped his MP7, grabbed the M27, braced it against his right shoulder, and unleashed the beast. Firing on full auto, he disintegrated the basement's corner window and then guided the heavy gun gently to the left, sending rounds through wood and cinderblock. He emptied the magazine and then rammed home a fresh one. Aiming just above the prone figures of John, Bunny and Felix, and just over the dead grass in the front yard, he sent thirty more rounds through the basement walls and windows.

John was the first to get himself reoriented. This time, just like all the other times he'd been put on his ass by high explosives, there was always that brief moment when he wasn't quite sure if he was still alive or his soul was floating above his body on the battlefield. He didn't feel any pain and didn't think he actually lost consciousness, but he knew at the very least the air had been knocked out of him.

One moment there was silence. Then there was a ringing in his ears. Then he heard the crack, crack, crack of rounds from the M27 tearing into the house.

"Bear, hold your fire," he said, lying flat on his back with his MP7 across his chest. "Cover me while I check on Felix and Bunny."

"Got you covered," Bear said, as he ejected the near empty mag, slapped in a full one and searched for any movement in or near the house.

John stood up and walked over to Felix, who was lying on his side and gently shaking his head, trying to clear it.

"Am I dead?" Felix asked.

"That's déjà vu all over again, Cat," John said.

"What?" Felix said.

"Six months ago... We got flattened by the suicide bomber in Union Square Park, and you asked me the exact same thing. Word for word," John said.

"Oh yeah," Felix said, smiling. "I remember that now. Is Bunny okay?"

A solid three-foot chunk of a porch step had hit Bunny square in the chest, and his tac vest hadn't done much to soften the blow.

"Yeah, I'm good to go," Bunny said. He groaned a little as he sat up and then instinctively rolled over to his right, reached out and grabbed his MP7 that had been knocked out of his hands.

They could all hear sirens in the distance now. The front of the house was burning from the explosions, the barn was too, and the rat-tat-tat of the unsilenced M27 rounds had neighbors from more than a mile away frantically calling 911.

John pulled Felix up onto his feet and asked, "You sure you're okay?"

"Yeah, I am, but you're not," Felix said, pointing down at his cousin's right leg.

John initially thought it was a huge splinter, then decided it looked more like a wooden tent spike. The narrow end was stuck deep in his thigh. John hadn't noticed it or felt any pain until Felix pointed at it, and then his leg immediately started throbbing.

"This is One. Everyone okay back there?" John asked.

Christmas had been lucky. The dual blast from two of the three RVs had both blown upwards. He'd been peering around the left corner of the barn when the bombs went off, and he threw himself down into the grass. All the pieces of the roof and the blast debris rained down in a wider radius, and he was completely untouched and uninjured from the massive explosion.

"We're good," Christmas said.

"Shoot the back stairs to make sure there's not another IED in there, and make entry. We need to get inside and confirm if Tariq is among the dead," John said. "And be advised, we've got smoke coming from the front of the house, but no flames yet."

John yanked the eight-inch wooden spike out of his thigh and immediately felt the blood trickling down his leg. Felix got the first aid pack off his back, unzipped it and quickly found a tourniquet. Bunny reached for it and then tied it tight around the puncture wound to stem the blood flow until John could get to a doctor and have it looked at.

Bear was still searching for targets with the M27 when he came out of the woods, crossed the street and said, "Nice catch, Johnny. You boys would've been in pieces if you'd been any closer to that porch when it blew."

"Yeah, our missing tango must've seen us and set it off," John said.

"We've got a fire," Felix said, pointing at the house.

The front side of the house was gone and they could actually see inside. John, Bunny, Felix and Bear all looked through the heavy cloud of smoke and saw the bright red and orange flames rising from what had probably been the living room, and licking up towards the second floor.

"This is One. Everyone okay back there?" Stand down. We've got a big fire in front and I don't want you guys in the kitchen when it blows," John said, and then directed Felix, Bunny and Bear to move farther back away from the house.

"Copy that," Neville said from the kitchen.

He'd gone in through the back door with Mace. They both saw the smoke seeping through the floor and under the door, and felt the kitchen heating up from the fire in the living room. They worked fast. Two of the bodies still had heads attached to them and Mace took pictures, getting closeups of their faces. The third terrorist had been wearing the S-Vest and he was splattered all over the kitchen's walls and ceiling. Mace looked around and saw the back of the bloody head on the floor near the dishwasher. He rolled the head with his boot and saw that the terrorist's face had been caved in by the blast, but he took some pics anyway just in case the tango could somehow still be identified.

While Mace was snapping photos, Nev grabbed a bunch of papers that were scattered all over the floor and on the kitchen table.

"Let's get out of here," Mace said.

Mace was leading the way through the back door when Nev glanced back and spotted two cell phones in an open kitchen cabinet. He ran back in, grabbed them and sprinted after Mace into the back yard.

They made it to where Christmas and Chago were standing when the fire hit the gas line, and the room they'd just been standing in erupted in a fireball.

"Shit," John said. "If Tariq was in there, I'm not sure anyone's gonna be able to identify him."

"But if we don't know for sure, where does that leave us?" Felix asked.

"Until there's a hundred percent certainty that he's dead, we'll assume he's still alive," John said.

"We got facial photos and other intel from the kitchen," Nev said over the radio. "And just so you know… we were already inside the house when you told us not to make entry."

"Great job," John said, just as he got a glimpse of something moving through the smoke along the left side of the house.

He raised his MP7 as he walked forward and said, "We've got a live tango crawling between the houses."

The house was fully engulfed in flames as John half limped, half ran along the path separating the two houses. A gust of wind swirled away the smoke for a moment, and just then he saw the guy crawling towards the back yard.

"Careful, Johnny," Bunny said from over his right shoulder.

They could both see him clearly now and he wasn't wearing an S-Vest over his coat, but there was no way to tell what he may have under the North Face parka.

"Don't fucking move," John said.

Felix ran up on John's left with his weapon trained on the terrorist, who was still crawling through the grass between the two houses.

"Check those basement windows," Bunny said to Felix, pointing with his left hand to the three knee-high windows in the second house that faced the path they were on.

Felix swiveled and checked each window. He could see the gray minivan that had followed them off the highway, now parked in the basement that was also a two-car garage. Other than the minivan, the garage was empty and he couldn't see any movement.

"Clear," Felix said.

"Stop," John shouted at the terrorist on the ground.

When his second command was ignored, John aimed and fired one shot into the sole of the bad guy's black Nike Air Max sneaker. The instant the bullet tore through the arch of his right foot and exited through bones on the other side, the crawling stopped and the screaming started. He reached down to grab his foot and John gave him another stern warning.

"Don't move. The only thing you need to do is place your hands flat on the ground," John said.

The terrorist kept reaching towards his left foot with his left hand. John fired again, hitting the knuckles of the middle and ring fingers. Both digits landed in the grass two feet away.

"You cannot do this," the eight-fingered terrorist cried out in heavily accented English.

"I can do this all day, and glad to know you understand me," John said. "What's your name?"

"Jibril."

"Jibril, very slowly... let me see your right hand."

"I am unarmed. You cannot shoot me," Jibril said, still lying on his stomach with his right hand balled in a tight fist near his head.

John backed away and motioned for Bunny and Felix to do the same before he shot Jibril through the back of his clenched hand.

Jibril screamed and shouted, "I know the law. You cannot do this."

"There's only one law here, asshole, and that's Bishop's law," Bunny said to Jibril.

"You are Bishop? The famous John Bishop?" Jibril asked.

"I am," John said.

"Can I turn over to see you?" Jibril asked.

"Very slowly," John said.

After John shot Jibril in his right fist, the terrorist had opened what was left of his hand, and it was clear there was no way he was holding onto any type of detonator. John, Bunny and Felix still weren't taking any chances with this guy. They were twenty feet back from Jibril with their fingers on the triggers and ready to fire as they watched him slowly roll himself onto his back with his blown-apart hands held out like a doctor who just scrubbed up before surgery.

"It is good to meet you, John Bishop," Jibril said.

"Way too friendly for a guy you just shot three times," Bunny whispered.

"Why is that, Jibril?" John asked.

"Because, I have a message for you."

"Let's hear it," John said.

"Tariq says hello."

"That's it? You got yourself shot up and all your men killed just to say hi?" John asked.

"We were going to New York to give you the message there," Jibril said.

"Figured I'd save you the trouble," John said. "So what's the message and where's Tariq?"

"Tariq said that he is too busy to meet you in person, but that you must die for killing Aziz Khan."

"Where is he, Jibril?" John asked.

"Doing God's work… As am I," he said as he quickly swung his right arm down towards his chest.

Bishop saw Jibril move and fired his MP7 again. This time he hit him in the right elbow. The bullet shattered the bones and cut through tendons, leaving Jibril's forearm dangling uselessly at an odd angle.

Jibril screamed louder this time, but John saw that even through the pain and shock of being shot four times, he was still intent on pressing some kind of triggering device inside his jacket. Bunny ran forward and stomped on Jibril's shattered left hand, pinning it under his boot.

The terrorist howled again. John ignored his screams. He moved up and stood over the man Tariq Hassan had sent to kill him. John bent down and carefully patted the pockets of the North Face before he slowly unzipped the front of Jibril's parka.

"Sneaky fucker," Bunny said when they both saw the remote trigger that was attached to a silver chain hanging from Jibril's neck.

"I thought you would shoot me in the head when I moved," Jibril said.

"Thought about it, but we need you alive for questioning," John said.

Jibril started laughing.

"What's wrong with him?" Felix asked as he came up and stood next to his cousin.

John knew.

"Grab him," he shouted.

They were at the midway point between the street and the back yard, and the smoke was getting thicker and heavier from the burning house on their right. Bunny coughed, slung his MP7 behind his back, and hooked his hands under Jibril's armpits. He hoisted him off the ground while Felix got hold of Jibril's right ankle and John grabbed hold of the foot he'd put a bullet through. Together they all ran towards Bear—who was still standing guard in the street—with Jibril screaming at every bounce and bump.

"House two is gonna blow. Run," John shouted into his mic.

They double timed it along the smoking pathway, hooked a left when they hit the street and kept going. They didn't stop until they were a good three hundred yards away up the middle of the street. Then they stopped and let go of Jibril, which brought on more screaming and cursing when his back slammed into the concrete.

They stood there for a moment, staring past the roaring flames of house one when a thunderous explosion from somewhere inside target two disintegrated the house and lit up the night sky.

"Damn," Felix said.

John looked down at Jibril and said, "We're gonna put some Band-Aids on your booboos, and then we're gonna have a nice little chat, my friend."

Jibril smiled and said, "Do what you will. As Allah is my witness, I will die before I ever betray my brothers."

John didn't say anything. He just leaned over and stared down at his prisoner, his yellow eyes blazing as bright and hot as the burning houses down the street. Jibril retreated under the stare and looked away.

"Everyone talks, dude," Bunny said. "Some last longer than others, but you? I can see you're a straight-up bitch. A hundred bucks says you give up your boy Tariq for a blanket and a chocolate bar."

Police cars and fire trucks were racing up Hansen Road from the east when Christmas, Nev, Chago and Mace came in from the west with both cars. They braked to a stop a few feet in front of John and hopped out.

"You guys good?" Christmas asked.

"All good," John said and then pointed down at Jibril. "Load this asshole in the back seat."

John was reaching towards a pouch in his tac vest to call Clayton when the secure satellite phone started vibrating. He punched the send button and put it to his ear.

"I see you blew up an entire suburban neighborhood," Clayton said coolly.

"Are you interested in results or property values?" John asked.

"Did you get Tariq?" Clayton asked.

"Unknown," John said. "We took out eight bad guys, got a lot of intel and we're standing over a prisoner."

"Great work, Johnny. What do you need?"

"An escort out of here, a safehouse and a medic," John said.

"Done. Look for the guys with gray suits and skinny ties driving the black SUVs."

Three Chevy Tahoes with flashing lights drove past the fire trucks and pulled over next to John.

"Hop in," the driver said. "Leave your cars and toss your gear in the trunk."

John nodded and said, "Got any water back there?" as he opened the rear door of the first Tahoe.

"Yeah, but we brought beer too just in case you're actually thirsty," the driver said.

"Beer? I fucking love this guy," Bunny said as he lifted Jibril and loaded him into the back seat next to John.

As they drove through a line of cars and trucks from several different branches of local and federal law enforcement, John asked the driver to stop for a second. He hopped out and walked over to a group of FBI guys holding M4s and dressed in full combat gear.

"Help you?" one of them asked.

"Just a heads up. There are several unexploded IEDs back there in the woods, in the back yard and along the side of the farthest house," John said.

They all looked at each other and then back at John.

"Thanks. Anything else you can tell us about what happened here?"

"You'll find three bodies in that house and five more in the other one," John said, extending his arm and using his index finger to indicate how many bodies were in each house.

"Who are you?" the FBI guy asked.

John didn't see any point in lying.

"Name's Bishop. John Bishop," he said.

Just then, three men in suits and an Army two-star general walked up behind John, flashed their credentials and said to the FBI SWAT team, "Mr. Bishop was never here and by order of the president of the United States, this entire scene needs to be locked down for reasons of national security."

John nodded at them, turned around and climbed back into the waiting SUV. They all stood there watching Bishop drive off into the night.

CHAPTER 39

JIBRIL

Fort Dix, NJ

THE CIA SAFEHOUSE was technically not on the Fort Dix Army base. It was a quarter mile away. It gave John and his team along with the CIA interrogators a free hand at questioning Jibril, while also being close enough to get all the medical equipment they needed to patch him up.

Jibril went in and out of consciousness on the drive along 276 East from King of Prussia to the Fort Dix safehouse. The caravan of SUVs kept their flashers on and roared along the highway at over a hundred mph, making the fifty-six-mile trip in just twenty-five minutes. Once they arrived, they carried him inside and a medical team stripped off his clothes and went to work.

"You must take me to a hospital," he croaked. "I am an American citizen. I demand to see a lawyer and be taken to a hospital."

"Dude, your only shot at getting anything other than a slow agonizing death is for you to tell us everything you know," John said.

"I know nothing," Jibril said.

"Nothing, huh? A few minutes ago you were sending me a goodbye message from Tariq, and now you know nothing?" John said.

"I will never betray my brothers," Jibril said.

"Asshole, in case you're too dumb to get what's happening here, these guys are gonna stitch you up and as soon as they're finished, they're gonna leave," Bunny said. "Once they're gone we're gonna go to work on you. We'll cut, peel, slice and dice you for as long as it takes, but one thing I can guarantee is that you're gonna tell us everything."

John and Bunny stepped out of the room and nodded at Christmas, Mace, Chago and Neville. John sat down and extended his leg, and another doctor cut off his pants leg and examined his wound.

"Stabbed you right in the muscle. You're going to need seven or eight stitches. Four inside and three or four out," the doctor said.

"Can you hold off for twenty or thirty minutes?" John said then nodded his head towards Jibril's room. "After he spills his guts you can stitch me up, okay doc?"

The doctor said that was fine and that he'd wait outside in his car until John was ready for him. John thanked him and limped over to the CIA interrogators, who were watching Jibril through an eight-foot by four-foot one-way observation window.

"Look, I know you guys are pros, but me and Jibby here have a prior relationship," John said.

"Meaning you shot him four times and he's missing two fingers?" one of the interrogators asked.

"Well, there's that, but I guarantee you if you give me and Bunny a few minutes alone with him he'll talk," John said.

"How?" the interrogator asked.

Bunny clapped the guy on the shoulder and said, "Don't worry about a thing. We've got this."

Bear and Felix walked in through the front door. Bear was carrying a big bright orange bag that read Home Depot on the outside.

"You got it?" Bunny asked.

"Yup," Bear said and handed the bag to Bunny.

Bunny looked inside and said, "Beautiful."

The three-man medical team stepped out of the interrogation room. One of them said that they cleaned and stitched all four wounds, but that the shattered elbow was pretty serious and he was going to need major surgery to save the arm. He added that their temporary patch job should give them several hours to "debrief" Jibril, but they should get him to a hospital in the next few hours if they wanted to keep him alive.

John thanked the doctor, gave a thumbs up to the interrogation team, who just shrugged, and then he went back into the room with Bunny trailing him.

"Showtime, Jibril," John said.

"I'm cold," Jibril said.

"We thought you might be so we had one of our guys run to the store for this," Bunny said, pulling a handheld propane blowtorch out of the Home Depot bag.

Bunny quickly examined it and fired it up.

"What… what are you doing?" Jibril asked, his voice shaking with fear.

"You said you're a little chilly so I'm gonna use some focused flame to warm your ass up, motherfucker," Bunny said.

"You can't do this!" Jibril screamed.

"We can do whatever we want, asshole," John said. "Bunny, start with his feet. That's what Benji used to do."

John was referring to Benji Medina, who had been fond of the "feet to the fire" interrogation method before he took a bullet for John less than two weeks ago.

"He sure did," Bunny said and then narrowed the flame into a white hot dagger and moved menacingly towards Jibril.

"Wait. Wait. I will tell you what I know!" he shouted.

John looked over at the mirror and beckoned with his hand for the CIA guys to come in. A moment later, two of the three CIA interrogators walked into the room.

"Tell them everything you know, Jibril," John said.

Bunny turned off the torch and said, "We hear one fucking lie come out of your mouth, I'll relight this bitch and I promise you I'll start barbecuing your ass."

It took just over an hour to get everything they needed. John and Bunny left the room and the two members of the three-man CIA team followed them out.

"Can't say I approve of your methods, Bishop, but you got him talking faster than we ever would've."

"You're welcome," John said just as Clayton Unser came in through the front door.

"Nice work, gentlemen," Clayton said, speaking to all of them.

"You heard?" John asked.

Clayton nodded. He listened in to the entire Q&A session on the helicopter ride up from CIA HQ in Langley, Virginia.

"There's a lot to unpack here, but my biggest concern is the number of cells," Clayton said.

Jibril had said the two houses in King of Prussia were the weapons depot for the ISIS cells along the East Coast. He supplied weapons, explosives and comms gear to kill teams in DC, Philly, New York and Boston. He didn't know for sure, but he thought there were other cells in St. Louis, Chicago, Cleveland, Las Vegas, Phoenix and LA.

"How the fuck can ISIS have this many guys in all these cities and we didn't know anything about it?" John asked. "Did they all of a sudden get way smarter and become masterminds of tradecraft?"

Despite the laws that protected US citizens from religious persecution, everyone in the intelligence community knew that many mosques in America were recruiting grounds and safe havens for the guys who swore to give their lives to destroy the country that was actually protecting them. Since local law enforcement was no longer permitted to monitor and surveil the mosques, it was up to the clandestine services to fill the void.

That was where things got dicey. The CIA wasn't permitted to conduct operations on US soil, so they outsourced the work to contractors who could operate without restrictions. Those contractors were then tasked with penetrating the mosques that had been red-flagged for having militant clerics and suspicious activity. The problem was that the numbers just didn't add up. There weren't enough skilled guys out there who spoke Arabic and could walk into a mosque without raising the alarm.

Even though it was an uphill battle and the numbers were stacked against them, it was still hard for John and Clayton to believe that there were this many cells with that many bad guys out there. Most of the "ready to die" sickos just weren't that bright. That was why they were so easily brainwashed into committing murder, but it was also the reason a good number of them got caught before they could act. They either bragged to friends or boasted on social media about how many Americans they were about to kill, and then they got busted. The fact that none of the members of these cells had made a mistake or drawn any attention to themselves was rare… and it made the threat even scarier.

"I agree. Hard to believe there's that many jihadists running around the country and we didn't get a whiff of it. That said, we've got to assume Jibril is telling the truth… at least for now."

"Wish he had more on Tariq. Jibril said he called him twice tonight, but he didn't have a cell phone on him when we snatched him," John said.

"The two cell phones you guys got from the kitchen may lead us to Tariq. We're checking their call histories and looking at the cell towers now. If Jibril used either phone we'll know soon enough where Tariq was when he picked up," Clayton said.

"Well, whatever Tariq has planned it's coming this week. Thanksgiving is Thursday. The parade?" John said, more of a statement than a question.

"Could be, but is that big enough for him?" Felix asked. "I mean, he came all this way to make a statement. Don't get me wrong. Blowing up civilians at the parade would be fucking awful, but is that big enough for him?"

"I think Felix is right," Clayton said. "Outside of 9/11, most al Qaeda and ISIS attacks have been small bombing or small arms attacks… That's been the norm, but I agree that Tariq has something much bigger planned."

"Good points all around. Hopefully your analysts will get a location on him and we can go in and end it," John said, then rubbed his leg and yawned.

Clayton looked down at John, who was sitting in a chair

with his pants leg cut off, a bloody bandage wrapped around his wound, his face and clothes covered in dirt and dust, and the strong smell of a wood fire rising off him. He turned to look at the rest of John's team and saw they were all just as cut up and dirty as John was… minus the leg wound.

"You guys look like shit," Clayton said.

John smiled and said, "And you're looking clean and crisp as always."

Clayton was wearing light blue khakis, gray bucks and a dark blue V-neck sweater over a white collar shirt. Even though John was giving Clayton a little dig over his wardrobe, he actually liked his style and he knew Clayton wasn't some overdressed desk jockey. Clayton was one of them. He'd been wounded several times in covert operations and as good as he was with a gun, he was famous for his knife work. According to John's Uncle Gonzalo, he'd personally seen Clayton take out four armed men with just a seven-inch blade… No easy task.

"Let me ask you something," Clayton said.

"Would we have done it?" John asked.

"Yeah. Would you have let Bunny use that torch on him?" Clayton asked.

John sat in silence for a three count and then said: "Maybe, but we talked about it amongst ourselves, and we were ninety-five percent sure Jibril would start yapping as soon as Bunny lit it."

"And if he didn't?" Clayton asked.

"Honestly?… Maybe. I saw the fear in Jibril's eyes when we first took him down. His eyes told me he wasn't sold on the promise of seventy-two virgins waiting for him with open arms, and he was more concerned with survival. But… if he didn't start talking would we have done it? Yeah, we would've," John said.

"You know, they say torture doesn't work," Clayton said.

"Yeah, I saw what you guys did at Abu Ghraib, and last year I read the summary report of the Senate investigation, and I agree that *those* enhanced interrogation techniques don't work," John said.

"You read all five hundred and fifty-four pages?" Clayton asked, unable to hide how surprised he was that a Green Beret in an FOB (Forward Operation Base) in Afghanistan would know that a summary report of the seven-year investigation even existed.

The United States Senate Select Committee on Intelligence (SSCI) conducted a seven-year study into alleged misconduct by the CIA and its contractors at post 9/11 detainee Black Sites. The six thousand seven hundred page full report remained classified, but the five hundred plus page summary report was made public by the head of the SSCI, a California senator.

John nodded. "Had some downtime in between ops in the Stan," he said, referring to his last deployment to Afghanistan. "But if you want to know the real reason, it's that I always want to know what motivates our enemies. Word on the street was that the summary report was going to be a great recruiting tool for Al Qaeda, ISIS, the Taliban and all the other psycho terror groups out there trying to kill us. I wanted to know what it said."

"Makes sense and I don't want to beat this to death, but what's the difference between what those guys did at Black Sites to detainees and the blowtorch tonight?" Clayton asked.

"Those guys threw a wide net and were using prolonged torture to fish for broad pieces of intel. Most of the guys they waterboarded were foot soldiers who didn't know shit about post 9/11 attacks coming to the US, or even the structure of the organizations they were fighting for," John said.

Bishop hesitated for a moment before he went on. He'd seen some horrific things done by both sides to captured prisoners during his fourteen years at war, and he didn't condone any of it. He didn't condone it, but he understood it.

Throughout all his deployments, he'd had to use some "come to Jesus" interrogation techniques himself a few times. In one instance, Captain Burke, the OIC (Officer in Charge) of John's A-Team was captured by a particularly vicious Afghan warlord. John knew they had to get Burke out before the warlord did his signature move and plucked out Burke's eyeballs. He snuck into the compound with Bear, Mace, Bobby and the rest of Team Razor. Once inside the perimeter, they snatched the warlord's top lieutenant and John repeatedly slashed the guy's face, and then cut off the tip of his nose with a combat knife to find out where they were keeping his captain. John cut the guy's throat before they went in and rescued Burke, and he had no regrets about it.

After reflecting on what he'd done to save his captain's life, John got back to answering Clayton's question:

"With Jibril here, he already told us he was connected to Tariq. But honestly, even if he hadn't, yeah we would've done it. You had me put this team together to kill bad guys, and that's what we're gonna do. And, we'll do whatever it takes to stop an attack. If it saves just one innocent life, then yeah, I'll hold the torch myself next time," John said.

Clayton nodded his approval and said, "Glad to hear you say it," just as they carried a sedated and unconscious Jibril out on a stretcher to get him to an operating table.

"As soon as he's out of surgery, we'll go back to work on him and see what else he can tell us," Clayton added.

Clayton's mention of Jibril's surgery reminded Bishop about his leg. He looked at Felix and said, "Cuz, can you get that doc in here? This leg is screaming on me."

"Will do," Felix said and then hustled out the door to get the doctor.

"What now?" Christmas asked.

"After I get patched up we're gonna rack out at Dix," John said. "We'll hit the showers and get a few hours' sleep at the Fort. If Clayton's analysts track Tariq and get a location, we'll roll out from there to take him down."

"Sounds like a plan, brother," Christmas said.

"I need to speak with General Truesdale, so I'll head over to the fort with you," Clayton said, referring to the Fort Dix base commander.

"That works," John said.

They all chugged bottles of water while John was getting stitched and bandaged. When the doctor left, Neville, Chago, Mace, Bear, Bunny, Christmas and Felix formed a semi-circle around their team leader.

"Great work, Johnny," Bear said, speaking for all of them. "Perfect decision-making under fire. You brought us all home tonight and we took down a bunch of really bad dudes."

Bear reached out with a closed fist to give John a dap and the rest of the team followed suit.

Clayton watched the tight group of battle-tested warriors acknowledge John's leadership. It was no small thing. Clayton knew most of them had fought together in the past in countless Special Forces operations, but this was different. They were an autonomous unit tasked with protecting the homeland from all enemies, foreign and domestic, and operating in that gray area where they would technically be breaking the law to execute their missions. Clayton knew they would eventually come together as a team. He just didn't think it would happen this fast.

CHAPTER 40
CLAYTON

Fort Dix, New Jersey

CLAYTON THOUGHT BACK to last July, when he was sitting next to John's uncle at Gonzalo's personal prison in Mexico. Clayton had been reading John's OMPF (Official Military Personnel File) that listed all the medals and citations for valor he'd received. During his fourteen years as a Special Forces operator, Bishop had worked on hundreds of CIA-sponsored operations. Bishop's track record of successfully executing reconnaissance and capture and kill missions was off the charts, but Clayton had still been beyond impressed by what was in John's OMPF.

From what he had read then and from the team's performance tonight in King of Prussia, Clayton knew his instincts had been right. Even with the protections of presidential pardons, being tasked with operating outside the law was a heavy burden to bear, and for several of the men Clayton handpicked in the past, the burden had become far too great.

Clayton had recruited fearless and dynamic leaders from the military and from the CIA's Special Activities Center

(SAC). SAC was the division within the agency that focused on covert and paramilitary operations. With each new team leader and the teams they put together, a disturbing pattern emerged.

The kill teams started out laser focused on their objectives, and their actions absolutely stopped terrorist attacks here and abroad. The problem was that power corrupts, and the team leaders gradually started developing a God complex. Once that happened, the abuses followed. The teams would start making questionable kills and occasionally take out wealthy peripheral players so they could confiscate their cash. One of the teams went completely rogue and actually started doing hits on the side for a Colombian drug cartel.

So far at least, the guys who knew they could do anything and had the full backing of the United States intelligence services had tended to cross the line. That led to Clayton having to send in new kill teams to terminate the rogue ones.

With John, Clayton knew he'd found the right man for the job. Add in the rest of the guys John recruited, Clayton knew he finally had his dream team. Even though they were just getting started, there was no chance Bishop and his men would do anything other than hunt down bad guys and terminate them with extreme prejudice. He was staking his career on Bishop's integrity, because above all else Clayton was a patriot, and as a patriot he knew that America and its allies needed a man like Bishop operating with a free rein to hunt down and kill the enemy.

Clayton had come up through the ranks of the CIA and his entire career had been devoted to clandestine operations within the SAC. After twenty years of running counter-terrorism ops out in the field, the agency now leveraged his expertise by having him oversee operations from CIA headquarters in Langley, VA. Clayton appreciated the magnitude of the responsibility that had been thrust upon him. He was up for the task, but the politics and the bureaucracy he had to deal with often made him want to smash his head against a wall.

Politicians trying to make a name for themselves and career bureaucrats doing their best to avoid getting noticed were his sworn enemies. Clayton had seen members of both camps derail operations that were critical to the safety and security of American citizens, purely to fulfill their own misguided and perhaps even treasonous self-serving interests. On his mental threat board, Clayton had politicians and bureaucrats listed right up there with Middle Eastern terrorists, Russia, China and North Korea as true enemies of the State.

Clayton was also a student of history and what he'd learned through his studies actually terrified him. He understood something that most people failed to realize: civilizations come and go, and democracy above all others has been the rarest and by far the most fragile type of governance. And, when democracies fail, as they all have, they are replaced by dictatorial regimes where genocide and mass murder soon follow.

Fortunately, Clayton was part of a confederation of like-minded patriots in powerful positions across the country who did their best to stop America from eating its young and destroying itself from the inside. They didn't swear an oath, use secret handshakes or meet once a month in a dusty basement. Rather, it was informal cooperation among experienced men and women who had been downrange and understood that the United States of America was at risk of collapsing without their help.

Part of the cooperation was sharing intel and helping each other avoid the all too common interagency turf wars.

More importantly, it was about working together to overcome the "cover your own ass" and "it's safer to do nothing" mentality that had infected so many members of congress. Clayton had been in countless meetings where he and his clandestine operators were ordered to ignore actionable intelligence for purely political considerations that had nothing to do with stated US foreign policy or national security interests.

It wasn't just congress that had him worried, either. Clayton was far from convinced that President-elect Stamper would actually honor his word about the CIA directorship and the promise of the NSA going to General Palmer. Stamper's shady business dealings and potential Russian mob connections aside, Clayton had seen too many men say one thing and then do the opposite once they had their ass planted in the most powerful seat on the planet. That was one of the reasons he wanted John and his team in place and going on the offensive before inauguration day on January 20th.

The commander of Fort Dix, General Truesdale, was one of those patriots who understood the challenges the military and the intelligence services were facing. Truesdale had been briefed about Tariq and the presence of ISIS terror cells in his AOO (Area of Operation). Since the safehouse was so close to the fort, Clayton decided to share what they learned from Jibril in person with the general.

Clayton told John and the team to get cleaned up and get some sleep, and before shaking hands and quickly saying their goodbyes, he said he'd let them know if the analysts pinpointed Tariq's location. When Clayton made his way over to his security detail, he noticed a dark-colored sedan parked about a hundred yards up the road from the safehouse. There was nothing ominous about the car, but Clayton noted it because it was an odd place for it to be parked. Once he climbed inside the Chevy Suburban with his three-man security team, he made a few quick calls and the sedan was gone from his mind.

After his meeting with Truesdale, they shared a light meal and a cold beer before they said their goodbyes. Two hours after entering the fort, Clayton and his team headed out into the night on their way to New York City. They were about two miles from the fort when Clayton glanced out the window and saw the same dark sedan on the side of the road, but this time it was parked on a different street.

"Pull over," Clayton ordered.

"What's wrong, sir?" Dan Milton, his head of security, asked from the front passenger seat.

Clayton filled him in on his concerns about the sedan.

"Let's take a look and see what the deal is, Dan," Clayton said.

"*We'll* take a look. You stay in the car, sir," Milton said.

One of his men was a former Army Ranger, the other a Force Recon Marine, and Dan was once a Delta Force team leader. They stepped down onto the street, spread out into a practiced three-man formation, and walked twenty feet back towards the sedan. The car turned out to be a dark blue Toyota Camry and as they approached they could see a man sitting behind the wheel.

They saw the driver's door open, but the interior lights didn't go on, which was a big red flag for all three men. They pulled their guns and aimed them at the driver, who slowly stepped out of the car.

"Freeze! Don't fucking move!" Dan shouted.

David Tringa watched the three men walk towards him. He could tell they were well trained soldiers by the way they moved and how they held their guns.

Too bad. They should have kept driving, David thought.

He was annoyed with himself for not killing Bishop when he saw him limp out of the house a few hours earlier. When he started following the caravan of SUVs, he thought they were heading back to New York and he figured he'd tag along and kill John when he got home. When they drove into the fort, David contemplated going in after him, but figured it would be easier to wait outside for Bishop to leave.

He couldn't wait right outside an active military base without drawing attention to himself, so he found a secluded spot along the most obvious route and waited. After a few hours he assumed that Bishop was spending the night at the fort, and Tringa was getting ready to drive off when the SUV pulled over and the three guys with guns came at him.

"Hands over your head!" Dan Milton ordered.

"You want me to raise my hands?" Tringa asked.

"Yes, hands up," Dan said.

David had been standing casually with his hands at his sides waiting for the three men to come in range.

"Okay, I'm putting my hands up. Don't shoot me, okay?" Tringa said.

His palms were facing away from the three men and they couldn't see the steel tipped throwing arrows that David held between his fingers. When he raised his arms he did a backhanded flick of the wrist that sent the weighted four-inch black spikes at the security team.

Dan Milton, who was slightly in front of the other two, didn't even see the small black arrow that hit him in the throat. The projectile hit with such force that it tore through the soft tissue and then severed Dan's spine when it reached the back of his neck. His eyes bulged and he reflexively squeezed the trigger on his SIG .40 as he fell. The other two members of the security team were each hit with a spike in the eye, one in the left, one in the right. They were both dead before their bodies hit the ground.

Clayton had always been a man of action, and despite his senior position he wasn't built to stay in the car when his team was engaged. As soon as his men had raised their weapons he pulled his Glock 19 out of the shoulder holster tucked under his left arm, quietly opened the door, and slid along the side of the Suburban. He saw the man standing calmly next to his car, but couldn't clearly make out his features.

White guy, maybe Asian, just under six feet. Something's off here, Clayton thought just as the guy moved.

All three of his guys were down on the ground before Clayton's brain could register what happened. He opened up with the Glock, but each time he fired, the man was somewhere else. Then Clayton saw his gun fly out of his hand a second before he heard the crack from a perfectly placed kick that shattered his right wrist. Clayton swore in anger and reached around to his back with his left hand. He pulled out the combat knife he always carried and crouched in a defensive position.

David Tringa appreciated the man's bravery as he watched the guy in the V-neck move forward and try to cut him. He stood there smiling, waiting for Clayton to come to him. The smile enraged Clayton.

"I'm gonna kill you, motherfucker," Clayton shouted, ignoring his own mantra of never threaten, just do.

David sidestepped a backhanded slash that he knew was coming, then spun and hit Clayton in his left side, shattering several ribs. The lightning bolt of pain was more intense than anything Clayton had ever experienced. He doubled over and his legs buckled, but digging deep into his warrior soul, he somehow willed himself to stay on his feet and to hold onto the knife.

"Who sent you?" Clayton croaked, barely able to speak.

"You think I'm here for you? I don't even know who you are," David said.

"Then who? I saw you at the house."

"Bishop," David said.

"*Bishop?* Why?" Clayton asked.

"Doesn't matter. Just something I've got to do," David said.

"Then why did you kill my men?" Clayton asked, glancing down at the bodies of Dan Milton and the rest of his security detail.

"I kill anyone who points a gun at me. Just a rule I have. You and your boys should have kept driving, old man."

"Old man? I'm fifty-two," Clayton said with a grin, then coughed up blood and spat it out on the ground.

"Hope you enjoyed it while it lasted," David said.

Clayton had never seen anyone move so fast or hit so hard. One moment the guy was standing there talking and the next thing Clayton knew, he was on the ground looking up at him.

David knelt over Clayton, who looked up at him and coughed up more blood.

"The blow to your side shattered your ribs. You're bleeding internally," David said.

"Lost a few fights over the years, but never like this. You kicked my ass, dude," Clayton said.

"Nothing to be ashamed of. I've been training my whole life," David said, then glanced behind him, turning towards the sound of cars coming fast in the distance.

"Got to go. So long, pops. You won't feel a thing," David said as he raised his fist.

Clayton coughed again. His eyes fluttered, wanting to close. His brain and body going into protection mode, trying to shut down to rest and recover. Fighting to stay awake and fighting to stay alive, Clayton never heard the gunshots fired from a Fort Dix military Jeep filled with base security MPs. Everything just went black a moment before David Tringa punched down with the death blow.

CHAPTER 41

SHOW YOUR TEETH

TARIQ GOT UP at 5AM, hit the bedroom floor for his morning prayers, then did his daily exercise routine of six sets of fifty pushups followed by six sets each of dips, sit-ups and planks. He wished he could go for a run to really work up a good sweat, but he knew he'd never jog again. At least not until he reached Jannah (paradise). He pictured himself in the afterlife. Saw himself running along a white sandy beach towards seventy-two virgins. Each of the beauties frantically waving at him, beckoning him to her bed, pleading with him to be the first to be mounted.

He shrugged his shoulders at the thought. The jihad-ist and devout Muslim side of him wanted to believe in the seventy-two-virgin dream. His far more practical and cynical soldier side wasn't sure what—if any—true glory awaited after death. Either way, millenniums with virgins on the beach, or an eternity of nothingness, he would willingly gamble his soul to avenge his warlord, Aziz Khan. Six months ago he stood over Aziz's mangled body, and nothing would stop him from fulfilling his blood oath to the man he secretly called father.

Tariq showered, dressed and went down the stairs of

the two-story, two-family house to get some breakfast. The women had prepared a simple meal of bread, jam and labneh (strained yogurt). Sitting on a beat-up sofa that was covered in dark quilts, he robotically scooped up the labneh with pieces of the warm bread.

All of Tariq's attention was on the forty-inch television that sat on top of a waist-high light-blue dresser across the room. He didn't even realize he'd taken a sip of the strong dark tea until the hot liquid hit his throat. Images of the smoking ruins of the two safehouses in King of Prussia filled the TV screen. He listened to the male and female co-anchor news team take turns describing the scene in their rehearsed rhythm of you go, then I go.

"In their initial statement, local fire department officials have said that both house fires are being investigated, but at the moment there are no indications of foul play," the male anchor said.

The female anchor raised an eyebrow and tilted her head back slightly. The move was more subtle than exaggerated… just enough to let her viewers know how skeptical she was about the statement from the fire marshals.

I wonder how many times you practiced that move in the mirror, Tariq thought as he watched her partner pause dramatically and she jumped in:

"Two houses burn to the ground and so far they've removed eight bodies from the rubble, and they're saying there's no sign of foul play here?" she said in disbelief.

"There's more, Katie," the male anchor said.

"I *bet* there is, Bill. What has your investigation uncovered?" Katie asked, leaning in to hear the information as if she hadn't already been briefed before they went live for this segment.

"Well Katie, neighbors from all-around said it sounded like World War III with gunfire and multiple explosions," Bill said, shaking his head dramatically.

"Gunfire? What kind of gunfire, Bill?"

"Machine guns, Katie. Neighbors said they could hear the sustained firing of automatic weapons," he said.

"Explosions, machine gunfire and eight bodies in two different houses in the Philadelphia suburbs? What's really going on here, Bill?" she asked incredulously.

"I agree, Katie. Something very fishy is happening here. We also have multiple eyewitnesses who confirmed that there were heavily armed FBI and Homeland Security agents, and even military personnel on the scene and throughout the neighborhoods surrounding the two houses," Bill said.

Then, one of CNN's on-scene reporters appeared in a split screen with a couple who looked to be in their mid-sixties. Tariq tuned out the interview and the couple's recounting of all they saw and heard the night before. The one thing that stuck in his mind was the reporting that only eight bodies had been found.

Was one of them taken alive? he asked himself.

Jibril was the head of "Bell Team." So named because Jibril's nine-man team was the Philadelphia cell, and because he often had them meet near the actual Liberty Bell in Independence National Park. Jibril had called Tariq twice last night. He was calm on the first call. He let Tariq know that he believed an FBI SWAT team was heading towards the houses.

Tariq had simply said, "You and your men know what you must do, my brother."

Jibril said they wouldn't let him down, and that they would kill all the FBI pigs before they died.

The second call had been more frantic. Screaming over

the sound of machine gunfire in the background, Jibril said that all his men were dead and he was surrounded by hundreds of law enforcement agents.

"Hundreds? Tariq asked.

"At least! They are firing from all sides!" Jibril had screamed.

"What will *you* do?" Tariq had asked him.

"I… I… I will be a martyr for our cause. Once the agents come inside I will blow up both houses," Jibril had said nervously.

"Your sacrifice will soon be rewarded. I will meet you and your men in paradise in just a few days," Tariq had told him.

From the images on the screen, it looked like Jibril had been true to his word and blown up both houses. The question was, did he remain inside when he pressed the buttons, or had he tried to save himself? Tariq replayed the conversation and recalled his impressions of Jibril when he met him at the safehouses three days ago.

Jibril had presented himself as a determined and committed soldier in complete command and control of his unit. The reports from his handlers here in the US and from the leadership council back in Raqqa had all been perfect. Jibril had carefully selected his team and when he had been forced to personally kill two members of the cell for questioning his orders, he immediately reported it. He had even requested that two Mujahideen replacements be sent through the Turkish-Costa Rican pipeline so that there could be no doubts about the integrity of his unit.

Despite all the reports and the success Jibril had had in finding the safehouses and obtaining the huge stockpile of weapons and explosives, there was still something about

Jibril that had made Tariq wary. He continued to think things through and dissect the news reports.

What if he is alive? Tariq thought.

If Jibril was taken alive and is being questioned at this very moment, what are the consequences?... None, he concluded. Then revised his thinking:

It is actually a good thing.

Gretchen had been watching him from across the room. She saw that he was working through the potential problem of the safehouses, and she hadn't wanted to disturb him, but when she saw his expression relax a little, she walked over with a fresh pot of tea and refilled his glass.

Tariq didn't thank her for the refill, and she hadn't expected a thank-you. She sat down on the far end of the couch, giving him the appropriate amount of space. Gretchen understood that her job was to fulfill his needs and help him in any way she could to complete the mission. Intimacy, or even the appearance of it by sitting too close to him, was not something that he wanted and was definitely not something that would be helpful to the team's overall health.

"Do you think they're all dead?" she asked him.

"I hope not," Tariq said.

She thought about that for a moment and then asked him why.

"It will make the hunters chase their tails. They already know we are here. Jibril and his men had no idea about the details of our mission or even our targets," he said.

"But can't they describe all of us? Tell the cops what we all look like?" she asked.

"Yes, Gretchen. The FBI and the police will know what some of us look like, but we will be... How do you say it?... A needle in the hay?"

"Needle in a haystack," she said. "But that was good."

"What *is* a haystack?" he asked.

"Just a big pile of hay that farmers stack up to feed their cows and horses," she said.

"And if you lose a needle in the stack then it is hard to find, isn't this correct?" he asked.

"Almost impossible to find… At least until you jump onto the stack and the needle sticks you in the butt," she said, smiling.

Tariq nodded his head and asked, "That happened to you?"

She was tempted to lie to make it more personal, but quickly decided to tell it straight.

"No, not to me. It's just a saying… Something Americans always say, but I'll bet it happened to someone a long time ago."

Tariq nodded in understanding and said, "We will be like the needles. We will move among them, walking with the crowds and when we strike, it will be far more painful than a poke in the butt. We will burn down all the haystacks."

Gretchen felt her face flush at the thought of what they were about to do. In just a few days, America and probably the world would change dramatically.

Our sacrifice will uplift generations of our oppressed brothers and sisters and Adeeb's murder will finally be avenged, Gretchen thought, picturing Adeeb's kind eyes and his handsome face. *I hope you are proud of me, my love.*

They heard Marwan and Lisa come through the front door, and the rustle of plastic bags as they made their way down the hallway and into the kitchen. They handed the groceries off to the three women who were busy wiping down the countertops and washing dishes before the couple made their way into the living room.

"Big day today," Lisa said. "Huge," she added, bursting with energy.

"What happened?" Gretchen asked.

"He smiled!" Lisa said.

"The baby?"

"No. The man killer holding the baby is the one who smiled," Lisa said, aiming her thumb at Marwan, who was carrying a sleeping two-year-old inside a baby Bjorn.

"Impossible," Tariq said just as the little lady strapped to Marwan woke up and started wiggling and writhing in her pink winter onesie.

Tariq wasn't a laugher, but seeing the big scowling Syrian with the baby flailing around on his chest brought a broad grin to his face.

"Didn't think your face could do that," Gretchen said to Marwan.

"This one," Marwan said, giving a thumb back to Lisa, "told us we have to show our teeth to the infidels."

Finally, Gretchen thought.

Throughout all their training and role playing sessions back in Raqqa, Lisa, Gretchen and the other American jihadists had tried their best to explain things to Tariq, Marwan and all the Syrian, Afghan, and Saudi team members. The United States was a melting pot of people from all over the world. Basic English was helpful, but foreign accents in and of themselves wouldn't make people nervous. It was the stiff jaws and hate-filled eyes of the foreign fighters that would get them noticed.

Men like Marwan and Tariq had been at war for most of their lives. Smiles were reserved for standing over the mangled body of an enemy or recounting a deadly battle where they had outwitted and outfought the opposing force. Simply walking down the streets of New York and smiling at strangers was a concept so distant from their daily reality that all the American jihadists had spent a great deal of time practicing with the non-Americans.

After countless hours of role playing, the best Tariq, Marwan and the others could do was to respond to a "good morning" or a "how's it going?" with stiff nods or way too formal return greetings, like, "I am well, how may you be?" Tariq, was by far the most open-minded, but even he had trouble understanding why this was important.

"We are going there to kill these dogs, not to make friends," Tariq had said.

Gretchen and Lisa hadn't let up. They let him know that as big and heavily populated as their targets were, the people there were still on the alert after 9/11, and there were cameras everywhere. Walking around any American city with rage on your face and murder in your eyes would definitely draw unwanted attention and potentially jeopardize the mission.

"We're traveling as couples on vacation. People smile when they're on vacation, Tariq," Gretchen had said.

"What is the meaning of this *vacation*?" Marwan had asked.

"Think of it like this," Lisa had said. "The fighting in Iraq breaks for a week or two and you go back home and take your sons to visit their grandmother."

"My mother died birthing me," Marwan had said. He thought for a moment and then said, "When each of my sons turned five, I brought them to the training camps to teach them how to shoot and make bombs. Is this the vacation you mean?"

"*Um*, yeah, something like that," Lisa had said.

Based on those many months when they had worked with the men, Gretchen understood why Lisa was now so excited about Marwan's breakthrough.

"What happened at the market?" Gretchen asked.

"I was getting food off the shelves when an old woman came up to Marwan and asked how old our baby was. The big guy smiled down at the old woman and said twenty-two months. Just like that," Lisa said, snapping her fingers for emphasis.

"Guess all our hard work finally paid off," Gretchen said then raised her palm up and high-fived Lisa.

"Very good, my brother. We will keep smiling at these devils, and in a few days we will smile much bigger when we kill thousands of them," Tariq said, showing his teeth.

CHAPTER 42
YOU HAVE QUESTIONS

GENERAL TRUESDALE WENT to the Dix barracks where the team was spending the night. Before Clayton left the fort, he told the general that Bishop had been pushing himself and his men to the limit for the past few days, and asked Truesdale to make sure they weren't disturbed unless there was a real emergency. Truesdale figured they couldn't have been asleep for more than a few hours, but knew he had to wake them.

At Clayton's request, Truesdale had posted half a dozen sentries around the barracks as an added layer of security. The sentries stiffly came to attention when they saw their base commander approaching the barracks. Truesdale gave them a quick salute before he hustled up the steps, opened the door and turned on the lights.

Even though the general knew these were all elite fighting men, he was still impressed by their reaction time. All eight of them went from sleeping soundly in their bunks to being instantly awake and on their feet with pistols in their hands.

Damn, Truesdale thought. *These guys don't fuck around.* "At ease, men," he said.

John and the men all lowered and holstered their sidearms.

"General," John said, nodding his head in greeting. "Do you have a target package for us, sir?" John asked, wondering why he didn't get a phone call about Tariq's location, and why the general was there delivering the news in person.

"Negative. This is something else… Clayton and his security detail were attacked twenty minutes ago when they left the base," Truesdale said.

"Attacked? Attacked by who?" John asked.

"One man. He disappeared into the woods when MPs fired on him. I've got a hundred men and local area law enforcement on the hunt. They'll run him down," the general said confidently.

One man? John asked himself, not liking any of the possible answers.

"How's Clayton?" Bear asked.

"Dan Milton, Jimmy Suggs and Bill McHugh are all dead. Clayton is critical, but still alive," the general said.

"*Dead*? Milton was Delta and Jimmy and Bill were two of the toughest dudes I know," Bear said.

"Was it a big bald guy shooting from long range?" Christmas asked.

"No. It was a small guy with dark hair. Killed all three of them with darts," Truesdale said.

"*Darts*? What do you mean *darts*?" Bear asked.

"He killed them all at close range with some kind of metal projectiles. That's all we know so far. You guys better come with me."

They grabbed their coats and weapons, following Truesdale, who raced out the door to a truck that was idling in front of the barracks. As soon as they piled into the back, it took off for the short ten-minute drive to the Deborah Heart and Lung Center, where Clayton was being treated.

"Deborah is one of the best. The MPs saw he was bleeding internally so they didn't risk bringing him to the base clinic," Truesdale said.

The general was a big guy in his late fifties. John noted that time behind a desk had taken its toll on the man and he estimated Truesdale had gained at least fifty pounds since he'd last seen him a few years ago. He also knew the sweat pouring down the general's face wasn't weight-related. He and Clayton had been friends for half of their lives and there was no hiding the man's concern.

When they got to the hospital John led the way in with the out-of-shape Truesdale calling out orders and running interference from behind. Staff members directed them to the critical care room and they hustled down the hallway towards the big double doors. As soon as they got there they entered the room and immediately saw that Clayton had several doctors and nurses working on him. The hospital's vascular surgeon walked over and gave them the details of Clayton's multiple injuries, and explained that he would be part of the team that was about to operate.

One of the nurses working on Clayton looked up and called out: "Is there a Bishop here? John Bishop?"

John trotted across the room and bent over Clayton. He saw his friend's face was taut, his skin pale and waxy. He looked like he'd aged thirty years since they said their good-byes three hours ago at the safehouse.

"Johnny… before they put me to sleep…. gotta tell you… the guy… not there for me…he was waiting for you," Clayton whispered.

John pulled a photo out of his jacket pocket and held it up so Clayton could see it.

"Is this the guy?" he asked.

Clayton nodded. The pain from the slight movement made him bare his teeth. "Yeah... that's him... Killed my guys... Who is he?"

"His name is David Tringa. He's a Pakistani assassin," John said.

"Pakistan?" Clayton said.

"Yeah. The Tringas are a murder for hire family that have been in the game for about a thousand years. Aziz Khan put the hit out on me before my Uncle Macho killed him, and David Tringa is here to complete the contract," John said.

"Fuck," Clayton said. "I had a gun and a knife, and he kicked my ass with his bare hands... Never seen anything like him before."

"I'm so sorry, Clayton. We'll get him," John said.

Clayton shook his head again. The slight move made him grimace more than he already was.

"Tariq...Tariq first... Then... *Then* you kill that guy for me," he said.

"Understood, sir," John said.

The anesthesia in the intravenous drip flowing into his arm was putting him down, but right before he went under, Clayton said, "Tariq" one last time. Then he was gone and the nurses wheeled him away to get him to the operating room.

Truesdale stayed at the hospital and told the team he'd update them as soon as Clayton was out of surgery. They all thanked him before they headed out and took the short trip back to Dix. There they quickly grabbed all their equipment and then headed over to the helipad, where the newly leased Valdez company helicopter was revved and waiting.

The two-pilot, nineteen-seat, Sikorsky S-92 flew the team through Jersey, across the Hudson River, over Manhattan, across the East River, through parts of Queens and then into Long Island. Twenty minutes after takeoff they touched down on the great lawn at the seventeen-bedroom Valdez estate.

It was exactly 3AM when Gonzalo and Bobby greeted them at the door. Bobby had bandages covering most of his face with spaces for his eyes and mouth. His left hand was also heavily wrapped in white gauze.

"*Mummy*. Oh, how I've missed you, *Mummy*," Mace sang to Bobby with his hands on his heart.

"Fucking asshole," Bobby said, then the two of them came together and gave each other a long hug.

"So fucking happy to see you, bro-ham," Mace whispered in Bobby's ear before they let go.

All the team members took turns embracing their wounded brother and told Bobby how glad they were that he was going to be okay. After the hugs John introduced Chago and Neville to his Uncle Gonzalo. Everyone else said their hellos and then they all trudged into the main dining room. They put their bags and gun cases in a corner of the room before they all sat down at one end of the massive dining room table. John sat across from Gonzalo, Felix was next to John, and the rest of the team was seated along both sides. There were platters of hot and cold sandwiches, some pasta dishes and several ice buckets filled with water, beer and sodas spread out along the table.

"Gentlemen, please eat," Gonzalo said, gesturing towards the food with his hands.

They all tore into it like a pack of famished wolves. John hadn't realized how hungry he was until he devoured a turkey sandwich and chugged an ice cold lemonade. He was debating on whether to go for turkey sandwich two or switch to freshly made Cubano sliders when Gonzalo asked:

"How's Clayton?"

"He's really messed up, Tio. Severe internal bleeding from three shattered ribs, a broken wrist, broken leg and a serious concussion," John said.

"He confirmed it was David Tringa?" Gonzalo asked.

"Yes, he did. Tringa was there for me and Clayton somehow saw him and went to investigate. He's lucky to be alive. We know the guys who were on his security detail. They're all married with kids and all three are, *were*, some badass dudes. Tringa went right through them. Killed them all with some kind of homemade throwing darts," John said.

His jaw kept clenching and unclenching. His brow was knotted and the scar running down into his cheek looked like a dark red river of rage and anger flowing across his face.

Gonzalo watched him closely for a few moments. He understood all the guilt and turmoil that was torturing his adopted son. Gonzalo felt exactly the same way after he loaned his baby sister his car for a Bishop family outing on a summer morning twenty-five years ago. Assassins thought Gonzalo was in the car when they opened fire. The gunmen massacred his youngest sister Christina and her husband Michael Bishop. John was the only survivor, but the face and heart of the nine-year-old had been scarred for life.

"You feel responsible for this?" Gonzalo asked him.

"Tio, do you have *any* idea how many good people have died because of me?" John asked without looking up at the man who raised him.

"Yes, I see your point," Gonzalo said.

"This is *all* on me," John said.

"I understand," Gonzalo said. "You blame yourself for

your cousin Chris being killed by Amir Khan's suicide bomber. For your friend, Sergeant Able Diaz, getting killed on the ship in Yemen. For your Uncle Macho dying in Afghanistan. For your Uncle Sesa getting shot. For Boogie Washington getting killed trying to rescue Maria from the Con Ed plant. For Alastair and Benji's murder. For all of our men who were killed by the Russians and by Connie Belusci... and now for Clayton and his men... Oh yes, and Bobby here."

Gonzalo gestured with his left hand towards Bobby and said, "Bobby would still have his fingers. Did I miss anyone?" Zalo asked.

John looked up and locked eyes with the man he called Tio. He called him uncle, but he truly loved him like a father, and that was exactly what Gonzalo had been to him for most of his life. Despite John's unconditional love and the deep feelings of gratitude he felt for his uncle for raising him, and in truth for saving his life, he could never bring himself to call him Dad. He always felt it would somehow erase the memory of his murdered father, Michael Barrington Bishop.

"Of course I blame myself, Tio. If it wasn't for me they would all be alive," John said, his voice rising as he fought to contain his anger.

Like John, Felix had been raised by Gonzalo and he knew enough about the man to see what was coming. Christmas had been Gonzalo's head of security for eleven years, so he knew too. Bunny, Mace, Chago, Bear, Neville and Bobby weren't sure what was happening, but they were all sharp enough to get that it was something major. They all stopped eating, carefully put their drinks down, and sat back in their seats to watch.

"And your wife? She would still be here, wouldn't she?" Gonzalo asked, his voice calm and quiet.

"Yes!" John shouted. "She's gone and that's on me!"

Gonzalo nodded his head in understanding. "Yes, I see your point," he said softly. "But if we go back to the beginning…Back to where this all started… Haven't all our family and friends died and your brother here got wounded because you saved a park full of innocent men and women? … A playground full of children? … Because you saved thousands of people from being killed by suicide bombers and a truck filled with explosives?"

John couldn't hold his uncle's eyes and looked back down at the table.

"Yes… but…" John couldn't finish the sentence.

"You wish you hadn't intervened? You wish you hadn't even been walking in Union Square Park with all those mothers pushing babies in their strollers? With all the kids laughing on the swings and running through the playground? And with all the thousands more shopping at the farmers market? Yes, I get it. It would've been so much easier for you and our family if you could've just read about the slaughter in the paper the next day. You could've talked about how fucked up the world is over a latte and we could've all prayed for the murdered innocents at the memorial the city built for them."

"That's…that's not…No, that's not what I'm saying, Tio," John stammered.

Gonzalo slammed his palm on the table.

"Then what the fuck *are* you saying!?" he shouted.

John opened his mouth to speak, but nothing came out.

Zalo softened his voice. "Do I wish Benji, Chris, my brothers and all the others were still alive? Of course I do. We all do. We cherish the memories of all those we've lost, but we can't let that pain stop us from moving forward. And as for your wife. I'm glad Maria left," Zalo said.

"You don't mean that," John said.

"You better believe I do. Ask me why."

"Why?" John asked, his voice barely above a whisper.

"Because she's safe, and like it or not you've been chosen for something much bigger than yourself. Bigger than just this family. If she were here you'd be so worried about her and the baby you'd get distracted. That's the hard truth of it, my son. You saved all those thousands last summer, and now Clayton and the president of the United States have asked you to save thousands more. This mission needs your undivided attention."

John knew his uncle was right, but still couldn't come to grips with the unfairness of it all. He understood that he'd been somehow chosen for this. Perhaps it was only by coincidence and by circumstance at Union Square, but now he'd been chosen because of his unique ability to kill the enemy.

"Look around you. Look at the men you are leading," Gonzalo said.

John looked up and made eye contact with everyone at the table.

"These are *men*," Gonzalo said, spreading his arms out wide to include them all. "They're the brightest, strongest and best trained fighters in the world. They dropped everything to join you and they're risking everything, including their lives to follow *you*."

"I know they are," John said.

"*Look*, I'm not saying all this to embarrass you in front of your team. We are all family now and one of the most important things we can do for each other is to speak the truth. Our truth is that life just ain't fair. We've all been tasked with carrying burdens that would break weaker men. Yes, we suffer. Yes, we grieve, but we continue to do what we're here to do. I know I don't need to remind you that there is no greater calling than being chosen to protect those who can't protect themselves," Zalo said.

"You don't, Tio. It's who we are and what we do," John said.

"Good… There's also no greater honor than being chosen by the best of the best to have you lead them. Clear your mind and harden your heart so you can use all your power to lead them well. Everyone here knows this is life and death. Some of us may not survive this war, but no matter what happens, you have to keep moving the team forward to complete the mission."

"What if the mission never ends?" John asked.

"I've been at war my whole life. Over one hundred men and family members were killed on my watch. Has it been hard? You bet. In the end I think I saved many more than we lost… I hope so anyway. Either way, that is the price of leading men into battle. The price at times may seem unbearable, but a true leader gives everything of himself to save as many as he can."

John nodded.

Got me again, he thought. *Every time I steer off course he's here to get me back on track.*

John got up and walked around the table and Gonzalo rose to meet him. They wrapped their arms around each other.

"Thank you, Papi," he said into Zalo's ear.

Gonzalo kept his composure. The word meant so much to him and he knew how big a deal it was for John to say them. He felt a huge ball of emotion rising in his chest, but he pushed it down. *No time for tears here,* Gonzalo thought. His heart was soaring, but he didn't say anything in response.

Just gave John a light slap on the back before they broke the huddle.

John looked around the table and zeroed in on Chago and Neville.

"Now you see how my family operates. We're an open book and as my uncle said, we speak the truth… especially when it *needs* to be spoken. No doubt I've been hit with a lot lately, but there's too much at stake here and way too many bad guys out there to let anything else matter," he said.

"Wish *my* family talked like that," Chago said.

"Damn straight," Neville said, then stood up to address Gonzalo and John. "Don Valdez… John… I joined kinda thinking this was just gonna be an adventure. I knew we were gonna see some action and I was getting involved with something pretty big. I just didn't know how big. Now that I see what this is and the importance of what we're doing, I just want to thank you for asking me to join the team. I'm truly honored to be here," Nev said.

Neville looked up and down the table making sure he got a head nod from everyone except Felix, who wasn't sure what was going on.

"John, I'm also gonna speak for the team and let you know that we talked amongst ourselves a few days ago. Christmas and Bunny filled us in on everything that's happening with you… basically because with this much at stake, we all deserve to know if there's anything personal that could hinder a team member's performance.

"You're our team leader. Period. That said, in the event that something prevented you from leading… God forbid if you got hit or if it *was* something personal… then we voted the order for who's next," Nev said.

"Next team leader?" John asked.

"Yes, exactly," Nev said. "We voted and the vote was unanimous. Bear would be next. Then me. Then Christmas. Then Bunny. Then Mace. Then Bobby. We figured if all the rest of us were dead, then all hope was lost and Chago and Felix could just surrender."

That got everyone laughing before Bear cleared his throat and looked over at Felix.

"Cat, this was no disrespect to you. We voted several days ago, and the only reasons we didn't invite you in at the time was, one, because you're family and we weren't sure if you'd feel conflicted or think that we were somehow asking you to betray Johnny, and two, because we weren't sure if you'd get the importance of laying out a chain of command within a combat unit."

"Thanks, Bear. I get it and I totally understand why you voted without me," Felix said, meaning it. "Is it okay if I vote now, though?" he asked.

"Uh, yeah. Sure," Bear said.

"My chain of command votes for following Johnny are, Bear, Nev, Christmas, Bunny, Mace, Bobby and then Chago," he said, smiling.

"Well done," Bear said to him and then turned to address their team leader.

"Johnny, as Don Valdez pointed out, we're all men here and we're a mission-first unit. Despite all these threats from David Tringa, Connie, Meecham and the Russians, taking out Tariq is *the* mission. Like Neville said, you're our team leader. Period. None of us doubt your capabilities. We all know you're the best, but with everything that's happened with Maria, we just weren't a hundred percent sure you could *be* your best. Know we all already said it at the safehouse tonight, but just want it on the record that you erased any doubts with your instincts and decision-making in King of Prussia, and you reminded us why we all volunteered to be here," Bear said.

"Thanks Bear… Thank all of you and thanks for putting the COC in place. That's something I definitely overlooked, and I'm relying on all of you to speak up if there's anything else you think we should or shouldn't do going forward," John said.

He paused for a moment. He knew it was late and wasn't sure whether he should bring it up now or save it for the morning.

We're all up anyway, he thought.

"Since we're having an open forum, I want to ask your opinions about something else," he said.

"Omar?" Felix asked.

"Yeah. Exactly," John said.

John turned to his uncle and started to tell him about the surprise visit from Omar at the training camp in Phoenicia. Gonzalo put up his hand and said,

"Felix called me and told me all about it."

John couldn't hide the look of surprise on his face, but quickly recovered and said, "Okay, good. Glad you're in the loop, Tio." Then he turned back to the team and asked, "So… how do you guys think we should handle the Omar situation?"

"Look," Bunny said, "I'll be honest. She scares the shit outta me. I shot her in the chest with a .45 from ten feet away and she just ate it and went on her merry way. That said, I'm not sure what changed her, but she seems like she wants to help us. The question is, can we really trust her?"

"I feel the same way. Just not sure. What if she's giving Johnny a temporary pass until she kills David Tringa and then flips on us when we least expect it?" Christmas said.

"If she's really with us… I mean all the way… she's a powerful ally to have on the team," Neville said.

"Yeah, Nev, I agree, but since she did almost cut my head off a few months ago, you can understand why I'm conflicted," John said and then turned to Felix and asked: "What do you think, primo?"

Felix looked at his cousin and then around the table before speaking and finally said:

"If I were in your shoes I'd feel the same way. I saw what she did at the Con Ed plant and what she did to Johnny… did to me too," Felix said, touching the scar that ran horizontally across his right cheek. "All I know is she's changed since then and she really does want to help us. With Tariq and all the other threats… not just with Tringa."

"How do you know all that?" John asked.

"I've been talking to her," Felix said.

"What? When?" John asked.

"When I was in the can," Felix said.

"That's why you kept going? Thought you had the squirts," John said, smiling.

"Don Valdez, what do you think?" Bunny asked.

"You want to know what I think?" Gonzalo asked.

"Yes… we really do," Bunny said.

"I think you should ask her yourself," Gonzalo said.

There was stunned silence when Omar walked into the dining room and Gonzalo directed her to a seat next to him at the table. She smiled at Felix, waved at him and then looked around at each member of the team.

"You guys have some questions for me?" she asked.

CHAPTER 43

WAITING

Long Island, NY

THEY ALL SAT there with their mouths open staring at her. Gonzalo was the first to speak.

"Gentlemen…This is Nikita," he said.

"Please… Call me Nicky," she said.

Everyone introduced themselves and then there was a long thirty seconds of awkward silence.

"Pretty strange, huh?" Nicky said to John.

"Uh… yeah. About as trippy as it gets," he said.

"I'm going to say a few words to get things started, and then you can all take it from there," Gonzalo said. "First, Nikita has been staying here for the past few days and over that time we've gotten to know each other. She is a guest in this house and as my guest she will be treated with courtesy and respect.

"Second, and more importantly, she has disavowed her Tringa oath and offered to swear her allegiance to the Valdez family. I am ready to accept her vow of loyalty. As the head of the Valdez family, I can do this now without your consent, but in this case I won't. Not unless all of you here at the table agree to it.

"Based on your past encounters with her, some of you may have your doubts about her sincerity. That is completely understandable. Take your time. Get to know her as I have and then tell me what you decide," Gonzalo said.

He got up from the table, looked down at Nikita and placed his hand on her shoulder, gave it a squeeze, then looked at John and said: "I've said my piece. I'll leave you to it. See you all in the morning."

They all wished him goodnight as he walked out of the room and then all their eyes turned to Nikita.

"Why?" John asked, getting right to it.

"Which why? Why did I disavow my oath to kill you? Why am I helping you now? Why am I here?" she asked.

"Yeah, all of it," John said.

Despite Bishop's trust in his uncle's judgment, it was hard for him to forget looking into her eyes six months ago when Omar, now Nikita, had nearly cut his head off. Her eyes had been dead. At that moment when she swung the sword down at his neck her eyes had seemed almost shark-like and completely empty of emotion. Since then he'd actually had a few dreams about her. Nightmares really, where Omar's shark eyes appeared out of nowhere and her sword whistled towards him before he popped awake.

As he stared at her now she seemed like a completely different person. *Seemed* was the key word here. Her eyes were alive and almost...*kind*? She was beyond beautiful and had a sweet demeanor about her, but sitting across the table from the monster that came to kill him in his dreams was still very unsettling.

Nikita told them her story. About the old man coming

to her family's farm on her fifth birthday and buying her from her father for a bag of jewels. About how her father and the men of the village had followed her and the old man the next day. How they attacked him, thinking he had more riches hidden amongst his meager belongings. How she watched the old man effortlessly kill them all. How she stood over her father's body, her bare feet red with his blood as it flowed out onto the road.

She walked them through her fifteen years of Tringa survive-or-die training where children were forced to fight to the death on a daily basis. About all she endured at the hands of her Tringa masters as they relentlessly drove her to become the world's ultimate assassin.

Nicky was truthful. Telling her truth as she had to Gonzalo over the past few days. The telling of it as much a form of therapy and self-healing for her as it was to explain to the men at the table what led her to be sitting there amongst them. She gave them the high-level details about the many Tringa contracts she'd completed over the past ten years. She also told them to feel free to ask her anything about what she'd done and who she'd killed.

Nikita went on to explain that she now realized that over the past twenty-five years, she'd been living an almost out-of-body experience. At least that was the best way she could describe it. Throughout all the training and all the killing it was as if she was watching someone else do it all. Then she got to what finally changed her.

"Honestly, John. It was seeing you after your friend Benji and your father-in-law were killed by the Russian," Nikita said.

"You were there?" he asked.

"I was dressed like an old lady. Watching from across the

street. I saw you all come out of the freight entrance with the bodies. You looked so broken when your wife drove off. Deep down I've always felt sad and ashamed about being Omar the Tringa killer, but for the first time in my life I actually felt sad about someone other than myself. I basically knew in that moment that I couldn't kill you. It was the first time that's ever happened to me… Wait, no… The second," she said.

"What was the first?" John asked her.

"Felix. Felix, you were the first," she said, staring at him with warm eyes and a shy smile on her face. "I could have easily killed you after you hit me with the pipe… but…."

"But what?" Felix asked.

"Well… you were just so damn handsome I thought it would be a shame," Nicky said, blushing.

"So on your first date you cut him across the face and put a knife in his leg?" Bunny asked, rolling his eyes at her.

"I guess. I wouldn't call it a date, but definitely the first time we met," Nikita said.

"I'm really glad you didn't kill me," Felix said, giving her a big toothy grin.

"Me too," she said and winked at him.

"Nicky, I'm sorry," Bunny said. "What I just said was rude and as Don Valdez said, you're to be treated with courtesy and respect," he added.

"I understand why you have concerns about me, Bunny. You're the protector. John leads and you're always right behind him watching his back. I *was* the enemy. All I can tell you is that your enemy died when you shot her in the chest six months ago, and I thank you for it," Nicky said.

"You're thanking me for shooting you?" Bunny asked her.

"Yes, I am. For the first month… when I was lying in bed

recovering... I only heard my Tringa voice. Omar's voice. But then, slowly, gradually I heard *my* voice. The voice of my true self. I remembered my given name for the first time in... I don't know how long, but I completely forgot that many years before I became Omar I was just a little girl named Nikita. I finally remembered my mother calling me Nicky.

Now, Omar is gone and all that's left is me. Me," she said, pointing her thumb at her chest, "the woman sitting across from you now, is your ally and I'm your biggest fan," Nicky said to Bunny.

"So... just for the record... You're not going to kill me?" John asked her, his face softening a bit.

"Never," she said. "I don't expect you to just take my word for it, but know this... I pledge my life to protect you and all of you here. If you'll let me, I'll help you hunt these terrorists and I'll kill David Tringa."

"Tringa murdered some of our friends tonight," Bear said.

"I know," she said. "He won't stop. He'll keep coming and if any of you get in his way he'll kill you too."

"You're saying there's nothing we can do?" John said.

Nikita's long jet black hair swayed across her shoulders as she shook her head.

"No, of course not. He *can* definitely be killed... but unless one of you shoots him in the head he'll go right through you. He's just that good," she said.

"Can *you* kill him?" Neville asked.

"Yes," she said and then looked up at the ceiling for a moment. "Maybe," she said thoughtfully.

They talked for another half an hour, probing her for how and when she thought Tringa would attack, before John called it quits for the night.

John stood up and said, "Nicky, we've been going hard for two straight days and we'll be rolling again the second the intel boys get a location on Tariq."

He walked around the table and stuck out his right hand. "There's a lot more to talk about and we can pick this back up in the morning. For now I just want to say thanks."

She got up and shook his hand and asked, "For what?"

"For *not* killing me at the compound the other night and for your promise to help us," John said, meaning it.

"Thank you for letting me share my story and thanks for letting me stay. Your uncle has been very kind to me, but I know he would've told me to leave if that was your decision," she said. "Also, if you decide you *do* want me to go, I'll completely understand. Trust has to be earned and based on what you know about me there's probably still a lot of uncertainty. No hard feelings either way… and whatever you decide I'm still going to help you."

Nikita nodded, said goodnight to them all, then walked out of the dining room and headed upstairs.

"Well?" John asked, looking at Bunny.

"Honestly? I believe her. She still scares the shit outta me, but yeah… she's got my vote," Bunny said.

They all followed Bunny's lead, voting yes to add Nikita to the team. Neville was the lone holdout.

"She's a tremendous asset to have on our side, but I have two questions which we can't answer tonight. One, can she work as part of our team? I mean, she's always been a lone wolf killer. Can she now follow your orders?" he asked.

"Good question," John said.

"That was one. What's the second question?" Felix asked.

"You already know it, man. It's you. How does your involvement with her impact the team? Are *you* going to be able to put your feelings aside if and when Johnny sends her into a dicey situation?" Nev asked him.

"Yeah, I am. I know how many lives are on the line and I support anything we have to do to get the job done," Felix said.

"That's good enough for me," Nev said to him.

"Okay, we'll ask her in the morning about being a team player and taking orders. For now we all gotta get some sleep. There's plenty of bedrooms upstairs. Make yourselves at home and grab whatever bed is free. See you manana," John said.

Bishop led the way. They all grabbed their gear and trudged up the stairs behind him. He heard Felix directing the other team members to their rooms, but his cousin's voice seemed far away. He stopped at the door to the big bedroom he'd shared with Maria up until two weeks ago.

It's only been weeks? Feels like she's been gone a year, he thought.

He went in and saw that the rest of her clothes and shoes were gone. That was the last thing he remembered before he passed out at four thirty in the morning. John woke up at eight and checked for messages about Tariq's location and Clayton's condition. There was nothing new on Tariq. Truesdale sent a text letting him know that Clayton had been upgraded from critical to serious after the surgery. The patient was still sedated and for now it was just wait and see, and pray that no post op infections set in.

John thought about getting up and hitting the shower, then decided he should take advantage of the moment and let himself go back down for a few more hours. He popped back awake at ten thirty feeling rested and recharged. After a shower and a shave he got dressed and looked around the room. The envelope with Maria's goodbye letter was still on the nightstand. He opened it and quickly reread the letter one more time. He felt himself drifting back into sadness and he quickly reset himself.

"She's alive. She's safe and so is my baby. That's all that matters right now," he said aloud.

He'd forgotten all about the second letter. Maria's typed notes with her thoughts on how to find and kill John's long list of enemies. He started to open it, but was interrupted by a soft knock on the door. He quickly refolded the letter and tucked it into the back pocket of his black jeans and said, "Come on in."

Gonzalo opened the door and peeked in.

"Figured you were up," he said.

"Morning, Tio."

"Most of the team is downstairs having coffee. Breakfast will be ready in ten minutes. Before we join them… What do you think of her?" Zalo asked.

John told him there were concerns about her relationship with Felix and questions about whether she could follow orders.

"That's understandable. I hope she can take orders, but even if she can't I'm happy she's with us. A woman with those skills? That's a powerful asset to have on our side. As to Felix… I think he's in love so there's really nothing we can do besides cross our fingers and hope it works out," Gonzalo said and held up his crossed fingers to emphasize his point.

"I agree, Tio. I'm not gonna try to talk him out of it. You know something? After the fight at the Con Ed plant he talked about her. He was recovering from the leg wound she gave him and he went on and on about how beautiful she was. I told him to put two bullets in her head if he ever saw her again."

"Love at first sight? Stranger things have happened in this world," Zalo said.

"Let's go ask her if she thinks she can be a team player," John said.

Gonzalo agreed, turned to leave, then paused in the doorway. He turned back to John, then grabbed him and put him in a big bear hug.

"I'm so proud of you, my son," he said.

"Thanks for last night," John said. "I was kinda strung out. Overtired and overstressed. Your kick in the ass got me refocused."

They gave each other a few rapid-fire love smacks on the back before they broke and headed downstairs. When they got to the kitchen they both poured themselves cups of strong coffee. Their movements were identical and they took their coffee exactly the same way. A quarter inch of heavy cream and one half teaspoon of sugar.

The resident chef was cooking up a feast and told them breakfast would be ready in five minutes. Bishop and Gonzalo each grabbed a piece of crispy bacon and felt the mouth-watering crunch as they chewed on their way into the dining room.

"What the hell happened to you, Cat?" John asked when he saw his cousin slouched in a seat at the table.

Felix's face was puffy and he looked kind of beat up.

"Looks like he stopped by Nikita's room last night," Bunny said, a huge grin on his face, shaking his head in disbelief.

"*Damn* son, she really put it on you," Christmas said.

"Looks like total domination. Did you even compete?" Mace said.

"You need a blanket? Maybe some tea?" Bear asked.

"You look worse than Bobby. What the hell did she do to you?" Nev asked just as Nikita walked into the room looking fresh and beautiful as ever. She had a spring in her step, her hair was up in a long ponytail that bounced from side to side as she moved, and she had a slight glow in her cheeks.

"All we did was cuddle," she said, shrugging her shoulders as she looked around at the team and then blew on her coffee before taking a long sip.

They all pointed at Felix and started howling with laughter. He looked at Nikita and smiled, then put his elbows on the table and put his face in his hands. Even Gonzalo joined in and was doubled over next to John.

When they were all laughed out John walked over to the big bay windows and looked across the great lawn and up towards the hill where Benji, his parents, his Uncle Macho and all the other Valdez family members were buried. The gravestones, new and old, brought his thoughts back to the threat from one of their own, Nestor, AKA Geronimo Valdez. Over the past week John had been so preoccupied with getting the team together, finding Tariq, the firefight with Connie and the attack from David Tringa that he'd pushed the problem with Geronimo to his mind's back burner.

He leaned in close to his uncle to speak privately and asked: "What happened with the sixty-seven million?"

Before Gonzalo could answer, Felix joined them and asked, "Are you talking about Geronimo?"

John nodded.

"Well? Did you give him the money?" Felix asked.

"No. I never gave it to him," Gonzalo said.

"Have you heard from him?" John asked.

"He called last week and asked me where his *hundred* million was," Zalo said.

"*And?*" John asked.

"I said I needed more time and he hung up."

John thought about that for a moment and then switched gears. "Tio, where's Antonio?"

"He said he needed some time alone… Because of Benji," Gonzalo said.

"I don't believe that and I know you don't either," John said.

"Do you think he's with Nes… with Geronimo now?" Felix asked his uncle.

Gonzalo paused a moment before answering. Antonio was his nephew. The son of Sesa Valdez. Out of all of Zalo's eleven brothers, Sesa was the one he had always been closest to. Over the past fifteen years the two of them had carefully groomed Antonio to be the next head of the family. Now Sesa was dead. He was still on life support from Connie's head shot six months ago, but Gonzalo had already accepted the reality that his lifelong advisor and beloved brother was gone forever.

As the head of the family and because Connie had been gunning for him, and not Sesa, Gonzalo felt responsible for his brother's death. His feelings of guilt were powerful, but purely personal. They didn't spill over to his decisions on how he guided the family and doing what was best to protect the many… Not the few.

He looked at John and then at Felix. His dark, scarred face was blank and void of emotion. No one, other than his two adopted sons standing before him, would've been able to detect the sadness in his yellow eyes.

"Yes, Felix. Antonio has left us. He's an Apache now," Gonzalo said.

"You don't think…?" Felix asked.

"No, I don't think. I know…They're coming to kill you, Tio," John said.

Gonzalo nodded. "I was hoping they would come before you and your men arrived. I don't want them distracted by Valdez family business," Gonzalo said.

"Tio, you were open and honest with them last night. We've got too much coming at us to hold back now," John said.

He turned to the team and asked them to listen up. All the side talk died instantly and they either sat up or moved in closer to hear what he had to say. Bishop didn't sugarcoat it. He broke it down and explained to them that his uncle and cousin would be showing up at some point with murder in mind.

"Johnny, you gotta tell us how you want us to handle this. I mean, they're your family. We're ready to do whatever you need us to do, but with this there can't be any gray area," Bear said.

"Yeah, you're a hundred percent right, Bear. I guarantee you when they get here we'll go to the study and that's where they'll make their move. I want you guys out of the way and out of sight," John said.

Gonzalo nodded in agreement and added: "Anything that happens with my brother and nephew is between the three of us," he said pointing to John and Felix. "My brother's men are a different story."

"Geronimo will have a security force with him. Your job is to take them out… but if shit goes south and the three of us are all dead, we'd really appreciate it if you'd blast Geronimo and Antonio out of their socks. Then it'll be up to you to take out Tariq. Deal?" John said.

"We got you," Bear said.

"Can I make a suggestion?" Nikita asked.

When she was done John nodded his head in approval and said, "Solid plan. If he shows up we'll go with that, but in the meantime let's refocus on Tariq. Tomorrow is Thanksgiving. No way he waits around until Christmas to make his move. I gotta believe Thanksgiving is when Tariq and his crazies are gonna strike."

They spent the next hour examining Tariq's possible targets and then laying out their strategies to take him down. They all agreed that no matter what Tariq's plan was, he was going to have unidentified bad guys hiding in the crowds, ready to back shoot or blow up the team once they were engaged. The key was to have two long guns on overwatch and then mount a staggered attack with primary shooters in front with backup trailing twenty or thirty feet behind.

The tactical planning session was cut short when a member of Gonzalo's security team walked in and announced there were some guys at the front gate demanding to be let in.

"Send them up," Zalo said, leading the way to the front door.

"Geronimo?" Christmas asked.

Gonzalo shook his head no. "This is something else," he said.

CHAPTER 44
TAXES

Long Island, NY

JOHN FOLLOWED HIS uncle to the door with Felix trailing a few steps behind them. They watched three cars drive through the main gate, then wind their way along the quarter mile curving driveway before they pulled up to the front entrance. The car doors popped open and twelve guys in dark suits, white shirts and a mix of blue and black neckties stepped out of the vehicles. All twelve men had their jaws set in determination and were staring intently at John as they marched towards him.

"John Bishop?" the man in front asked. He had a flattop haircut and wore thick-framed black horn-rimmed glasses.

"Yep," he said. "Who's asking?"

"The IRS and the Southern District of New York," horn rims said.

"The IRS? You guys are making house calls now?" John asked.

"The Criminal Investigation Division does," the agent said.

"Okay. Why are you here and what do you want?"

"I'm Senior Agent Hastings and you're coming with us, Bishop."

"That's not happening. I'll ask you again… What do you want, Hastings?"

Hastings opened his jacket and pushed it back over his hip holster. "Watch your tone or you're getting cuffed and going face down before we drag you out of here."

John immediately saw what this was. He knew these clowns were sent on Caleb Meecham's orders to harass and intimidate him. That was never going to happen, but Bishop still made one last try at defusing the situation:

"Look Hastings, I'm in the middle of something right now, but I can stop by your office one day next week to discuss my tax returns. Just leave me your card. You have my word— I'll call and make an appointment, okay?

"No way, Bishop. I'm *not* going to tell you again. Get in the car. Now!" Hastings shouted, inching his hand closer to his pistol.

John moved forward. Agent Hastings tried to step back, but his CID guys and the Southern District investigators were packed together and standing too close behind him to give him any place to go. John got right in his face and then shot his left hand out, grabbing and twisting Hastings's right wrist in a vicelike grip. His face remained calm and relaxed as he forced the agent's hand onto the butt of the Smith & Wesson in his hip holster.

"Pull it," John said, nearly nose to nose with Hastings.

"You just assaulted a federal officer! You're under arrest!" he squealed.

All the agents were completely focused on John and didn't notice Bunny, Christmas and the rest of the team spread out in a semi-circle around and behind them. The twelve suits also had no way of knowing there were over thirty guns zeroed in on them from concealed positions around the property by Gonzalo's security detail.

"Assault? All I did was hold your hand, Hastings," John said.

"Dumbass. You touch an agent in any way, it's automatically assaulting an officer."

"Fuck it then," John said. He raised his right hand and slapped Hastings hard across the face. The horn-rimmed glasses went flying and both lenses shattered when they hit the paved driveway.

"Now, all you boys have a simple choice. You can get in your cars and get out of here or you're the ones who're gonna be face down and shackled with your own cuffs." Bishop hadn't raised his voice, but there was no mistaking the menace in his tone.

"You know how much trouble you're in, Bishop? I've got eleven witnesses here who are all going to testify to what you did. You'll be lucky if you're out in ten years," the red-faced agent said while he rubbed his left cheek.

John cracked him again, striking with his left hand this time.

"Make it twenty," he said.

Hastings reached for his gun and John gave him a swift knee in the nuts. That doubled him over and he slowly sank down to his knees, holding his balls with both hands. A few of the agents moved their hands towards their weapons, but John and the entire team could see their hearts weren't in it.

"Easy, boys," Bunny said. "We don't want any of you accidently discharging a weapon so we're gonna need you all to place your hands behind your heads."

The agents looked at Bunny and saw the MP7 in his hands. Then they glanced around and saw the rest of the team surrounding them with a mix of handguns and semi-automatic weapons. They all quickly raised their hands and grabbed the backs of their heads.

Felix, Neville, Mace and Chago disarmed all the agents including Hastings, and then removed the magazines from their pistols. They racked each of the weapons, checking to see if any of the agents had bullets chambered and ready to fire. None of them did. These guys weren't streetwise law enforcement officers ready for a firefight. They were basically accountants with concealed carry permits.

John looked at the line of agents and zeroed in on a pudgy one with dark hair and a close-cropped mustache. The guy's blue eyes were darting back and forth and his legs were shaking with fear. John grabbed him by the arm, guided him away from the others, and asked him what his name was.

"Jerry. Jerry Rosen," he said.

"Why are you guys here, Jerry? I know this isn't about my tax return. What's the real reason?"

"A guy named Meecham came to our office and met with Hastings. After Meecham left, Hastings said we had to go arrest somebody. Which was weird because that's not at all what we do."

"Arrest people?" John asked.

"Yeah. We don't do that. We follow the money and work with the DOJ to hand down indictments, but we don't put people in handcuffs. At least I've never heard of it. Even if we did, we all know who you are. Know you're a hero and all. None of the guys wanted any part of this, but Hastings is the senior agent. He's a real prick and he already makes our lives a living hell," Rosen said.

"Thanks, Jerry. I promise you that Agent Hastings will permanently be out of your hair as of tomorrow morning," John said.

"You don't mean?" Rosen made the sign of a gun with his fingers.

"C'mon, Jerry," John said, shaking his head. "Hastings is losing his job for sure, but there are some people above me who may want him in a cage for a few years because of this bullshit."

"I'm sorry. We all are. We just didn't know what to do and we definitely didn't have any idea what we were getting ourselves into," Rosen said just as they heard the sound of truck engines in the distance.

John pulled Jerry with him as he ran back to the house.

"What's wrong?" Rosen said.

"Trouble," John said as he looked back at the long line of SUVs and Hummers heading towards the main gate. "Jerry, we're going to throw your weapons in the trunk. Pack up your people and start the cars, but don't make a move until I give you the word, okay?"

Rosen couldn't hide his fear but John was impressed by the man when he asked, "Do you need our help?"

"Appreciate the offer, Jerry, but we got this and I don't want you or any of your guys getting hurt… Remember… wait for my signal before you pull out, and when you do… pull out nice and easy."

All the pistols were tossed into the trunk of the first car. Then they picked up Hastings, who was cursing and shouting at John as he got dumped in the back seat of car two. All the agents climbed into their vehicles and slammed the doors just as the SUVs pulled up alongside and behind them.

On John's signal Bunny, Christmas, Bear, Mace, Nev,

Chago and Bobby had all disappeared through the front doors and gone into the house before the caravan of trucks arrived. John, Felix, Gonzalo and Nikita were the only ones left standing outside to meet Geronimo and his Apaches.

"Hello, big brother," Geronimo said as he stepped out of the second SUV.

Gonzalo didn't return the greeting. He saw the SUV's back door swing open and watched Antonio hop out and walk towards them.

"Tio," Antonio said to Zalo.

"You're an Apache now?" Felix asked Antonio.

Geronimo answered for him. "No, nephew. Antonio is my partner."

"Yeah, sure he is," Felix said.

Geronimo looked at him and gave him one of his long silent stares.

"Who's this?" he asked finally, looking Nikita up and down.

"My girlfriend," Felix said.

Another silent stare.

"Who're the guys in the cars?" Antonio asked.

"IRS," John said. "I'm getting audited. They're just leaving."

He walked over to the first car and nodded at Rosen, who was in the front passenger seat. The cars eased out, made a wide turn in the open area in front of the estate's garages and guest house, and then drove back down towards the main gate.

"Zalo, we're here to talk," Geronimo said.

"Talk? Sure. Go ahead," Gonzalo said.

"Let's go inside. I feel guns on me out here. My

compliments to Christmas and his men. I can't see any of them, but I know they're out there," Geronimo said.

"Where is Christmas?" Antonio asked.

"In the city with my team. There's a group of ISIS terrorists planning a Thanksgiving Day attack on New York and we're going to stop it," John said.

"ISIS terrorists? Here in New York? We can't have that," Geronimo said, then held out his hand and said, "After you" to Nikita as they all went inside.

CHAPTER 45

GERONIMO

HE HAD BEEN busy over the past few weeks. After decapitating the Russian Mafia's management teams inside all the prisons under his control, he turned his attention to the Aryan Brotherhood, the Mexican Mafia and the long list of prison gangs across the country.

Geronimo's business model was simple. He already controlled eighty percent of the US state and federal correctional facilities. Inside the razor wire-topped walls he was willing to let criminal organizations continue to exist with some semblance of autonomy. More like the appearance of autonomy. He would allow their leadership to pretend to operate semi-independently as long as the cash flowed without interruption and every one of their members understood that his Apaches were untouchable.

He made it clear that this was the only deal on the table. They could keep a small piece of business. If they bent the knee he'd let them hold on to just enough to make a living. Otherwise they were getting wiped out.

The Mexican Mafia, La Familia, Barrio Azteca, Neta, the Black Guerilla Army, the Aryans and some of the other gangs had collectively given him some stiff resistance over the past few weeks. The fighting had been bloody and his targeted attacks on their leadership had spread outside the prisons and into the streets. Geronimo knew they wouldn't bow down without taking some major losses, so he'd mapped out a list of high-value targets long before the fighting started.

He went after what they all loved. Their mothers, fathers, brothers, wives, sons, daughters and even grandchildren. It didn't matter where they lived. From El Salvador to Sinaloa, from El Paso to East L.A. When entire families disappeared from their homes without a trace, the men behind the concrete walls quickly waved the white flag.

He was expanding from city to city and would soon own the streets too. For Geronimo, prisons were the foundation. He'd started with just two Apaches. Now he had an army of nearly five thousand, and that number was growing every day.

His vision was to reverse engineer the way many of the false kings who came before him tried to control the global drug markets.

In the early eighties Escobar had leveraged his ownership of the Colombian coca fields and labs to wear the crown for a few years. In the late eighties the Mexicans had taken over when Miguel Ángel Félix Gallardo organized all the Cartels by using the power of their cross-border transportation routes. That had only lasted until all the Cartels went back to war with each other, and it had been chaos ever since.

Geronimo locked down distribution first. He was close to owning transportation and then the final piece would be controlling the source. He knew the Colombians and Mexicans wouldn't go down without a fight, but he was looking forward to it. He'd seen his future and within a year it would all be his.

He'd own it all. Everything from the fields to the labs, the global transportation routes to the street corner and of course the penal systems around the world. Prisons, corrections officers, cops and judges. After that it was the military and the beating heart of the government itself. Congressmen, senators, cabinet members and eventually the president. They would either all work for him or be publicly executed as a warning to anyone else foolish enough to defy him. Bend the knee and stay in line… or die bloody. It was that simple.

Geronimo had been going over his battle plans for years, reviewing and modifying his tactics and strategies like a three-dimensional chess master. When he ran the numbers from his jail cell he anticipated losses of around five thousand Apaches. Even if he doubled it to ten thousand or more, the losses were still acceptable. He wanted his army strong and battle-tested, and those who survived the initial wars would be forged into an unbreakable fighting force.

As for his enemies, he figured he'd have to drop at least five thousand bodies here in the US It would probably be three or four times that number as he continued his expansion across the border into Mexico and then down into Central and South America. Five thousand, ten thousand, twenty, or even thirty thousand enemy dead were all numbers he was ready for.

The one thing Geronimo didn't want and couldn't afford was a protracted war. Swift surgical attacks were the key to victory. Every prominent gang leader was already on his kill list, and for the more structured organizations that had succession plans in place Geronimo sent in his Apache army to do what he called a cleansing. For the cleansings there could be no survivors. Every member of the gang was to be hunted down and executed.

So far, all his carefully orchestrated strategies were going according to plan… as he knew they would. Over the years he had seen the outcomes so clearly in his dreams that everything he was experiencing now felt like déjà vu. He started having vivid dreams when he was a boy, but once he got to prison his dreams had evolved into something else. They became premonitions. In them he saw his victories because he knew in advance where all the pitfalls and dangers lay in wait.

That was one of the reasons he had never been concerned about his brother Gonzalo. Zalo wasn't a threat to him. Geronimo had added his brother to his mental kill list years ago and he was hoping Antonio would man up and take care of it for him. Either way Zalo was a dead man.

Antonio stepping up would actually save a lot of lives. Geronimo hoped he wouldn't have to order the cleansing of the entire Valdez family. He had seen one version of the future where the bodies of his former relatives and all the Valdez soldiers were being bulldozed into a mass grave. He also saw another reality where everyone except his brothers Gonzalo and Sesa, and his nephews John and Felix were alive and well.

In truth he didn't want to have to cleanse them. He didn't really know John, but had always admired what he accomplished in the military. Felix, though. Felix was different. Geronimo spent four years with his nephew when Felix was doing his time in El Mira State Penitentiary. Geronimo always liked him and he remembered saying to himself, *If I ever had a son I'd want him to be just like Felix.*

It was too bad. He realized he was actually going to miss Felix. Deep down, in some remote part of him, he was saddened by what was about to happen. The feeling was there, but as distant as a star in the sky.

They headed through the house to the study. When they

got there, Geronimo led the way in and walked over to the big mahogany desk. He went around it and sat down in Gonzalo's high-backed executive chair. Three of his Apaches followed them in, then stood in front of John, Felix and Gonzalo and held out their hands.

Each of the Tres Gatos (three cats), so named for their matching yellow eyes, slowly pulled pistols from their waistbands and handed them over to Geronimo's security detail. The three Apaches then walked across the room and stood at parade rest, waiting for further orders.

"Please have a seat," Geronimo said, directing John and Gonzalo to the couch and Felix and Nikita to a matching leather loveseat.

"I don't suppose you have a pistol on you, do you, little lady?" Geronimo asked Nikita.

She smiled and shook her head no. "I don't care for them," she said.

"Bueno," Geronimo said. "You're far too pretty to be playing with guns."

She smiled at Geronimo again, but didn't say anything in response to the compliment. Then something caught the attention of both her and Felix. They watched Antonio casually glide over from the study's doorway to a few feet behind the big couch. It was a subtle move, but Nikita and Felix noted it because Antonio was now standing directly behind Gonzalo.

Geronimo leaned back in the high-backed swivel chair and looked over the desk at his former family with indifference. He knew they were all going to arrive at this moment together. He'd seen it in his dreams. The only person he hadn't seen was the girl. That bothered him.

Why didn't I see her? he asked himself.

He dismissed the thought and took it all in. It was a scene in a movie. A scene that he'd scripted and watched many times over. Every actor was queued for their lines and sitting or standing exactly where they were expected to be.

Geronimo spun himself around in his "director's chair" and stared at the character playing the role of Wild Bill Hickok.

My foolish brother doesn't know he's holding Aces and Eights… The dead man's hand, he thought.

"Gonzalo… Why did you make it come to this?" Geronimo asked.

"Not sure what you mean, little brother."

"You were supposed to deliver my hundred million a week ago. I've been busy with more important things since you missed the deadline… But *now*? Now I'm here."

There was another one of Geronimo's sixty-second pauses. Gonzalo broke the silence.

"Okay, you're here. What do you want to discuss?"

"I want to know what you think your punishment should be," Geronimo said.

"*Punishment*? I don't know. A late fee I guess," Gonzalo said, shrugging his shoulders.

"Late fee? This ain't about library books. You owe me money, but the truth is it's really not about that anymore," Geronimo said.

"Then what's it about?" Zalo asked.

"In a word… Respect."

"I've always respected you. We're family. You're my brother, Nestor."

"There it is. You were already a hundred mil in the hole and now you're givin' me another dis?" Geronimo asked, but the question was rhetorical.

"I'm done with the Geronimo bullshit," Zalo said. "Wake the fuck up. You're Nestor Valdez and nothing will ever change that."

"That's where you're wrong, Zalo. I *am* Geronimo. More importantly, we're not brothers anymore."

"That's what I thought, but I just needed to hear you say it. So… What happens now?" Gonzalo asked.

"What happens now is you have to be a true leader," Geronimo said.

"How?"

"By making the ultimate sacrifice to save the Valdez family. You die and they live on."

"You're going to kill me, Nestor?"

"No. Not me," Geronimo said, smiling.

CHAPTER 46
ANTONIO

HIS MIND WAS racing as he stared at the back of his uncle's head. Gonzalo had handpicked *him* to be his successor. To be next in line to lead the Valdez family. This was no small matter… especially with Gonzalo's father-and-son-like bonds to both John and Felix.

Antonio knew what an honor it was to be the chosen one, and for fifteen years he had greedily soaked up the daily lessons from his uncle and from his father, Sesa Valdez. He listened, observed and waited patiently for them to hand over the reins.

Antonio's apprenticeship was just beginning when Gonzalo announced that he was taking the family out of the drug game. Although he was firmly opposed to the decision, he'd kept his opinion to himself. He was shocked that Gonzalo and his father didn't seem to have any remorse about turning their backs on hundreds of millions of dollars, but that was their choice.

He had his own vision and his own plans. Once he became the new Don he would quickly retake abandoned territory and return the Valdez family to its glory days of ruling a drug empire. He was already getting the pieces in place and identifying which of the New York kingpins he would have to wipe out. Starting at the top, he'd kill the strongest ones first, and then see which of the weaker crews were willing to surrender and which ones wanted to die bloody.

Gonzalo had never given him a sense of when his time would come, but Antonio marked his own mental calendar with a target date. That date had come and gone two years ago. Since then he continued to respectfully bide his time, and with growing impatience, wait his turn.

As for his father's death, Antonio didn't blame Gonzalo for that. It had just been Sesa's bad luck that he'd bent down and picked up Gonzalo's hat and then put it on his own head a moment before the sniper fired. Part of him, a part buried deep down in the recesses of his soul, had been relieved that his father was gone. He loved his dad, but he craved the throne even more, and his drive to rule the family trumped love. Once Antonio knew for sure that his father would never wake up from the head wound, he finally felt free to take what he knew was his.

Antonio wanted the transition to appear natural and the key was all in the timing. He needed Gonzalo to stumble badly. To make a mistake that would force the family to look to a younger, more capable leader to run the show. When Gonzalo announced that the Valdez family was turning its back on the streets to become military contractors he could barely contain himself. The move was so insane that Antonio had been about to stand up and take his seat at the head of the table right then and there. Gonzalo completely ruined the moment and stole his glory when he showed the CIA contract and handed out the six-figure paychecks.

That day had been one of life's insane roller coaster rides

where men make plans and God just laughs and laughs. One minute his dreams were shattered and they were all getting ready to start business classes. Then the next thing he knew he was standing over Benji's body with the Valdez army ready for war.

When Antonio shot the Russians in cold blood at their waterfront warehouse in Red Hook he was genuinely enraged over Benji's death. Benji Medina had been a brother from another mother since elementary school and he had big plans for the deadly Valdez family enforcer when they retook control of the drug trade.

Sad and angry as he was, deep down Antonio wanted to thank the Russian hitman who'd killed Benji and Alastair Williams. The angrier everyone was and the more chaos there was surrounding the family, the easier his coup would be.

What he hadn't considered in all his grand plans were his cousins. With Gonzalo moving the family into this business venture, Antonio knew it was pure fantasy to think his uncle would step aside voluntarily. The harsh reality was that he would have to kill the man who trained and mentored him, and he was ready to do it.

But John and Felix?

He somehow missed that. Maybe because it was too awful a thought to entertain and his calculating mind had shielded his heart from the truth. His Uncle Geronimo had unceremoniously pulled back the curtain and showed him what the true cost of becoming Don Valdez would be. Both his cousins would have to die too.

And the girl, he thought.

There couldn't be any witnesses. All of the staff and the security detail had to go too.

What's the difference? a voice in his head said. *After my uncle and cousins, who cares about another twenty or thirty bodies?*

Antonio pulled the .40 cal Glock 27 from his hip holster and let it hang by his side for a moment.

"Ah. I see," Gonzalo said without turning around, and still keeping his eyes locked on Nestor's. "You're not going to kill me, little brother. You're going to have our nephew do it for you."

"Thought you would've seen it coming, Zalo. Shows how you're slipping. A few years ago?… No way you would've missed it," Geronimo said.

He took his eyes off Gonzalo and looked above him to stare at Antonio.

"Go ahead. Put him out of his misery," Geronimo said to him.

Antonio raised his gun and pointed it at the back of Gonzalo's head. He held it there for what seemed like an eternity. Antonio was six-four and powerfully built, but the Glock suddenly felt heavy in his hand.

"Do it," Geronimo commanded.

Antonio shook his head. He raised his gun a few inches higher and pointed it at his other uncle. The one sitting behind the desk.

"I can't, Tio," he said.

Felix was next to Nikita. Their legs and shoulders had been touching until she shifted slightly to her left, creating some space between them. The subtle move got his attention. Felix kept his breathing steady while he planted his feet firmly on the floor and tensed his legs. Sensing she was about to act; he was poised and ready to back her up.

Inside the wide sleeves of her light jacket Nikita kept six throwing knives hidden in sheaths wrapped around her wrists. In a practiced move she placed her elbows on her knees and put each of her hands in the sleeve of the other arm. Her jacket didn't move when she smoothly unsheathed the blades, three in each hand, the flat black daggers held between her fingers in a closed fist.

The three Apaches carefully watched Antonio, just as Geronimo had ordered them to. When they saw the threat from their boss's nephew, they didn't hesitate. All three raised their weapons. The Apache in the middle was slower and tried to lift his gun to shoulder height and take aim. He was dead before he could put any pressure on the trigger of his 9mm SIG. The other two fired from the hip and managed to get off a round each before Nikita's hands went up in a blur.

Six knives flew across the room and all three Apaches were dead before they hit the ground. The tattooed man on the left and the one on the right both had blades buried up to the handles sticking out of their eyes. The man in the middle had one knife in his throat and another in his chest.

Nikita lifted her left pants leg and pulled a Taurus PT638 .380 auto from an ankle holster. She stood up and pointed it at Geronimo.

Felix stared at her and thought… *Damn, my girl is on another level.*

Nikita never took her eyes off Geronimo, but she was thinking about Felix. She'd felt it when he got himself tensed and ready to join the fight.

My man was unarmed and ready to face guns for me, she thought.

"Who are you?" Geronimo asked her.

"Like we told you. I'm Felix's woman," Nikita said.

"So strange that I never saw you," Geronimo said, his brow knotted with confusion.

She had no idea what that meant, so she didn't say anything.

Gonzalo and John both hopped up, walked around the couch and looked down at Antonio. He'd been hit hard by the shots from the two Apaches and had both hands pressing on his stomach. They knelt on either side of him.

"I couldn't do it. I'm so sorry, Tio," Antonio said, his eyes wet with regret.

"I knew you couldn't," Gonzalo said.

"You were willing to bet your life on it?" Antonio asked.

Blood was coming up from his stomach wounds. Two wet lines of red flowed from the corners of his mouth and down across his cheeks.

"I told him he was crazy to risk everything for you, cousin, but Tio said there was no way you'd kill him," John said.

"I was supposed to kill you too," Antonio said, coughing up more blood as Felix joined them and knelt down next to Gonzalo. "Was supposed to kill all of you."

"We know. Tio swore you'd come back to us before anyone got hurt," John said.

"I fucked up. Big time… Johnny… Felix… I'm sorry. I'm sorry for all of it… Know my Dad's gonna be pissed when I see him."

John, Felix and Gonzalo all placed their hands on top of Antonio's as his eyes darted to each of theirs.

"First he'll slap you. Then he's gonna hug you tight," Gonzalo said.

"Don't stress it, cuz. We got you," Felix said.

Antonio's eyes went wide when he suddenly remembered his sister. "Oh man…Silvi… Tell her… Just tell her I said…"

He died before he could give them his final message for Silvi.

"Such a waste," Gonzalo said.

"He made some bad choices, but he came back to us in the end. He died a Valdez. Not a fucking Apache," Felix said.

"Speaking of Apaches," John said, nodding his head towards the other side of the couch. "What're you gonna do with him?"

Gonzalo locked eyes with John, but didn't answer. He got up, wiped his bloody palms on his pants legs, then walked over to Nikita, who was still pointing the Taurus at Geronimo.

"Can I have that?" Gonzalo asked, extending his right hand.

She passed him the gun and moved a few feet away just as John and Felix came over and stood on either side of their uncle. All four of them were in front of the desk facing Geronimo, who hadn't moved since the shots were fired and the knives were thrown. He seemed lost in thought, staring blankly at some faraway place.

"Such a waste, little brother," Zalo said.

Geronimo came back from his dream state and said, "I still don't know why I never saw her."

"Nikita?" Zalo asked.

"Yes. I never saw her in my dreams."

"Doesn't matter now," Zalo said.

"No, it doesn't," Geronimo said and then stuck a few fingers in his mouth and whistled loudly.

"They're not coming," John said just as Christmas and the team came through the door.

They were all wearing body armor and tac vests and carrying silenced MP7s. They walked in and looked down at

Antonio, and then at the three dead men with Nikita's knives sticking out of them.

"All good?" John asked Christmas.

"Yep. The Apaches are all dead," Christmas said.

"Well played, big brother," Geronimo said.

"Five minutes ago we weren't family and now you're my brother again?"

Geronimo shrugged and said, "More Apaches will come."

"We'll deal with them when they do," Zalo said. He paused for a moment and then added, "You know…. You pissed off some very powerful people."

"Who're you working for, Zalo? The Mexicans or the Colombians?"

Gonzalo laughed.

"Neither. I was at Camp David two weeks ago and the president said *you* are an imminent threat to the safety and security of the United States. He put you on his top ten kill list."

"The fuckin' president put a hit on me?" Geronimo asked.

Gonzalo nodded. "He considers you and your Apache nation a terrorist organization right up there with ISIS and Al Qaeda. Our new business deal is contingent on you being gone… Out of respect, they asked me if I wanted to handle it personally or have them send in a kill team."

"Why'd you wait? Why didn't you act sooner?" Geronimo asked.

"Because of Antonio. I owed it to Sesa to see if his only son would wake up before it was too late," Zalo said.

"Very noble of you," Geronimo said.

Gonzalo shrugged. "Like I said, I wanted to give Antonio a chance. As for you… I shed a few tears when I took the contract, but my eyes weren't leaking for *you*. It was for the kid I once knew and loved.… I don't know who you are or what you are, but I *know* you're not a Valdez anymore."

"Like I told you the day I got out of prison, I made my own family," Geronimo said.

"Yeah, you did. That's why we're not burying you up on the hill. In fact, we're not burying you at all. The cleaners are gonna grind you up, incinerate your ass and then dump the ashes in the trash along with the rest of your crew."

"Wow. Very scary, hermano. Enough with all the drama. Put the gun down and let's talk."

"Not interested," Zalo said.

"Wait… Just listen to my counter-offer."

"Goodbye, Nestor."

Zalo squeezed the trigger and hit Geronimo center mass. The .380 hollow point mushroomed on impact, tearing through his chest plate and ripping through his heart and lungs. Nestor Valdez died with his eyes open, giving them another one of his weird silent stares. They all stood there looking back at him for a long thirty seconds, wondering if the monster was really dead.

"You okay, Tio?" John finally asked.

"Yes. I'm fine. He was my brother once, but I don't recognize this man," Zalo said.

"He was a fucking lunatic and I'm glad he's dead," Felix said.

John watched Nikita go over to the three Apaches and retrieve her throwing knives. She wiped all six blades on the dead men's shirts before she re-sheathed them along her wrists.

"Nicky. Welcome to the team," he said. "You still scare the shit outta me, but I'm really glad you're on our side."

"Thanks, John. I've never worked with a team before, so

just let me know what you need me to do and how you want me to operate," she said.

"Quick question. How did the knives get in those Apaches?" Bunny asked.

"I barely saw her move. She was next to Felix on the small couch. From a seated position she threw all six blades... Three from each hand. Nestor's men had their guns up and they were dead before they hit the floor," John said.

"Jesus," Mace said.

"I'll tell you how we want you to operate... You just keep being you, girl," Bunny said to her, shaking his head in awe.

John turned to face the team and asked, "How're you guys doing?"

Bear, Nev, Mace, Chago, Bobby, Christmas and Bunny just stood there staring at him.

"What?" John asked.

"Johnny, we've all seen and done some insane things over the years, but... I mean... C'mon man... You gotta admit this is some otherworldly, beyond surreal shit you've got surrounding you," Nev said.

"Haven't had time to step back and really look at it, but I see your point. Not much we can do about it except put these crazy motherfuckers down one by one," John said.

"No argument here, brother," Nev said.

"What now?" Felix asked.

"Tomorrow is Thanksgiving. Since we're all in agreement it's the day Tariq's launching his attack, we're relocating to the city," John said.

"Campos Plaza?" Felix said.

"Yeah. It's a bunker with plenty of beds for all of us and we can be on target anywhere in Manhattan within ten minutes," John said.

Several of the team members tensed and turned their heads towards the sound of loud engines coming up the driveway.

"You can all relax. That's the cleaning crew. They're here to dispose of this garbage," Gonzalo said, nodding at his former brother.

"What about Silvi? Her father's on life support and now her brother's dead. She's gonna be really fucked up over this," Felix said to his uncle.

"She's at Campos. When we get there we'll tell her what a hero Antonio was. How her brother saved our lives today," Gonzalo said.

They all nodded their heads in approval then stood there, not sure what to do or say until John snapped them out of it.

"Gather your gear and be ready to roll out in ten minutes," he said.

There were four armored SUVs revved and waiting for them when they went outside with their gun bags and backpacks. The Valdez cleaning crew had already loaded up the fourteen dead Apaches who had been scattered around the driveway and slumped over in their bullet-riddled vehicles. The cleaners turned on the heavy vacuums to suck up the brass and soak up the pools of blood before they turned on the hoses to do a final washdown.

"Like I said… Beyond surreal," Nev said as they drove away.

CHAPTER 47

TURKEY DAY

Bushwick, Brooklyn

WHEN TARIQ WOKE up at 6AM he felt an instant rush of adrenaline. Today was *the* day and it was nearly impossible to contain his excitement. His heart began beating rapidly and his thoughts immediately started racing. He blinked several times, then closed his eyes, forcing himself to slow his breathing and calm his mind.

No mistakes today, he said to himself, then rolled out of bed and got down on the floor to begin his morning workout. The routine of pushups, dips and sit-ups got him refocused. He went at it a little harder than usual, doing three sets of one hundred pushups instead of his usual seventy-five.

Why not? This may be the last day I live in this body.

By the time he finished he was damp with sweat and mentally locked in. Then he shit, showered, shaved and quickly dressed. Tariq headed downstairs wearing dark blue Gap jeans, a white tee under a black turtleneck and Merrell high-top walking boots.

The team was already gathered around the table sipping

Arabic coffee and dipping warm bread into bowls of labneh and honey. After the morning greetings he paused for a moment to take it all in. Every member of his team was calm and cool. None of them displayed any signs of being scared or nervous, and he couldn't have been prouder.

You have trained them well and they are ready, he thought.

When they finished eating, one of the women who traveled with them from Seattle approached him…

"Tariq, you haven't told us when we should head back home with the children. Do we leave this afternoon or wait a few days after your mission has been completed?" she asked.

"I am so sorry, mother. We have been so focused on what we are about to do, I forgot to give you your instructions," he said.

"Oh yes, we all understand and we are only here to serve you," she said, waving her hand to include the five other mothers who were standing in the living room.

Some of them were holding their toddlers in their arms as they smiled at Tariq and looked upon him with love and adoration. He was a living hero to all of them and they felt blessed and honored to have played even a small part in helping launch the attacks.

"Allah blesses you all for your sacrifices," Tariq said. "We need you to remain here for just a few more days. The cars and a van will arrive on Sunday to bring you back home," Tariq said.

"Wonderful. Thank you, Tariq. May God protect you and welcome you all into paradise," she said.

Tariq smiled at her and nodded. "We have a few more hours of work to do, mother. Would you mind waiting for us downstairs? We'll stop down and say goodbye before we leave."

The women all hustled out of the room and headed down to the furnished basement that also had a playroom for the kids.

"Now, let's do a final weapons check and then one final mission review," Tariq said.

The team got to work. They checked their guns first, fieldstripping their Beretta APX 9mm subcompact handguns and their 9mm Micro Uzis. All their weapons and ordnance had to be easily concealed, and the APX's three-inch barrel and light weight (only nineteen ounces) made it the ideal handgun for them. Each of them would carry two of the Berettas and four extra eight-round magazines in their jacket pockets.

The Israeli-made Micro Uzis were their street sweepers that would flatten anything on the receiving end of seventeen hundred rounds per minute of 9mm slugs tearing through them. The Uzis, with their extended magazines, were too big to conceal under coats, but they fit nicely into backpacks and carry bags.

Tariq and the team checked every weapon, and unloaded and then reloaded every magazine before they turned their attention to the explosives. They slowly and meticulously examined every wire, every remote and handheld detonator, and then made sure all the C-4 was molded to perfection. When they were done, Tariq congratulated them on their attention to detail and then reminded them again that the mission was far from over.

"We strike in two hours. Remember all your training. Think about the millions of dollars that were spent and all the lives that have been sacrificed to get us to where we are today. Let nothing stand in our way. We owe it to ourselves and to the many thousands of our brothers and sisters who have been massacred by the Americans. We will not fail them. We will not fail ourselves and most important, we will not fail God... Allahu Akbar!"

"Allahu Akbar," was repeated over and over again until they were worked into a frenzy.

Tariq finally raised his hand and the room was instantly quiet: "Before we go, we must bless and say goodbye to those who helped us get here," he said.

The basement of the two-family house was big. So big that it had been divided into four separate rooms. One was a playroom for the children, two were storage rooms and the biggest one had cots, day beds and a full bathroom.

The six women were in a corner of the big room in a semi-circle, sitting on hard plastic folding chairs. They all jumped up when they heard Tariq and the team coming down the creaky wooden stairs.

"You are leaving?" the spokeswoman for the women asked.

"Yes, mother," Tariq said. "We just wanted to come down and thank you one last time."

"Allah yusallmak (May God protect you)," she said and all the women nodded.

"And you. Goodbye, mother," Tariq said, smiling.

He kept smiling at her as he pulled his Berretta. The subcompact APX was considerably longer with the threaded six-inch silencer attached to the end of the barrel. Her lips parted to say something that would forever remain unsaid when the 9mm round hit her between the eyes and crumpled her to the floor.

The other five women stood there frozen in shock and horror. He fired quickly, hitting two more of them in the head before they could fully react. The last three grasped hands, got on their knees and closed their eyes. They were praying to Allah when Tariq walked over and one by one placed the hot silencer on their foreheads and fired.

"Gather the children," he said. "It's time to go."

Ten minutes later they left the house, walking along the quiet streets of Bushwick, Brooklyn. They headed east on Eldert Street towards the L train to make the thirty-minute trip into Manhattan. The few people they passed on the way to the Halsey Street station nodded and gave them warm holiday greetings.

The team of jihadists pushing toddlers in C-4-loaded strollers and wearing baby Bjorn's over their S-Vests showed their teeth and said, "Happy Thanksgiving."

CHAPTER 48
THANKSGIVING

Manhattan's East Village
AKA Alphabet City
AKA The Lower East Side
AKA The Lower

FELIX WAS RIGHT about Silvi. Things were rough when they broke the news to her about Antonio. They spent several hours consoling her and telling her over and over again about how her brother had saved them all. Silvi finally fell asleep on one of the couches around 2AM and then John, Felix, Nikita and Gonzalo tiptoed to their own rooms to get a few hours of sleep.

Bishop's eyes popped open at 6AM on Thanksgiving morning. Even though he'd been asleep for less than four hours, he felt instantly wide awake. His mind started racing through the long list of things he had to do to kill the bad guys and keep his team alive.

He closed his eyes, slowed his breathing and calmed himself down. Then he hit the floor for three rapid-fire sets of one hundred pushups to get himself refocused. Bishop followed that with an intense core workout of sit-ups to hollow mans, planks, v-ups and bridges.

Pushups hurt. The bullet that bounced off the top of his vest during the shootout at Jacob Riis had his right shoulder screaming whenever he overworked it. Planks hurt too. Twelve fresh stitches in his leg from getting blown up at the battle in King of Prussia gave him a blast of pain every time he flexed his quads.

He knew how to embrace it. To move through it. To find that place where the pain tried to make your brain shut down and make you physically retreat inside yourself. Once you were there, the key was to drive through it. To force yourself past it and retake control of your mind and body.

The years of Special Forces training had taught him how. How to handle the pain and stay in the fight. How to endure and survive what few other men ever could.

Bishop knew that the team's combat skills and his own ability to lead were going to be sorely tested today. If he wasn't at the top of his game innocent people were going to get hurt, and there was no way he'd let a few booboos slow him down.

After a shit, shower and a shave, Bishop quickly got himself dressed. His shoulder bit him when he pulled a black tee and a dark blue sweater over his head. Then his leg wound gave him a shoutout when he put on his black jeans, and again when he bent down to tie his boots.

As soon as he left his room he was hit with the aroma of fresh brewed Café Bustelo hanging in the air. Eager for a caffeine boost, he made his way to the kitchen, poured himself a steaming mug, then headed to the main dining room.

Campos Plaza had been the Valdez family's HQ for more than thirty years. Whenever the family was on a war footing they utilized eight interconnecting apartments that had twenty-two separate bedrooms. There was also a large common area with a massive dining room table that could seat forty people.

The entire team was sitting at the big table, sipping coffee and picking at a light breakfast. There were "good mornings" and "how'd you sleep?" all around, but no one offered up a Happy Thanksgiving. This year's holiday celebration was on hold until they killed Tariq and his men.

"After we eat we'll check our weapons and comms gear," John said.

"Sorry to even ask this," Bear said to Nikita. "But seeing how you've always worked alone… Are you familiar with communications equipment?"

"No apologies, Bear. It's a reasonable question and yes, I can work any radio or listening device. I've often used comms for surveillance… Just to listen in… I'm looking forward to finally being able to *send* and receive," she said.

"Good," Bear said.

"What are we using today?" she asked.

"Let me show you," Bear said. "We're operating undercover today, so our comms have to make us look like civilians talking on a Bluetooth or cell phone. We also don't want to all be walking around with identical earpieces."

"Because it would make it easier for a bad guy to spot us," Nikita said. A statement, not a question.

"Exactly," Bear said, nodding his head.

"Nicky," John said. "I want you on point. Me and Felix have been in the papers enough lately that Tariq's team might recognize us. The rest of these guys have all done undercover ops before, but they have a military stink on them that's hard to wash out."

He waited for the laughter and the side jokes to die

down before he continued: "You said you were dressed as an old lady at my father-in-law's building. What other disguises do you have? Not an old lady, but just not, you know… you."

"Not me?" Nicky asked, not quite sure what John was saying.

"What he means is *you're* just too damned fine to be strollin' 'round as yo' natural self," Nev said in a New Orleans deep Southern drawl.

That got everyone nodding their heads in agreement and laughing again.

"Not an old lady, but just make it so you don't stand out," John said, feeling slightly embarrassed.

"I'll get to work on it," she said.

"Before you do. What weapons are you using?" he asked.

She grabbed her kit and laid her equipment out on the table. They'd already seen the six throwing knives and the Taurus .380 auto, but there were plenty of oohs and ahs when the team looked over the rest of it.

"I was planning on swapping the Taurus for FNS-9s," she said, picking up two short-barreled automatics. "I'll shoot .40 cals to make sure my targets go down, and I'm using hollow points to avoid any ricochets. I usually hit what I aim for, but in case of a miss I don't want anything bouncing off a wall and clipping an innocent bystander."

"Makes sense. What else?" John asked.

"I'll have three short throwing knives on each wrist, a longer fighting knife in each of my leg sheaths, my sword and a spear in my light backpack."

"A spear?" Felix asked.

"Yes. I made it myself," she said, holding up what looked like a handful of ten-inch-long black sticks. Nicky flicked her wrist and the sticks clicked together into a five-foot-long steel rod. Then she gave the full length weapon another flick and a vicious seven-inch spearhead popped out of the far end.

"Jesus. Maybe we should just sit this one out and let Nicky handle it," Mace said.

"Wow," John said, taking the spear from her and feeling the balance in the deadly weapon. "Impressive. Is that it?"

"Yeah, that's basically it. I mean… I usually carry a few wads of C-4 and detonators in case of emergencies, but for this mission I don't think I'll need it."

They all watched and listened, trying to take it all in and not show her how dumfounded they were. Then all of them, except for John, turned their attention to Felix and glared at him with green-eyed envy.

"Yes, I know. I'm a lucky man," Felix said, grinning from ear to ear.

"You better believe it," Nicky said and then asked the team about their weapons.

Christmas, the former Navy SEAL, said: "Every gunfighter has his own preference for concealed carry pistols, but we all agreed to carry Glock 19s today."

"Why?" Nicky asked.

"We all like the way the 19 shoots, it's concealable, and if needed we can share or swap out 9mm mags. Can't imagine us being in a sustained firefight with Tariq and his boys, but as always we try our best to anticipate and plan for worst-case scenarios."

"That makes sense. What about the Mk 12s?" she asked, pointing to the two SPRs (Special Purpose Rifles) that were lying side by side on the table.

"I see you know your guns. Once we have a target location, me and Mace will get to the high ground and be your overwatch. Once you ground-pounders identify our targets, we'll knock 'em down for you," Christmas said.

"What about knives?" Nicky asked.

They all pulled out their blades that were a mix of KA-BARs, Mk IIIs, Strider SMFs and Green Beret fighting knives.

Nicky nodded her head in approval and said: "When this is all over I'd be happy to show you guys how to use those things."

They all smiled, thinking she was joking. When they realized she was serious and that there was no doubt they could learn a few things from anyone formerly known as Omar the Blade, the smiles quickly disappeared.

"That would be great. Thanks Nicky," John said, just as his iPhone vibrated in his pants pocket.

"It's Clayton," he told the team when he looked at the caller ID.

Bishop asked Unser how he was feeling and after listening for twenty seconds John said, "Okay, I'm putting you on speaker."

They could all hear the pain in Clayton's voice when he croaked out a greeting to the team.

"The little guy you put all the holes in just told us something you all need to know," Clayton said.

They all knew that the "little guy" was Jibril, the terrorist John had shot four times.

"We already knew that Tariq might have some radicalized Americans with him and Jibril just confirmed at least four of them are women," Clayton said.

"Women?" Bear said.

"There's a possibility of children too."

"They're gonna use kids as shields?" John asked.

"Not just kids… Babies. Jibril couldn't confirm whether

Tariq was just using them as cover to get across the country from Seattle, or if the babies are actually part of the mission, but he said he got a bad feeling when he saw the infants in PA," Clayton said.

"Jesus," Nev said. "How do we shoot women holding babies?" he asked.

"How? Five pounds of pressure on the trigger, the same way you drop any other murderous asshole trying to kill civilians," John said.

"You got that right," Clayton said. "Baby or no baby, you get any of those traitorous bitches in your gunsights, you put two in their fucking heads. This was their call and we all know why they're here."

"Nothing about who or what Tariq's targets are?" Christmas asked.

"Jibril's in the dark, but same as us, he knows it's big. Something that's gonna shake up the world," Clayton said.

"What the fuck are we missing?" John asked, then got up from the table and started pacing across the room.

"We've locked down every major event and every high-profile monument, and we've got a whole bunch of really smart guys trying to figure out where he's going," Clayton said.

John put his hand in his back pocket and felt a folded piece of paper. He pulled it out and realized it was Maria's analysis. Her writeup on all the bad guys who were coming at them that she added to her goodbye letter. He glanced at it and tossed it on the table without reading it.

"What's that?" Felix asked, picking it up and unfolding it.

John gave him a short and terse recap of what it was while Felix started reading:

Johnny,

I did my analysis and here's what I came up with. You obviously have a long list of very dangerous and very powerful enemies. I'm no soldier and this may be a waste of your time, but I'm writing this all down in case there's even a small chance that something here may help you.

As painful and personal as this is for me, this list is prioritized in ascending order. Even though the Russians murdered my Daddy, that was a personal attack to try to get to you (as are most of the others). Tariq/ISIS? That's different. As much as he's coming for you, he's also here to kill innocent people. Don't let him get away with it.

The Russians: They killed my father and I already told you what I want you to do. They're murderers and criminals, but they think like businessmen. You don't have to go to Russia. Tear down their businesses here and the men responsible will come to you.

Connie Belusci: He's one man and you have all the resources of our government, law enforcement and the intelligence agencies behind you. Use them. Put the squeeze on Belusci from all sides. He's a six foot-seven bald guy with a crooked nose. A guy who can't blend in or hide out. Have his picture posted on the news and let the cops take him down.

Caleb Meecham: Watch out for this guy. He's a billionaire with a vendetta and, like his father, he didn't hesitate to hire a hitman to get revenge.

The Politicians: If it weren't for the Tringas and ISIS

I'd put these guys as enemy number one on this list. They will use you and I guarantee that eventually they will set you up by sending you out on a bogus mission to get you killed. Either that or they'll try to use what you've done for them to lock you up in a cage.

The Tringas: The fact that this family of assassins even exists defies reason and reality. I have no idea how to find them or kill them, but if you can, lure them into a trap and ambush them.

Tariq Hassan and ISIS: I spent a lot of time trying to figure out where Tariq and his cell will strike. The amount of money and logistics it's taking to get him and his followers halfway around the world is significant here. It tells me that his target(s) are probably more than just blowing up a parade, monument or a building.

I'm obviously not a counterterrorism expert, but assuming Tariq doesn't have some sort of nuclear device or biologicals, he only has a small group of terrorists that will attack using conventional weapons.

So, I tried to figure out how he can maximize pain and suffering with a small group of people. My conclusion is that his intended victims were not randomly selected. They are a very specific group. Most high level officials (congressmen, senators, joint chiefs and the president) have heavy security around them and the chances of a group of Syrians and Afghans getting close to them is basically nil. But what about the families of those government officials? How much security do their mothers, fathers, brothers, sisters and children have around them? Does the secret service provide 24/7 protection for all of them?

I obviously don't have the answer, but I can't imagine there's enough to keep them all safe. Anyway, I hope and pray that this helps you and it wasn't a complete waste of your time.

Johnny, please stay alive. Even though we're not together I need to know you're always going to be out there somewhere protecting us.

Love always,

Maria

"Wait, wait…wait…" Felix said. "Johnny, have you read this?" he asked, holding up Maria's one-page analysis.

"Uh… no not yet," John said. "Been meaning to, just kept getting sidetracked."

"Some of this is personal, but listen to what Maria says about Tariq," Felix said and began reading the relevant paragraphs about the Afghan terrorist.

They heard Clayton say: "Jesus Christ," over the speaker phone.

"Clayton, we need a list of close relatives that are here in New York today. Especially spouses and children," John said.

"I'll call you right back," Clayton said and hung up.

"Not something we can find in a Google search, but if Tariq found them then there's got to be a way we can too," Christmas said.

"Call Danny," Gonzalo said.

Danny was Danny Jones, the Valdez computer expert

and a world-renowned cyber hacker. Christmas was still on the phone with Danny when Clayton called back and John again put him on speaker so the entire team could hear the news.

"There are fourteen possible targets in New York City for Thanksgiving…"

Clayton was going down the list of who was in town, their names, family connections, and where they were eating their holiday meals when John stopped him:

"President-elect Stamper's daughter is here?"

"Yes," Clayton said. "Stamper and his daughter have been estranged for a long time. She actually started using her mother's maiden name, Sillo, after Stamper left them for another woman, the soon-to-be first lady, twenty years ago."

"Where is she?" John asked.

"Kelly Sillo volunteers every Thanksgiving at the Bowery Mission. They hand out free meals in front of Tompkins Square Park."

"That's six blocks from here," John said, pulling on his Kevlar vest. "Does she have a security detail?"

"Yes. Secret Service keeps a spotter on her. Just a watcher. Not close-protection," Clayton said.

"We're moving. We'll be there in three minutes," John said.

"Glad you're already on-site, but for this I'm alerting everyone… Secret Service, DHS, FBI and NYPD. I'll make sure they give you and the team time to get in position, and have them move in quiet. No lights or sirens," Clayton said.

"Understood. Just make sure they know there's a counter-terror team in civilian clothes going on-site to extract Stamper's daughter," John said as he started moving towards the front door with the entire team behind him.

"Will do… and John…"

"Yeah."

"One more thing… Kelly Sillo has her six-year-old daughter, Kristin, with her."

CHAPTER 49
IT'S ALL ABOUT SURVIVAL

Trappe, Maryland

THE THANKSGIVING DAY feast was laid out in the mansion's small dining room that seated twenty instead of the sixty-seater in the big ballroom. The chefs cooked an incredible holiday meal that was going to be impossible for two people to come close to finishing. An eighteen-pound turkey, Cornish hens, a ham, steaks, stuffing, yams, cranberry sauce, mashed potatoes, gravy, and much more were spread out in front of the emaciated thirty-year-old billionaire and the three-hundred-pound Albanian contract killer.

Caleb sat at the head of the table. He stabbed an extra rare piece of filet mignon and let the sterling silver fork hover in front of his mouth for a moment. He watched the mix of blood and dill butter drip off the meat and splash down on to his Astbury Black dinner plate.

"How are you feeling?" Caleb asked and then popped the chunk of bright red flesh into his mouth.

Connie grunted and took a huge gulp of the Lafite-Rothschild Bordeaux.

"You're supposed to sip it," Caleb said, quickly doing the math of what four ounces of red wine just cost him at thirty-five hundred dollars a bottle.

"Fuck that," Connie said.

He refilled his crystal wine glass and contemptuously drained it all in another long open-mouthed guzzle.

"You seem upset, Connie," Caleb said.

"You're wise beyond your years, young man."

"What are you mad about?"

"Let me see. I'm the best contract killer on the planet and Bishop is the only guy I've failed to hit."

"Are you?"

"Am I what?" Connie asked.

"The best. Ever since my Dad hired you, you've had one fuckup after another."

"Careful, kid. I'm in no mood to be messed with."

"Kid?"

"Okay… *Caleb*. You happy now?"

"Seems like you're trying to pick a fight or at a minimum just doing your best to disrespect me," Caleb said. "Either way, I don't care for your tone, and I definitely don't like the way you're drinking my Lafite."

"It's not about you, Meecham. Bishop just won't die and he fucking shot me," Connie said, pressing his hand to his side.

"You're sure it was him?"

Connie waved his massive hand dismissively: "No way to tell. Doesn't matter whether it was him or one of his guys. Either way they put a fucking hole in me and killed my crew."

"You managed to get away, though. End of the day it's all about survival," Caleb said.

After Bishop and his team ambushed him on the plateau,

Connie had rigged his claymores and then sprinted down the back side of the mountain in the rain. The bullet hole in his hip was pumping blood and he was lightheaded by the time he got down to the Ford Yukon he'd stashed in a thick stand of trees. He did a quick Google search for local veterinarians and drove flat out to the only one that showed a home address.

As Caleb had just said, it *was* all about survival. A quick home invasion, followed by the threat of raping the vet's wife and killing his two kids, was all it took to get him patched up. Once the bullet was out, after getting stitched and bandaged, all he'd wanted to do was sleep.

There was no time to rest. He knew he had to move. He left the doggy doc and his family tied up in the kitchen, got in their sensible Subaru Forester and drove south. Once he made it to Baltimore he dumped the stolen car at the airport and took a taxi to a downtown Starbucks. From there he called Caleb, who sent one of his flunkies to pick him up and bring him back to the Meecham estate.

Despite the top-notch medical attention, the gourmet food and chugging four bottles a day of Caleb's fine wine, Connie had been too angry to appreciate or enjoy any of it. He couldn't understand why this contract had been such a pain in the ass... And in the hip.

He sat there replaying all the times he'd missed Bishop over the past six months. His brow was knotted and his lips were squeezed in a tight angry line when he sensed the movement behind him. Connie turned his big bald head just as the taser was pressed to the back of his neck. Fifty thousand volts blasted him off his chair and left him shaking and twitching on the white marble floor.

When he came back to life his brain wasn't working

right. He had no idea who or where he was. From some far-away place he heard someone saying the name Connie.

Connie? That's me, he thought, but not a hundred percent sure that was right.

He opened his eyes, couldn't see anything clearly, then blinked a few times to try to get his brain working again.

"Welcome back," a voice said.

"Where am I?" Connie asked.

"On my wall," Caleb said.

Connie shook his head and regained some situational awareness. He realized he was naked, spread eagled and shackled by his wrists and ankles to the torture wall in Caleb's basement.

"What's going on here, Meecham?"

"Introductions," Caleb said.

"The fuck are you talking about, you little shit?"

"Connie Belusci… It's my pleasure to introduce you to Yakov and Sasha Skobelev," Caleb said.

Connie tried to maintain his composure when the two brothers walked into the room and stood before him.

"He hired me," Connie said, nodding at Caleb. "Him and his father. It was all their idea."

"We know," Yakov said. "But you killed my only son."

"So you shoot me and he gets a pass?"

"Shoot you? No, we're not going to shoot you, Mr. Belusci. But you're going to wish we did. You're coming with us back to Moscow," Sasha Skobelev said.

"And this piece of shit? What happens to him?" Connie asked, looking defiantly at Caleb.

"We came to an agreement," Caleb said. "Less than a year from now, with the help of my new friends here, I will be Senator Meecham."

"Bullshit."

"Like I told you, Connie, it's all about survival. Some of us just do it better than others."

"Why the fuck would you give this kid a pass, let alone make him a senator?" Connie asked the brothers.

"He gave us you," Yakov said.

"Plus three hundred million to ease our pain and suffering," Sasha said.

"Add to that, once I'm in office I'll give them anything they need, from intel to legislation that helps their businesses," Caleb said.

"I'll crush your fucking skull, you little punk," Connie shouted, his muscles bulging as he strained to free himself.

Caleb smiled. "Yakov… any preference?" he asked, nodding at his wall of toys.

Yakov walked over to what Caleb called his *toy store*. Hammers, knives, bats, screw guns, drills and power saws were laid out in neat rows on metal shelves and were hanging from wooden pegs stuck in the wall. He picked up several different tools and finally settled on a curved dagger.

Caleb licked his lips in anticipation. He'd tested out most of the tools on Valdez family soldiers who had the misfortune of being pinned to the wall just like Connie was.

"Yakov. May I make a suggestion?"

"But, of course," Yakov said.

"Try this," he said and handed Yakov the bullwhip.

"I've never used one."

"You're gonna love it. Take a few practice swings. You'll see. Once you get the hang of it it's better than sex."

Yakov raised his arm and swung the whip at Connie. The end gave the big man a soft slap across his bare chest. He tried it again and had the same disappointing result. Yakov grunted in frustration and Connie winked at him.

"Let me show you," Caleb said.

Yakov handed him the whip and stood back. Caleb raised his arm and flicked the bullwhip back and forth.

"Pick a spot," he said.

"Right nipple," Sasha said.

Connie had witnessed firsthand what the whip did to men. How it tore off flesh and cut them to the bone. He steeled himself for what was coming.

I can take it. No matter how bad it gets. No matter how much it hurts. I can take it, he thought, but when Caleb took his practice swing and the whip cracked like a gunshot against the wall next to his head, the terror took over and Connie's bladder released.

"Damn that stinks," Caleb said, wrinkling his nose. "Happens every time."

He walked over to a table in the corner, pulled open a drawer and took out a jar of Vicks VapoRub.

"Put a dab of the Vicks under your nose. It'll cover the smell," he said to the brothers.

"Right nipple?"

Sasha nodded.

"Come on, Caleb. Please don't do this," Connie pleaded just as the tip of the whip flew at him and hit his chest with a loud crack.

Caleb and the Skobelev brothers were so excited they barely noticed Connie's screaming and cursing.

"Bingo!" Caleb shouted.

"Bravo," Sasha said, clapping.

"Well done, Senator Meecham," Yakov said, reaching for the whip.

"My turn," he said to Connie.

"Nose or cock?" Sasha asked.

"I will start with his nose and work my way down," Yakov said as he swung the whip back and forth over his head and got a nice rhythm going.

Chapter 50

Sacrifice

Tompkins Square Park
Manhattan's East Village

THIS WAS *HIS* neighborhood. John grew up playing basketball in Tompkins Square and he could visualize every store and building surrounding the park with his eyes closed. The fact that Tariq was on his turf gave him a tactical advantage… He hoped so anyway.

John pushed open the Campos Plaza exit door on East 13th Street and Avenue C and waited a moment for the rest of the team to make it out of the complex. As they gathered around him all their phones vibrated when images of Kelly Sillo and her daughter Kristin arrived in a group text message sent by Danny Jones. Each of them took two seconds to memorize the faces of the next president's daughter and granddaughter, and then John gave the team their orders:

"Nicky, no time for disguises. You're a millennial out for a run. You go on ahead of us. When you get to the Avenue B side of the park I want you to jog through it and when you hit Avenue A, head south towards 7th Street. That's where the Bowery Mission always sets up its trucks and food stations.

"Bobby, there's always a long line of homeless waiting for the free meals along Avenue A. You look so beat up you'll blend right in. Move to the front of the line and see if you can spot Kelly and Kristin.

"No call signs today. Use your names to identify yourselves when you transmit... and remember, Tariq and his people are going to be out in the open, hiding in plain sight. Consider everyone you see a bad guy until we know they're not," John said.

Gonzalo's voice came through their Bluetooths and earpieces: "We have a top floor apartment at 98 Avenue A. It's next to the Blink Fitness gym between 6th and 7th Streets. Christmas, you can look right down at the park from the windows. The doorman is waiting for you and he'll let you in."

A black Toyota Camry pulled up next to them. Christmas hopped in with his Mk 12 in a big Nike gym bag and the driver took off.

"Mace, we have another apartment on Avenue A and St. Marks Place that faces the park. Felix has been there and he'll take you up to the sixth floor. The super is waiting outside to let you in," Gonzalo said.

Another Camry roared down Avenue C, braked hard and came to a stop a few feet ahead of them. Mace and Felix jumped in the back and they were flying west on 13th Street a second later.

"Okay, let's move. Nicky, you sprint. We'll jog along behind you," John said.

"Will do," Nikita said and took off running up the block. She quickly put herself in another gear to be their eyes and ears and the first one on the scene.

John, Bunny, Bobby, Nev, Bear and Chago were running at a slower pace a hundred feet behind Nicky when Clayton's voice came over their secure net:

"John, we just identified another potential target. General Palmer's mother, his sister and his three nephews are in the West Village for a holiday meal. They're at his sister's townhouse on Charles and Washington Streets."

John didn't hesitate to split the team: "Bear. You, Chago, Nev and Bunny get over there," he ordered just as another Valdez driver in a gray Nissan Quest minivan pulled over with both of the rear sliding doors already open.

Bunny wasn't comfortable watching John head towards the park on his own without backup. He understood the order to go with Bear, Nev and Chago, but he couldn't help feeling uneasy about it. In all their recent battles John led the way in and Bunny was always on his six.

Who's gonna watch your back, Johnny? Bunny thought as the minivan took a hard right on 11th Street and headed west across town.

Everything was happening fast. Despite the transition from examining weapons and having no idea where Tariq was ten minutes ago to running down the street into battle, John knew the team was ready. Every one of them had been in countless firefights and they all knew how to slow everything down and instantly transition from planning an operation to successfully executing it at a moment's notice.

John got to East 10th Street and entered the park through the basketball courts he grew up playing on. It was too cold for a full court, but even at midafternoon on a cloudy Thanksgiving Day there were more than a dozen people shooting around. He jogged over to a teenager who was dribbling a red, white and blue basketball and wearing a black Brooklyn Nets cap.

"How much for the hat?"

The kid smiled at the question. Then he saw John's eyes and the expression on his face.

"Twenty," the kid said nervously.

John pulled out some cash, peeled off three twenties, put the hat on his head and started running through the park, angling south.

"I see them," Nicky said into her Bluetooth. "Kelly and Kristin are behind a table handing out hot meals. Just off the corner of 7th and A."

"Bobby here. I see them too. I'm walking towards them on Avenue A. No sign of Tariq or any threats yet."

"Overwatch one in position," Christmas said to the team.

"Two in position with eyes on mother and daughter," Mace announced.

"Felix here. I'm heading back downstairs. I'll position across the street from the park."

John processed all the info as he hustled through Tompkins Square. Instead of going east to west, from Avenue B to Avenue A, he ran diagonally across it and came out on the 7th Street side of the park. Once he made it out onto the street he slowed down to a brisk walk and came up behind the line of more than five hundred people waiting patiently for their free meals.

He stood back and watched the line. It was easy to spot which were members of the Lower East Side's broken, homeless, drug-addicted community, and others who had fallen on hard times and were just unemployed and hungry. He scanned for anomalies. Anyone who was too young and too fit to be a part of this beaten-down LES tribe.

He looked at clothing too. No matter how hard they tried, John knew ISIS terrorists couldn't match the look and feel of true New Yorkers. Even if there were some traitorous American jihadists amongst them, he knew there was no chance they came from the mean streets of LES, and LES had its own unique style and dress code.

There.

He spotted a couple near the corner who didn't look right. A smaller dark-haired woman with a baby on her chest and a tall, strong-looking guy with his hands on a stroller. Their clothes and the stroller were too new, and the guy was too fit.

Could be a guy who just got out of prison, John thought and then quickly dismissed it. His gut registered *soldier*, not *ex-con*.

"Listen up," John said quietly into the mic attached to his earpiece. "I've got eyes on two possible tangos just east of the corner of 7th and A. Woman with a baby. Man with a stroller."

"Good copy. Overwatch one has eyes on both targets," Christmas said.

"No way they're alone. The other tangos are probably dressed the same way as these two. Look for new clothes," John said.

There were acknowledgments from the team as they searched for the enemy amongst the crowded sidewalks around the park.

"Clayton, you still on?" John asked.

"I'm here," he said.

"Patch me through to the Secret Service agent. We need

to know where he is and he needs to know we're the good guys so he doesn't shoot us."

There was a long thirty seconds of silence and then Clayton came back and said, "He's not responding."

"Bad sign," John said, knowing that for a protective detail on-duty agent not to answer his secure phone he'd have to be dead or at best unconscious.

He stayed close to the line, trying his best to blend in with the hundreds of people who were patiently waiting for a hot meal as he moved. The big man looked back in his direction and John froze and turned to speak with two elderly Asian women. Neither of them spoke English, but he kept talking to them anyway. When he glanced back towards the corner the couple was gone.

"Tangos are moving. Heading towards the president's daughter," Christmas said from his sniper's hide in the fifth floor apartment overlooking Avenue A and the park.

John ran forward. He got to the corner and turned right. Heading north on Avenue A, he slowed back down to a walk when he saw the couple were only fifteen feet in front of him. Their backs were turned and he moved up behind them, ready to draw and shoot.

"Should I take the shot?" Christmas asked.

The guy pushing the stroller must have sensed something. He turned casually and looked back, turned away and then stopped and looked back again. He locked eyes with Bishop.

"I know you," the big guy said. "John, isn't it?"

Bishop instantly realized his mistake and let everyone know it. "Stand down! They're not our tangos. He's an off-duty cop. Repeat. Off this target and keep searching the crowd."

"Mike?" Bishop asked. He recognized the cop from the 9th Precinct, which was just three blocks away. He also had a quick flashback of playing hoops with him at the 14th Street Y more than fifteen years back.

"Yeah, that's right. Everything okay?"

Bishop smiled and said yeah, everything was fine, but his eyes told a different story. John leaned in, pulled Mike close as they shook hands and said softly, "You need to get your family out of here right now. Turn around and go the opposite way."

Mike nodded his thanks, said something to his wife and guided her into a gentle U turn just as Felix's voice came through John's earpiece: "I've got a couple crossing the street behind Kelly and her daughter," he said.

John was twenty feet away from the Sillos. He saw Bobby walk right up to the table and start speaking to them, then two massive explosions gently shook the ground and froze everyone in place. John could tell the blasts weren't local. He gauged they were around twenty blocks away, which meant they came from the West side. From where General Palmer's daughter lived.

He pushed aside his concerns about Bunny, Bear, Nev and Chago and ran towards the food tables. John heard Bobby shout a warning just as a big Bowery Mission delivery truck pulled up behind Kristin Sillo and her daughter.

There was a short burst of automatic weapons fire followed by two quick shots, and then Christmas's voice blared in everyone's ear:

"Take cover! I put two tangos down in the back of the truck. Both wearing S-Vests!"

As soon as the shooting started there was a loud roar of shouting and screaming from the crowd. The screams were momentarily silenced by the dual blasts from the rear of the truck. The silence was short-lived. Once the shock wore off, the maimed and injured started shrieking in pain and crying out for help.

John had a Glock 19 in each hand as he ran forward. The passenger door of the delivery truck was already open and a tough-looking blond-haired guy was moving towards Kelly and her daughter. John fired both of his Glocks and hit the tango with three rounds along his right side: ear, shoulder and armpit.

He saw Kelly Sillo on the ground and then caught the flash of terror in her eyes as she reached for her daughter, who was ten feet away. A young dark-haired woman with a small scar on her forehead ran over and grabbed six-year-old Kristin. Her fanatical scream of, "Allahu Akbar," was cut short when John shot her in the crescent moon-shaped scar between her eyebrows.

Everything after that happened in slow motion. John saw the dead man's switch in her left hand. The wires that ran up her sleeve were connected to the suicide vest she wore over her coat. Her right hand was gripped around little Kristin's arm and as she fell backwards she was pulling the next president's granddaughter down with her.

John saw Bobby dive at the jihadist. Saw him knock Kristin aside and land right on top of the dead terrorist and hug her tight. The S-Vest detonated just as John screamed, "Noooo!"

CHAPTER 51

THE FOG OF WAR

BOBBY WRAPPED HIS arms and legs around the dead woman. He tucked his head next to hers and felt her hair tickling his ear. A whiff of her shampoo was in his nose. His brain tried to identify the brand, dismissed it and then focused on the shiny brown penny on the ground just a few inches from his face. The penny, with the words In God We Trust above the image of Abraham Lincoln, was the last thing Bobby saw. His body absorbed the blast wave, but the bolts, nails and screws packed into the wads of C-4 ripped him apart and sent pieces of him flying all over the street.

John felt a splash of Bobby's blood hit him in the face and saw his brother's shredded body parts scattered all around him. He pushed the pain and sorrow aside and ran over to little Kristin. There wasn't time to check her vitals. He picked up the unconscious girl just as Felix ran in and threw Kelly over his shoulder.

Both cousins knew there could be more jihadists in the area. Carrying the Sillo girls, they hustled across Avenue A and ran towards the corner of St. Marks Place. When they saw Nikita standing on the sidewalk they both shouted, "Run!"

Nicky ignored them. Standing her ground with her arms extended straight out, an FNS-9 in each hand, she unleashed a barrage of fire on two men who were chasing John and Felix. More shots came from the high ground as Mace and Christmas identified and took out targets the moment they showed themselves.

John and Felix got Kelly and Kristin around the corner to safety just as they heard the sirens and then saw the squad cars flying down St. Marks Place. They stood in the street forcing the NYPD rollers to screech to a stop a few feet in front of them. The cops were getting out and drawing their sidearms when John ran over to them.

"This is President Stamper's daughter and granddaughter. Get 'em to the hospital."

"But our orders are to…"

"Fuck your orders. You want to tell the next president you let them die? An IED lit off right next to them. They both need X-rays and a trauma surgeon and they need it now!" John shouted.

The female officer who had been riding shotgun opened the rear door and climbed in.

"Pass me the girl first," she said.

John and Felix helped put mother and daughter in the back seat with the officer while her partner got behind the wheel.

"Back up and take them to the NYU ER. A Secret Service detail is meeting you there," John said, conveying what Clayton was saying to them over their comms.

The cop hit his siren, put the car in reverse and floored it. John and Felix watched until the car made it to the next corner and then roared up 1st Avenue towards the hospital.

"What now?" Felix asked.

"We go kill Tariq," John said.

"Where is he?"

"He's sitting with a blond-haired woman in Odessa," John said.

Odessa was an old-school Ukrainian diner that opened up across from Tompkins Square Park more than fifty years ago. It had long been the go-to breakfast and lunch spot for LESers looking for a cheap meal, and John and Felix had probably eaten there a couple hundred times since they were kids.

"Motherfucker," Felix said.

Strange things happen in the fog of war and John recognized that this was one of those bizarre moments. When he'd run across Avenue A something had caught his eye. Something out of place. Not movement. Just the opposite.

While shots were being fired and bombs were going off across the street from the Odessa diner, a man and a woman sat at a table by the shattered front windows. They weren't panicked. They weren't hiding *under* the table. They were just sitting there… watching.

It was only for an instant, but as he ran with little Kristin he made eye contact with the man, and in that brief moment John saw recognition in the guy's eyes. More importantly… he saw the hate.

John's gut said, *Tariq.*

"Christmas, Tariq is in Odessa. Do you have a visual?" John asked.

"Negative. I have eyes on the exterior, but can't see inside," Christmas said from his sniper's hide.

John turned to Nikita, who was standing a few feet in front of him and Felix:

"Nicky, cross Avenue A and see if you can see them from the park side."

She nodded and took off.

"Mace, you okay?" John asked as he started walking down St. Marks Place towards the corner with Felix next to him.

"I'm looking at pieces of Bobby scattered all over the fucking street," Mace said from the window of the six-floor apartment.

"I know, brother. Let's smoke all these assholes and then we'll take care of Bobby," John said. "Bobby saved a whole lotta lives today. Not just ours. Not just the mother and daughter, either. There would be thirty or forty bodies on the sidewalk if he hadn't tackled that bitch and smothered the blast."

Odessa's glass doors and all the front windows had shattered from the explosive force of the S-Vests that detonated on the two dead jihadists in the back of the truck, and on the woman Bobby jumped on. Nikita had a clear view inside the diner from across the street.

"I don't see Tariq or a girl. There are six or seven people huddling together in the back, but they all look elderly," she said into her Bluetooth as police cars, an EMS crew and fire trucks raced in from multiple directions, converging on the scene.

"Tariq can't be far. Mace, check the park. Christmas, look west on 7th Street."

"Copy that," Mace said.

John and Felix both looked down and saw *the* crack in St. Marks Place sidewalk. It was the same wide crack that Felix had tripped over on the night of John's eighteenth birthday when they were running from the cops after they were attacked in the West Village. A few months after tripping on the crack, Felix was in El Mira State Penitentiary doing time for John's crime.

"Almost fifteen years and they still haven't fixed that shit," Felix said.

"Nope," John said, then turned suddenly and pushed Felix aside.

John used his shove against Felix to torque his body. Twisting from the hips, he brought his Glock up and began applying pressure to the trigger before he got eyes on the threat he sensed was there. Once he got his head around, he saw Tariq and the girl aiming at him from twenty feet away. Then he saw the babies strapped to their chests.

John went for head shots, snap firing two quick rounds before his world blew up and he was down on his back looking up at the clouds. The shots that hit him had come in close together. Four rounds from two different guns. The two in his chest and the one in his left side felt like someone smacked him with three rapid-fire swings from a baseball bat. The Kevlar saved his life, but the energy from the 9mm rounds traveling at 1,180 feet per second with a muzzle velocity of 386 foot pounds when Tariq and Gretchen fired their Berettas knocked him flat.

"Johnny's down!" Felix shouted as he crouched over his cousin, raised his Glock 19 and fired. "Tariq and the woman are running west on St. Marks!"

Police converged on John and Felix with their guns drawn and screamed at the cousins to toss their guns.

"Freeze!"

"Drop your weapons!"

John was getting his breath and bearings back when Nikita stepped in front of the five cops aiming their pistols at him and Felix.

"No. Don't hurt them," John said to her. Then into his Bluetooth he said: "Mace, get up on the roof. I think I hit Tariq. You finish them off."

Clayton had been working the phones behind the scenes and a uniformed police lieutenant ran over and told his officers to stand down.

"Bishop. You okay?" he asked.

"I'm fine," John said. "Can't believe I let that motherfucker bushwhack me."

He grabbed Felix's outstretched hand with his right, and was pushing himself up with his left when his arm collapsed and exploded in pain.

"Shit," he said.

"What?" Felix asked.

"He's been shot," Nicky said.

It wasn't the first time he'd been hit and didn't know it. In one prolonged firefight in Iraq it wasn't until Bishop and his team were back inside the wire, the adrenaline was wearing off and he was taking off his gear that he realized he'd been shot twice.

"Help me up," he said to Felix.

Once he was up on his feet Nicky helped him get his jacket off and rolled up his sweater to examine the wound.

"Looks like it sliced right through the outside of your bicep. It's a bleeder and you're definitely going to need surgery," she said, then put a cinch around his left arm above the wound and pulled it tight.

"So fucking annoying," John said just as Mace's voice came through their earpieces.

"I see them running up the block. There's too many people... Can't..."

They all heard the shot. The cops and several bystanders

flinched, ducked and looked up to the rooftops. They spotted Mace holding his Mk 12 with the rifle's long barrel extended over the roof's edge.

"That's my guy! Hold your fire," John said to the police lieutenant and the cops aiming up towards Mace.

"I got her in the leg. Right calf," Mace shouted so the cops below could hear him. "There's a crowd of people helping them. I can't take another shot without hitting civilians… They're moving. Getting into a car on 1st Avenue… Looks like a black Camry."

Several cops took off running up the block, two more jumped in a squad car, and the lieutenant snapped orders on his radio.

"We'll get them," the lieutenant said to John.

"Nice work, LT. An FBI SWAT team is on the way and you need to get a bomb squad over here to look inside the Bowery Mission truck."

"Thanks, Bishop. My guys already cleared the truck," the lieutenant said, extending his hand. "I'm Davis."

They shook hands and Davis said, "Appreciate everything you did here. We'll secure the crime scene. You get yourself to a hospital."

"Gotta go see my guy first," John said.

Davis nodded: "I'll walk you in."

John, Felix and Nicky walked solemnly behind Lt. Davis. When they got to the corner they saw Mace burst out of the building across the street and run over to what was left of Bobby. Christmas was already there, kneeling over him.

As they crossed the avenue John reached down and picked up an arm. He knew it was Bobby's because of the bandages wrapped around his left hand where it was missing fingers. The fingers he'd lost in the firefight with Connie Belusci.

Mace rolled Bobby over, took a knee, and placed his hand on his brother's head.

"You God damned hillbilly. Why'd you have to go and do that?" Mace said, thick wet tears rolling down his cheeks.

John carried the arm over and gently laid it next to Bobby. He knelt beside Mace, and then Felix and Nicky did the same. They bowed their heads until they heard a car screech to a stop. They looked up and saw Bear, Bunny, Nev and Chago explode out of the rear doors of the minivan and come running over.

"Oh my God," Bear said. "Oh my God."

"What is his name?" Davis asked.

"Staff Sergeant Bobby Floyd. US Army Special Forces. One of the greatest warriors to ever wear a Green Beret, and the best friend any man could ever hope to have," John said, his eyes welling up.

"A brother like no other," Bear said.

Davis took a knee and bowed his head in prayer.

"General Palmer's family?" John asked Nev.

"All okay. The crazies couldn't get through the reinforced front door and they blew themselves up in the street," Nev said. "Three civilians got hurt, but none are critical."

"Thank God," John said.

"You okay, Johnny? You're looking kinda pale," Bunny said.

"I'm fine," John said, just before he fell forward onto Bobby.

CHAPTER 52

WHAT'S UP, DOC

"IT'S OKAY, CHRIS. Jump. Jump and I'll catch you… Daddy's got you," he said to his son.

Chris was stuck in a tree. Afraid to climb down and too scared to jump. John knew this was a big moment for his little dude. The five-foot drop was a long way down for a three-year-old, but John kept encouraging him and letting him know that he wouldn't get hurt. Chris was ready to overcome his fears and launch himself off the tree when John felt a hand on his shoulder, and the image of his son faded to black.

"Johnny? Johnny, wake up," Felix said.

Bishop struggled to open his eyes. His lids felt like they were glued shut. He blinked several times to clear his vision.

"Where am I?" he asked.

"Hospital… NYU," Felix said.

"How's the girl?"

"Mother and daughter are bruised and only slightly broken. Little Kristin has hairline fractures in her wrist and elbow from the fall she took when Bobby shoved her aside, and they both have mild concussions from the force of the blast wave."

"Thank God," John said. "But wait…What happened? I remember we were kneeling over Bobby. Then nothing after that."

"You lost a lot of blood and passed out," Felix said.

"You're telling me I fainted in front of the entire team?"

"Sounds pretty fucked up when you say it like that, but yeah, you did," Bunny said.

"Jesus Christ," John said, knowing he'd never live it down.

"Don't beat yourself up over it," Bear said. "You took three 9mm rounds to your chest plate and the bullet wound in your arm was way worse than it looked. You nearly bled out."

"How bad?" John asked as he sat up in his hospital bed, slid his legs over the side and placed his feet on the floor.

"The bullet hit the outside of your bicep, which would've just meant a whole lotta stitches, but it angled in and clipped the humerus on the way out. That caused some bone splinters which put a few holes in your brachial artery," Bear said.

"Did you scrub up and do the surgery yourself, Dr. Bernstein?" John asked.

A few lifetimes ago Bear had completed two years of medical school before dropping out to fulfill his childhood dream of becoming a Special Forces operator.

"I could've patched you up with some tweezers and a sewing kit, but since the nation's top vascular surgeon was handy, I let him take a shot at it."

"Thanks for that," John said, smiling.

He looked down at his heavily bandaged left arm and the sling that had his forearm tucked in against his stomach.

"Man, my chest is killing me… I guess the good news is I can't feel the arm, and the stitches in my leg aren't hurting either."

"Three hits from a nine at close range will do that to you," Bear said.

"No doubt," Bunny said.

"Wait… What time is it? How long have I been out?"

"It's Friday morning. You've been down for eighteen hours," Bunny said.

John knew it was a combination of the anesthesia and the trauma to his body that made his brain temporarily shut down, but he still shook his head in disbelief that he'd been unconscious for nearly a full day.

"Did they get Tariq?" he asked.

Bear shook his head no just as the rest of the team and Gonzalo came in. After they all gave him the standard "how're you feeling" and "thank God you're okay" routine, they got down to business.

"How'd Tariq and the girl get away?" John asked.

"They had a pretty elaborate escape plan," Bear said.

Bear described how Tariq and his female accomplice had so far managed to elude a citywide search. He was going over the details when Clayton Unser called in on his phone and Bear put it on speaker.

"Glad you're okay, Johnny, and really sorry about Bobby," Clayton said.

John's jaw clenched and his amber eyes narrowed at the mention of Bobby's name, but he didn't say anything in response. After a pause Clayton continued, "As for Tariq, the only piece of good news is that you shot him in the shoulder and Mace shot the girl in the leg. They're both wounded and holed up somewhere, but their pictures are on every news channel and my people, the FBI, DHS and the NYPD counter-terrorism unit arc all on the hunt. We're tracking their every move before and after they got to the diner," he said.

"Can't see how they managed to get out of the neighborhood with our people and cops everywhere, but so far Tariq has been a step ahead of us," Gonzalo said.

"What about the Secret Service agent?" John asked.

"He's dead," Bunny said. "Surveillance cameras show the blond bitch with the baby approaching him and probably asking for directions or something. He was smiling when she shot him with a silenced pistol."

"What was his name?"

"Raymond DaSilva. Former Ranger. Seven years on the job. Married with three kids," Bunny said.

"So… Bobby's dead, Agent DaSilva is dead and Tariq and the woman escaped. We stopped the attack and we only have three civilian casualties, but overall we completely failed to execute our mission," John said.

"We stopped him here, Johnny, but Tariq's other cells…"

"Other cells? I thought it was just Tompkins Square and the failed assault on General Palmer's family."

"There were eleven other suicide bombing attacks across the country. They murdered a senator, four congressmen, a cabinet member, the CEOs of Boeing, Raytheon and General Dynamics, and two prominent evangelical clergymen. They went after their families, Johnny. Tariq killed women and children on Thanksgiving and we didn't stop him. You're right in your assessment. We failed, and two hundred innocent people are dead because we didn't do our fucking job," Clayton said, the rage and pain in his voice cutting through them all.

John sat on the edge of the bed in stunned silence. He took a few seconds to process everything he'd just heard, then tightened his jaw. He reached down and pulled out the IV that was in his forearm feeding him post-surgery antibiotics and fluids.

"Pass me my clothes, Cat," he said to Felix, then stood up and took off his hospital gown. "Clayton, let us know as soon as you get a scent trail on Tariq."

"Will do. Where are you going?" Clayton asked.

"We're gonna work the streets and see if we can find him on our own. One way or another we're getting payback for Bobby… and for what he did to all those families."

"Understood. Before you kill him make sure you squeeze him dry. Find out everything he knows about additional cells and the ISIS pipeline that got him here from Syria," Clayton said.

"Will do," John said before Clayton ended the call.

To the team in the room he said, "You all head back to Campos with my uncle. I'll ride with Nicky, Felix and Bunny and meet you there."

The rest of the team and Gonzalo filed out of John's private hospital room into the hallway in the east wing of NYU's Langone Center.

"Why'd you send them ahead?" Felix asked.

"Didn't want them seeing you put my belt on me and tying my shoes. No way I can get them on by myself."

"I'll do the shoes," Nicky said, picking up John's boots and directing him to sit in the chair.

"Thanks… and nice work out there," he said.

When she was done she tapped the top of his boots and stood up. John pushed himself up off the chair and Felix came over with the belt. He slipped it through the belt loops on his cousin's pants and buckled it.

"You need help with your guns?" Felix asked, nodding his head towards the two Glock 19s in clip-on holsters that were laid out on the bed.

"Thanks, Cuz. I'm good," John said.

"I hate hospitals," Bunny said, with good reason. He'd spent nearly a year at Walter Reed recovering from wounds he received on his final deployment to Iraq. "Let's get the fuck outta here," he said and walked to the door.

When he pulled it open, a doctor was standing there in front of him. At six-five Bunny towered over the five-foot-nine-inch doctor who had NYU Hospital Langone Center embroidered on the left breast of his lab coat, a stethoscope draped around his neck, and a patient chart in his hand.

"What's up, Doc?" Bunny said, smiling at his own joke.

"Hello, Mr. Brown," the doctor said.

Bunny's brow creased as he tried to figure out how the doctor knew his last name. While he was pondering, the small man smashed him in the face with the metal chart and fired a straight-on kick into Bunny's groin. The big man's eyes rolled back in his head and he crumpled to the vinyl floor. The doctor stepped over Bunny's prone body and looked around the room.

"Hello, Mr. Bishop," David Tringa said.

CHAPTER 53

SOME THINGS ARE WORTH DYING FOR

NYU Hospital
1ˢᵗ Avenue and 32ⁿᵈ Street

FELIX REACHED FOR his gun. He did a cross draw with his right hand from the holster on his left hip. His grab and pull was smooth and fast. Just not fast enough.

David Tringa flicked his wrist and two metal darts flew across the room. Felix was focused on putting holes in Tringa and didn't bother to duck. The darts would have killed him if his girlfriend hadn't shoved him aside. One dart flew past his right ear and the one that would've gutted him struck Nicky, burrowing deep into her chest.

John charged across the room, yanked his left arm out of the sling as he ran and threw himself at the Pakistani assassin. Tringa watched Bishop flying towards him, as relaxed and unconcerned as a cat would be if the mouse decided to attack instead of run.

With his guns on the bed and out of reach all John could think to do was get his arms around Tringa. Get the killer on the floor and try to hold him down until help came. He ignored the bolt of pain that shot through him when he extended his arms and the stitches from his surgery ripped loose.

Grab him, he thought.

He was right there. Only inches away when Tringa blasted him with a double palm strike to his shoulders. The blow stopped him in mid-air and dropped him to the floor like a bag of cement, smashing his nose and chin when he landed.

Felix pushed the vision of the metal spike in Nicky's chest out of his mind, got his gun up and squeezed off three shots. Tringa darted away before Felix could fire again, then shot his leg out and shattered Felix's wrist.

Felix had black belts in Kendo, Karate, and a brown belt in Brazilian Ju Jitsu, but all his years of training didn't add up to much when it came to hand-to-hand combat against David Tringa. He feigned a kick with his right foot, swiveled his hips, lunged forward and wrapped his fingers around David's right wrist. Before he could rotate Tringa's wrist inwards, the assassin ducked under his armpit and came up behind him. The blow to the back of Felix's head sent a jolt of electric light through his brain and a blast wave of pain through his body that buckled his knees and left him spasming on the floor.

David walked over to Nikita. She was on her back struggling to breathe as her punctured right lung filled with blood. He stood over her and shook his head in disgust.

"You betrayed your Tringa honor for *them*? For *these* animals?" he asked her as she pushed herself towards the wall with her feet and then used her arms to sit up with her legs splayed out in front of her.

"They're not the animals, David. We are. They're better and more honorable than you or I will ever be."

David laughed at the absurdity of her statement. He laughed and the corners of his mouth rose a bit, but his eyes didn't smile. "You made your choice, Omar. You broke your oath and now you're going to die for it."

"I'm not Omar. My name is Nikita, and some things are worth dying for."

"You're still the same dumb-peasant-bitch you always were. Ever since we were kids, I knew that one day I was going to have to kill you," David said.

He heard movement behind him and turned to look at John, who was back on his feet, but swaying like a drunkard.

David glanced down at Nikita and said, "I'm not done with you. Don't die until I destroy this man you claim is better than me."

John managed to clear his head and get ready for what was coming. He got his fists up and his feet set as Tringa came at him. John could feel Tringa's energy. The Pakistani killer emitted a deadly force that seemed to fill the room.

Fuck it, John said to himself, preparing for the inevitable, but determined not to go down without putting up a fight.

When Tringa came in range, John took a step forward and threw a solid front kick with his already injured right leg at David's gut. The execution felt right… until Tringa's foot flew out and hit him just below the knee. John heard and felt his leg break in the same instant. As he fell backwards he managed to grab hold of Tringa's lab coat and pull him down with him.

David Tringa looked down at John, his dark lifeless eyes seemingly searching for something as he raised his fist to deliver the death blow.

"Don't know what she saw in you, but it's all over now, Bishop."

David flinched, reached around and grabbed the handle of Nikita's throwing knife that was stuck in his back. He pulled it out and stared back at her in disgust. He watched her sucking air like a fish out of water and willing herself to stay conscious long enough to throw another blade at him.

He beat her to it. Once again he flicked his wrist and sent her own knife flying across the room. The blade went through her forearm, pinning it above her head against the wall.

"Don't die yet," he said. "I'll be right there to finish you off."

Tringa sensed the movement underneath him and managed to get his left hand out in time to block John's upward knife thrust. The tip of the four-inch narrow blade that was attached to John's belt buckle went right through the palm of Tringa's hand. John shoved upwards with everything he had. The blade extended out another quarter inch through the back of Tringa's hand, and just enough to graze his neck before the killer used his power and his positioning over John to use his own weapon against him.

"Nice try, Bishop," he said.

Oblivious to the pain, David grinned down at the man so many had tried and failed to kill. They were lesser men. Omar was inferior too. In part because she was a woman, but she was also a peasant. No matter how much time and training David's grandfather had devoted to his pet project, a farm girl could never be compared to a pure blood Tringa.

David knew he was the last of his kind. A true Tringa with a family legacy that traced back to a time before the prophet Mohamed... a time before Jesus. All that history, the legacy of never having failed to kill a target in twelve hundred years, was all coming to a close today. Bishop was the final act of fealty and honor to his ancestors. The last contract his family would ever fulfill.

He twisted his hand, reversing the tip of the blade to point it downwards, and using his leverage to turn John's knife against him. Even though only two inches of the blade was protruding through the back of his hand, David knew it would be more than enough to do the job. John fought him, but David tensed, squeezed and pushed down with all his might.

John felt his wounded arm giving out as he fought. He had a clear view of the knife tip moving relentlessly closer and closer to his right eye. It was a quarter inch away when he was blinded by a wet spray. He felt Tringa jump off of him and John reflexively rolled away and blinked his eyes to clear his vision. He pulled himself to the bed, yanked off the blanket and caught his guns as they fell to the floor.

He pulled the 9 from its holster and aimed at Tringa, who was leaning against the far wall with both hands pressed to his neck. Blood was pouring down between his fingers, turning the top of the white lab coat a bright crimson.

Gotcha, John thought, realizing that his upward thrust with the belt knife must have nicked David's carotid artery.

Nikita was directly across the room from David. She looked into the eyes of the man she'd known since she was a child. She saw the arrogance… and the hate.

"Told you he was a better man," she managed to croak out. "Goodbye, David."

Tringa knew he was dying, but there was no way he would die without fulfilling his contract. He smiled at Nikita, shook his head no and made his move. His hands left his neck and flew down to his waist. He managed to get the knives in his hand and then his body was slammed back against the wall.

John, Bunny and Felix fired at the same time. John hit Tringa twice in the head and once in the throat. Bunny gave him a double tap to the heart, and Felix—who was still dizzy from the blow to the back of his head—shot him once in the belly button and twice in the groin.

David Tringa slid down the wall and toppled over just as the door burst open and Bear, Nev and Mace charged in with their guns drawn.

"Fuck," Bear said.

Felix scrambled across the floor to Nicky and pulled the knife out of her wrist, unpinning her from the wall.

She looked up at Felix and smiled.

"Kiss me," she said and then her head fell forward.

"Get a doctor in here!" he shouted.

CHAPTER 54
PEACE OFFERINGS

Long Island, NY

TWO DAYS AFTER the fight with David Tringa at NYU, most of the team was back at the Long Island estate. Felix and Nicky were still in the hospital and had just been upgraded from critical to guarded. Felix had a soft cast on his right forearm, but his broken wrist was minor compared to the head trauma. Tringa's punch to the back of his head was nearly a death blow, and a neurosurgeon had to cut through his skull and drain the blood that was pooling around his brain.

As for Nikita, if she'd died anywhere other than in a hospital room, she would still be dead. A team of specialists managed to restart her heart, re-inflate her lung and repair the severe internal damage. She was still intubated, but the doctors gave her sixty-forty odds of pulling through. The team knew the doctors had no idea who their patient was, so they all upped the odds to ninety-nine to one in favor of Nicky getting out of bed in a few more days.

Although Felix and his girl were the most critically injured, John was by far the worst looking of the wounded warriors. He had two black eyes and a broken nose from when his face hit the floor, his left arm was back in a sling after the doctors re-stitched him, and his broken right leg was in a cast up to his thigh.

It was hard getting around with a sling on one arm and a cast on the opposite leg, but he was getting better at balancing with one crutch under his right arm and using his left leg to hop around. Lulu Medina, Benji's brother, who was wounded in the shootout with the Russians in Red Hook, was giving John pointers on how to avoid falling forward or backward. Lulu had been shot in his leg and shoulder and had gone through the single crutch-sling routine for a week before he ditched the crutch and switched to a cane.

Bunny was beat up too. Like John, he had a set of black eyes and a severely broken nose from Tringa smashing him in the face with the metal clipboard. He was still seeing lots of weird colors and getting stabbing headaches if he looked at a bright light or a TV screen, but that was minor compared to the pain in his nuts. Tringa had kicked him so hard in his balls that they were swollen tight, and it hurt so bad to piss he did everything he could to hold it. Whenever he was finally forced to squeeze one out, the toilet water turned pink from the blood.

John, Lulu, Bunny, Christmas, Nev, Mace, Chago, Silvi Valdez, Gonzalo and his brothers were all waiting in the big study. None of them spoke. They all stood and watched silently as Yakov and Sasha Skobelev entered the room with a small security detail. No one shook hands. There was still too much simmering anger and resentment for all the lives that had been lost.

"Thank you for meeting with us," Sasha Skobelev said.

"There's been a lot of bad blood between our families,"

Gonzalo said. "Come in and let's talk. Yakov, please take the seat of honor."

"No, I couldn't," Yakov said as Gonzalo guided Yakov to the big executive chair behind the mahogany desk.

"I insist," Zalo said.

Yakov nodded and said, "Very well. Thank you for the honor, Don Valdez."

After they were all formally introduced and seated, Yakov opened the meeting:

"My brother and I are here to make peace and to acknowledge that we made some mistakes that affected all of you very personally."

"We appreciate you coming here, but these mistakes you speak of. When did they happen? When did you know you were acting on bad information?" Zalo asked.

"When your nephews attacked my warehouse in Red Hook and took my money. John told me that one of our soldiers went rogue and killed his father-in-law and almost killed his pregnant wife. I offer you my deepest condolences for this. I was very angry when I found out about it, and as you know we immediately ended hostilities from then on."

"There can be no peace without honesty and account-ability," Zalo said.

"Yes. That is true."

"Then why are you lying?" Zalo asked.

"You are calling me a liar?" Yakov said, his brow knitted in anger.

"I am," Zalo said. "Your only son was shot down in the streets, and the man who killed him made it seem like we did it... By the way, how was your meeting with Connie and Caleb?" he asked, trying to defuse Yakov's anger.

"Very productive. Mr. Belusci has decided to spend some

time with us in Moscow. As for Mr. Meecham, we came to an understanding. He will no longer be a problem for you, and perhaps even become an ally when he is elected to the senate next year," Yakov said.

"Excellent. Connie was obviously a peace offering from us to let you know how sincere we are about wanting to move forward," Gonzalo said.

"We appreciate the gesture, but let's get back to your accusation," Yakov said.

"I'm not making an accusation. I'm stating a fact. Your own security team informed you that the Valdez family had nothing to do with your son's murder. It was *after* you received that information that you hired Vorovka and sent him here to kill my nephew."

Zalo raised his hand like a stop sign when Yakov started to protest and declare his innocence.

"Don't bother. I have a copy of the PowerPoint presentation. The question is, how do we move forward if you're going to sit here and lie about your crimes?"

"We can't," Sasha said and got up from his seat on the couch. He turned to John and said, "Mr. Bishop, I am truly sorry for your loss and I apologize for the terrible mistake my brother made."

"Sasha. Sit Down. You don't speak for me, and regardless of what happened I'm not apologizing for it," Yakov said defiantly.

"I know, Yakov, but we came here to make a peace offering, and this is it."

"What is?" Yakov asked.

"This," Sasha said, pulling a Colt 1911 .45 from his shoulder holster. From eight feet away he fired one booming round into Yakov's chest and said, "Goodbye, brother."

He holstered the Colt, stared at Yakov for a moment and then turned to face Gonzalo.

"I heard you recently had to kill a brother as well."

Gonzalo nodded. "He was sitting in that very same chair when I shot him."

"The things men must do," Sasha said.

"True leaders make the hard choices," Zalo said.

"I have one more peace offering for you," Sasha said. He snapped his fingers and his two-man security detail hustled out of the room. They returned a few minutes later with an elderly man.

"This is Vorovka," Sasha said to John. "He is yours. Do what you want with him."

Sasha's men gave the old man a hard shove. He fell to the floor, landing on the rug in front of John and Gonzalo.

"You intentionally targeted and killed Alastair Williams?" John asked.

Vorovka shrugged. "I was doing my job. He hired me," he said, tilting his head towards Yakov's body. "I did what I had to do to get the job done."

The sling, the cast and the crutch made it hard and painful to move. John had swapped out his double shoulder rig for a single cross draw holster that was clipped below his wounded arm on his left hip. Bolts of pain shot through him as he balanced on his left leg, and with his right hand he slowly and methodically pulled out his Glock 19.

Vorovka got up from his prone position on the floor and onto his knees. With his back straight he stared defiantly up at John.

"I hear you've murdered a lot of people," John said.

"Not murdered. Just like you, my clients hire me to eliminate targets."

"We're nothing alike, Boris. I serve my country. No one else."

"So you know my name. Good. As coworkers we *should* be on a first-name basis."

John wrinkled his eyebrows and asked, "What's that supposed to mean?"

"The Central Intelligence Agency is your current employer, is it not? CIA has hired me more than any other government, group or person over the past forty years," Vorovka said.

"Bullshit," John said.

"Up until a year ago, when I announced my retirement, I was kept on a retainer of three hundred thousand a year by your government. I don't have an exact count, but there was a six-year period when I was getting a minimum of three target packages a week from the CIA's station chief in Moscow."

"I don't believe you."

"Is true," Sasha said. "Everyone knew Vorovka was on your CIA's payroll, but he always got FSB or GRU approval before each job, so as far as hitmen go, the old man was untouchable."

"Doesn't matter who he worked for in the past," Bunny said. "He killed Alastair and Benji. Why should we care whose payroll he was on?"

"You're right. It doesn't matter," John said.

Still on his knees, the old man stared back indifferently as John held the gun on him. Everyone in the room knew Vorovka deserved to die for the heartless way that he'd killed Alastair, and they all stood there waiting for the shot that never came. Despite his promise to Maria, John just couldn't bring himself to squeeze the trigger.

"My father-in law, Alastair Williams, was a civilian. You didn't kill Alastair—you murdered him."

Vorovka shrugged. "And? I use anyone around my target to get to my target. No one is off limits."

"That's the difference between us. We're not colleagues and never could be. I'd never kill a person in cold blood," John said.

"Not yet, but you will."

"Not ever," John said.

"Really? Then why are you about to shoot an unarmed seventy-year-old man who's on his knees?"

"Two reasons. One, you're not a civilian."

"And?" Vorovka asked.

"I promised my wife," John said. "*But* I'm breaking that promise… I'm not going to kill you, Boris."

Vorovka seemed to relax a little, until he saw John pass his gun to the man standing next to him, leaning on a cane.

"What's this?" Vorovka asked.

"An introduction," John said.

"Who are you?" Vorovka asked.

"I'm Lulu Medina. You killed my brother Benji."

"Wait…" Vorovka said, raising his hand like a stop sign as Lulu limped forward, aimed from just two feet away and squeezed the trigger.

Vorovka's eyes were wide in surprise as smoke drifted out of the hole in his forehead. He hovered on his knees for a moment before toppling backwards with his legs folded underneath him.

"Are we good?" Sasha asked.

"Yes. Yes, we are," Gonzalo said and then asked, "What would you like us to do with your brother?"

"What did you do with yours?"

"Ground him into little pieces and tossed them in a landfill," Gonzalo said.

Sasha nodded his approval. "I think the best way to end our misunderstanding is to have our brothers' bones and ashes mixed together with the trash."

The two of them shook hands to formally seal the end to a war that never should have happened.

"Where's Connie?" Christmas asked Sasha.

"He's outside. You want to say goodbye?"

"I definitely do," Christmas said.

"We all do," Gonzalo said.

They all walked through the house and out onto the driveway, where Sasha's soldiers were standing around with a much larger Valdez security detail of twenty men keeping them company. The new head of the Skobelev crime family snapped his fingers and pointed to the Mercedes G 65 Wagon. One of his personal bodyguards hustled over and opened the back door.

Connie was curled up on the floor of the Benz's rear hatch. The once powerful and intimidating Albanian bar brawler, turned German Special Forces soldier, turned contract killer, was almost unrecognizable. If it was anyone else, Christmas, John, Gonzalo, Felix, Silvi and the rest of the Valdez family would have felt a twinge of sympathy. Not for Connie Belusci.

"Have a nice trip, Connie," Christmas said.

"Kill me, Christmas," Connie pleaded. "Please. Kill me."

"Tempting, but I'm gonna let bygones be bygones. Enjoy your extended vacation."

Silvi pushed the men away and stared at Connie for a few moments.

"You shot my father," she said finally.

"Who was he?" Connie asked.

"My Daddy was Sesa Valdez. He was a great man and by Valdez law I could claim my right to kill you here and now… But I won't. I'm forgoing my right to vengeance. I know Mr. Skobelev is going to keep you alive and make you suffer for a very long time for murdering his nephew."

Connie didn't say anything and Silvi stared at him for a long time before she said, "Hold out his right hand."

Sasha's men reached in and pulled the zip tie that bound Connie's hands together. The big man was past the point of resisting. He looked on almost indifferently through his one remaining eye and watched as Silvi pulled a pair of garden shears from her purse.

"Right index finger," she said to the Russians.

Connie tried to pull away, but the two men guided his hand and his finger towards her.

"I heard you're a righty, so you must have used that finger to shoot my Daddy."

She turned and looked back at Sasha. "Whenever you think he's suffered enough and you're ready to finally kill him, would you please make him suffer some more for what he did to my family?"

"It will be my honor, Ms. Valdez," Sasha said.

"Thank you," Silvi said. "As for me, I'm taking *this* as a peace offering."

Connie was already in shock and in so much pain from the bullwhip session on Caleb's wall that he didn't scream or even make a sound when Silvi snipped off his index finger. She tossed away the shears and wrapped the appendage in a black handkerchief with a pink and yellow flowered pattern.

"I'll put it in my father's suit pocket before we bury him so it will always be with him," Silvi said.

CHAPTER 55
REST IN PEACE

THE DAY WAS cool and crisp with a cloudless powder blue sky and a breeze strong enough to keep all the flags, large and small, waving on the wind. The midafternoon sun reflected brightly off the more than four hundred thousand white marble headstones laid out in neat rows in Arlington National Cemetery. John wondered if any of the fallen heroes knew or cared about all the pain and suffering evil men had caused in the past few days. He hoped not. It was his job to hunt down and kill the monsters. For these heroes, all that was left was to rest in peace.

John sat with his broken leg extended out in front of him while he listened to Bear give a heartfelt eulogy for their fallen brother, Staff Sgt. Robert "Bobby" Floyd. President Carson, the first lady, President-elect Jeff Stamper, his wife, his ex-wife, Kelly and Kristin Sillo, General Palmer and his family, Clayton Unser, Team Razor, the Floyd family, the Diaz and the Valdez families were all sitting and listening too.

Bear mixed in stories of Bobby's heroism with hilarious moments they'd shared with the Kentucky mountain man during their multiple tours and years of frontline combat duty. He also talked a lot about the comedy duo of Bobby and Sergeant Able Diaz, and the love the two men shared for each other.

"It's only fitting that Bobby and Able are together again," Bear said.

He wiped tears from his eyes, glanced over to the right of Bobby's final resting place, and nodded at the white marble headstone with Able's name engraved on it.

"They came from different parts of the country, from different backgrounds, but their love for each other and the way they moved as one across a battlefield was something all of us on Razor will never forget. Born of different mothers, these two heroes were true brothers in life. We honor Bobby Floyd and Able Diaz by reuniting them and laying them side by side for all eternity."

Bear went on to talk about Bobby's selfless sacrifices and what Bobby once told him:

"In his thick country boy accent he said, 'If I gotta die young, the only way I wanna leave this here Earth is giving it all to save someone else.'… Well, we all know that's exactly what he did. God bless you and rest in peace, brother."

After the eulogy, the rifle volley and the folded flag being handed to Bobby's mother by General Palmer, all the mourners got up and talked in small groups for a while. After a lot of tears and hugs, people began to disperse and head to their cars. It was then that Kelly Sillo and her daughter made their way over to John and the team.

Kelly wore dark sunglasses and a thick gray coat over a black dress. She also had a big bandage on her forehead and several smaller cuts around her face. Kristin was wearing black pants and a thick sweater under her North Face down jacket, with only her left arm through the sleeve. Her fractured right arm was in a brace and tucked inside her zipped-up coat. Like her mom, she had several Band-Aids on her face.

Kristin walked right up to John and put her good arm around him: "Thank you, Mr. Bishop. My mom told me who you are and how you carried me to safety after Mr. Floyd…" She started to break down, but kept it together so she could finish… "After Sergeant Floyd saved our lives. I spoke to his mother and showed her this." Kristin unzipped her coat a bit and touched the heart-shaped locket that hung from her neck. "It has a picture of Sergeant Floyd on the inside and I'll never take it off. Never ever," she said.

"I know Bobby is smiling down on us right now. He's going to be honored to travel through life with you and stay close to your heart," John said.

Kristin nodded and wiped away her tears. Kelly came in, gently put her arms around his neck and kissed him on the cheek. She did the same for every member of the team.

"Thank you all and God bless you," she said.

She took her daughter by the hand and the two of them turned and walked away, surrounded by their upgraded Secret Service detail. When they were a good distance away, President-elect Stamper came over and put his hand on John's shoulder.

"Thank you, John. Thank you all. You saved my babies, and whatever you may think or may have heard about me, the one thing everyone knows is that I always repay a debt. This ain't about money or politics or anything else. Just know that from here on, you need anything, and I mean anything, you just call me directly and I'll get it done."

"Appreciate that, sir."

Stamper waved over the others who had respectfully given him a private moment with the men who saved his family. John watched the most powerful men in the world march towards him. President Carson, Clayton Unser, General Palmer, Jim Masterson, the head of the Secret Service, and FBI Director Brian Quinlan spread out in a line facing him and the team.

"We've reviewed all the intel and the after-action reports. The bottom line is we're all in agreement that you and your team are the only ones who successfully executed their mission. You stopped the New York attacks, saved a lot of innocent lives, and actually managed to shoot Tariq and the girl. That's way more than the rest of us were able to accomplish," President Carson said.

"What now, sir?" John asked.

"For now, you and your team stand down. Take some time to rest and recover. We've got every federal, state and local law enforcement agency in the country hunting for Tariq. If you guys can figure out where he's hiding, call me and let me know, but barring that, we need you healthy and fully operational. I'm assuming by that time my watch will be over and you'll be working directly with President Stamper. Help him. This is a very different type of war we're fighting and the country needs you and your team to protect it... Now more than ever."

"Thank you, Mr. President," John said to Carson. Then to Stamper: "We'll be ready when you need us, sir."

"Heading back to New York?" Clayton asked.

"The service for Agent DaSilva is here at Arlington later this afternoon. After that we'll head back home to bury my uncle Sesa and my cousin Antonio," John said.

"So much death," Clayton said.

"We've lost too many good men."

"We pay a high price to be the guardians against evil," Clayton said.

"They're the ones who're gonna pay once I'm back on my feet," John said.

Clayton nodded and shook John's hand. Carson, Stamper and Palmer did the same and then they all turned and walked away, surrounded by a ring of security.

"You trust Stamper?" Bunny asked.

"Not sure and don't care. We're going on offense as soon as Felix and Nicky are ready for action and I'm healed up. In the meantime, we focus on finding targets. Here or overseas. Wherever they're hiding, we're gonna find 'em and take 'em out," John said.

"Amen, brother."

"Now give me a hand. My crutch keeps sinking into the grass."

They stopped at Bobby's grave, gave him a final salute, did the same for Able, and then slowly walked away. There were three more funerals to attend, and after that some downtime. But soon, very soon, John and his team were going to track down every person who had a hand in the Thanksgiving Day attacks and leave a trail of blood and death in their wake.

Epilogue

Tariq Hassan
Wildwoods, Missouri

TARIQ WAS SPRAWLED on his bunk, his head propped up on two pillows as he watched a 60 Minutes Special Report titled "Where is Tariq Hassan? The Search for the Mastermind Behind the Thanksgiving Day Assault on America."

The twenty-minute segment included a short bio on his life and some odd assumptions about his motivations. The piece also included an interview with the newly appointed directors of the FBI and Homeland Security. Both men tried not to sweat under the glow of the camera lights as they were grilled on how all of Tariq's terrorist cells could have operated undetected on American soil and why, with the vast amounts of intel and resources the directors had at their disposal, they couldn't figure out where he was hiding.

"I'm in Missouri, you idiot," Tariq said to the TV.

Gretchen limped into the room with a tray of hot tea. She set the tray down and handed him a steaming mug.

"Thank you," he said.

She smiled and sat down next to him on the bed. Her smile broadened and her eyes brightened as she watched the two squirming directors try to explain the failure of each of their agencies to prevent the attacks.

"Tariq, you outsmarted them all and when Stamper is inaugurated this week, he's going to send the Army into Syria."

"Maybe," Tariq said. "But if he was about to send in battalions of Marines and US Special Forces, they would already be mobilizing. Stamper would have worked it out with Carson."

"You may be right, but Stamper has to do something right away. He has to go on the offensive and if he doesn't start with a full-on invasion, we'll force his hand with a few more attacks on his inner circle. Once they send in the Marines, moderate Muslims will rally to our cause… and *then* the real war begins."

"The chaos of war will turn a billion sheep into God's warriors. Our army will lay waste to the infidels. We will cleanse the Earth with American blood and the blood of all its allies," Tariq said.

He sat up in the bed a little too quickly and the shoulder bit him. He pushed the pain aside … and his anger at himself for not doing a better job of hiding it. It irritated him that she saw him flinch. She pretended that she didn't, but he saw her eyes momentarily flare with concern.

Despite his anger, Tariq knew he was lucky to be alive. He thought back to nearly two months ago. To the moment on Thanksgiving Day when they took aim at Bishop and his cousin from just a few yards away. Tariq had been shocked by how fast Bishop moved, and couldn't believe that the man managed to turn and fire twice before he and Gretchen hit him with four shots.

One of Bishop's rounds went right past Tariq's ear and the other blasted him in the left shoulder. His shoulder wound and the big hole in Gretchen's leg from the sniper's bullet had both become badly infected during their escape from New York and their trip to Missouri inside the filthy tank of an oil truck.

He'd healed faster than her, and the doctor treating them said he might have to amputate Gretchen's leg in order to save her. It took seven days of intravenous antibiotics to bring down her fever and kill the infection. Two months later, she still had a pronounced limp from the big chunk of muscle missing from her calf.

For her part, Gretchen knew that she too was lucky to be alive. During her fever-induced delirium she had seen Tariq's eyes when the doctor mentioned removing her leg. At that moment, she knew he was thinking about killing her right then and there. She was grateful that he hadn't and she was now more determined than ever to prove her worth.

She placed a hand on his leg: "How long will we stay here?" she asked.

Tariq looked around at the battleship gray concrete floors and matching walls of their tiny room inside the bunker. Theirs was one of dozens of connecting rooms along the tunnel that was more than fifty feet below ground. As spartan as it got, there was nothing aesthetically pleasing in any of the rooms Tariq and Gretchen had been allowed access to.

The Johnson Group had spent five years building their end-of-life sanctuary, and they hadn't been concerned with building something pretty. The underground bunker was designed for one thing: survival.

When Tariq asked the bearded and checked-flannel-shirt-wearing Johnson Group members where they got the name, one of them handed him a DVD. It was the movie *Jeremiah Johnson* starring Robert Redford. Tariq and Gretchen watched it together and later discovered that the Johnson Group's manifesto was loosely based on the fictional story of a mountain man who turned his back on civilization in the late 1800s.

"We may be here for quite a while," Tariq said to her.

"Do you trust them?" she asked.

It was a good question. When the ISIS council members had told him about a newly formed alliance with a small group of white supremacist/doomsday survivalists, he was dumbstruck. He didn't understand until the council explained that the Johnson Group was tired of waiting around for the superpowers to launch their nukes at each other. They were eager for Armageddon to start now. The council told him that the Johnsons would assist him with his escape from New York and provide him with a safe place to operate.

"Coordinate your attacks from their underground tunnels and drive America into an all-out war with Islam. We will do the same with our brothers here, in Europe and in Asia. Together we'll set the world on fire," the head of the council had said.

"Yes, Gretchen," Tariq said. "Our mission and theirs are the same. They want to destroy their country and live below the ruins for a few years before they emerge as the sole survivors. As long as we can keep launching attacks, they will protect us."

"Okay," she said. "It's just hard to wrap my mind around white supremacists helping and protecting Muslims."

"War makes strange alliances, and don't forget... they're not just offering us weapons and a secure headquarters. They're taking direct action too," he said.

"Bishop?"

"Yes, my dear. They have already assigned one of their top killers to get close to Bishop. Someone he'll never suspect."

"When?" she asked, licking her lips in anticipation.

"Soon, my dear. Very soon," he said.

She batted her eyes seductively: "What should we do until then?"

He smiled, then pulled her farther onto the bed and helped take her top off.

President Stamper
Washington, DC

This was the fourth of six inaugural parties the newly anointed President Jeff Stamper had to attend tonight. His face hurt from smiling and his feet ached from all the standing and dancing.

What I'd give for a shower and a foot massage, Stamper thought as he worked the room.

He shook hands, laughed at inside jokes, and clinked glasses with staffers, Republican donors, senators, congressmen, and diplomats from countries all over the world. He gave each of them their moment of glory. Depending on their level of importance, he let them paw at him and warm themselves in the bright light of his presidential orbit for anywhere from five, to as painfully long as thirty seconds.

Paul Simms, Stamper's former personal attorney and newly appointed chief of staff, came over and pulled him away from a small group of businessmen from Arkansas and Louisiana.

"Enjoying all the ass kissing?" Simms asked.

"A little too wet for me," Stamper said.

Simms tilted his head questioningly.

"Nothing wrong with a little ass kissing, but not when the guy does it with his tongue out."

Simms held it for a moment and so did Stamper before they both cracked up. While they were laughing, Simms steered him out of the main ballroom, down a wide hallway and finally to a door that led to a small anteroom. Stamper told the four-man Secret Service team to wait outside for a moment and he followed Simms through the door.

"Congratulations, Mr. President. So wonderful to see you again," Damir Goncharov said.

Russia's US ambassador extended his hand and gave Stamper an insider's triple pump shake.

"Thanks for meeting me, Damir," Stamper said.

"Anytime and anything you need; I am here, Mr. President."

Stamper nodded and turned to look at Caleb. He tried to hide his shock at the young man's transformation. Meecham's once pale and sickly complexion had been replaced with a healthy bronze tan, and he looked quite dashing in his custom-made tuxedo.

"Good to see you, Caleb. You clean up nice," Stamper said.

Caleb thanked him as they shook hands, and then he asked: "What can we do for you, Mr. President?"

"John Bishop," Stamper said.

"What about him?" Caleb asked.

"Leave him alone. He saved my daughter, *and* my granddaughter's life. I owe him and I don't want to hear about any more IRS audits or Russian hitmen blindsiding him."

Caleb asked, "Is that an order?"

"It is. You've made some powerful friends in Moscow, and I'll put the full weight of the Republican Party behind you to guarantee your Senate seat, but you keep your hands off Bishop. Understood?"

"Sounds like you have more than just a casual interest in his wellbeing," Caleb said.

"You're right, I do. I'm about to unleash him. He's going to be my tip of the spear and I don't want him looking over his shoulder when he's hunting down and killing every bastard that had a part in the Thanksgiving Day attacks."

"Speaking for Moscow, we fully support you, Mr. President, and our issues with Mr. Bishop have already been… *resolved*," Damir said.

"Excellent," Stamper said.

"No problem from me either," Caleb said.

After they all shook hands and the president and his chief of staff left the room, Caleb dipped his chin and looked at Damir.

"We'll let Stamper play in the yard with his new pet for a while," Caleb said with a devious smile.

"Your hands and ours will be clean when the time comes. Our Federal Security Service is already working on scenarios. When Bishop goes up in flames, it won't tie back to either of us."

"Excellent," Caleb said, rubbing his hands together in anticipation.

John Bishop
JFK International Airport

The leg hurt. He'd worked it a little too hard over the past few days, and walking nearly a mile through Kennedy Airport to his departure gate added to the steady throb he felt below his right knee. It pissed him off that the recovery from David Tringa breaking his leg was taking so long, but he also knew he was lucky to be walking at all. Tringa's kick had shattered his tibia and the doctors originally said he'd be in a cast for a minimum of six months. Thankfully, the X-rays revealed far more rapid healing and the cast was cut off in less than sixty days after the fight in his NYU hospital room.

Felix and Nikita had been lucky too. Both had fully recovered from their injuries and they were roaming around the Long Island estate like a couple of high school sweethearts. It had bothered John more than it should have and it took him a while to figure out why. Deep down he was happy that Felix was in love, but he made every excuse he could to get away from them.

Ultimately, it was John's Uncle Gonzalo who had opened his eyes to what was going on:

"Have you made your choice?" Gonzalo asked as he uncorked a second bottle of red wine.

"About what?" John asked.

"Her or them?"

John wasn't following.

"Are you going to find Maria and your son, or are you going after Tariq and the girl?" Gonzalo asked.

John didn't say anything for nearly an hour. He stared down at the rug, drinking steadily while Gonzalo kept refilling their wine glasses.

"I can't choose, Tio," he said finally. "I have to see my son, but I have to kill Tariq too."

"You can't do both, my son. If you go to Maria, I don't want you ever coming back here. You put down your gun for good and stay out of this life."

John had nodded, kissed his uncle on the top of his head and gone up to his room. That had been a week ago. He'd struggled with the decision for days, his heart and brain battling over the choice between love and death. Ultimately, he chose love.

He made it to the gate with only a few minutes to spare. He sipped a Starbucks coffee and pulled out the map he'd marked up. There were over two thousand inhabited islands in the Philippines and John knew his wife and newborn son were on one of them. One of the remote islands as far from suicide bombers and contract killers as any place on Earth. He smiled at the tiny dots that translated into an image in his mind.

He saw himself walking along an empty white sandy beach. Following the curve of the island, he would come around a corner and there they'd be. He pictured himself and Maria running into each other's arms. Kissing and hugging as they had just a few short months ago. Then he would lift his son high in the air while Chris's little eyes sparkled and he squealed with joy.

The moment was interrupted and the image faded with the sound of his phone ringing. He stared at it for a moment, reluctant to answer, and then he hit send.

"John," Clayton said.

"Yes, I'm here."

"I'm with the president in the situation room."

"What's happened?" John asked.

"We have a target package for you," Stamper said. "How soon can you and your team get moving?"

John looked back at the gate and the passengers who were already boarding. Then he looked down at the dotted map in his other hand.

"John? Are you there?" Stamper asked.

"Yes, sir. I'm here. Twenty minutes, sir. We'll be ready to roll out in twenty minutes."

"Excellent. Clayton will coordinate the mission with you. Go get 'em and good hunting, John," Stamper said eagerly.

"Thank you, sir," John said.

He carefully folded the map and stuck it in his back-pack. He took one last glance back at his gate, then turned and hustled through the airport. He tried to choose love, but once again death had pulled him back. John set his jaw and got himself refocused. He returned to what he was: the yellow-eyed God of war marching forward to slaughter every enemy in his path.

About the Author

Rafael Amadeus Hines comes from a diverse family background with Panamanian, Jamaican, and Irish roots, and is a native New Yorker, born and raised on Manhattan's Lower East Side. Dipping into his early Alphabet City memories, he loosely based many of the characters in the Bishop series on the people he grew up with, and adapted many of his own experiences into the book as well.

A former Jazz club owner and restaurateur, Rafael has worked in the financial and energy markets for over 20 years. On 9/11 he watched his office along with all the others in The Twin Towers come crashing down and, like many New Yorkers on that day, he anticipated follow-up attacks to take place throughout the city. Years later he envisioned a lone citizen soldier preventing these attacks and the hero Sgt. John Bishop appeared on paper.

A voracious reader of suspense thrillers, Rafael's writing career was inspired by legendary artist-authors Elmore Leonard, John Sandford, Vince Flynn, Stephen Hunter, James Lee Burke, and Tom Clancy. He is currently working on the third novel in the Bishop series.

AWARDS

Rafael has recently been added to the list of the **World's Top 200 Most Influential Authors** (https://richtopia.com/inspirational-people/top-200-authors) and in addition to becoming an Amazon International Bestseller, his debut novel, **Bishop's War,** is an **IPPY (Independent Publisher) Suspense-Thriller Award Winner**, **New Apple Literary Award Winner for Best New Fiction**, **New Apple Literary Suspense-Thriller Solo Medalist**, a **Global eBook Suspense Award Winner**, **Book Excellence Gold Medal Winner**, **Pinnacle Book Achievement Award- Gold Medal Winner**, **Top Shelf Magazine- 1**st **Place Winner,** the **IAN Book of the Year,** and the **Book Viral Millennium Book of the Year**.

www.rafaelhines.com
https://twitter.com/RafaelWrites
https://www.facebook.com/RafaelHines.Author/

KJC 12/2020

Made in the USA
Coppell, TX
19 July 2020

31275274R00282